DEEPER

ALSO BY JEFF LONG

FICTION

The Wall

The Reckoning

Year Zero

The Descent

Empire of Bones

The Ascent

Angels of Light

NONFICTION

Duel of the Eagles: The Mexican and U.S. Fight for the Alamo

Outlaw: The Story of Claude Dallas

DEEPER

JEFF LONG

ATRIA BOOKS

New York • London • Toronto • Sydney

ATRIA BOOKS

A Division of Simon & Schuster, Inc.
1230 Avenue of the Americas
New York, NY 10020

First Atria Books hardcover edition August 2007

ATRIA BOOKS and colophon are trademarks of Simon & Schuster, Inc.

For information about special discounts for bulk purchases, please contact Simon & Schuster Special Sales at 1-800-456-6798 or business@simonandschuster.com.

Designed by Dana Sloan

Manufactured in the United States of America

10 9 8 7 6 5 4 3 2 1

"China Bills U.S. $1 Million for Plane's Stay" reprinted courtesy of CNN.com.

Reprint of Pat Robertson/Jerry Falwell dialogue on Christian Broadcast Network falls under the fair use rule as provided for in Section 107 of U.S. Copyright Law.

Library of Congress Cataloging-in-Publication Data
Long, Jeff.
Deeper : a thriller / Jeff Long.—1st Atria Books hardcover ed.
p. cm.
I. Title.

PS3562.O4943D44 2007
813'.54—dc22   2007003862

ISBN-13: 978-0-7432-8454-7
ISBN-10:   0-7432-8454-2

To Ada

ACKNOWLEDGMENTS

My deepest gratitude to the following.

Emily Bestler is one of those rare and magical editors every writer dreams about, an editor who rolls up her sleeves, tackles your language, and tames your story, all with a Southern accent.

Equal parts gentleman, gladiator, and prophet, my agent, Sloan Harris, continues to light my path and guide me through the wilderness.

For some reason, film agents never seem to get mentioned in literary acknowledgments, maybe because real writers aren't supposed to be starving for Hollywood's attention. The fact is that my remarkable film agent, Josie Freedman, has helped keep the wolf from our door for years now.

The greatest fly fisherman in the world, Cliff Watts, has been doctoring both the town of Boulder and my fictional walking wounded for the last three decades. Any and all errors should prove once and for all that you probably ought not go to a novelist for your brain surgery.

Finally, Barbara and Helena, thank you for lending me to the dark depths for so many years. Now let us ride off into Mustang dawns.

And in the lowest deep a lower deep
Still threat'ning to devour me opens wide,
To which the Hell I suffer seems a Heav'n.
                    (Satan peering into the abyss)

—JOHN MILTON, *PARADISE LOST*, BOOK IV

PROLOGUE

Ike surrendered.

As he stole from bed, naked, the cave dust in his old wounds and tattoos flickered like lightning. He paused at the door to listen. Ali was seven months pregnant and seemed to have found all the sleep Ike was losing. But he could not hear her soft breath, only the song.

For more than a month it had been waking him in the middle of the night, always the same song sung by the same woman, or maybe it was a child. Ike couldn't decide what to call the thing, a war hymn or a ballad. Or the death of him. Bottom line, he knew, the abyss was fishing for its faithless son. His time had come.

His pack was ready inside the garage, behind the garbage can. Tomorrow was pickup day. Ike dutifully lugged the can to the road, one final chore in this world. Then he saddled on the pack and set off into the moonlit hills.

When the song first began, Ike had blamed his ramped-up senses. All those years in the deep had retooled him, inside and out. Metamorphosis came with the territory, a medical fact. Everyone changed down below, some more than others, he more than most. The depths had spared him disfigurement, but left him half-animal. Tonight, for instance, he could count the birds in a tree by the rustle of their wings. The moon literally uplifted him: its gravity pulled the fluid in his spine. He could hear his child's heartbeat . . . still growing in the womb.

Thinking the song might be coming from a sleepless neighbor or someone's radio, Ike had spent a week of nights prowling through the yards in his bare feet. But the source eluded him, even as it grew stronger. He wondered if something in nature might be calling to him, some creature, say, or the sea. Maybe the muse was teaching him a song. Maybe this agitation was how you came to create something.

But a few days ago, at last, he had tracked the song to the mouth of a cave. That was his destination tonight. A short walk brought him to a gash in a limestone cliff. He stood there, facing the source. It did not exactly invite him with its dung and rot. But Ike was a veteran of such places. In a sense, he had been born in there.

The song guttered out from the cave. It lured him with his memories of the deep earth. The words were indistinct at best. Maybe Ali, the linguist, could have made better sense of them. What he perceived was what he imagined: *come away, leave the golden apples of the sun.* Or whatever. With a last glance back at the world, Ike nodded good-bye and began to descend.

Over the coming days, the abyss acquired him at an average rate of seventy-five heartbeats per minute. That was how calmly Ike abandoned all that he loved in the world. One step at a time, inching down his ropes, braving the tunnels and subterranean seas, Ike cast himself into the stone.

A week passed. His food ran out. His batteries failed.

Most people would have turned back. Most people never would have come down. Ike just kept on sinking deeper. From his days of captivity, he knew tricks for seeing in this infinite night.

Drink from black rivers.

Eat the flesh of midnight animals.

Listen for colors.

Smell for shadows.

The darkness unfolded before him.

For a while, Ike recognized the veins and cavities and chambers, not by name, but by the scent of their subterranean animals and minerals. Gradually, with intent, he got lost. No map, no memory, no compass served to guide him. Ike simply navigated through the planet's basement by the tug of gravity, that and the slivers of meat left for him to find.

The meat was bait, he knew. The cave tribes were luring him into the depths, or thought they were. In fact, he was as much a creature of the void as they were. This labyrinth of tunnels and holes was his home, too. The only difference between him and those feeding him was his relentless quest. They were bottom dwellers, but not really, because this was not yet the bottom. They had their limits. He had none. They were hiding from humankind. He was trying to save it.

Every now and then, Ike scratched his initials onto the pillars and walls. He wasn't quite sure why he bothered. His mark wasn't meant to guide others who might follow, nor to point his way out. He did not harbor the slightest expectation of emerging. Unlike his other descents, this was a one-way ticket. Whatever waited for him down below—whatever had been infecting his dreams, whatever ruled this place—would never let him go, he was sure of it.

Once upon a time, he might have come for the pure adventure. As a young man, Ike had been a climber and trek guide, a professional vagabond and survivor, and that was the beginning of his curse. While muscling through the Himalayas, he had accidentally strayed into the planet's far-flung cave system and its terrible mysteries. In reaching for the sun, he had ended up reaching for the darkness. By going high, he had been going deep all along. Everything in his life seemed to have been a prelude to this final descent.

In his wildest imagination, even stoked by Afghani hash or Johnnie Walker red, he could never have conjured up this world within the world. In retrospect, it should have come as no shock to him or anyone else that hell really existed, a vast network of arteries and chambers inhabited by primal nomads and lorded over by a sovereign of sorts. Since the beginning of time, mankind had suspected as much. One civilization after another had built a vocabulary of demons, ogres, and vampires to explain the predation from below. When the occasional human escaped and brought up wild tales, he or she was thrown into a dungeon or an insane asylum, or burned at the stake, or made the subject of some epic poem. As it turned out, shamans and exorcists had been trying to repel the darkness since the invention of fire.

Not so long ago, he had guided a scientific expedition into the tunnel complex riddling the Pacific Ocean subfloor. Along with a single other survivor, Ali, he had barely managed to claw his way out from the depths before a plague swept the inner earth. Afterward, people were convinced that all subterranean life had been exterminated, and that the devil was dead.

But now, as Ike soloed down into the bowels, it was plain as day that people were wrong. The abyss had never quit living. Some restless spirit existed down below. It was singing to him. And it wanted out.

1

BENEATH THE INTERSECTION OF THE PHILIPPINE, JAVA, AND PALU SEA TRENCHES

He snapped his fingers. *Let there be light.* And they popped the flares.

The faces of his crew sprang from the darkness, flinching. The flare light hurt their eyes. It painted them green and hungry.

The city of stone materialized around them.

Clemens gave a nod. The clapboard snapped shut like a gunshot. In grease pencil: "HELL, scene 316, take 1. IMAX."

"Dead, all dead," he intoned as the camera panned across the city. It was a bony thing, hard and empty, ancient long before Troy was built, before Egypt was even a word. Walls stood cracked or breached by geological forces. Arches hung like ribs. Windows stared: blind sockets. The camera stopped on him.

Clemens turned his head to the lens. He gave it the tired bags under his eyes, and his shaggy salt-and-pepper beard, and the greasy hair, and the bad stitch job along one cheekbone. No makeup. No concealment. Let the audience see his weariness and the marks of five months spent worming through the bowels of the earth. *I have sweated and bled for you,* he thought. *I have killed for you. And for my cut of the box office.* He put fire in his blue eyes.

"Day one hundred and forty-seven, deep beneath the deepest trenches," he said. "We have reached their city. Their Athens. Their Alexandria. Their Manhattan. Here lies the center."

He coughed quietly. The whole film crew had it, some low-grade cave virus. Just one more of their shared afflictions: a rash from poison lichens, fouled stomachs from the river water, lingering fevers after an attack by crystal-clear ants, rot in their wounds, and headaches from the pressure. To say nothing of the herpes and gonorrhea raging among his randy bunch of men and women.

Clemens approached a tall, translucent flange of flowstone. It had seeped from the walls like a slow, plastic, honey brown avalanche. A carefully placed flare lit the stone from behind. The dark silhouette of a man hung inside, like a huge insect caught in amber.

Clemens glanced at the camera—at his future audience—as if to ponder with them. *What new wonders lie here?* He pressed his flashlight against the stone, and peered in. *Through my eyes, behold.*

He moved his light. Inch by inch, the shape revealed its awful clues. This was no man, but some primal throwback. A freak of time. The camera closed in.

Clemens illuminated the pale, hairless legs covered with prehistoric tattoos. His light paused at the groin. The genitals were wrapped in a ball with rawhide strips, a sort of fig leaf for this dreadful Adam. That was the creature's sole clothing, a sack tied with leather cord from front to back across the rump. Leather, in a place devoid of large animals . . . except for man. These hadals had wasted nothing, not even human skin.

"We were their dream," Clemens solemnly intoned to the camera, "they were our nightmare."

He scooted the light beam higher. The beast was by turns delicate, then savage. Winged like a cupid, this one could not have flown. They were more buds than wings really, vestigial, almost comical. But this was no laughing matter. Like a junkyard mutt, the creature bore the gash marks and scars of a hunter-warrior.

Moving higher, his headlamp beam lit the awful face. Milky pink eyes—dead eyes—stared back at him. Even though he'd seen the thing while they were setting up the shot, it made Clemens uneasy. Like the crickets, mice, and other creepy crawlers inhabiting these depths, it was an albino. What little facial hair it had was white. The eyelashes and wisps of a mustache looked almost dainty.

The brow beetled out, heavy and apelike. Classic *Homo erectus*. This one had filed teeth and earlobes fringed with knife cuts. Its crowning glory, the reason Clemens had picked this over all the other bodies, was its rack of misshapen horns. Horns upon other horns, a satanic freight.

The horns were calcium growths, described to him as a subterranean cancer. These happened to have sprouted from its forehead, which fit his film's title to a T. Every hell needed a devil.

Never mind that this wasn't the devil Clemens had come looking for. This was not the body of Satan, said to be lying somewhere in the city. Never mind that through the millennia man's demons had been ancestors of a sort, or at least distant blood cousins. Clemens would deal with the family tree later, in the editing room.

"Now they're gone," he spoke to the microphone clipped to his tattered T-shirt. "Gone forever, destroyed by a man-made plague. Some call it genocide, others an act of God. This much is certain. We have been delivered from their reign of terror. Freed from an ancient tyranny. Now the night belongs to us—to humanity—once and for all."

Clemens stood back and gazed upon the horror, like Frankenstein contemplating his monster. He held his pose to the count of five. "And cut," he said.

The cameraman gave a thumbs-up from behind his tripod. The soundman took off his earphones and signaled okay. A clean take.

"Get a few close-ups of our friend here," Clemens said. "Then break down the gear and pack up. We're moving on. Up. There's still hours in the day." A running joke. In a place without sun, what day? "We're heading home."

Home! For once the crew jumped to his command.

The exit tunnel lay somewhere close. It would lead them to the surface in a matter of weeks. For the millionth time, he pulled a sheaf of pages from a waterproof tube and studied its hodgepodge of maps.

The pages came from the daybook kept by a nun, one of only two survivors to emerge from this region three years ago. It was the ghosts of her doomed expedition that Clemens was chasing on film. Hers had been one of the most audacious journeys in all history, one to rival Marco Polo's or Columbus's, a six-thousand-mile passage through the tunnel system riddling the bedrock beneath the Pacific Ocean. It had been a journey with a punch line, a journey of scientists who bumped smack into an unpleasant article of faith. For here they had found the home of Satan, or the historical Satan, the man—hominid, take your pick—behind the legend. The leader of the pack.

The nun, a scholar cunt named Ali Von Schade, had written of meeting him. The city had still been alive back then, the plague not yet released. The last she'd seen of this Satan, he was wearing a warrior's suit of green jade platelets. For three days now, Clemens had been scouring the city for the body or skeleton, looking for his film's money shot, the one that would shock and amaze and bring the story all together in one image. He'd found a suit of jade armor all right, but it was empty, discarded, ownerless, not a bone in it. Despite his disappointment, he kind of liked that. In the end, Satan had been nothing more than an empty suit.

Clemens had made numerous requests to Von Schade for an interview, all in vain, always meeting the same polite refusal. *I don't wish to share the details of that disaster.* As if the story belonged to her. As if intellectual property had some sacred protection. Cunt.

He and Quinn, his film partner, had needed her maps and clues to plan this journey. Clemens had tried flowers, dinner invitations, offers of money, even a percentage of the film's net profit, yeah, net, not gross, an old Hollywood joke. Nothing worked with her. Zip. Nada. Quinn said to leave her alone. Instead Clemens had hired a burglar to steal her journal, copy it, and then return it. What was the harm? If she wouldn't talk, her diary would.

Von Schade's maps were as much memoir as cartography, laced with fanciful tales and ink-and-watercolor sketches of the Helios expedition's progress. Along the way, every time Clemens was sure she must be wrong or had made something up, her maps would prove to be right.

A waterfall thundered in the darkness, hidden in the distance. That was on the map, too. Bound and blindfolded at the time, Von Schade had later recorded it in her daybook, an acoustic landmark. Through the waterfall lay their shortcut to the sun.

Long, ghostly strips of clouds drifted overhead. The cavern was so big it generated its own microweather. Geologists theorized that millions of years ago great bubbles of sulfuric acid had eaten upward from the earth's deeper mantle, carving out this labyrinth of cavities and tubes known as the Interior. The perfect hiding place for a lost race.

Clemens rolled up the pages of Von Schade's diary and switched off his headlamp. They were running low on batteries, and everything else, for that matter. But the shoot was largely over. His crew had reached its summit, so to speak, this dead city in the deepest reaches of the sub-Pacific cave system. Now they could ascend, back to the surface, back to the sun. Back to Clemens's faded name and glory.

Most of the kids on this crew hadn't even sprouted pimples when he'd won an Academy Award for his documentary, *War High,* about jackass athletes braving international war zones in their search for the ultra-extreme. After that, he'd coasted on his Oscar laurels, getting work as a second-unit director on Hollywood action vehicles.

Then the earth's Interior had been "discovered." Overnight, everyone's attention had shifted to this vast, inhabited labyrinth right beneath their feet. The market for movies and books about adrenaline junkies had gone out the window. Clemens learned the hard way that there was no competing with the demons and fiends of religious lore. Within a year, he was bankrupt, divorced, and shooting porn videos for $200 per day.

Around that time, Quinn had come into his life. Quinn was an old-fashioned explorer who had dipped his toe in the subterranean world and had a film in mind, this film, about an expedition following in the footsteps of an expedition into hell. In a coked-up revelation, it had occurred to Clemens that in order to beat the devil, he needed to be the devil. And so—fifty-two years old—he'd convinced Quinn to partner with him on the production. Together they had assembled this desperate, calculated slog through the earth's basement. Clemens figured that if "Hell," splashed upon giant IMAX screens, couldn't revive his career, nothing would. He'd have to go back to work for the skin mafia.

Unfortunately Quinn had proved to be a problem. Quinn the decent. Quinn the grin. Quinn the Real McCoy. Quinn for president! The crew had loved Quinn's easygoing style and his insistence on safety. And his sense of story and scriptwriting that made Clemens look like a dumb-it-down hack. Which Clemens was. But which he didn't need to have the little people snickering about. Thus, Quinn the scream. Quinn the dead.

After his partner's disappearance, Clemens had assumed things would get better. But the crew only grew more disrespectful of him. They suspected him. Idiots. Murder didn't exist in a wilderness with no laws. And besides, no body, no crime. Quinn had chosen a bottomless pit to fall into. It had been easy, the slightest of nudges from behind, barely an ounce of adios, amigo. Clemens had made a few attempts at placating the crew, even giving them two days to search for their fearless leader. Then it was crack-the-whip time. On with the show.

Joshua. There it was again, that whisper. Clemens whirled around.

He jabbed his light left and right. As always, no one was there. It had been going on ever since they'd entered the city. The crew was screwing with him, whispering his name with Quinn's voice, winding him up.

"Fuck ya," Clemens said to the darkness.

"Likewise," said a woman's voice. Huxley came striding into his light. "What do you think you're doing?"

"Was that you?" said Clemens.

"Yeah," she said. "It's me. You said we were making camp here."

Huxley was a veterinarian Quinn had hired to be their medic. It was the pet doctor's unsteady needle that had sewn together Clemens's cheek after a rockfall in the tunnels system. He could guess what she wanted.

"Those wings," she said. She went to the creature suspended in flowstone, the mineral seepage. "I need to take his measurements and get tissue samples. And I want those wings for my collection. The wings of an angel. A fallen angel. This specimen is unique."

My ongoing rebellion, thought Clemens. The crew was an inch away from outright mutiny. They couldn't wait to get out of here. Daylight was waiting up top. They could practically taste it. And Huxley wanted them to stay?

"You've been saying that about every bone and body we've stumbled across," Clemens said. "We're done here. Onward. Upward. Miles to go before we sleep, all that."

"You don't understand," Huxley said. "Wings on men? And we saw that one yesterday with amphibian gills. And the reptile lady last week."

"What do you want me to say?" said Clemens. "They're hadals. Mutants. A dime a dozen down here. A dime a thousand. Besides, you've got your degree, Doc. What more do you want, the Nobel?"

"I don't know," she said. "What more do you want, another Oscar?"

It wasn't Huxley's ambition that Clemens resented. Once this was over, each one of them meant to squeeze the lemon for all it was worth. He'd been hearing their big plans for months. The kayakers were going to buy ad space in *Outside* and *Men's Journal* to lure adventure travelers. There were dark, class IV tube rapids down here, and river beaches made of polished white marble. The cinematographer wanted to open an art gallery and publish a coffee-table book with her still shots of the Interior. Three of the climber types meant to incorporate, raise venture capital, and return to prospect the outrageous veins of gold they'd all touched, but left behind.

In short, there was money and reputation to be grabbed down here. Huxley was no different from the rest of them. Having suffered the darkness, she wanted her piece of the pie. But the thing about Huxley was that she didn't have manners. Just because she'd been Quinn's girlfriend didn't exempt her from the rules. This was Clemens's show. Everyone else, even the hotshot climbers, had asked his permission to capitalize on the expedition. Not Huxley, though. She treated him like he was stealing the descent.

"We had a deal," she said.

"What deal was that?"

"I came along as a scientist."

"You came along as a medic," Clemens said. "That's your job, to tend the sick and wounded."

"You said we were camping here one more night."

Clemens stared a hole through her. "End of discussion," he said. "We're leaving."

"I'm staying."

"By yourself? In this place?" The flares were dying. The shadows loomed.

"You're not a man of science," Huxley said. "You wouldn't understand."

Clemens thought for a minute, not about staying with her, but about getting shed of her. He wasn't born yesterday. She was going to try to bring a murder charge against him once they got up top. That or slap him with a lawsuit. Lien him to death. This was his retirement she was threatening here.

Clemens shrugged. "You got to do what you got to do, Doc."

Huxley blinked. She'd been bluffing. Too late now. Clemens gave her his crocodile grin. "That's right," she said. "I've got to do what I've got to do. With or without you."

"We'll be on the trail leading up," Clemens told her. "You go through a waterfall and there will be a tunnel. Don't forget."

Huxley lifted her chin. "This won't take more than a few hours. I'll be right behind you."

"You'd better be. I'm telling you, man, don't miss the bus. Because nobody's waiting for nobody anymore. It's dog-eat-dog, Huxley. You hear me?"

She stared, as if he'd just confessed. "I'll catch you before night."

Night. There it was again, their strange conceit. Even, in this lightless place, they clung to convention, calling their wakefulness day, and their sleep night. Never mind that their bodies had forgotten the sun and they dreamed in shades of blackness.

They left Huxley in a tiny puddle of light. *Good night, sweet princess,* thought Clemens. Fantasizing, he began to write the sad loss of Dr. Huxley into his mental screenplay.

For three days they had been meandering through the city, gathering a bounty of images. It was like Pompeii among these ruins, with this difference: instead of being locked inside volcanic ash, the dead hung in translucent flux. The plague had killed them; the mineral ooze had made them immortal. You could see them underfoot, suspended in the flowstone, hundreds, no, thousands of them. For three nights they had slept atop the last resting place of the ultimate barbarian. Now they were done with it.

A gigantic waterfall seemed to block the end of the cavern. They shot a flare into the heights. As it drifted down, the spray lit with rainbows in the blackness.

"Lord," one of the kayakers said. That said it all.

Just as the nun's daybook promised, a tunnel lay behind the central waterfall: caves within caves within caves. It was like Swiss cheese down here.

Clemens tried to get his crew to set up the camera and take a shot of him entering the falls tunnel. But they pretended not to hear him. He had been waiting for their muttering and scowls to spill over into actual defiance, and now that it had, now that they had broken from his command, he was relieved. Finally he could quit lashing them deeper. He could just float back up to the world.

The path led up and up in giant circles. The stair steps, carved from solid stone by a subterranean civilization that some scholars dated to twenty-five thousand years ago, had been worn to faint corrugations. The stone was slick from the humidity that blew at their backs on a warm, steady draft.

It didn't take long for Huxley to change her mind about staying behind. Clemens was at the back of the line for a reason. Her voice began echoing up to them after the first hour, but Clemens was the only one to hear it. He couldn't make out her words, but her distress was clear. Maybe her batteries had run out. More likely she couldn't find the tunnel entrance. Bummer.

Soon her echoes grew almost faint enough to ignore. Almost. The whisper still reached him. *Joshua.* How did she do that?

The tunnel walls tightened. The current of warm air quit rushing from below. Clemens could sense the space closing around him by the change in his hearing. Things just sounded closer.

Joshua. He ignored her.

As they went on, Clemens kept looking for debris, bones, or other signs of the original expedition. Funded by the Helios conglomerate, the party of scientists, soldiers, and porters had numbered over two hundred at their start beneath the Galapagos Islands.

Following their lead, Clemens and the crew of nineteen had hiked, climbed, and rafted some six thousand miles. They had retraced the Helios expedition's route by its remains, finding clues to its long breakdown in their graffiti, trash, dried dung, and, near the end, their bones. Quinn had likened the doomed explorers to Lewis and Clark crossing America, except the sub-Pacific journey was almost three times as long, and they had been slaughtered by the natives, these so-called hadals of this geological Hades. Only Von Schade and the expedition's scout had lived to tell the tale, though they had barely told it. The scout had vanished without saying a word about anything. The nun had gone into therapy, and then academic seclusion. Which had left their story ripe for the picking.

Finder's keepers, thought Clemens. It was his now, the scraps of diaries and logbooks, the rags of uniforms, the broken instruments, the forlorn skulls mounted on stalagmites, the hadal bones lying where the plague had felled them . . . all collected and digitized on large-format tape.

Climbing higher, they found hadal symbols cut into the walls or floor. One, in particular, suggested they were on track. It was a simple, recurring spiral shape. For months, they had been seeing different versions of it, like a blaze mark, only more beautiful and ornate. The closer they got to the city, the more elaborate the spirals had become. Here, for instance, the spiral was woven so deftly into an arabesque engraving that it seemed to be hiding.

Clemens still found it hard to believe the brutish hadals had once conducted an empire that extended throughout this tubular maze. While humankind was still learning to make fire, the hadals had been busy constructing a metropolis far from the sun. Some experts even claimed the hadals had tutored man at the dawn of agriculture and metallurgy.

A lot of people objected to the notion. *Us? Schooled by them?* Now that he'd spent time down here, though, it made terrible sense to Clemens. Why not get your meat to grow its own food, to breed, and to cluster in villages and cities? Fatten them up before bringing them down.

At a fork in the trail, the group halted for the night. Without a word, the men and women shucked their packs and laid out their sleeping pads. The daybook said nothing about a split in the trail. Indeed, it said almost nothing about the ascent from the city. Apparently the nun had been in shock after her captivity and rescue there. That or she had intentionally concealed where the tunnel exited in New Guinea.

Bobbi, another one of the alpha females, took it upon herself to reconnoiter ahead and determine which of the two trails they should follow in the morning. Within minutes her shout for help rang down the tunnel walls. Immediately everyone got to his or her feet. No hesitation. Out came their motley collection of rifles and handguns.

Not once in eight months had they needed to fire a single shot. There was nothing left to shoot down here. The darkness had been sterilized. The Interior was scrubbed clean of threats. Exorcised, as some put it. The pandemic had erased the hadals from existence. Haddie was out of business.

They found Bobbi in a broad hollow, speechless and pale beneath her subterranean pallor. She pointed up the trail. Clemens watched as the women gathered around their sister and the men flocked ahead with their firearms. They rounded the corner.

"God help us," barked a man.

A long row of human mummies stood tied on either side of the trail. There were thirty of them, still wearing pieces of military webbing, boots, and uniforms . . . with the sun and wings of the Helios corporation logo on their shoulder patches.

"Finally," said Clemens.

They looked at him. "Finally?"

"The lost patrol," he said. "I wondered where they went."

For the past three hundred miles, Clemens's crew had been finding what was left of the Helios scientists, but always absent their hired guns. Here at last were their bodyguards, dried and arrayed for public view, complete with arrows and darts and various death wounds. A black obsidian ax blade with a broken haft jutted from a skull.

"What is this? What happened here?"

"Stone Age taxidermy," someone said.

"Custer's last stand, dude."

Their soundman murmured, "Like sinners burning in hell."

Bound with ropes, their jaws agape and flesh shrunk to the bone, they did look tortured. A chorus of the damned. No wonder mankind had feared the underworld. The subplanet really had contained the torments of legend.

The money shot, Clemens was thinking to himself.

They walked up and down the line like visitors in a darkened art museum, shining their lights on different mummies. The soldiers looked alien to Clemens, like barrel-chested insects with bulging eyes.

Then he saw the incisions. Their rib cages seemed so huge because their abdomens were so small. The men had been gutted. Their eyes had been scooped out and replaced with round white stones that stared into eternity. Their shriveled thighs and biceps all bore the same cut marks, some kind of ritual mutilation.

Their assault rifles lay at their feet, stocks splintered, so much kindling wood. Except they were plastic. Broken into pieces. Clemens could almost see the hatred in it. The hadals had despised these men.

"What's this?"

"Christ, it's his heart. They tied his heart into his beard."

Clemens went over. Sure enough, the dried fruit of muscle was a heart knotted into a man's black beard. "But why didn't they eat it?" Clemens asked. "That and the rest of their bodies?"

Bobbi stared at him. "What are you talking about?"

"There must have been two thousand pounds of meat here when they were fresh," Clemens said. "But instead of eating them, they dried and displayed them. I mean, why go to all this trouble preserving them?"

Hunger ruled this world within the world. No protein went wasted. From what they'd seen, the remains of the scientists, and even of the hadals, were always eaten to the bone, and the gnawed bones broken open for the marrow. And yet these bodies were whole, or mostly so.

Clemens's crew was somber. He listened to them trying to make sense of the atrocity.

"It's a warning," a climber said. "Keep out. Beware of dog. Here dragons be."

"The Romans used to do this. Crucify prisoners on the roads leading into the city. Behave, or else."

"No, no. It's like a trophy case. These are their war souvenirs."

"Why did they do that to their eyes?"

"Jeez-is, would you look, they're castrated, too. The bastards cut their nuts off."

That got them, the men especially. "There, but for the grace of God, go I."

"You think any of them are still around?"

"You saw the city. They're extinct. Dead and gone."

"But what if some of them survived?"

"Impossible."

"There are always survivors."

"She's right. The place is one giant hiding place."

Their lights spun this way and that, scouring the blackness.

"Impossible."

They were freaking themselves out. "Go get the camera and sound gear," Clemens said. "The least we can do is record them for posterity."

This time no one balked at his command. When they went, it was all together, leaving Clemens alone with the bodies. He began framing camera angles and composing narrative.

Pan left to right. "These few, these lucky few, this band of sons and brothers."

He edited himself. People didn't go to IMAX to hear Shakespeare. Give the crowd their boom, bang, kapow. He started over.

Shock cut to a mummy's face. Pull back to show the dead. I step from their midst.

"Since the beginning, man has been at war with the dark side . . ."

He walked down the line, shopping for the right face. Their bared teeth gleamed. The stone eyes stared. Blackbeard, he decided. The one with the heart dangling from his chin.

He strode on and picked his mark, and backed between two bodies. The wall was cool. They smelled like a tanner's shop, and a gym, too. Even dead, their different body odors clung to them. Leather and sweat. Dry as cornhusks.

Joshua.

The whisper jolted him. How could Huxley's voice reach him here? Or was it another one of them messing with his yin/yang?

He shoved away from the wall, out from the carcasses. "Who is it?"

He thrust his light beam up and down the tunnel, hunting for the trickster. But he was alone.

Joshua. Again.

He splashed light across the faces, each grinning his death grin. The air, he decided. It moved in these tunnels. It made them whistle and moan sometimes. That was all. The whispers were just air.

In the middle of the night, Clemens woke with a start. He sat up and shook his head, looking around. This evening's choice of chemical night-light was orange. His little tribe slept all around him in a jumbled orange clump, their limbs tangled and heads pillowed on one another, breathing each other's breath. A fortress of snores and twitches. And guns.

The clustering had become a reflex. By day they were a bold bunch, all muscle and trash talk, itching to beat every cliff, river, or squeeze chute that got in their way. But when it came time to sleep, they huddled like children lost in a forest.

Joshua.

It slid in from the outskirts, a kitten of a sound, barely a breath of a word. He scanned the sleeping pack. None of them was the culprit. The whisper had come from beyond their bubble of orange light.

And then again, *Joshua.* So soft it might have been in his head. Was he dreaming? No. He was wide awake now.

"What?" He kept his voice low.

Joshua. It called to him. Someone was out there.

He counted them and, sure enough, came up one short. Then he remembered Huxley. She'd never shown up. In all the excitement about the mummies, they had forgotten about her.

"Huxley?" he whispered.

One of the women stirred. She lifted her head. "What's wrong?"

"Nothing," he said. "Go back to sleep."

Her eyes closed.

He sat there for another few minutes, listening intently. But the tunnel was silent again. He lay back and tried to sleep. No dice. Voice or not, Huxley was in his head now. She was alone down there, terrified no doubt, probably lost. She'd asked for it, staying back. Accusing him with her glares.

At the end of a sleepless half hour, Clemens sighed and stood up. He didn't believe in conscience. But the voice had him going now. Screw it, he thought. Bring her in. Maybe she'd show a little gratitude.

He stood up and tiptoed from their orange halo. No sense waking anyone. By morning, he'd be back, with Huxley in tow. One more rebel to add to his collection.

As he headed down the tunnel, the image came to Clemens of an immense throat about to swallow him, and for a minute he almost returned to get his sawed-off shotgun. But his knees were bad enough without the extra weight. Besides which, for the past six thousand miles they had found nothing alive larger than a lobster. *Satan is dead. Long live . . . whatever.*

Down he sank through the tunnel. The thunder of the waterfall grew louder.

Huxley was waiting just inside the entrance. Her pale face appeared in Clemens's light. The whites of her eyes bulged. She looked indignant.

"I told you not to stay behind," he said to her.

She didn't say anything. Sulking. Probably hungry. It was going to be a chore prodding her up the trail.

Just the same, Clemens was glad he'd come to fetch her. He would work it into his script, the tale of his midnight rescue. Never mind that it had taken him less than three hours to descend. He'd make it eight hours. Hours? Days. Milk it for all it was worth. People would hail his compassion. Reviewers would note his guardian care of the crew. Couldn't save everyone, *poor Quinn,* but not for lack of trying. Everything helped during awards competitions.

Huxley went on staring at him. She didn't make a move to come up the trail. "So let's go," he said, descending the final stretch.

She glared at him.

"Can't we just get along, Hux?"

Clemens stopped. Now he saw the blood painting the spike between her legs. Her mouth was sewn shut. She was impaled on a stalagmite. "Jesus, mother," said Clemens. He stepped back from the mess.

Huxley's eyes followed him. *Impossible.* She was still alive.

Joshua.

Clemens knifed at the shadows with his light. The darkness parted. It sealed shut again. The walls glistened with waterfall sweat. There was a crevice. Something moved in there. He thrust the light at it.

Eyes glittered back at him. A face in there. It spoke his name again. But this time it was out loud. "Joshua."

Clemens jumped. "What?" The thing didn't answer. For a moment, he thought his buddy in the flowstone had come back to life and broken free. But the eyes weren't pink. There was no rack of horns. He had a tattered, greasy cowl of hair and a ragged beard, years long.

The beast eased from its womb of a crevice.

Stone scraped on stone as it emerged. To Clemens's shock, it was wearing that suit of armor made with green jade Clemens had found on the ground. The green platelets tinkled like chandelier glass.

The stone tube began crying from above. They sounded like puppies. The men's screams were even shriller than the women's.

Reject. Refuse. Make it go away. Clemens tried to pace his breathing. This couldn't be happening. The city was dead. Killed. Just bones.

Clemens remembered his camera. Even as he backed away, he could not help thinking what a great shot this would have made. In the belly of the abyss, in a city of lost souls, out of sweating stone . . . Satan was resurrecting himself.

ARTIFACTS

The United Nations Subplanetary Treaty

Recognizing that it is in the interest of all mankind that the subplanet shall continue forever to be used exclusively for peaceful purposes and shall not become the scene or object of international discord; acknowledging the substantial contributions to scientific knowledge resulting from international cooperation in scientific investigation in the subplanet; etc. . . . The signatory governments have agreed as follows:

Article I [The Subplanet for Peaceful Purposes Only]

1. The subplanet shall be used for peaceful purposes only. There shall be prohibited, inter alia, any measures of a military nature, such as the establishment of military bases and fortifications, the carrying out of military maneuvers, as well as the testing of any type of weapons.

Article IV [Territorial Claims]

1. All previously asserted rights of or claims to territorial sovereignty beneath the international waters of the Oceans and Seas shall be frozen for the duration of this treaty.
2. All previously asserted rights of or claims to territorial sovereignty beneath the existing boundaries of sovereign nations shall hold jurisdiction over their own nationals in those contained areas.
3. Nothing contained in Article IV re territorial claims shall overrule Article I. There shall be no military measures of any nature in the subplanet, whether beneath the Oceans and Seas or beneath sovereign nations.

2

SAINT MATTHEW ISLAND, FAR WESTERN ALASKA

Mommy?

The little voice floated through the blue fog.

Ali straightened in the long cut of earth. It had rained last night, turning the sedge emerald green. The muddy bones were spattered with white drops.

She stood still for a minute, listening for more, trying to make sense of the haunting. The heart is an echo chamber. Memories round on you. Ali accepted that. But her daughter had been dead for seven years now. Maggie had finally let go of her.

It was the bones, she decided. All these children's bones.

"Maggie?" she whispered.

The fog made no answer. The presence faded. Ali looked down. Her yellow galoshes glistened beside the tumbled ribs and skulls.

Sleep, baby.

Ali returned to her work. Summer was nearly over. In a few weeks, the island would return to the wind and ice. The dead could have their peace.

Like so many digs, this one resembled a sewer project with its trenches, shovels, string, and colored pin flags. Besides the bones, the dig held the usual pottery shards, carved trinkets, and bric-a-brac of days long gone. But there was no Babylon under here, no lost Atlantis, no gold of kings. Only mystery.

Math-3, as they had dubbed the third of the St. Matthew's excavations, was a common, even sorry, place. Yet it promised to change the story of man. Her task was to decipher the slaughter of these Ice Age children.

After seven weeks of soggy work under a midnight sun, they were close to solving the mystery. Ali could feel it. The bones were guiding her someplace. Going forward meant seeing . . . seeing like a hadal, not a human. But she kept bumping up against the Sape barrier.

"Sape" referred to *Homo sapiens,* and barrier referred to an engrained mind-set. It was probably going to take another generation before people finally came to accept that they and their ancestors had been sharing the planet with a separate and once superior species of man until just a few years ago. Technically both species were human, but that offended the hell out of folks, so the street divided them into human and hadal.

A little over one decade had passed since the planet's Interior had been "discovered." That was when it became clear that *Homo hadalis* (for Hades Man) had preceded his cousin throughout early Europe, Asia, and the Americas, including this island that was once part of the Bering Strait land bridge. Archeologists had gone scurrying back to their supposedly exhausted sites—ancient tells, pyramids, and middens—to figure out how they could have missed an entire epoch in mankind's history. Digging deeper, down through the Sape barrier, they were uncovering a tale of codependency, competition, and racial warfare that dated back twenty thousand years or more.

Even with all the renewed archeological vigor, Saint Matthew Island should have been irrelevant. It was an uninhabited flyspeck in the middle of a hostile sea. Before World War II, the U.S. Coast Guard had placed a small, irrelevant installation here that lasted barely three years. In between storms, an intrepid seaman named Jones had gone exploring the island on foot and strayed across odd petroglyphs half-buried at the root of the grassy mound that Ali now stood before.

Shortly afterward, Jones had gone AWOL. Until getting here, Ali had not realized how unlikely going AWOL would have been. The frigid sea chopped at the island, a relentless boundary. Swimming would have been impossible. A raft would have been swept away. The tallest vegetation stood no higher than your ankle. There was no place to hide, no way to escape. Ali wondered about foul play, or suicide. At any rate, the commander had written off Jones's glyphs as "Eskimo scrawl," and they were forgotten about.

Then a year ago, a grad student from northern Spain had stumbled across the old Coast Guard file with its black-and-white photos. Suspecting these might be pictures of hadal glyphs, young Gregorio Montaña had taken them to the Institute of Human Studies, Ali's brainchild. In short order that had led to this fogbound excavation.

Ali was a linguistics expert, not an archeologist. She had come for glyphs, not bones. But when she and her team had peeled back the thick lichen mat—on a whim of hers, a whispered suggestion—they had found the bones waiting. Ever since, she had been wrestling with them.

Forty-three sets of children's bones lay in a row at the foot of the mound and its wall of glyphs. The children—all girls, all Ice Age humans—had been ritually sacrificed. Even Ali's untrained eye could read the knife marks on the front of their neck vertebrae.

"Here you are, Alexandra."

The voice jerked Ali from her thoughts. What emerged from the fog was the handsomest man she had ever seen. It was not a matter of personal taste. Some creatures are simply born perfectly formed. With his long black hair and Basque cheekbones, Gregorio was one of them.

"It is like hide-and-seek with you," he said, waving at the fog by way of explanation. But also he meant the kiss. Things had actually gone that far last night. Just one quick good-night peck. Enough to crack the earth open. "You like to be by yourself too much."

Ali saw the bouquet of little wildflowers in his fist. Gregorio was in full siege mode.

"I'm trying to make sense of things," she said. "Before it's too late." She gestured at the bones by way of explanation. But she also meant the kiss.

For some unfathomable reason, this god had decided to fall head over heels in love with a woman fourteen years and three months his senior, a woman who had been a nun before she became a mother, a wife who had never been married, a widow whose husband might not even be dead. Ali still didn't know what to do with Gregorio, scold him or run from him. Or jump him. For what it was worth, Gregorio didn't know what to do with himself.

"Yes," he said, turning to the bones. "It is time to put the children to bed for the winter."

Unable to properly excavate the site, they had decided to leave everything in situ and cover it over again with the blanket of lichen mat. A larger team would come for the bones the next summer.

As if suddenly noticing the bouquet in his hand, Gregorio laid it beside a skull. That eased some of the tension. Now they could be on the same page, he and Ali, attending to the mystery of the bones.

"This is eating me up," said Ali. "Why kill these children? What a horrible day that must have been."

Gregorio shrugged. "Savage gods," he said. "One more sadness in the universe."

Ali could smell him. "There are too many of them," she said. "All killed at once. All females."

"An orgy of blood," he said. "A hadal thing."

"That's what gets me, though," she said. "It's *not* a hadal thing. There is not a single instance of child sacrifice in their world. They were vicious, but when it came to human captives they were pragmatists. The women were used as breeders. The men became slaves. But it was the children who were the real treasure. They were integrated into the life cycle of the underworld. They were beloved, especially the girls. There are captive tales of hadals sacrificing themselves in order to protect a human child."

"There is a limit to love," Gregorio declared.

"Excuse me?" Just last night he had declared the very opposite.

Others in the office made do with Greg. But from the very start she had pronounced every vowel in his name. It sounded rounder and richer. And it drew out his presence, even when he wasn't in the room. Also, of course, it was his actual name. In turn she was Alexandra. Alek-sondra. And Gregorr-io. Only slowly had she become aware that their courtship was a public affair, or even that it was a courtship. Everyone in the office listening to their weaving of sounds could tell something was in the works.

"What I mean is, we were just animals to them," he said.

"Agreed," said Ali, "but child sacrifice wasn't their style. Capturing humans meant training hunters and sending expeditions to the surface and maintaining a slave network. Their empire was built on slaves. We've found codes of law that dealt with the treatment of slaves. Killing a slave was a serious offense. How do you explain this then? Forty-three children, in one fell swoop, their throats cut, their bodies abandoned. And these were girls who could have produced hundreds of more children for them." *Girls*, she thought, like her Maggie.

"It was evil." Gregorio said it very quietly. He knew about Maggie. He let Ali have her anger.

Breathe, she told herself. Maybe she didn't have any business among the bones this morning. But day after day, the long-lost children kept pulling her up from camp. It was as if they needed a mother. And she needed a daughter. It was that simple.

"There is no evil," she said. "Satan is dead. I saw him killed. He was just a man in a mask."

In a sense, that incident had closed the book on hadal civilization. The man, a Jesuit named Thomas, had recruited her to join the first scientific expedition beneath the Pacific. Her mission: to hunt for the historical Satan. It had made a sort of holy sense at the time. Hell was freshly opened, and she was a nun and he was a priest. Only later, after the hadals captured her, had Thomas declared himself to be the same immortal creature he had sent her to find. She had fallen for his deadly charade, just in time to see him gunned down.

"Then he wasn't Satan." Gregorio glanced around at the fog, as if his *basajaunak,* the shaggy ancient ones of his homeland, might hear her blasphemy. "Because there is still evil in the world." At times like this, he seemed very young to her.

"Evil doesn't need a name, though," she said.

"But it does," Gregorio insisted. "We need the devil." He touched his heart. "In here, it feels only half complete without him."

"Why? Because if he's dead, God is dead?" That was the hand grenade in the theologians' shop these days. It was something of a religious crisis. Unless evil had a face, man was left alone looking in his mirror. "We had to grow up eventually," she said. "We're all alone now. There is no one else to blame for the wicked things that happen to us."

Gregorio gestured at the skeletons. "So it is okay for the children to die?"

Her eyes dropped to his bouquet of wildflowers by the skull. "I'm simply saying there's no use in blaming it on wicked spirits," she said. "The best we can do is to make the universe speak for itself. Language is our salvation. Without it there is only chaos."

"Music, I think," he said. "Music is our salvation." His great work in progress was a symphony for prehistoric instruments. What a sight and sound that was going to be, the bone flutes and violins with sinew strings.

"Words or notes," she said, touching the long wall that girdled the mound, "we are left with only glyphs for our clue."

Standing a foot high, the glyphs ran the length of the exposed stone. They were like a badly weathered jigsaw puzzle in a language from another planet. Some of the symbols already belonged to her growing database of hadal alphabets and pictograms. The rest were so ancient, they had probably gone extinct long ago.

"I still can't figure out how that Coast Guard boy found them in the first place," she said. "What possessed him to walk across the island to this spot?"

"Voices." Gregorio said it without hesitation.

It startled her. "Voices?" He heard them, too?

"Well, not real voices. Memories. In the case of our friend Jones, he was hearing the voice of his dead lover," Gregorio said. "I am reading between the lines of the commander's report. But after she killed herself, I think Jones had a curse on him."

"His girlfriend was a suicide?" Ali had glossed over that part of the report, going straight for the old black-and-white photos of the glyphs.

"She was pregnant by him, and they were not married yet, and her parents were very religious," Gregorio said. "She killed herself. It was only a matter of time before he did the same, don't you think?"

"Not necessarily."

"He went missing on the anniversary of her suicide. It's completely obvious. She was calling to him. He was haunted. I think he jumped into the sea."

"Come on, haunted?"

"Yes, I know, my Old World superstitions."

"Okay, a broken heart and guilt might explain Jones's wandering, but not his discovery," she said. "Something tempted him to pull away the vegetation and find the glyphs." Just like something had tempted Ali to pull up part of the lichen mat and find the bones.

Gregorio laid one hand on the stone. "Luck," he said. "His, then ours."

Ali looked at him, then looked again, but this time over his head. Last night's rain had washed away a chunk of the mound's green turf. Something lay underneath, carved from the rock face. "Is that a stair step?"

Gregorio grabbed a shovel, but couldn't reach the step. He tossed it, and the shovel head rang on the stone.

"Give me a boost," she said.

"You want to go up there?" Gregorio's expression darkened. "No. I will go."

"Just give me a boost."

She stood in the stirrups of his hands, then on his shoulders, and got a good grip of the sod. Her misplaced husband, Ike, the mountain climber, would have waltzed up. Ali thrashed and flailed without shame. The turf sheeted off below her waist.

"That's high enough," said Gregorio. Covered with mud and wet grass, he stood ready to catch her.

The prospect of climbing down was worse than going up. Struggling higher, she reached the step. She tore away more of the turf. "There's more than one step. It's a whole staircase."

The edges of steps laddered higher. "Go get the rest of the gang," she said. "Something's on top of the mound. Or inside it."

"I'm not leaving you," he said.

He looked so small down there. To his left and right, half digested by the fog, the bones rested in a long line of white piles. They were arranged at the base of this buried staircase. It was so obvious from this height. The children had been sacrificed to the secret in this mound.

"I'm not going to fall," she said. "Start them digging from the bottom up. Expose the stairs."

"Don't go any higher."

"I promise."

The moment he vanished, she started higher, attacking the turf with her bare hands. The mud was chilly. It avalanched past her legs. None of the bones lay in the fall line. The children were safe.

The stairs rose into the fog. She lost sight of the ground. The mound was not natural. Massive blocks of stone lay buried under the dirt and lichen. Someone had built this small mountain by hand, and then someone else had buried it. But why?

The summit was a disappointment, flat and empty and viewless. Tufts of grass jutted from the stone joints. Bits of broken blue eggshell littered the tufts. Ali walked around, hunting for hints of what the pyramid might once have balanced on its head. She bent to examine a long furrow, partially grown over, that offered the possibility of more recent activity up here. She pressed her fingers into it, then heard someone huffing for breath behind her, and stood.

Gregorio arrived, smeared with mud and carrying his shovel. He blew a cloud of frost. Far below, the ocean broke against invisible cliffs. "What have you found?"

"I don't know. The glyphs at the bottom are hadal. This must have been an outpost, the farthest reach of their empire. Beyond this point, the surface held only an Ice Age wilderness. Does that explain the sacrifices? Were they trying to hold back the forces of nature with a blood sacrifice? Or warn away their human rivals. Or . . . what?" They were close, but winter was closer.

"We are not done yet, Alexandra," Gregorio vowed. He struck his shovel at the inscrutable earth.

Without a sound, the ground opened at his feet. It swallowed him to the hips. One moment he loomed head and shoulders above her, the next she was staring down at the top of his head. There he stood, a man with no legs, still gripping the majesty of his shovel.

Ali burst into laughter.

Gregorio made a face. He patted the dirt at his waist. "This is funny?"

His wounded dignity only made it worse. "Stop," she said. "Give me your hand."

"Never mind," he said. "I'll work from where I stand."

He began sawing away the grassy carpet from around his hips, widening the hole. The hole contained steps leading down inside the mound. Gregorio started down, then looked up and saw her hesitation.

"Maybe we should wait for another day," he said.

She had every reason not to go in. People were pouring into the earth's caverns by the thousands each day, seeking their fortunes, finding their dreams. But for Ali, the Subterrain remained a nightmare. It had stolen the father of her child, and then stolen her child. It had stolen her life, or one of them. That's how it felt.

She had made a career of staring into the abyss, but from a distance, in the safety of her institute in San Francisco. Eventually she was going to have to go under, though. She felt halfway gone from the world anyway.

"We don't want to be wondering all winter what's in here," she said. "Show the way." She had a flashlight in one pocket, a compulsion, light. She handed it to him.

The stairs snaked down. What began as a man-made structure with quarried stone soon married an old volcano vent. The passage followed nature's lead.

The rewards came almost immediately. Untouched by the elements, glyphs in pristine condition decorated the walls. Ali and Gregorio wound deeper into the tube.

"The volcano was like a throat singing words into the wind." He shined her light here and there. "But what was it singing? Who was it singing to?"

"Have you noticed this symbol?" Ali pointed to a mark similar to a bent *N*. "It keeps repeating. And the deeper we go, the more frequently it repeats, like a drumbeat practically, drowning out all the other sounds."

Soon the walls bore a steady stream of nothing but *N*'s. The glyph teased her. She felt like she should know it. Her head tilted. The glyph fell into position. "It's an aleph."

Gregorio came back up the steps.

"Do you see it?" She traced a modern aleph beside the incision in the stone. "It's from the Semitic alphabet, the first letter, a silent letter. But this symbol must predate that by ten thousand years or more." Ali glanced around. The alephs spiraled upward. "How elegant."

Gregorio waited, helpless.

"It's the sound of silence," she said. "See how silence turns into words as it ascends."

Her intuition shocked Gregorio. "That has to be it."

"I could be wrong," she said. But she was right. She knew it in her gut.

"How deep does this go?" Gregorio said.

"If it connects to the network of tunnels, and I suspect it does, then you've discovered a new entry point. Congratulations. You can add your name to the register." Once upon a time that would have been unique. Anymore, it was like climbing Everest, a dime a dozen.

"We can't stop here," he said. The hook had set in him that quickly.

"And when the battery goes dead?" she said. "And, let's see, I have a Luna bar for my lunch. Oh, and a bottle of Aleve." For what she feared were hot flashes, she did not say. "How about you? Got all the descent gear?"

"The deeps provide," he said. "You told me so."

"To those who know them, they provide."

He handed her the flashlight. "Then you guide me. This is your province."

"It's not that easy." In fact, it was. Going down into the earth was as simple as breathing. Climbing back out, though—leaving hell and all its magic behind—that was the challenge.

"Here's a path. Our very own. Think what we might find, Alexandra."

"Another time."

"Just a little farther."

They did not have to go far.

Gregorio saw the body first. He froze and crossed himself. Ali went around him and kneeled by it.

More bone than leather, the carcass rested at the foot of a raw stone column. The man had been wearing a heavy, cable-knit sweater and sailor's pants.

"Petty Officer Jones," she said. She had no doubts. Here was the Coast Guard boy, the would-be Orpheus. He had descended barely a quarter mile before lying down for a nap here. Maybe he had died dreaming of his dead sweetheart.

Gregorio took off his wind jacket and covered what remained of the face. He straightened. And hissed. "And what is this thing?"

Ali followed his eyes and ran her light up the pillar.

"A Minotaur?" she said.

It was a statue, two stories tall, grotesque in the classical sense, part man, part beast. The thing had been carved from a single twisting column of stone. Spiraling up from the base, veins of dark granite served as mineral ropes. The sculptors had begun their work at its stomach, leaving coarse chisel marks and gouges at the start, and refining their strokes as they went higher. In effect they had partially freed the man-bull creature from his roots. But they had, fearfully it seemed, not freed him entirely. Only the horns were polished.

"This is what killed the children," said Ali.

"A fairy-tale monster?" Gregorio circled the pillar like a moth.

"Here is the voice of the aleph," she said. "It fits perfectly. The aleph and the ox's head."

"What are you talking about, the ox's head?"

"Ah, grasshopper," she said. It was one of their private jokes, the wise teacher and her intern. With her fingertip she sketched the symbol's evolution. "The Phoenicians drew it with horns."

"Here is the shape of a head, here are the horns. The horns became legs, this went here, that went there."

It came tumbling out of her. She was excited. "The aleph is the origin of the first letter in our alphabet, a celebration of our contract with nature's power. It's the beginning of our written language, an animal turned into a picture turned into a letter. A humble letter. A powerful letter. Written on the head of the golem, it was the letter that brought it to life. Did you know the aleph is the first letter of God's mystical name in Exodus? *'Ehye 'Asher 'Ehye.* 'I Am That I Am.'"

"Yes, Alexandra. But this is no golem. This is not God. It's a monster."

"It must have been their god," Ali said. That sculpted mouth, half open, was roaring the silence that became language. "The aleph made flesh. Or stone." She spoke a word in the hadal's click language. It meant "Older-Than-Old." *Their god, our devil.*

By accident, it seemed, lured by a memory of her daughter's voice, she had jumped twenty thousand years back in time. Long ago, a simple letter in the alphabet had lived in these dark caverns in the form of some monstrous cult. But also, she suddenly realized, not so long ago.

"I've seen this before," she said. "It was a different version and grown over with scar tissue. But it was the same thing, an aleph."

"Scar tissue?"

"They cut it into Ike when they captured him." Gregorio's little smile faded. Ike, again. Though Ike was probably dead. As dead as poor Jones. "It was at the base of his spine," she said. "He told me it was an ownership mark."

"He belonged to this?" Gregorio shoved at the stone column as if his hand could topple it. But the statue was immovable. It almost seemed to support the earth on its shoulders.

"He had no idea what it meant or who had owned him. It was different from all the other slave marks. It bothered him. Obsessed him. He said it was like being an orphan who didn't know his father's name. I think it's why he abandoned us." Us: she and Maggie and all his own kind.

Even before his daughter was born, even before Ali chose her name, Ike had vanished back into the earth, leaving one child fatherless while he searched for a name and a father that were not his own.

They stood quietly. Water drip-dropped in the shadows. Otherwise, the place was silent as a tomb.

Ali shined her light into the tunnel. It wound deeper. "We should go. The others will wonder where we disappeared to."

Suddenly he was alarmed for her good reputation. "Yes, immediately. We must tell them about the tunnel." He looked down at the body. "What about him?"

"We'll inform the authorities. But for now, poor Jones has his tomb."

"Good. Very good." Gregorio's face blossomed with relief. Someone else could handle the dead.

"You might as well take your jacket with you."

He shuddered. "Let him have it. For his journey."

They started back. Partway up the steps, Ali felt something, not quite a hand, but a grasp nonetheless, reaching for her.

Mommy.

She froze.

Ali glanced up the stairs at Gregorio striding on. Plainly he hadn't heard a thing. She stabbed her light at the lower reaches, searching for the voice. The stone Minotaur seemed to be watching her.

"Maggie," she whispered. She waited for the voice to speak again. It didn't. *Sleep, baby.* Turning, she climbed after Gregorio, unaware of the lullaby on her lips as she hurried toward the light.

ARTIFACTS

THE WEATHER CHANNEL
A COLD DAY IN HELL

A persistent tubular airflow will continue to cool the Nine Rivers Gorge region. Patchy fog early, then clear and unseasonably chilly. Highs in the upper 40s to low 50s. Lows, the same.

River levels—steady at norm. Be alert for flash flooding.*
Interior extremes (last week)
High—148 degrees in Wink, Grosse Tunnels, Arctic
    provinces
Low—39 degrees in Nueva Loca, Argentine
    Protectorates

ALERTS: a fast-moving cloud of sulfur will reach the Henners network late today. Expect olfactory distress. Tube 666 in the L-Zone is closed due to electromagnetic storms.
SUPERALERTS: a methane plume has been detected in the Xining-New Toronto territories, at minus-3 miles elevation and rising. Methane is combustible. Mixtures of 5 to 15 percent in air are explosive. Methane is not toxic when inhaled, but can produce suffocation by reducing oxygen concentrations. Carry gas masks. Observe flame discipline. Be prepared. Be aware.

*Always wear backcountry survival beacons in case of rock slide, earthquake, flood, or animal attack. Always carry backup light sources.
Happy hunting!

3

BENEATH THE NORTH PACIFIC FLOOR

They paused in their great walkabout, lightless, nine of them, resting on their haunches. The last in line, Li, idly fiddled with the growths covering his head. His fingers toyed with the coral-like horns, tracing the bumps and buds that boiled from his skull. Every day the configuration was a little different, a little more advanced. Like their long journey, his helmet of bone was relentlessly building upon itself.

Up the line, one of them groaned quietly. For three days he'd been trying to pass a stone in his urine. No one suggested slowing down for him. Each of them had suffered torments along the way, and you kept up for the sake of the band. You just did. Pain couldn't kill you, and there was too much territory to cover with too little time. They were in a footrace against the hordes of man.

Li didn't need his nose anymore to smell the human trespass. You could taste it in the air. The rancid stench breathed through the living tunnels. For days now, he and his comrades had been picking up traces of the colonial advance. Sewage and chemicals poisoned the subterranean waters that flowed down to them. It burned their skin and roiled their stomachs. Man was a curse. A weed.

He wished he could lead their little band away from the civilization looming ahead. For almost two years they had been picking their way through the remotest arms of the deepest mazes, keeping one step ahead of the mushrooming colonies. Before it was too late, before the hordes completely overran the warren of tunnels shooting through this part of the planet, they were visiting what remained of the People, to bear witness.

In one collapsed city after another, Li and his comrades had clambered among painted acropolises, and coliseums carved in one piece from the bedrock, and spires whittled from stalagmites, and passageways decorated with cryptic lettering and images. Where rivers had cut underground canyons, they had walked between giant statues of kings whose names were probably lost forever. Ancient canals had worn away to broad mineral deltas. What you took from the stone returned to the stone.

The faintest tap-tap of an insect's feet came to Li's ear. Slowly, still squatting, he turned to face the wall. As his eyesight had atrophied, or rather altered, his other senses had sharpened. He could smell the difference in minerals. He could feel shapes by the sound of his voice bouncing back. He could sense colors without seeing them.

It came again, that slight tap-tap, the cautious telegraph of escape. The insect sensed his presence. Too late. With a swift motion, Li trapped it under his cupped palm.

He removed it carefully, still alive, and let the details tell him what kind of insect this was. It mattered. Some carried bizarre toxins in their vessels. Inside their bodies, some had barbs built that released during digestion. This one was harmless. It had the familiar length and weight of a common cave beetle. *Coleoptera bailey,* he had named the species.

With a flick of a finger, he killed it. He broke off the wings and the head with its long antennae, opened the body, and stripped out its innards. The meat and shell crunched between his teeth, nutlike. Yes, beetle, definitely.

They were constantly on the prowl for such snacks. Insects, lizards, fish, snakes: anything that had survived the plague, and wasn't poisonous, fueled their pilgrimage. Living off the land had changed their metabolism. There wasn't an ounce of fat on the bunch of them. They slept three hours a night. Every five days or so, Li laid a hard little turd, which he saved and dried and contributed to the rare campfire.

He had found the rhythm of the depths. Here was home. Unfortunately, not enough of them felt the same way. They were the ones pulling their dark voyage back to the light. Surrendering to nostalgia. It was a useless, one-way longing, though. They were forgotten by now. And there was still so much to record down here. But the majority ruled, and that was that. In these outlands, cohesion was everything. Dissent was death.

"Light," their leader warned up ahead.

The coral man shielded his eyes. A blue penlight clicked on. It burned too brightly for a minute, or seemed to, then dimmed to a bearable round bead.

"John," said his neighbor.

John Li took away his hands. He blinked at the sight ahead.

Dressed in rags, or loincloths, some of them, his comrades looked like a row of monstrosities. In fact they were, *lusus naturae*, freaks of nature . . . bearded, shaggy haired, bearing satchels and backpacks and scratched, battered tubes and boxes housing their scientific instruments. Every man sported sores, fungal rot, spider and sand-lice bites, scars in various stages of healing, bruises, and the burn marks they'd gotten while crossing an intramarginal hot zone. What really made them birds of a feather, though, were their deformities.

The depths had grown on them in more ways than one. Even as they had acclimated over the months to the darkness and isolation and endless hunger, even as they had acquired some sense of the flora, fauna, geology, and lost culture of this realm, even as Li and others had fallen in love with it, the subterranean world had quietly been at work infecting them.

They had come prepared, or so they'd thought. But their motion sensors had proved useless, for there were no large animals, much less hadals, left to defend against. Their radiation badges and gas detectors had alerted them to the defined dangers, but not the undefined ones. They had learned the hard way that there were rare gases, acids, salts, and liquids never classified by man. Once they got back to the surface with their discoveries, the table of elements was going to grow another few appendages. In short, the explorers had unwittingly become guinea pigs in the Subterrain. For what it was worth, they weren't the first. The hadals had been enduring—indeed, celebrating—these and other mutations for millennia.

Skeletal warp, it was called. *Osteitis deformans,* or Paget's disease. Skeletal tissue went wild, raging through cycles of breakdown and rampant growth. As a result, Li and his companions all had misshapen skulls and bizarrely shaped horns. The good news was that the disease was not a cancer. The bone growth didn't invade their cranial cavities. It didn't impair their intellect.

The bad news was that, in varying degrees and shapes, NASA's North

Pacific Subterrain Exploration team number two had turned into a pack of elephant men. Or a flock of fiends. Or a gaggle of gargoyles. They had made a game of it, sitting in the darkness, cracking each other up. A pride of ogres. A murder of monsters. A drift of demons. A sleuth of brutes. Maybe, Li thought, the bone growths had impaired their intellect after all.

Li preferred the term "charm," used for goldfinches, or better yet, "watch," as in a watch of nightingales. Personally he saw nothing ugly about their metamorphoses. It was a mark of passage. God's way of speaking through your body. But Li understood the group's black humor. Underneath all the quiet joking, they were terrified. Most had families out there. One version of them had gone down into the earth, and another version was about to come out. Would their children and wives still recognize them?

"The station can't be far now," said their leader, Watts. He had a Medusa head of calcium serpents. Next to him, holding the penlight, Childs—who knew more sheep jokes than any other man alive—had a unicorn shaft growing from his forehead. In the orb of blue light, Watts rolled up his dog-eared maps.

They were describing a huge two-year circle, returning to their departure point, the Sitka Station beneath Baranof Island, off the Alaskan shore. If not for circling back upon themselves, their maps would have been useless. They only knew where they'd been, not where they were going. GPS didn't work down here. Magnetic north got fouled by gremlins in the Subterrain: strange, wandering electromagnetic fields. Most radars couldn't penetrate this deep. Only low-frequency radio waves worked, though even they were subject to still unexplained anomalies.

"We don't need to do this, you know," said a half-naked biologist wearing Adidas running shorts.

"We know, Bill," someone said.

"We can still go back," said Bill. "Down. Deeper."

"Bill, we voted."

"But think about it," Bill said, "think about the things waiting for us."

It was true. Who could say what else lay in the far tunnels? They had sampled just a tiny fraction of the underworld. They had found strangeness and beauty, like in a dream.

Li remembered. They had crossed a bottle green desert made of ground limestone, fine as powdered sugar, with little tongues of flame for flowers: a hot five days of trekking.

Braced for more and more fierce heat, because the inner earth was supposed to be a place of fiery rock, they had descended instead into cold zones with ice that threatened to clog the passageways. The ice came from glaciers dyed pink and orange, whole fields of crevassed glaciers filled with plankton, yes, plankton carried from ancient, now buried seas. Still alive, too. Thaw the ice and they wriggled about under the microscope.

In one tunnel they had walked barefoot upon an anaerobic moss that was the largest living life-form on the planet, miles long and eons old.

They had found the bones of bizarre animals that could have wandered straight out of—or into—a Hieronymus Bosch painting. The species variation was incredible. The mutation rate was off the scale.

Somehow evolution had superaccelerated down here. More astonishing yet, acquired traits got passed along as inherited traits. The trend ran counter to all that was Darwinian. It verged on Lamarck's theory, which held that giraffes stretching their necks for food would have offspring with longer necks. No one had bought that idea for almost two hundred years. But here it was, a menagerie of proofs, in effect, that pigs could fly. Or hadals, apparently, some of them. Wings. Webbed feet. Scales. Claws. You name it. Remarkable, truly.

And then there were the ancient cities melting away as minerals invaded, and the seemingly endless network of paths, lanes, stairways, and bridges over black rivers . . . the architecture of a once great people. And their bodies and bones. Tens of thousands of them, unceremoniously felled by the plague and left unburied. In the beginning, Li and a few others had attempted mass graves. But there were too many remains and it took too much energy, and future colonists would only excavate the bones to grind for animal feed and fertilizer.

For that very reason, when four of their members had drowned in a river accident eighteen months ago, they'd gone to great lengths to mark their graves as human. Li was pretty sure even that wouldn't stop the colonists, though. Everything was getting ransacked down here. Progress was the watchword. It was Manifest Destiny all over again, except this time the Wild West was four miles deep and perforated the crust of the entire earth.

What more might be waiting for them deeper? More gold, more glory, more species, more cities. Someone else would have to find out. Team two of NASA's Subterrain Exploration was going home.

No one replied to Joe. It was over. At some point it had to be over.

Li had to restrain himself. Like Joe, he would have been happy to stay under for years to come, meandering and exploring. But unlike Joe, he had not fought when the group voted to turn around and finally start their retreat. For months he had been hearing the yearning when they murmured in their sleep. You could not fight heartache. Yes, their grand exploration was drawing to a close.

Their team of geologists, biologists, and a botanist had been dispatched to map and catalog regions lying beneath the northern third of the North Pacific Ocean. Sooner than later, like it or not, the stone frontier was going to be occupied and stripped of its natural resources. Like true field scientists, even the Republicans among them had come to wish this dark wilderness could be preserved as it was.

There were wonders down here that defied their combined sciences, a design whose shape and purpose Li had merely glimpsed in this darkness. He had always prided himself on his atheism. It was a measure of his rational mind. How ironic then that this literal, physical hell should usher God into his life.

He had always disliked those scientist-believers who couldn't seem to come down on one side or the other of the issue, the types who rigorously arrived at a big bang theory, for instance, and then conceded it might represent the divine spark. To him such gymnastics amounted to intellectual schizophrenia. To superstition dressed in wire-rim glasses.

Yet here he was, swept away like some Biology 101 student by the balance and symmetry and mystery of it all. Just when science had finally nailed together a tidy explanation for the workings of the planet, this other planet inside the planet had wrecked the whole neat scheme. Humans, meet your long-lost cousins. It was like suddenly meeting a secret roommate who has been sharing your skin with you since birth. Most troubling. In such close quarters, sharing this chunk of rock circling the sun, how could they never have met?

In the old days, mapmakers had concocted fictional continents called Australia and Antarctica to serve as counterweights to real continents.

And then the fictional continents had become real ones. Such was this, a secret mirror reflecting the unknown to the known, an inner world that inverted the outer world, a dark truth to match the sunlit one above, a perfect balance of stone, air, and animals.

The yin/yang of his revelation embarrassed Li, and so he had not spoken about it to anyone else on the expedition. Indeed, for a time he dismissed his notion of harmony as a cosmological itch born of his Chinese-American heritage. But then Li discovered he wasn't the only one thinking such thoughts, nor the first, not by a long shot. He had found his notion confirmed, *exactly* confirmed, written in stone. Carved in it. By hadals.

Not being a cryptographer or archeologist, Li had no definite idea what the hadals had been communicating with their glyphs, writings, and other cave art. Like the others, he had snapped photos of the more remarkable examples, and speculated on the meaning of this or that rune or symbol. Underneath their bloody-mindedness, the hadals had apparently been a whimsical race. They had left stylized depictions of flowers, animals, the sun and moon, along with murals and tableaux of wars waged and humans sacrificed, their hearts pulled out, their heads chopped off, their skins flayed. Very Aztec.

Then one day Li had found something that took him beyond the superficial, and turned his universe upside down. Or inside out. There, cut into the base of a high obelisk, was a yin/yang symbol. It was unmistakable, the circle enclosing conjoined opposites . . . and yet probably fifteen to twenty thousand years older than the Chinese sign.

That had been the beginning of his sympathy for the devil, so to speak. He was doing his best not to get carried away with it. Only a fool would romanticize the hadals as noble savages. Everywhere Li looked, he had found a culture built on slavery and murder. Even at the height of their civilization, they had used humankind as their cattle. In their pictograms, in statuary, in the iron chains and shackles and cages used to secure human prisoners, in the drinking cups made of human skulls, the hadals had celebrated sadism and bloodletting and predation.

And yet, at the same time, only a fool would ignore the civilization they had built down here, so far from the sun, one might almost say so far from God. For two years now, the ghosts of the hadals had been speaking to him, not with their sad piles of preserved flesh and bones, but with the glory of their ruins.

While humankind had still been figuring how to put iron in the fire and seeds in the ground, the hadals were sculpting domed monuments to emperors. Their Michelangelos were engraving magnificent bas-reliefs, their da Vincis were inventing, their Newtons were arriving at basic truths. Li had found math equations etched into slabs overgrown with yellow and blue lichen. Yes, whole theorems, using hadal numbers and symbols!

In this perpetual night, dynasties had replaced other dynasties while their cousins, *H. sapiens,* were still loping about on the surface terrifying the mastodons to death. While man was just beginning to daub ochre bison onto cave ceilings, the history of the hadal empire had been written and forgotten. And not only the history of their empire, but also of their religion. Because Li was convinced they had worshipped a single deity.

The rest of his team refused to grant the hadals a god. It was still an affront to them that an offshoot of *H. erectus* had preceded man in every aspect. That the evidence now showed human civilization had probably leaked to the surface world, borne by escaped slaves. That man was not the first. How could it be that mutants, mere hominids, these slope-browed primitives, these living fossils, could have been our superiors, ever? God was the answer, or so the politicians and evangelists—more and more they were the same—would have you believe. Something had to distinguish us from them, and so people had fastened on to monotheism as the grand event that had catapulted humans past hadals.

But Li had walked through huge structures that could only have been cathedrals and temples at one time. Even after all these eons, their acoustics were crisp and precise. A voice at the front carried through the whole chamber. Whose voice but a hadal bishop's or rabbi's or imam's or rinpoche's?

And how else did you explain the presence of the same recurring glyphs and images and spirals carved in the walls leading to the most impressive buildings in each hadal city? Prehistoric graffiti, his scientific companions said, dismissing it. God, Li knew. The hadals had found the sacred down here. How could they not? Who else but God could have created—and hidden—a world of such beauty and wonders? The only question in Li's mind was what kind of god they had worshipped, a dark one or a light one, or one that embraced it all, including the crickets.

"A little more," Watts said to them. He stood. The rest of them stood. Their coral branches of horns scratched against the tunnel ceiling. After two years of walking, they were all leg muscle.

Bill stayed squatting. He wasn't going any farther with them. It would mean the end of him eventually. There were no hadals to dodge. But somewhere in the darkness a rock slide or a swift current of black water or an insect with venom had his name on it. Or he would simply starve. No one argued with him. He no longer existed. They walked past him. Not one so much as murmured a good-bye.

Li was the last in line. "Tell me what it was like," he said.

Bill gave a grin with what was left of his teeth.

Farther ahead, Morris, the geologist with the kidney stone, grunted as he walked. The team had run out of pain medication ages ago. The colony would have drugs and a doctor. Their suffering was nearly at an end.

But two days later, when they reached the outskirts of the well-lit colony, Li realized their suffering had only just begun. Bill was right. They should have kept going deeper out there.

There was no challenge, no warning. A gunshot snapped through the tunnel. Brooks, their botanist, dropped in a heap.

"Don't shoot," Watts yelled into the blinding light. "We're friends. Don't shoot."

A man's voice said, "They talk?"

Li and the others were quiet as mice. Quieter. Almost as quiet as Weber.

Another man shouted from the light, "Lay down. Right now. Noses into the floor. Kiss it. Anyone moves and we open up on the whole shitload of you."

After a minute, Li heard boot steps. There were seventeen of them. They had been eating beef, he could smell the grease in their pores. Deodorant. Skoal's chewing tobacco. Quartz dust in the cleats of their boots. Gold miners.

"This one's dead. You got him through the eye."

Brooks had been the one pressing hardest to go home. Two years of surviving in the tubes, just inches away from the ride home . . . he'd almost made it.

Watts started talking fast, part plea, part blame. "We're team two with NASA. The space agency. Only inner space. Scientists. Unarmed. What have you done? Don't shoot. Isn't this the Sitka Station? We left here twenty-three months ago. Is Graham still in charge here? I want to see the person in command. Right now."

"Enough of that," a big man said. "Calm yourself down."

"He has a family. You just shot him. Calm myself? Six thousand miles. We were here. We made it back. What have you done?"

Li could smell the inside of Brooks's head. The blood traced past his fingers along a runnel in the floor.

"Let's see some identification, mister."

"Here, in my pouch, take it, damn you."

After consulting one another, the men let them stand. But they kept the rifle muzzles trained at their faces, fingers on the triggers.

"Talk some more," one demanded.

"Talk?" Watts snapped. "You've killed a man. A good man. Are you crazy? Lower those damn weapons."

"He speaks English," one of the men slowly observed.

It hit Li. The sentries thought they were hadals. Even up this close.

"They're human?"

"What the hell happened to you boys?"

"Take them in," a big man said.

What remained of team two entered the colony in a line, tentatively, barefoot and blinded. Li's head throbbed. The acid light burned his eyes.

Blurred shapes bracketed the path. Voices fenced them in. Li heard them clearly.

"Who are they? What are they?"

"Team two, NASA, that lost bunch. Feds."

"But they died out there."

"Not a word in two years."

"What happened to them?" Over and over, that question. "How could this happen?"

"Mommy, that one's crying."

Tears were running from Li's eyes, flushing the smog and blaze of light. And the sickness in his heart.

"He's coming home," said the mother. "He's just glad to be back."

That wasn't it, though, far from it. Li tasted the salt. He had made a mistake. *Bill.*

"Simms shot one. Hell, look at them. Horns and near naked. How were we supposed to know? Shoot first, ask later."

The air gagged Li. It reeked of diesel fuel and engine grease and electricity and cement dust. Leftover food lay rotting in their homes. Even their sewage was ripe with waste. Overfed, their bodies had cast off the abundance.

He felt panic. *What have you done?* He didn't belong here. This was a terrible mistake. But it was too late to run. They had him hemmed in from behind.

The shapes clarified. The crowd took on substance, lots of it. Subsisting on protein bars and whatever they could catch, his sticklike comrades had become the norm. These settlers shocked him with their immense shoulders and chests and padded stomachs. Even the thin ones seemed plump. *Like cattle.* He shut out the thought.

He should have known better. He *had* known better. And yet he was here.

No one offered water, or rest, or even a hey or a nod. No one spoke to them, only about them, as if they were wild animals sliding through. Li could feel their fear. It went beyond that. Revulsion. It was hard not to take it personally, but he tried. They were defending themselves. It was that simple.

Driven by poverty, greed, desperation, or dreams, these people had descended from all that was familiar to find what they were missing in their lives. They had carried light into the darkness, full of blind faith, believing their rewards lay just around the next bend. Now this little NASA parade of monstrosities had appeared from deeper yet, and it threatened them. It terrified them. They had thought they could muck around in the basement of the earth and not be changed, at least not like this. They had thought they could have deliverance without transformation.

"They must have done something wrong."

"Went too deep, that's what. It happens. Those boys went to the wrong place at the wrong time."

Li's misshapen companions were silent, because now they had their answer. The loathing would only get worse as they neared the surface. They could no longer pretend the Interior had not left its mark on them. Their wives would flinch. Their children would have nightmares about the creature in their house.

As he walked between the gawking settlers, Li withdrew deep into himself. He pictured Bill wandering like a monk into the core of darkness, padding through the tunnels, roaming through the hollow cities. He imagined Bill slowly starving or falling through a shaft or losing his mind among the empty temples and fortresses, and thought, *What glories will I never see?*

ARTIFACTS

THE WALL STREET JOURNAL

The Underground Economy: "Deep Dollars" Both Boom and Bane

Fueled by a surge in raw exports, the Subterranean economy grew an astounding 282.1 percent last year. Meanwhile tax revenues, corporate profits, and earnings sent home by workers in the Subterrain, have sent federal and private spending on the surface into overdrive.

Fueled by "deep dollars," the U.S. has seen a boom in spending in all sectors, from health and education to information technology, transportation, and the military. Analysts predict the recent record deficit will be wiped out in the next two months. Unemployment rates have tumbled. Wall Street broke 15,000 last week.

And yet President Wayne Burr has called for a range of economic sanctions to be imposed upon the entire Subterrain. "Plain and simple, we are getting bought off by rogue states," Burr said. "While we spend the riches sent up from below, Subterranean regimes are building armies, stockpiling weapons, and trafficking in humans and drugs. The international order is disintegrating before our eyes, undermined by warlords and modern-day conquistadores using petroleum and precious metals to bribe the surface nations. Unless we reject their temptations and take control, we will find ourselves hostage to our own appetites."

Of particular concern, says Burr, is the recent spate of coups in sub-Atlantic regions, the assassination of UN peacekeepers in sub-Africa, and China's continuing violation of immigration limits throughout the Pacific commons. Numerous terrorist organizations are known to have bases under the surface.

But one man's terrorist is another's revolutionary, at least according to several Subterranean politicians. On a recent swing through the Subterrain, this reporter found uniform consent among colonists that surface fears are overblown.

"If anything, it is we who are being held hostage to the needs and demands of surface nations," said Tommy Hardin, the disgraced ex–House representative from Texas, and now a governor within the Pacific Confederacy. "We are subject to taxation without representation. Surface tariffs cripple our factory goods. Food, medicine, and other critical supplies are sold to us for outrageous profits. UN troops are garrisoned in our settlements at our expense, where they act above our laws."

President Olmec of the Correo Pacifico Sector has set off alarms with his pledge to seize control of all drilling and mining operations in his region. "There must be just compensation for our labor and resources," he says. "No more pillaging by the sunshine pirates."

4

BENEATH THE MUSICIANS SEAMOUNTS, NORTH OF HAWAII: 5,635 FATHOMS

You saw the most amazing things through a sniper scope.

At the moment, Ian Beckwith, Navy SEAL, was admiring a strange, leathery hummingbird licking the inside of a cave "flower" made of gypsum crystals. Hovering a few inches to the left of his target, at a range of 938 yards, it pulsed in his night optics. Unless he was wildly mistaken, this was a species never before seen. Later he would add the bird to his sniper log.

Every sniper kept a sniper log. The front page had handy algorithms for reckoning distances, plus human physiology factoids, like how long a head was, or how many inches it was from your neck to your navel. The rest of the book was for recording kills. This is where Beckwith kept his life list. Encrypted.

A life list was the birder's version of a sniper log. It listed every new species one saw. Beckwith's life list also served as a sort of memoir. Peregrines reminded him of a certain city where he'd stalked and shot a terrorist. Parrots summoned to mind a drug cartel he helped root out, one shot at a time. A whippoorwill once sang to him while he smoke-checked—shot dead—the leader of a Communist coup. In a sense, they became the souls of his kills.

To say the least, watching birds wasn't part of his job. He had to be careful. A gunnery sergeant once came close to finding him out. Luckily Beckwith was jotting down his sighting of a great tit flicker, and the gunny decided that if anything could be excused, it was most definitely that.

They trained you in sniper school to focus your mind the way you focused your scope. Dial it in. No distractions. Watch. Wait. Make the kill.
Pack up. Get away.

But Beckwith couldn't help himself. After a time, the targets reduced
to mathematical calculations. Whereas every time he uncapped his scope,
a whole new world lay waiting.

"Wind?" said Beckwith.

"One minute right," said his spotter.

A military sniper rifle is considered a crew-served weapon. It takes
only one finger to pull the trigger. But your spotter provides you with an
extra pair of eyes, and a second brain, and backup if the enemy starts to
close in.

"Elevation?"

The spotter told him the numbers. Beckwith adjusted the knobs. The
hummingbird flickered like a little tongue of fire inside that crystal flower.
So beautiful!

Until sniper school, Beckwith had never paid the slightest attention to
birds. He'd never been a hunter, a student of birds, or even much of an
outdoors person. Sniper school had changed all that. Now he hunted men
for a living. He lived outdoors mostly. And he was an avid birder.

The first time it happened he was on an exercise like this one, but up
on the surface. He was wearing a ghillie suit, one of those monstrously hot
and fetid lumps of garbage and grass they sometimes used for camouflage.
He had been dressed as a cow pasture that early morning, and was lying
next to a pile of flyblown shit, glassing the far-off weeds for a target, not
exactly hating his life, but not exactly loving it either.

He had joined the marines ten years ago, when the deeps were first revealed and Haddie seemed to be lurking in every shadow. Like so many
other young recruits, he had heeded the call of the president to "join up
and take the fight to hell and back." But by the time he finished basic, the
fight was over. Haddie had been exterminated. Mission accomplished, the
president announced. Beckwith had never even seen a live hadal, much
less shot at one.

Stuck with three more years of service, Beckwith had decided to im-
prove himself. One thing had led to another until the morning he found
himself sharing space with a pile of cow flop, peering through a sniper

scope, and contemplating his lowly station in the universe. That was when, through his scope, he strayed upon two creatures dancing face-to-face. Time had stopped for Beckwith. Wings spread, the two whooping cranes—he looked them up on his next leave—went on dancing and flapping and bobbing their heads hypnotically. After that, out in the field, whether training or manhunting for real, Beckwith could not seem to escape the beauty waiting in his scope.

"I'm holding center chest," he said to his spotter.

"Roger, on scope," his spotter said.

"On target." Beckwith exhaled half a breath and softly squeezed, taking up two of the three pounds of trigger pull. The hummingbird glowed.

"Fire when ready."

Beckwith finished the squeeze. His bullet left a vapor trail of disturbed air, but with a difference. Here in the darkness, lit by the optics, the hole in the air was full of rainbow colors.

"Hit. Center chest," said his spotter. "That's one dead piece of paper, Becky."

The paper target was an older version, left over from ten years ago, back when Haddie was a threat. The new targets had Chinese soldiers on them. The Chinese army used American soldiers on their targets. That was the point of these training exercises. Wars always loomed for the warrior. Eventually the paper would turn to flesh.

Beckwith lingered with his scope. The hummingbird was gone, though. "Shake a leg, Becky," said his spotter. "We're moving out."

Beckwith reached for his drag bag, sheathed his rifle, and started walking.

One by one, other sniper teams met them along the trail. None was in uniform. Loosely speaking, they didn't exist, not as marines and SEALS, not in the DMZ. It was just a matter of time before the niceties of international law wore out, though. Once the landgrabbing began at the international level, subterranean warfare was going to be the next big thing. Until that day, however, uniforms—and targets with Chinese soldiers on them—were forbidden down here.

Their cover—when they passed through the settlements and mining outposts—was a fictional NGO called Paramedics for Peace. Beckwith and his fellow snipers were supposed to act like barefoot doctors, never mind the rifle cases. People saw right through their disguise, but if it meant free medical care, they were happy to play along.

So it was in the town they now entered. Margaritaville was built into a cliff side. The citizens crawled from their burrows and caves like insects. Two navy corpsmen set up a medical clinic, and Beckwith got enlisted to help stitch some cuts.

Coming in, they had dispensed drugs, pulled teeth, and fixed a tree's worth of broken limbs. Cave life could be brutal. Walls collapsed, machinery ate fingers and arms, animals bit you, pockets of gas migrated, underground rivers flash-flooded, and miners got sloppy with their explosives.

It was all pretty standard until two miners carried in a man on a section of aluminum ladder.

The man was a mapmaker. His name was Graham. He looked tough as wire, more like an old-fashioned mountain man than a cartographer, whatever they were supposed to look like. Like Peter O'Toole at the beginning of *Lawrence of Arabia*, thought Beckwith. Not like this, slashed and mauled.

After getting raked by the talons of some animal, Graham said, he had crawled through the darkness for three weeks, to safety. The old mapmaker couldn't quit grinning. "Boys, I'm the luckiest man in the planet," he said. "I made it. I'm going home."

Beckwith and the corpsmen went to work on the slash wounds on Graham's chest and abdomen. A crowd of onlookers formed around them. Graham never quit talking despite his wounds. He was a contract worker for one of the big multinational land companies. He had gone out with a long-range surveying team.

"Where's the rest of your crew?" someone said.

"In the belly of the beast. The black beast."

"You left them?"

"There was nothing much to leave, believe me."

"Where are they, Graham?"

"I'm not telling you, boys. That's my gift to you. Because if I tell you, you'll go, and if you go, you'll die, too."

"They're dead?"

"They are. We trespassed on the beast, and it got us."

"What beast is that, old man?"

Graham's eyes shone with a damning gleam. The man was mad. Beckwith opened a stitching packet.

"By beasts, you mean animals?" said a lanky man. "Was it dogs?"

Beckwith had been briefed on the wild dogs. Left behind by miners or settlers who could take no more of the Hole, the pets went wild, packed up, and were prone to attack the unwary traveler.

But the mapmaker's wounds didn't look to Beckwith like a dog attack so much as a knife fight. That disturbed him. Tales surfaced now and then of remote outposts running out of food, and parties lost in the tunnels. It was a documented fact that a group of Japanese lepidopterists, trapped by a cave-in, had resorted to murder and cannibalism.

"Not dogs," said Graham. "There was just the one of him, and he was only part animal. The rest of him was man, or something like it."

"What are you talking about, Graham?"

"An ogre or a demon, I don't know what exactly. Something that's been living down there a long time, hidden away in the bowels of the earth. Leave him buried, boys."

"Where is this demon of yours living?"

"I'm not saying."

"Why is that, Graham?"

"No trespassing. Even here, we don't belong. That's the lesson, boys, don't go any deeper. Just pack it up and walk away. That's my plan."

That brought a chorus of snorts. Beckwith glanced around at the grim faces.

"There's no burying something like this, Graham. Tell us what happened. We'll decide how to deal with it."

Beckwith started sewing.

"We only saw snatches of it," said Graham.

"Start at the beginning, Graham."

"Promise not to go down there?"

"Convince us we shouldn't."

Graham took a breath. "It followed us for a week," he said. "Probably it was hunting us longer than that. We heard little noises but passed it off as our imagination, or the caves playing tricks on us. One of us would see something and everybody would hit his light. But there was never anything there.

"We blamed the water, or gases that weren't registering on our monitors, or the air compression. Your brain gets twitchy in all that dark, but not everybody's at the same time, not unless you're all drinking the same Kool-Aid. And the thing was that none of us was seeing the exact same thing as the other fellow or even the same thing we'd seen before. We were like blind men feeling different parts of the elephant. One of us would see the scales, another the paws, another its hands. It had all of those things. And a sort of shell for a head. See what I mean, different beasts, none of them real. Except they were all the same thing, and it was real."

Graham looked like something chucked out of a lawn mower, sliced right down to the white of his bones, and yet he went on with his concoction of a creature. Beckwith was impressed. You don't get through SEAL training without learning the thresholds of pain, and this old man raised the bar to a whole new level.

"A week goes by," someone said. "You're getting buggy. You're seeing things. Then what?"

"We kept doing our job," said Graham.

"You said something was hunting you, though."

"We didn't know that yet," Graham said. "But then Sheriff goes missing. We were setting up camp, and that was the first we noticed he was gone. We looked for him. We tried infrared for a heat signature. I rapped down a few potholes in case he had fallen. But there wasn't a trace."

The mapmaker looked at Beckwith. "A little more water would be nice." Beckwith held the bottle to his lips. "That's tasty," said the old man.

"Keep on with it, Graham."

"We decided that whatever happened to Sheriff, it was an accident. We only had another few days before the job was finished. So we kept working.

"Reilly was next on the menu. I was the one who discovered him. I smelled blood, and right away switched my night goggles to infrared, and by God if the walls weren't glowing with a heat signature. The blood was so fresh it was still radiating some of his body heat. It was like standing inside one of his arteries, that tube of stone all painted with blood."

"What next?" someone said.

"P.J. and I knew it was time to get out. We ditched the surveying equipment ..."

"Goddamn it, Graham," said a man, and one of the citizens walked away cursing. Beckwith guessed he was the owner of the surveying equipment, and that it wasn't insured. Probably nothing was down here.

"Cut to the chase, Graham," another man said. "If you're talking about Haddie, say so. Are you saying one of them lived through the plague?"

"This was no hadal," said Graham. "It was too big."

"A big hadal then."

"It had claws, and a shell for a head," said Graham.

"Okay, a big hadal with claws and a shell."

"And it ate hadals. Lots of them. Hadals and humans and creatures I've never seen. Ate 'em all."

That quieted the audience.

"Let the man tell his story," someone said.

Graham resumed. "We started out, not running, but always on the move. Two days and nights, never a stop. By the third day, we were getting punchy from the lack of sleep. We decided we'd outrun the thing, so it was okay to take a rest. It wasn't." He stopped.

"Go on," someone said.

"Our lights were off. We were sleeping. All of a sudden I thought I was on fire. At first I didn't know it was the claws going at me. In the darkness, it just felt like fire. Then it was P.J.'s turn. He started screaming. I turned on my light, and these eyes were waiting for me, eyes like ours, intelligent, but totally wild. Then my light got smashed, and those claws went at me again. They tell you to play dead with the bears and lions, right? I didn't have to. I pretty much died, I figure."

"You blacked out?"

"How can you black out when everything's already black?" Graham said. "Time passed. I felt pain. At some point I realized I'd been moved. This wasn't our tunnel anymore. It smelled like the inside of an intestine, like digestion and bad gas and shit. Then I heard the sound of teeth on bone, like a dog working for the marrow. Gnawing away. Splintering it. I realized that I was in this thing's den, and that it was saving me for later."

"What did you do?"

"Counted my heartbeats. Stayed still. Tried to think about something else, the sun, the blue sky, riding my Harley along I-70. Better times."

"Then what?"

"It spoke."

Beckwith paused in his sewing.

"It what?"

"It said something."

"It talked?"

"I know. Crazy. I thought, Graham, you're losing it. An animal that talks? But that's what it was doing, gnawing on bones and talking to itself, or trying to talk. That scared me more than everything else put together. This thing had the beginnings of a voice. It was alone and trying to talk to itself, but couldn't quite form the words."

The skeptics quit challenging Graham. Everyone listened in silence.

"Finally it left. I could hear its nails on the rock. Things got quiet. That's when I heard P.J. groan. He was alive. We found each other in all the bones and muck. In the darkness, I couldn't tell who was hurt worse, him or me. We lay against each other whispering, trying to decide what to do. P.J. said he still had his light. I said give it to me. He said no, it would only bring that thing back. The light would be the death of us. Finally I just took it from him and turned it on."

Beckwith gave him another drink.

"It was bad," Graham continued. "Reilly's head was up there. Yes, just his head. And a hand with Sheriff's Sigma Chi ring on one finger. P.J. was all ripped up. I saw the wounds on my arms and legs.

"We weren't the first of its victims. Like I said, it ate hadals, too. And it doesn't just eat, it collects. It had leg bones stacked like firewood, and skulls on a shelf, human and hadal and others. No animal does that.

"Then we heard it coming back. P.J. said Graham, you just fucking killed us. But I saw a hole at the back of the den. We crawled over and squeezed in, and sweet Jesus if it didn't hold a chimney going up.

"Well, we started climbing. The chimney was tight. It got tighter. We were both leaving skin and blood on the rock, and there was no rope to protect us if we slipped and fell. But what was our choice? That thing was coming right behind us, talking at us with its grunts and barking.

"We wormed up higher and higher, me first, and I was beginning to think we could beat it. Right about then, we came to a squeeze slot. I tried it one way and then another. P.J. was under me yelling hurry up, get it done, that fucker's coming. I would have let him try the slot, but the chimney was too tight to switch spots, so it was up to me. I stretched long and blew all the air out of my lungs, and it worked. I shimmied through the slot and the tube opened up. I saw a feeder tunnel just above. All P.J. had to do was finish the slot.

"But he was a big man, you boys remember? I turned myself around, upside down, and I told him the moves, one arm up, a foot there, now blow your air out. I held the light. I touched his fingers. I was sure he had it. Just a little more. But then he took a breath. His rib cage swelled up and that was that. He jammed in the slot as tight as a nail. He couldn't come up and he couldn't go down.

"I slid down some more. I reached his hand and pulled. You're killing me, he says. No I'm not, come on, you're almost there, I say. We go back and forth like that. I've got the light. His face is all red. His eyes are starting to get the black panic in them. If he loses his cool, I know it's all over. Smooth and easy, I tell him, just a little more.

"All of a sudden he gave a big jerk. His mouth opened up like a fish out of water. His eyes bugged out. He didn't scream. No air for screaming. He just looked at me. It was like the most terrible knowledge written on his face."

"What are you saying? Graham, what happened?"

"The thing had caught up with him and taken a bite. Then it took another. This little squeal came out of poor P.J., like air leaking."

"What did you do?"

"Well, I stayed with him as long as I could. Every now and then he would jerk hard and it was that thing tugging on him, trying to uncork the hole and get to me. But P.J. was jammed. So it fed on his legs. P.J. never quit looking at me. Finally his eyes glazed over. The light went out of them. I said good-bye, brother, next life, all that. I scooted myself around and reached the feeder tunnel and left him behind. Pretty soon, the battery died."

The mapmaker got quiet. His eyes closed. Beckwith thought the drugs had knocked him out. It seemed the old man might get a chance to heal and see the sun again. Beckwith hoped so. He didn't know the man from Adam, and this was none of his business. But he had come out of the infamous hell week convinced that suffering was ultimately redemptive. Whatever had happened down there, the mapmaker had definitely suffered.

"Hey," said a man with a bull's neck and shoulders. "We're not finished with you yet."

Graham's eyes opened. He looked around. The grin surfaced. "Here I am."

"You think we're fools?" said the bull. "An animal that talks killed everyone but you? And then you spend three weeks crawling, with no light, lost and alone? And somehow you land right back in Margaritaville?"

"He got lucky," someone else said. "Ease up, Mick."

"There's no such thing as lucky, not in the tubes," Mick said. "We've all been out there. We know what it's like. I say he planned it. It was premeditated, it had to be."

"Planned what, Mick? Look at him. Do you think he cut himself to ribbons?"

"He must have hidden caches of food along the trail when they were going down," said Mick. "And made secret marks in the tunnels to guide him back. There's no other way he could have made it out alone. I want answers. P.J. was my friend."

"You're right, Mick," Graham said. "The truth is, I wasn't alone. I got aided and abetted. I had help." He smiled. His eyes gleamed. "Inside help."

People muttered darkly.

"There," said Mick. "By God, who was in on it with you?"

Graham smiled a little wider. "P.J."

"What?"

"And Reilly. And Matthews."

"What are you saying, old man?"

"They talked me in. It was like a radio call, but without the radio."

"Quit your hogwash."

"I'm telling you straight," said Graham. "Whenever I wanted to quit, they kept me going. Wherever I got lost, they led me right. They were with me every inch of the way, whispering me in."

"He's lost his mind."

"God's truth, boys. Clear as crystal. Souls," said Graham. "Dead souls. Whispering away down there as real as you and me."

Beckwith would have told him to shut up. The fool was pouring gas on the flames with his crazy nonsense. But it was too late.

"First a demon creature, now dead souls," said Mick. "What next, angels with flaming swords? Out with it, old man. Where'd you leave the bodies?"

"Down where you're not going because I'm not telling," Graham said. "Now I've seen. There's places we shouldn't go. There's things we want to leave alone."

"You're hiding something more than bodies. What was worth killing three men for? Gold? Diamonds? What? Where'd you leave them, old man?"

"Not another word from me," said Graham.

"Tell us, you murdering bastard."

Beckwith felt a heavy hand on his shoulder. It was Mick. The veins stood out on his temples. "We'll take it from here," he said.

"I'm not finished," said Beckwith.

"Yeah, you are. Your work is done, mister."

Beckwith stood up. Like many men in special ops, he was under six feet and not heavily muscled. This pissed-off miner had a hundred pounds on him easily. "The man's hurt and tired and dehydrated," he said.

"Step away," said Mick.

"He's delirious. He doesn't know what he's saying."

"You're in my way," said Mick.

The corpsman folded his kit shut. He leaned close to Beckwith. "We're done here," he said.

"Not yet," said Beckwith. The corpsman glanced at the crowd and frowned at him.

Another of the snipers stepped in. "It's over, man. We're out of here."

"You know what's going to happen once we leave," said Beckwith.

"We can't save the world. Let's go."

"You don't just turn a man out to the wolves."

"We did our best," said the corpsman. "Let go, Becky. Walk away."

"They'll kill him. I'm not signing off on that." He sounded crazy, even to himself. The mapmaker was a complete stranger. His welfare had zip to do with their training mission. They'd descended to this region to shoot paper targets, not tangle with the locals.

"Saddle up, Becky. We're leaving."

Beckwith didn't budge. He looked around at the crowd and saw the bleakness and severity of this place on their faces. They belonged to the cave. They *were* the cave. Someone had to fight that. Otherwise the darkness won.

"I'll stick with you," Beckwith said to Graham. And he meant it.

The old man pushed at Beckwith's leg. "Thanks, but no thanks, friend. Get back to where you came from. Don't waste yourself on the dark places."

"You're going with me," Beckwith said.

He shoveled his hands underneath the mapmaker and started to lift him. It could have worked. The crowd would have parted for him and he could have carried the old man out of there. But Graham yelled out in pain, and Beckwith set him flat again.

"Fight," said Beckwith.

The mapmaker closed his eyes. "I'm tired, son. I hurt."

"You said you want to go home," said Beckwith. "Let's go home."

But Graham turned his face away.

"A savior with no one to save," Mick scoffed.

One of the snipers stepped forward. "If I were you," he said to the giant miner, "I'd quit crowing and go get drunk and thank the gods. Because today's the day you looked into the eyes of the angel of death, and for some fucking reason he let you walk away."

Mick's grin died.

An arm went around Beckwith's shoulder. It was his spotter. "Grab your gear, dude. You did your best."

Beckwith looked down at the old man on the ground with his half-sewn wounds and emaciated body, and for the first time in his life he surrendered. And it did not feel good.

ARTIFACTS

From NAVAL SPECIAL WARFARE BASIC SNIPER TRAINING

Equipment

The sniper should have with him the following items:

1. Suitable paper in a book with a stiff cover to give a reasonable drawing surface
2. A pencil, preferably a number 2 pencil with an eraser
3. A knife or razor blade to sharpen the pencil
4. A protractor or ruler
5. A piece of string 15 inches long

From CUSTOMS

A Medieval Carthusian Monk's Equipment

He (the monk copyist) should be given an inkwell, quill pens, chalk, two pumice stones, two horns, a small knife, two razors for scraping the parchment (one ordinary stylus and one finer), a lead pencil, a ruler, some writing tablets, and a stylet.

5

TEXAS

When the crickets started up, Rebecca laid aside her book and went to the window. Lightning flickered to the south. Something was coming in from the Gulf.

Jake was doing battle under the big oak, killing weeds and getting raked by the rosebushes and slaying the mosquitoes, all in the name of his so-called lawn. It was a ratty, sorry thatch of a thing, but that did not diminish his territorial imperative. Until the blue northers came breasting down from Canada with their hard cold, the suburbs would stay green. Meaning Jake would have his bit of grass to defend for at least another month.

Further out she spied Sam dancing on the edge, all too literally, and her mother's heart gave a squeeze. Sam was not a bold child in most things. The prospect of fourth grade frightened her. And she had what Rebecca considered a proper loathing of snakes, bees, doctors' needles, and dinosaur movies. But when Daddy was around, Sam had the courage of lions. Or cubs.

Just now Sam was performing bits of ballet upon the very lip of the limestone cliffs that fell straight to the river. Jake looked perfectly oblivious in his salt-of-the-earth way. It took everything for Rebecca to keep from rushing out. *Have a little faith.* Things were fine out there. Somehow, with Jake around, they always were.

By her Aggie standards, Jake was not so very big. But she had seen him lift fallen trees, and once carry a man with a broken leg over nine miles of bad trail, and hold her family strong after her father passed on. On a trip to Ireland, he had talked his way out of not one, but two sure brawls . . . and left the pubs with everyone in fine humor. Jake took care of things. Sam worshipped him. As did Rebecca.

Watching them together, she began to relax. Father and daughter were in perfect wordless synch. Without actually looking at each other, Sam never strayed more than twenty feet away from her daddy, nor he from her. They were like satellites orbiting each other.

Lightning stitched the horizon. There was no thunder. The storm was far away.

At last Rebecca went out onto the porch. "It's time, you two," she called.

Sam resisted. "Watch this, Mama." She did a pirouette. *Right on the edge.*

"Come away from there," Rebecca said.

"But Daddy said—"

"I don't care, young lady. You've gone plenty close."

"You worry too much, Mama."

Jake laid aside his bag of weeds and grabbed her. "Let's go, Junior."

That was her new handle, self-selected. When they'd pointed out that Junior was a boy's title, she had shrugged. She already went by a boy's name. And wasn't Daddy a room mom at school? If he could be a girl, she could be a boy. Or something like that.

Coming in, they smelled of grass and lemonade. "It's bedtime," Rebecca said.

Sam looked at her. She looked at her father. "Not yet," she said.

"Yet," said Rebecca.

"Please, Mama?"

"School starts next week, Sam. We have simply got to get you back on schedule."

The girl glanced down the hall at her bedroom door and gave it a moment's thought. She solemnly shook her head no.

"Not this again," Rebecca sighed. "You've had Daddy three nights in a row. When do I get him?"

"When they go away," Sam said.

Her monsters.

Jake thought it had to do with the recent and premature demise of Santa Claus, leprechauns, and the tooth fairy. The Baptist minister's boy had ever so helpfully broken the news on the playground. And it had happened with the minister right there watching, not saying a word. Rooting out the heathen from man's dark heart. Setting straight a child's beliefs.

Jake held up a finger, as if suddenly remembering something. "What do we have here?"

With a magician's flourish, he produced a small paper sack from the HEB store. Inside was a Disney mermaid night-light. "You won't believe how pretty this is in the dark. I asked the lady at the store. She said her little girl still uses hers, and she's off to college now."

Sam looked at the night-light. She admired it. But she didn't touch it. You couldn't buy her off that cheaply. "They're in my closet," she said. It was becoming a broken record.

"I checked last night, baby. And the night before that. There's nothing but clothes and shoes in there."

"I can hear them in the crawl space."

"I checked down there, too. Clean as an elephant's ear."

An elephant's ear? But Sam was in no mood for distractions. "Underneath the crawl space, then," she said. "They're hiding."

"Come on, Sam."

"It's true. I'm too young to lie. You said so."

It was a test. Sam was up for some imagination if they were. No Santa, then no monsters. But if there could be monsters, then there might be a Santa. Meaning, maybe the fat elf had some mileage left in him after all. If Daddy would sleep with her again.

Jake looked at Rebecca, who nodded in a sort of happy resignation. Monsters it was.

"Okay, kid," he said, and picked his girl up. "First the teeth, then the pillow. Do I get the outside of the bed again?" He headed down the hall with her slung over his shoulder. "I'm not sure we finished our story last night anyway."

"Are you sure there's no monsters?"

"There used to be, darlin'. In the old days."

"What about now?"

"What do you think?"

"Yes," she said. "There's monsters all right. Lots and lots and lots of them. They're just waiting, is all."

ARTIFACTS

THE WASHINGTON TIMES

China's Bare-Branch Policy Denounced

The secretary of the Interior Department today charged that China is waging a "shadow war" with the U.S. by flooding the Pacific underground with tens of thousands of its "surplus" adult males. This has created a "Chinese octopus," said Secretary Tom Tancredo, with tentacles now reaching over a thousand miles out from the Chinese coast.

"China is emptying its prisons and ghettos into the Subterrain," Tancredo said. "China offers financial incentives, pays for transportation, and provides housing and food for the criminals and gangsters going down. China is conducting a slow-motion conquest of international territory. This is a deliberate strategy aimed at destabilizing the entire sub-Pacific." He labeled this strategy China's "Bare Branches Policy."

For centuries China has preferred sons over daughters, resulting in an imbalance of 120 (some claim 150) males for every 100 females. With too few women to go around, poor, unskilled, and illiterate men are increasingly unlikely to marry. These are the fruitless "bare branches" who historically form gangs or bandit armies, control crime, and fuel nationalistic wars.

"China's population disaster is spreading disease, corruption, Han supremacy, and a culture of superviolence through the Pacific Subterrain," Tancredo said.

China's ambassador to the U.S. calls such language "inflammatory and counterproductive." The bare branches are "floaters," said Ambassador Yao Deng. "If they wish to leave the motherland to better their lives, we cannot prevent them. Freedom of travel is a human right, yes?"

6

DIALOGUES WITH THE ANGEL, NUMBER 1

The angel and his disciple are walking along a path. They come to a colony of ants. The angel stops and picks up one of the ants.

"You came to kill me," the angel muses to the disciple. His voice rings against veins of metal in the stone.

"I came to learn, Lord," says the disciple.

"To learn how to kill me."

"To learn how to kill evil, Rinpoche. But that was before."

"Before?"

"Before I realized that ignorance is the evil. Before I understood that you cannot die, Teacher. Before you taught me to renounce all violence."

The angel is amused. "And so I am no longer the source of all evil?"

"You are the diamond, Messiah."

The ant struggles in those marble white fingers. Hold it too hard, and the angel would crush it. Too lightly, and it would escape.

It is a lesson. Every motion, every step, every breath he takes is another lesson. The disciple watches everything. Nothing the angel does is accidental.

"Do you know how many assassins have come to me over the eons?" says the angel.

"Many, Lord." The disciple has seen the Collection.

"Do you know what I have done with them?"

"Destroyed them one by one, Ocean of Wisdom."

The angel places the ant to one side of their path, safely on its feet. "I offer myself to them. I try to overcome their unawareness, and in the process I re-call all the things I know about the universe."

"Yes, Lord." But the disciple has seen the Collection.

"Some I trained and sent back into the light of day. Some I dressed in my powers and let them pretend to be me, so that I could shape my legend. Others, like you, I keep with me in my solitude."

The disciple bows his head respectfully. But he does not lower his eyes from the angel's face. The angel has warned him. Never look away. I am a hungry god.

"Let us continue on your path to knowledge," says the angel.

"Lord, lead me on."

The angel turns. He goes on. The disciple watches as he crushes the rest of the ant colony beneath one foot. The disciple learns the lesson. Many are called. Few are spared.

ARTIFACTS

Diary Notes for a Symphony Subterranea *by Gregorio Montaña*

- As a boy I was spellbound by the discovery of the Neanderthal flute in 1995 by Dr. Ivan Turk of the Slovenian Academy of Arts and Sciences (SAZU). It was made from the femur of a cave bear and dated to forty-five thousand years old. Also by the discovery of the flutes (from the wing bones of the red-crowned crane) and tortoiseshell drums at Jiahu, China (7000 to 5800 bc), and a triangular-shaped lyre on a statue at Keros in the Aegean Sea (2700 bc). That was when I first thought of a prehistoric symphony. I made versions of the instruments and learned to play them.

- The oldest known song was recorded on Assyrian cuneiform tablets (2000 bc) and used harmony and the diatonic scale (do, re, mi, etc.).

- Then the inside of the earth was discovered, and I began to see instruments of every kind. Now, with my own lips, I have played notes from Subterranean flutes twenty-five thousand years old (standard diatonic to heptatonic, including a flatted la and a neutral third for mi, i.e., a blue note). I have translated fragments of hadal songs. I have listened to recordings of recaptured slaves singing. One woman has heard the hadals sing their own songs. After my doctorate I must get to America and meet her. Her name is Alexandra Von Schade.

- What does music have to do with the underworld? My professors mock me. I don't know the answer to my own question. It is like a riddle God has planted in my hands. The connection eludes me, but I feel it in the middle of the night, when everyone else is asleep. Somehow music is our salvation.

• Dr. Von Schade wrote back to me! Suddenly I am not alone. Now there is someone to discuss what came first, music or words. She is a linguist, and feels strongly for words. We argue in our e-mail. We have passion for what we believe. I feel drunken on this. Someday I will finish my symphony and dedicate it to her.

7

AMERICA

It was Halloween, the one night of every year that American parents can be depended on to send their children out into the darkness like eager sacrifices. The sun had barely set. Costumes were just appearing, a nation's little nightmares on parade.

With so many disguises that night, the task of distinguishing the missing from the dead would be all the more difficult come morning.

A dad—this one's name was Dave—was walking behind his little gypsy on her Schwinn. He'd taken off the training wheels that very morning. *Growing up. Too fast.* "Slow down, Jen." Of course she only pedaled faster. *Got to make more time for the munchkin.*

Down the path she wobbled, beyond the reach of the park's vapor lights. She gave Dad one glance over her shoulder. A smile. He was there. All was safe. Onward she went, into the darkening woods.

The orange-lit plastic pumpkin on her handlebars dipped out of sight.

"Jen."

Silence.

Louder. "Jenny."

A deeper silence.

Dave's dad alarm went off. Boogeymen sprang to mind, the gangs, the crackheads, the unregistered sex offenders, the homeless. Who knew what all lived in these shadows? They were legion.

He wasn't in the best of shape. Too many Dairy Queens on summer nights. Too much grazing in Costco. *Memo: Cut down, Dave.* Huffing and puffing, Dave pounded along the pathway.

It smelled of loam and rotting leaves among the trees. Water was trickling in hidden veins. Shadows loomed, a bony web of branches. The pale moon watched.

"Jennifer." Again. Strictly. They were going to have to have a talk. There is a time and place for games, but not in dark and dangerous woods. "Jennifer."

Animals skittered. Leaves stirred. He was getting a little scared, but had not the slightest doubt that everything was fine. He would find her around the next bend. They would have a story to share. *Remember that time in the park...*

Four kids—two Spidermen, one Jason, one Ring girl—crouched behind a swaybacked picket fence. Their target was an old ranch-style tract home. The lights were out. They were never on. The lawn hadn't been mowed for years. A Re/Max sign waggled in the breeze, long forgotten by its neglectful realtor.

Spiderman One: "There's two of them living in there."

Spiderman Two: "Three's what I heard."

Jason: "My dad says they're lesbians. Or Democrats."

Ring Girl: "That's mean."

Jason: "The country needs some spine. That's what my dad says."

Spiderman Two: "They're witches is what they are."

Spiderman One: "Vampires."

Jason: "They never come out. They don't have kids. My dad says they don't even own a car. Vegetarian dike atheists."

Spiderman One: "No car? So how do they eat?"

Jason: "Pets. Stray cats. Remember the Browns' dalmation?"

Spiderman Two: "You don't know that."

Jason: "Roadkill. And mushrooms."

Spiderman One: "I say we TP their trees."

Ring Girl: "Like they'd care. Look at the yard."

Jason: "Rock their windows then."

Ring Girl: "You're getting psycho, Billy. Again. They're just old ladies."

Spiderman Two: "Nan's right, man. What'd they ever do to you?"

Jason: "They don't belong. That's enough."

Ring Girl: "They could be your grandma."

Jason: "Or your mom."

Spiderman Two: "Whatever, Billy."

Ring Girl: "I'm going up there."

Jason: "Forget that, Nan."

Ring Girl: "I'm going to ring their doorbell. I'm going to say hi."

Spiderman One: "No you're not."

Ring Girl: "Watch me."

Spiderman Two: "Awesome. She's doing it!"

Spiderman One: "Nan, get back here."

Spiderman Two: "Now what?"

Jason: "What do you think? She'll tell everybody we were pussies. We have to go with her."

Spiderman One: "I'm not going up there."

Jason: "Pussy."

Spiderman One: "Take it back, Billy."

Jason: "Or what?"

Spiderman Two: "Hey, look. The door's opening."

Spiderman One: "She's waving to us."

Spiderman Two: "Nice, Nan. Now they know we're out hiding in the grass."

Jason: "Come on, you guys. Maybe they'll have some good stuff. Like poison apples."

Spiderman One: "Or eyeball soup."

Spiderman Two: "Or dalmatian burgers."

Spiderman One: "Hey, Nan, wait for us."

"Ten dollars a head," Reverend Robbins said to the couple.

"But I've got a coupon."

The reverend smiled. Joe Quarterback was trying to Jew him. Like Robbins was born yesterday. Like he couldn't take the musclehead down in a heartbeat. Pop his knee out, stomp his head. In one Rocky Mountain heartbeat.

"That coupon's from last year, son," he said.

"There's no expiration date. It says seven bucks. So here's fourteen for me and her."

"Twenty dollars, friend."

"I don't have twenty."

The girlfriend started pulling at the hero's big arm, like, let's go make babies in the parental SUV. Just then a bloodcurdling scream ripped from the mouth of hell. Robbins calmly kept his back to the maze entrance. He watched the effect on his two young customers. It sent a shudder through them. It made them think. It made them want.

The girlfriend quit trying to leave. She looked at the entrance to the maze. Oh, joy, her eyes seemed to say. Another scream—and these were real screams, that was the beauty of it, real teenage terror, nothing canned—and the deal was swung. "Fifteen dollars and twenty cents," said the golden boy. "That's all I've got."

Robbins looked out across the parking lot. More customers were approaching, all clean-cut Jesus types, the guys in Dockers, the girls prim, with long sleeves and buttons all the way to the throat, with little crucifixes on chains, like they were peasants in Transylvania or something. Lots of hormones in motion tonight. Not much T & A, though. A pity, some of these gals. But the upside of all the sanctity was no dopers, no inner-city gorilla eyes, no guns or blades, no trouble. Robbins didn't need trouble. Just lots and lots of clean green pouring in.

"Fifteen," said Robbins. "Keep the change. Just don't tell anybody I caved in for you."

Joe Quarterback brightened. He looked at Suzy Q like he'd just won state or something.

An hour went by.

Robbins sat there taking money, counting it up, listening to the kids scream their heads off. This year's "hell house" had cost him an extra fourteen hundred in lumber, paint, and accessories. It was a lot of money, but you had to keep up with the competition. An hour and a half up I-25, two Denver preachers—one a reformed felon like Robbins—were running their own hell houses.

There was good money to be made scaring the secular crap out of nice young Christians, and every year demanded new refinements to the art.

Not so long ago you could get away with a few gory dioramas of the punishments awaiting the needle fiends, glue sniffers, drunks, sluts, queers, Hollywood blasphemers, and other fuel for the evangelical flames. Anymore, though, you had to be Cecil B. DeMille.

This year, for instance, Robbins got a Toyota car body from the junkyard, and hung it in midflight as it careened off a fake cliff . . . with a horrified drunk driver at the wheel. Farther on, a wax figurine of the filmmaker Michael Moore was getting the radical fat roasted off him in a lake of red cellophane "fire." A perennial favorite was the evil abortionist, played by Robbins's brother Ted this year, who slowly turned from the metal gynecology stirrups (a pair of horseshoes spot-welded to poles) and held up a bloody fetus (a Wet Baby with the cry voice dismantled). In a nod to current events, the abortionist then sold the fetus to a stem-cell scientist. Another crowd-pleaser was the human vegetable, played by Ted's wife, who begged for her life while the atheists yanked out her tubes one by one. Farther on, a teacher was beating the snot out of a child for reading a Bible in biology class.

But the real scream machine, this year's big moneymaker, was the climactic "Inferno" display. Word about the exhibit had spread far and wide. Kids were driving from as far away as Cheyenne to take the plunge—down a plastic slide from Target—into the pit of hell.

Robbins had gone all out making this one, truly his masterpiece. It had pools of darkness, strobe lights, dry-ice fog, and "Sympathy for the Devil" playing really loud. And ghastly fiends that sprang from nowhere. Besides brother Ted and his wife, several more of the Robbins clan had driven all the way from Eugene to dress up as demons and jump out, grab hair, run around on all fours, moan, howl, bark, and generally terrify the sinners half out of their wits. Judging by the screams, Team Robbins was doing a damn good job in there.

Around nine or so, the first Concerned Parent came up. Every year there were Concerned Parents. They always parked at the far end of the lot, where their embarrassed sons and daughters consigned them. Every year they would approach about this time wondering where their Johnny or Corey was. As if he was a babysitter.

"You haven't seen a girl about this tall, have you?" the mom asked him. "She has blond hair and glasses. It's been almost an hour."

"She'd be inside," Robbins said, hitching a thumb at the hell entrance. "No one's come out yet. What the young people do is circle around in there. They're supposed to go straight through and come out. But they get all caught up."

A caterwauling shriek overrode the Rolling Stones. The mom jerked. Nice legs. No wedding ring. Robbins shook his head and chuckled. "They just love the fear."

A boy roared. It was a lion's roar of outrage and pain. *Not bad, kid.* It died away.

"Good lord," the mom said.

"Kids," said Robbins.

But she was staring past him, over his shoulder. "Sally?" she said.

Robbins turned.

A girl was standing there, clothes ripped, face slack, drenched in "blood." She didn't answer. Her thousand-mile stare didn't even see them.

Damn it, thought Robbins. *Didn't I tell Ted and them, no paint? And no goddamn rough stuff.* This was the problem with relatives. Upside, they worked for free. Downside, you couldn't fire them. Now he was looking at a bill for new clothes. And Sally here wasn't exactly dressed in Wal-Mart blue-light specials.

"Sally?" the mom repeated.

The girl collapsed in a heap.

"Jennifer!" Dave yelled again.

The Schwinn was lying at his feet. Her pumpkin bucket rested in a ball of orange light on the mat of leaves. Around and around, Dave turned. Where to begin? Moon shadows striped the forest floor. Crevices gaped like open mouths among the boulders. Not a soul in sight. And his cell phone was on the fritz.

"Jennifer!" This couldn't be happening. Any instant she would come bounding from the trees with a "boo" on her lips. But as the woods squeaked and scratched their branches and the seconds became minutes, Dave finally broke the peace and started hollering for help.

*   *   *

Spiderman One: "Nan?"

The boys entered the house tentatively, flashlights slashing at the darkness. There was no furniture. It stunk. Even to their boy nostrils, the place was a violation.

Spiderman Two: "What is that?"

Spiderman One: "Shit. Dog poop."

Jason: "That's not dog shit. It's human."

Spiderman Two: "On the carpet?"

There were piles of it all over the place. It shocked them. They were ready for bodies, eyeballs, skulls, or bat wings, the stuff of witches. But this house wasn't so different from their houses, and the women had used it like a way station. Like an animal den.

Spiderman One: "We don't belong in here."

Spiderman Two: "What about Nan?"

Jason: "Take a look in here, you guys."

It was the master bedroom, no bed, no bureau, no mirror. A fire ring set in the middle of the floor had burned right through the Berber carpet. The ceiling was black with smudge.

Spiderman One: "Are those bones?"

Like little twigs. Skulls like strawberries. The boys clustered.

Spiderman Two: "Squirrels."

Jason: "Or mice."

Spiderman One: "Cool."

Spiderman Two: "Where's Nan?"

Spiderman One: "Quit messing with us, Nan."

They found a briefcase lying on the kitchen floor. Among the papers was a real estate contract with the signature pages flagged.

Spiderman One: "What's that stink?"

Jason: "It's coming from the oven." The cold oven.

Spiderman Two: "Don't open it, dude."

Jason: "Voilà!"

Spiderman One: "What *is* that?"

Spiderman Two: "Meat."

Spiderman One: "Meat?"

Jason: "Old meat. It's all gray. There must be a hundred pounds in there."

Spiderman Two: "Maybe they got a deer."

Jason: "There's no deer around here."

Spiderman One: "Is that a fingernail?"

Jason: "No way."

Spiderman Two: "Don't touch it, numb nuts. Great, now you dropped it."

They stared at the thing lying on the floor.

Spiderman One: "A hand? Someone's hand?"

The oven door gaped at them.

Spiderman Two: "That's a person in there."

Spiderman One: "I'm leaving."

Spiderman Two: "What about Nan?"

Spiderman One: "Let the cops find her."

Jason: "We can't. They'll bust us."

A noise came from the open basement door. The smell of raw earth poured up from below. "Nan?" Another noise.

Spiderman One: "She's down there."

Spiderman Two: "I'm not going down there."

Spiderman One: "We have to."

They armed themselves with pieces of sharp bone or lumber torn from the walls for firewood. Down they went.

Their lights played over mounds of dirt. Mountains of it.

Spiderman Two: "Prairie dogs? In their basement?"

Jason: "It's a cemetery, stupid. They're serial killers."

Now it made sense. Ghoulish sense. They relaxed.

Spiderman One: "*Silence of the Lambs.*"

Spiderman Two: "*Texas Chainsaw Massacre.*"

Jason: "*The Devil's Rejects.*"

Spiderman One: "Uh-oh."

Jason: "Now what?"

They gathered at the edge of a hole in the back corner. Here was the source of all the dirt. The tunnel snaked down and under the concrete footer and far beyond the reach of their lights.

Spiderman Two: "Nan?"

The hole yawned.

Spiderman One: "Did you hear that?"

Dirt shifted in the corner, hissing faintly.

Jason: "We've got to get out of here."

Their lights slapped at the concrete walls. The stairs suddenly looked so far away.

Jason: "Run."

"Sam?" Rebecca spoke it from the bedroom doorway. Sam's bed was empty, though.

"No playing, Sam."

But Sam didn't play like this. Plus, she had a fever. Something was going around at school, and they'd finished their trick-or-treating early. Rebecca dropped to her knees and looked under the bed. Toys and a book. *Madeline.* The little Disney night-light blushed in the corner. That useless thing.

"Okay, Sam, you can come out now." She threw open the closet door. In her haste, she almost missed the hole under a pile of clothes. The floorboards had been pushed loose.

"Jake!" she screamed.

He came running, bare feet, bare chest, clutching the big Mag light like a club. He took one look at the hole and, like a bull, ripped more floorboards loose. It scared her even more. "What are you doing?"

He didn't answer. "Sam," he yelled into the hole.

"What is it?"

"I think I know," he said.

Rebecca stepped back, frightened by his strength, frightened by his certainty.

He jumped in, just like they say, with both feet. She peered through the lip of broken boards, and her husband was plowing at the foundation wall, tearing away cinder blocks. It was like watching him demolish their world.

"Jake?"

He didn't look up. He didn't say good-bye. Why should he? He just went right through the wall, from the inside of their safety and boundary to the outside.

Rebecca spun and darted to the window. Like a madman, or a werewolf in a movie, in his pajama bottoms, nothing else, he raced through the moonlight toward the cliffs above the river. The porous white cliffs. Riddled with lairs.

She tried not to read into what he'd just said. *I think I know.* But now she thought she knew, too. Which couldn't be. Jake had told Sam there were no more monsters. He'd promised her with a pinkie shake.

No, it had to be something else. Rebecca defied the evidence. She deliberately ignored the torn-up flooring and the hole leading to another hole to the holes in the cliff. Sam was sleepwalking, that was all. She had wandered off in a dream. Jake would find her. He knew all her hiding places.

But then the moon shadows came alive out there. They boiled up. The oak and the thorn brush and the toolshed suddenly vomited up a whole yard full of animal motion. Watching through the window, Rebecca almost screamed a warning. But the glass stopped her, that's what she would tell herself later. The impenetrable glass.

She was shocked by how quickly Jake went down. He took a few swings at the pale, moonlit things. He kicked. She heard his faint bellow. Then he disappeared under a small mountain of jackal frenzy.

Rebecca quit watching. She slid from the window. She clutched Sam's fallen pillow and breathed her baby's smell. *Sam. Sam. Sam.*

Later she would replace her cowardice with something stronger. Not tonight, though. Not this endless night.

What they found inside the reverend's hell house put to shame his little skits and interactive parables. The adults lay slaughtered and left behind, unwanted. To their credit, several of the football players had ganged together and made a sort of last stand. They were the easiest to identify because of the remnants of their letter jackets.

All the other children had been taken.

Hour after hour, they had come and paid in dollars for a taste of hell.

Then hell had come to get a taste of them.

ARTIFACTS

TUCSON, AZ—DAILY POLICE REPORT—10/31

Time	Offense	Comment
4:57	Dog Pick Up	2 dogs fighting
6:32	Disturbance	Reports loud music in area, contact made and will comply
7:15	Public Service	Deliver box of Halloween candy to YMCA
8:05	Disturbance	Barking dogs in area, no further assistance made, bring dog in
8:06	Battery	Reports hearing screaming in area, units in area
8:07	Residential Alarm	Basement alarm, Rp called back to cancel, false activation
8:08	Residential Alarm	Rear motion and basement motion, Rp did not want house entered
8:08	Shots	Shots fired in residence
8:08	**Disturbance**	**Children screaming, Rp elderly, officer explains it is Halloween**
8:09	Suspicious	Female heard screaming for help next door, no victim, no perp
8:09	Shots	25 shots fired in condos, units in area
8:09	Disturbance	Man yelling for help
8:10	Injury Accident	Homeless man runs into street, struck by car, medical aid on way
8:10	Disturbance	2 women screaming
8:11	Reck Driver	Reckless driver in area, units in pursuit
8:11	Animal Bite	Bite report, Rp not certain about animal ... etc.
8:24	Overdue Person	Children late, unit in area
8:24	**Injury Accident**	**Body reported**

Time	Offense	Comment
8:24	Reck Driver	Reckless driver in area, no pursuit
8:24	Overdue Person	Child missing, units in area
8:24	Injury Accident	Body reported
8:24	Medical Aid	Medical aid requested for fight wounds
8:24	**Animal Bite**	**Bite report, not dog; Rp claims hadal; med aid**
8:24	Shots	Shots fired
8:25	Overdue Person	Child missing, units in area
8:25	Injury Accident	3 bodies reported
8:25	Overdue Person	5 children missing
8:25	Shots	Shots fired
8:25	Medical Aid	Medical aid requested
8:25	Overdue Person	2 children missing
8:25	Overdue Person	Child missing ... etc.
8:26	Suspicious	Rp claims hearing loud thumps on roof, advise stay inside
8:26	Amber Alert	Amber Alert issued for missing child
8:26	**Emergency Alert**	**All off-duty officers recalled ... etc.**
8:38	Amber Alert	Second Amber Alert issued for 5 missing children ... etc.
8:49	Amber Alert	Sixth Amber Alert issued for missing child
8:49	Amber Alert	Seventh Amber Alert issued for missing child
9:03	**System Failure**	**Amber Alert system crashes**

8

THE MORNING AFTER

No parent slept that awful night. Those without televisions got the news from frantic relatives or from school districts on red alert. Police cars threaded the neighborhoods. Helicopters drifted overhead with spotlights filleting the alleys and overpasses. National Guardsmen appeared on lawns in pieces of uniform. In dozens of cities, trigger-happy citizens gunned down unfortunate burglars, vandals, graffiti artists, and pizza-delivery people.

At two in the morning, the president declared a state of national emergency. By dawn the nation's highways were empty. School and work were canceled. For some reason, despite the fact that the dangers were subterranean in origin, air traffic was shut down, too. Americans turned on their NPR or FOX or *Good Morning America* or Yahoo. Like intelligence analysts, they called each other to discuss every new blog, interview, factoid, theory, or video clip.

The U.S. had taken the brunt of the attack. Yes, northern Mexico was reporting an incident near the American border, quaintly linked in their media to the Day of the Dead. And yes, a portion of southern Canada had been struck as well. But clearly America had been ground zero. Her children had been stolen. Anyone defending them had been killed.

The figures varied wildly. Some reports suggested thousands of victims. More thoughtful commentators cautioned that the figure might be as low as several hundred or less. Even if it were several dozen, the terror would be the same. On our soil, in our homes, in our modern times, a monstrosity from long ago had once again trespassed against us.

"For those of you just joining us . . ."

". . . numbers continue to be revised. Reports are coming in from across the country. The official count keeps creeping up, Jim. Upward of twelve thousand . . ."

"White House press secretary Arthur Young has revised initial estimates of last night's toll—downward—to seventy-three missing and one hundred thirteen dead. He has assured us that fewer than five cities were affected, not the scores of cities that were reported in early reports. Those numbers could change. Meanwhile he is urging calm."

"And this just in. Los Angeles is reporting widespread rioting and looting. The governor is rushing in troops . . ."

"We will continue to bring you live, uninterrupted coverage of this . . ."

No one knew quite what to call the event. Each television anchor played off his or her own pet word or phrase. Midnight Raid. Halloween Invasion. Blitzkrieg. Not Since Pearl Harbor. Since 9/11. Vendetta. War of the Worlds. Slaughter of the Innocents. Was it an act of terror? An act of war? No one knew.

There was no question who the enemy was. Somehow the demon horde had resurrected itself. After eons of subjection, of slavery and night terror and serving as herds of sun-fed meat, mankind thought it had rid itself of hell. Now hell yawned at the foot of everyone's basement stairs.

No matter where people turned this day, horrific images and unedited footage that would normally never make it past the network censors awaited them.

"Please be advised that the following is not appropriate for children . . ."

"If your children are watching, please . . ."

"What you're about to see is unsuitable for children . . ."

Children. It was all about the children. That much was clear.

Certain footage kept replaying. The images began to take on a fame of their own. The Eugene Sighting. The Witches' Parlor. The Flayed Man. Hell House. Rebecca. Over and over again.

An ATM camera showed ghosts, white ghosts, moving very fast. Slowed down and computer enhanced, the ghosts became four hominids running down Main Street in Eugene, Oregon. The camera's time signature read 18:22. That would be Pacific time. The creatures were brazen. At that hour it had barely been dark in Oregon.

Yellow police tape girdled a house on the outer edge of an Atlanta subdivision. Cops mingled with black-clad SWAT commandos and National Guardsmen in old desert camouflage. A reporter was addressing the camera. Four Atlanta youths had last been seen approaching this residence last night while making their Halloween rounds. The telephoto zooms in on a Spiderman mask and a flashlight near the front door.

"According to neighbors, three homeless females were living in the vacated property. And, Monica, we're being told that a tunnel has been found in the basement."

Suddenly gunshots ring out. Everyone panics. The camera tilts at crazy angles. Men yell in the distance. "Take him down, take that fucker down. Get his gun."

The camera swings around to a bunch of cops pinning a man to the sidewalk. They don't want to punch or Taser him with all the cameras around.

Dressed in pajama shorts, the gunman keeps struggling and shouting. "Billy? Let me up, you sorry bastards. My son's in there. I'm going after him. Billy? I'm coming for you, son."

People mill around outside a police station. In another setting, on another morning, they might be zombies left over from Halloween. Their hair is a mess. Eyes are red and puffy. They shuffle about, crowding a bulletin board with photos and notes.

A woman glimpses the camera. She peels away from the rear of the crowd and approaches with a snapshot held in front of her. "Have you seen my son?" She says his name. "If anyone has seen him, please, please call. We let him go out with his friends last night. He asked and we let him. We let him."

More parents catch sight of the camera. A collective lightbulb goes on. Snapshots outstretched, they mob the screen.

*   *   *

Amateur video footage shows two joggers standing in Central Park among a stand of trees and massive boulders. It's chilly. They have lollipop-red cheeks. Frost blows from their mouths.

"Yeah, we take this loop most mornings. And you know, you find stuff at that hour, freaky stuff left over from the night before. But never anything like this."

The second jogger crowds into the camera. "At first we didn't even know what it was. I mean, we knew something organic, like off an animal. But who'd guess it was human."

The camera pans from the path to the boulders. An orange plastic pumpkin lies sideways on the mat of leaves. A child's Schwinn bike. The camera wobbles. Leaves crunch. The view goes in and out of focus as we approach.

The woods look hostile, its boulders glassy with ice. It looks almost like Christmas in here. Long pink ropes loop between the trees. Blue and gray viscera dangle from the boughs.

"Oh yeah, now I see it," says the camera guy. "Like he exploded. Wild. Is that the dude's kidney up there?"

The joggers come up. "Only in New York, man."

A woman's face fills the screen. Her beauty is startling in its purity. You cannot take your eyes from her. She could be a Viking queen with her blond hair loosely braided.

"Your daughter and husband went missing last night, Ms. Coltrane?"

"My daughter, yes."

"And not your husband?"

"He is dead, not missing. I saw that much. They will find him down-river, I am sure."

Silence, then, "Can you tell us what you saw?"

The woman looks at us. The television screen practically vibrates with raw emotion. This is almost too painful to watch. The widow and be-reaved mother will break down now. She will weep or curse or collapse. In-stead she speaks, simply. "I saw a man lose to wild animals."

A single tear runs down her cheek. She doesn't wipe it away. Her dig-nity breaks your heart. Her eerie strength might come from shock or insanity, and yet those green eyes are so crystal clear. The night has given birth to something extraordinary here, you can sense it.

"I know this is difficult for you, Ms. Coltrane."

"Rebecca," she says.

The interviewer is emboldened. "Rebecca, do you ever expect to see your daughter again?"

Rebecca does not pause. She knows her heart. "God is keeping her safe for me. I will find her and bring her back to the light."

The interviewer shifts uncomfortably. "God?"

"Of course. This is a test. We are in a war. There will be only one winner."

"You seem so certain." The interviewer tries to hide it, but she is as frightened and unsure as the rest of us. "How can you be so certain?"

The light on Rebecca's face brightens one degree. It is like watching her spirit show itself. She leans forward to touch the interviewer. This woman who has lost her entire world in a single night reaches out to comfort a stranger who has lost nothing but her courage.

"Believe me," she says. "Don't be afraid. We are God's people."

"So we will win?"

"I don't know about that. But one thing I do know is that the children will return to us. They will."

FOX NEWS

The Rob O'Ryan True News Hour

O'Ryan: "It was supposed to be over, General Lancing. The plague sterilized the Interior passages. That's what we thought. We were told Haddie had gone the way of the carrier pigeon. Dead. Extinct. Following the subterranean plague ten years ago, the U.S. government gave our citizens a green light. Over 1.3 million American pioneers are now engaged in developing the Interior, everywhere from the Atlantic Recesses to the Pacific Bowl. We thought the inlands were safe. Not so. Now we learn these things were alive and well all along. How do you explain this?"

General: "It may be that a group of them survived the plague in some isolated branch of the tunnel system. It may be that individuals were residing on the surface at the time of the plague, and that they are just now organizing."

O'Ryan: "Sleeper cells, is that what you're saying? That these things infiltrated our towns and communities a long time ago and have just been waiting?"

General: "We don't know yet. But I will say this. Americans have gotten complacent over the last ten years. The plague gave people a false sense of security."

O'Ryan: "We can't ever let our guard down, is that what you're saying?"

General: "That is the soldier's creed, Robert. Vigilance."

O'Ryan: "What now, sir? Hot pursuit? Special ops? Military occupation?"

General: "It's common knowledge that the previous administration signed off on the United Nations Subplanetary Treaty three years ago. Now the implications are finally becoming clear."

O'Ryan: "Don't blame me, General. I said at the time that the treaty was a mistake. But people see what they want to see. The treaty was sold to us as the blueprint for a new utopia. Peace forever. But the devil's always in the details. It may sound grand and noble to forbid all nations from annexing or militarizing the subocean territories. But now we find ourselves chained—shackled hand and foot, us, the American giant—by a world body that has always been hostile to our interests."

General: "My hands are tied, that much I know."

O'Ryan: "Outrageous. Really. This is crazy, General. The United States of America suffers a bloodbath on her own soil. Thousands of her children are kidnapped from their homes. And we have to sit on the sidelines begging for permission to defend ourselves?"

General: "The treaty, Robert."

O'Ryan: "This is giving me a stomachache, General. All right, enough of that for now. Let me introduce my next guest, Professor Alexandra Von Schade, an expert in hadal cultures and civilization. She joins us from our studio in San Francisco, where she is the director of the Institute of Human Studies. Welcome aboard."

Von Schade: "Thank you."

O'Ryan: "So they are alive after all, Dr. Von Schade. As someone who studies what we thought was a dead race, you must be awfully excited."

Von Schade: "Excited? A terrible tragedy occurred last night."

O'Ryan: "Committed by your hadals."

Von Schade: "They don't belong to me, Mr. O'Ryan. Until last night we had no idea that any had survived."

O'Ryan: "It's no secret that you are an advocate for them."

Von Schade: "I'm a student of their remains, linguistic, archeological, and cultural."

O'Ryan: "You're an authority on these things. They held you captive for a time. Can you tell us what lies in store for the missing children?"

Von Schade: "I can only guess. The initial phase will be shock. The violence of capture, the forced march through tunnels, the abrupt shift to permanent night, the change in diet, the homesickness, all these and other factors will stress their systems. In the first days and weeks, they face tremendous challenges."

O'Ryan: "Challenges? You make it sound like an Outward Bound course."

Von Schade: "The children will be given every advantage to survive. They will receive the best food and care their captors can offer. If there is any danger along the way, the children will be guided around it. You have to remember, the hadals value our children."

O'Ryan: "Especially the females, isn't that right? The breeders."

Von Schade: "For some reason it became difficult for Homo hadalis to reproduce among themselves. They had learned to reach across the species border, to create hybrids as a way of surviving. They had been doing it for so long, it became a cultural instinct."

O'Ryan: "A cultural instinct? Again, you make it sound so neat and painless and reasonable, Professor."

Von Schade: "Reasonable, yes. Not painless. Not neat. Not for the captives. Not for their families."

O'Ryan: "Is that what's going on then? Are they trying to repopulate their decimated ranks?"

Von Schade: "I don't know. It's possible."

O'Ryan: "Then why not take children from other countries? Why America alone?"

Von Schade: "That puzzles me, too. It has the appearance of a political act. An act of terrorism."

O'Ryan: "But these are apes. Or demons."

Von Schade: "In hindsight, we never should have gone down there. Once we discovered hell was a real place, an inhabited place, we should have roped it off and taken one giant step back and thought things through before attempting contact. Instead we rushed in. We destroyed their habitat. We wiped them out with some sort of biological weapon ..."

O'Ryan: "You persist in your conspiracy theory. There is no evidence to suggest the plague was anything but natural."

Von Schade: "I've seen the cylinders."

O'Ryan: "Which have been proved fakes."

Von Schade: "We upset a delicate balance. That is my point. Until then, we were in a sort of truce with them. Our monsters largely stayed down there. Except for the occasional literary hero, the Oedipus or Aeneas or Dante, we largely stayed up here. Then, suddenly, the hadal tribes had nowhere left to go. It may be they're trying to restore the earlier balance, us up here, them down there."

O'Ryan: "By going on a bloody rampage across America?"

Von Schade: "We exterminated them, including their children. We wiped out the future of an entire people. Here's what it feels like."

O'Ryan: "An eye for an eye then? You're saying America had it coming?"

Von Schade: "Of course not."

O'Ryan: "But what goes around comes around?"

Von Schade: "There are always consequences to one's actions."

O'Ryan: "But again, why America? Why not China or France or the Arab Emirates?"

Von Schade: "It may be they figured out that America was responsible for the genocide and this is payback. Basically, I think they just want to be left alone."

The screen splits, showing General Lancing, to O'Ryan's side. He is a picture of rage. The muscles are flexing in his head. He can barely restrain himself.

O'Ryan: "You claim that the hadals civilized mankind, Ms. Von Schade. That they planted in us the notion of pyramids, agriculture, and poetry, again your words. That without them, we would still be apes in the marshes."

Von Schade: "The facts are increasingly clear. We were mentored. We inherited civilization."

O'Ryan: "Civilization? We're talking about creatures that ate us. They used us as slaves and livestock. They stole our children. And yet you continue to humanize them."

Von Schade: "They humanized us. That is my point."

O'Ryan: "Let's look at some footage now from one of last night's kill sites. Please help walk us through the humanity of these things. A word of warning to all you parents out there, the following is not for younger eyes."

The screen fills with yet another image of last night's havoc. "Hell House," reads a roadside billboard, "Redemption Through Terror." The "house" is in fact an old circus tent pitched against a hillside. Portions have collapsed at the rear, revealing a mine entrance with a rusted metal door dangling by one hinge.

O'Ryan: "We obtained this from one of our correspondents in Colorado Springs. This was a sort of haunted house aimed at high school teens. Unfortunately it was placed next to an abandoned gold mine."

The scene shifts from outside to inside. The Colorado sunshine, so cheery in the early part, filters through blood-splashed canvas walls. Pieces of scaremongering exhibits litter the floor: a Bible, a plastic baby doll painted red, a car body gently rocking in midair.

O'Ryan: "Over the course of two terrible hours, twenty-three young people were kidnapped and taken down the mine shaft. But not before the raiding party killed all the adults and anyone else who resisted."

The first of the bodies appears on camera, tagged but not yet bagged or moved. The dead man seems astonished to find himself in this state. Naked as a hog, flat on his back, his body has been mutilated. Each thigh bears an identical wound, long and deep, exposing the red muscle. The camera returns to his face. His eyes are gone, replaced with pebbles. That explains the astonished look.

O'Ryan: "The bodies were butchered. Some were scalped and castrated. Five were decapitated. Meat was taken."

Most of the dead are men, thighs slashed open, pebbles for eyes. Several are buff younger hunks, athletes obviously. These are the ones who were beheaded and castrated. Their chest cavities yawn ajar, with ribs snapped. The camera moves on.

Near the back of the tent, we reach a woman. After killing her, they propped her sitting upright. She was a large woman. Her obesity is somehow more pornographic than her nakedness. She sits there in a great mound of her own flesh. The camera pauses at her enormous breasts. Each breast has been embellished with a vermilion stripe running around and around in a barbershop swirl to the nipple.

They did not cut her thighs. Instead, her plump white legs sprawl open, and a caramel apple, a Halloween fruit, rests on the ground in between. To her left and right sit the missing heads, five of them. With pebbles for eyes, they look ferocious, like bloody lapdogs. Some kind of meat spills from each of her hands.

O'Ryan: "As you can see, they vandalized this woman, arranging her like a mannequin or plaything."

The video ends. Cut to O'Ryan sitting at a table with the general.

O'Ryan: "And yet, Professor, you continue to call these things human."

Von Schade: "Because that's what they are. They are offspring of *Homo erectus*. Two different branches on the same family tree, or bush. They were far more advanced than what we narrowly define as human today. It's a mistake to call them monkeys or demons. In fact, at his peak, *Homo erectus* had a larger cranial cavity than modern *Homo sapiens*. Most likely it was *erectus* who discovered fire, and then went on to build empires predating ours by tens of thousands of years."

O'Ryan: "I must be missing something then. You saw evidence of human behavior in the footage we just showed?"

General Lancing: "Wild animals. Devils."

Von Schade: "They took time and put themselves at risk to prepare the bodies we just saw. They could simply and more safely have fled with their prisoners. Instead they took the time to honor the dead."

O'Ryan: "Slashed them. Ripped them open. Tore out their hearts. Cut off their heads. How is that honoring them?"

Von Schade: "Take the wounds in their thighs. Those are a form of signature. They designate the particular clan or tribe a warrior comes from. A different clan would have cut the biceps or abdomen. They were marking their enemy for others to know. But the wounds serve another purpose, too. They open the body to rebirth."

O'Ryan: "Rebirth? That's a bit unorthodox. Maybe you can explain that to those of us who don't live in San Francisco, Professor."

Von Schade: "Through these wounds, the spirit is able to escape and continue its journey and be reborn. That's what they believe. Also the wounds allow the body to start its own journey. By opening the closed flesh, the wounds allow in the insects and animals who will help render these people back to the sacred earth."

O'Ryan: "What about the eyes? Scooped out, all of them. You have an explanation for that?"

Von Schade: "The eyes were replaced with stones to give them eternal sight. The hearts were removed to be eaten. They were taken from the bravest fighters so that their courage can be recycled."

O'Ryan: "And that poor woman?"

Von Schade: "They probably mistook her for a minor deity. A fertility goddess. To them, the whole procession of people through the haunted house would have appeared to be a form of adoration. My guess is, they tried to take her along. When she refused, they killed her."

O'Ryan: "And then mutilated her."

Von Schade: "I didn't see a single mark on her."

O'Ryan: "Come on. They violated her body. They abused her flesh. Who knows what else?"

Von Schade: "Her body awed them. They would have worshipped her, if she'd gone with them."

O'Ryan: "Give me video." (The dead woman appears on screen again.) "This is worship? They drew obscenities on her. They turned her into a mockery."

Von Schade: "They turned her into a goddess. Look at her, the large breasts, the large stomach, the huge hips and rump. Anthropologists call her condition 'steatopygia.' Well into the twentieth century, tribes in Africa prized a woman like this. We've all seen artifacts from the Stone Age. She's the shape of their Venus. Abundance and fertility and nourishment, all in one package. This woman would have had a high status among them."

O'Ryan: "We're talking about slaughter, kidnapping, and a lifetime of rape."

Von Schade: "From our perspective, yes."

O'Ryan: "So now these creatures have a perspective?"

Von Schade: "For them this is all about survival. A competition for resources, if you will. They don't distinguish between us and them. From their perspective, we're all in this together, part of one great circle."

General: "For God's sake, woman, whose side are you on?"

Von Schade: "But they don't think in terms of sides, General. You need to understand that. They're not fiends punishing us for our sins. Although they do see us as very sinful, very unclean."

General: "Now it's our fault?"

Von Schade: "I didn't say that. I'm simply pointing out that they don't hate us any more than a predator hates its prey."

General: "So you admit that they're animals."

Von Schade: "Aren't we all?"

General: "You know what I mean."

Von Schade: "They have committed terrible atrocities. But over the eons so have we. The story fragments that we've been able to translate speak of us—the surface people—as the devils and beasts and barbarians. At least they never attempted to exterminate us. They culled the herd, as Mr. O'Ryan labeled us. But they never tried to kill us off wholesale. It's we who are guilty of genocide. The so-called plague was a man-made mass murder. It was planted by an American agent, or agents, on an American expedition."

General: "That's Chinese propaganda, and you know it. Congress investigated. They issued their findings. The plague was a natural disaster."

Von Schade: "Actually, that's American propaganda. American colonists were evacuated just before the plague was released. It was delivered in capsules with U.S. military markings. The capsules weren't meant to be found, of course. But every now and then a settler or miner still comes across them. We have several in our archives."

General: "What is it with you people?"

Von Schade: "We people?"

General: "We know who you are."

Von Schade: "Domestic surveillance is a slippery slope, General, if that's what you're talking about."

General: "There aren't many of you, thank God. Though I wonder why there are any of you. It's a testament to the First Amendment and the good graces of the American people that your institute is still standing."

Von Schade: "Sir, I'm . . . I don't know what to say. I'm sure you're not advocating violence against people who disagree with you. We all need to be careful with our words, especially now and in public. We are suffering a national crisis. These are dangerous times."

General: "These are times for patriots, madam, not excuses for the enemy."

Von Schade: "General ..."

O'Ryan: "You're a mother, Professor Von Schade, am I right?"

Von Schade: "I was."

O'Ryan: "Was?"

Von Schade: "She died."

O'Ryan: "I'm sorry."

Von Schade: "It was years ago. A flu brought up from below."

O'Ryan: "As a mother, doesn't this tear at you? How would you feel if something had happened in your home last night?"

Von Schade: "The same way you would feel, I'm sure."

O'Ryan: "Desperate? Frantic? Ready to die?"

Von Schade: "Yes."

O'Ryan: "And yet you defend these hadal animals."

Von Schade: "The hadals need us, that was my point. And once upon a time we needed them. They were our Adam and Eve, leading us from the wilderness into civilization. Fear is our greatest enemy right now. But peace is still possible."

O'Ryan: "What about the missing children?"

Von Schade: "I don't understand."

O'Ryan: "It's not a difficult question. The children. What about them?"

Von Schade: "I would do anything to help get them back."

O'Ryan: "Anything, you say?"

Von Schade: "That's what I said."

O'Ryan and the general trade a look. They seem to share some deep secret. Then O'Ryan faces the camera with the bulldog scowl that is his trademark.

O'Ryan: "Thank you for taking the time to join us, Dr. Von Schade. Now my next guest is ..."

ARTIFACTS

THE PRESIDENT'S ADDRESS TO THE NATION—NOVEMBER 1

"I know many citizens have fears tonight, and I ask you to be calm and resolute, even in the face of a continuing threat. I ask you to live your lives and hug your children.

"We'll go back to our lives and routines, and that is good. Even grief recedes with time and grace. But our resolve must not pass. Each of us will remember what happened and to whom it happened. We will remember the moment the news came, where we were and what we were doing.

"Some speak of an age of terror. I know there are struggles ahead and dangers to face. But this country will define our times, not be defined by them. Great harm has been done to us. We have suffered great loss. And in our grief and anger we have found our mission and our moment. Freedom and fear are at war.

"Our nation, this generation, will lift the dark threat of violence from our people and our future. We will rally the world to this cause by our efforts, by our courage. We will not tire, we will not falter, and we will not fail.

"Tonight, I ask for your prayers for all those who grieve, for the children whose worlds have been shattered, for all whose sense of safety and security has been threatened. And I pray they will be comforted by a power greater than any of us, spoken through the ages in Psalm Twenty-three: 'Even though I walk through the valley of the shadow of death, I fear no evil, for You are with me.'

"Thank you. Good night, and God bless America."

9

Ali hustled through the corridors behind her escort. Her hair was wet. A helicopter had delivered her here through a raging storm. Even deep inside this underground facility, she could hear the wind howling. They came to another security check and more guards with rifles. The doors opened upon more doors.

General Lancing was waiting for her, the same uniformed bully she'd just sparred with on television. He stuck out a big paw. "Thank you for coming, Dr. Von Schade."

She shook hands warily. He seemed different from the fire-breathing warhorse who had race-baited her on *The Rob O'Ryan True News Hour.* The trademark cigar was nowhere in sight. He looked intelligent and full of good cheer.

"I have to tell you, General, I had misgivings when you called for my help."

"You're talking about O'Ryan's circus for the masses," he said. "No hard feelings, I hope. His viewers like red meat, I went along and gave them red meat. I thought that was very sporting of you to volunteer to be his daily goat."

"You make it sound like a game."

"More like Kabuki theater," the general said. "Lots of ritual. O'Ryan's no dummy. He plays it for all it's worth, red versus blue, sage patriots ver-

sus spineless liberals, whatever it takes to stay on the air. We need his su-
pernationalism at times. Just like we need your insights now."

"So I'm not here to be burned at the stake?"

"Christ no. We need you. This is for the children."

It wasn't hard to guess. Her strength was linguistics. They would have
some hadal artifact for her to translate. Or to try and translate. It would
have been easier if they had flown it down to her archives. Her glossary
was not exactly enormous, but she had a foothold with the words and
symbols. Someday a Rosetta stone might turn up to bridge the gap between the writings left by the hadal empire and the modern languages of
man. Until then, she was it.

"I'll do what I can," she said.

The general paused at the door. "For the children," he said again, and
opened the door. The smell hit her. Feces, urine, and Lysol. And hadal. Live
hadal.

Inside was a darkened room with a table and chairs and a one-way
mirror window. Immediately she understood. This was not about documents or artifacts.

The window looked upon a white room. A monster lay strapped to a
hospital bed. A human, she told herself. *Homo hadalis.* But deeper in-
stincts prevailed: *monster.*

The creature looked all the more grotesque lying on top of the white
sheets. It was like a wild animal that has broken into your house and can't
find its way out again. *He,* not *it,* Ali corrected herself. He was rotting from
the hands and feet inward, as if the surface world were a cancer upon him.

"We captured it along the coast south of Portland last night," the general told her.

She had seen hadals in all shapes and sizes during her year with the Helios expedition. Some had vestigial wings or gills. Some had the long,
climbing arms of ape ancestors, perfect for the vertical shafts of the Subterrain. Some were half the size of humans, possibly the result of long isolation and poor diet. Some nested in pockets in the ceilings of caves.

Biologists and geneticists were at their wits' ends trying to explain the
outrageous variation. Mutation and genetic drift fell inside the scientific
norm. Wings and gills did not. The evangelical crowd gleefully proclaimed
that the hadal bestiary proved evolutionary theory was a false doctrine.

According to them, the hadals were the living progeny of rebel angels, and their deformed bodies were God's punishment.

His rib cage was barely moving. He cast a curious red shadow on the sheets.

"What's the bandage for?" It ran across his abdomen. Wires and tubes snaked out from the bandage.

"A pair of fishermen spotted him in the rocks. They thought he was a sea lion, which you're not supposed to shoot. But the sea lions eat the lobsters from their traps, so they opened up on him. He's lucky they were drunk and terrible shots. We collected fifty brass shells from the boat floor, but only one round hit him."

"Were any of the children with him?"

"No. But we backtracked and found a storm drain with a tunnel bored from below. And this." He held up a clear plastic bag with a child's muddy pajama bottoms. They were decorated with Pooh bear.

Ali had bought the whole series for Maggie. Time ran out before they'd managed to finish the first book.

Ali had a pretty fair idea what came next.

The general placed the pajamas next to a book. It was the only other thing on the table. *Army Field Manual 34-52.3, Revised Edition,* it said, *Interrogation Procedures.*

"Why me?" she said. "You must have people who can do this."

"Ten years ago, yes. But after the plague, we dropped it from the language school. We thought they were all dead. That leaves you as the expert. I don't know where else to turn. We need your talents."

In normal times, she would have walked away. In normal times, they wouldn't have asked her to come in the first place. These weren't normal times.

She could have put on airs and made him at least court her participation. But they were in a hurry, and she was old enough to know her heart and mind. Ali made her decision on the spot. "For the children," she said.

"We need to know where he came from, how he and his bunch managed to escape the plague, how many of them are down there, their organization, the nature of their leadership, their route of passage, their weaponry, their grand strategy. Is this the beginning of a larger campaign? What do they want? Where are they going with the children?"

The interrogation manual sat there like a family Bible, prominent and austere. "Why is this here?"

"To show you that we are civilized. We understand limits. We have rules. But none apply to him today."

"What if I say no?"

"Frankly, I'll be surprised if you say yes. I know how ugly this must be to you."

"I could go straight to the press. I could expose this whole operation."

"After last night, do you think anyone would care?"

He was right. For eons these creatures had been boiling up from the depths and dragging poor souls deep and doing unspeakable things to them. And, yes, people would cheer every terrible thing the military might do today or tomorrow, in this building or down below. None of which meant she had to participate in torture.

"I care."

"That is precisely why you're here. You know them. You've studied them. You lived with them."

She looked for bruises or burn marks on the hadal's body, but there were none, only the corruption of disease and his scars and the pale arabesques inking his skin. And the wires coming from the bandage. "What have you been doing to him?" she asked.

"Training him. He needs to understand this is not under his control. That's the key to any successful interview."

"Interview?"

"We ask the questions. He answers them."

"Those look like electric wires."

"To monitor his vital signs."

"How are you training him?"

"He was injected with a paralytic agent. His muscles quit working. He stopped breathing. He was fully conscious, he just couldn't move. Not for the life of him. We had to breathe for him. It's an old Mossad technique. After a few minutes, we restarted his body with a counteragent. It's harmless, but horrifying. People will do anything not to go through it twice."

"They're human, General."

"I don't care if he's my long-lost kid brother. He has struck at the heart of our country, kidnapped our children, and murdered our neighbors.

The nation is under siege." The general tossed another plastic Baggie on the table. It held a strip of meat. "We found that on him. Beef jerky. Except it's not beef. We're doing a DNA analysis to try and identify who it came from."

They were wrong if they thought she shocked so easily. "I know what it is," she said. "That was my food for twenty days straight. High in protein. Depending on the cut, we taste a little like chicken or pork."

He nodded. He got it. She wasn't a weak sister. Her objections weren't squeamish or prissy. "I need your answer," he said. "The clock is ticking. We've got teams down there looking for the children right now, but there's not a trace. The hadals collapsed the tunnels behind them. We're digging as fast as we can, and it's not fast enough. The children are sinking farther and farther away. The trail is getting colder by the minute."

"I thought the Chinese ambassador came out with a warning this morning. Didn't he tell us not to send in troops?"

"He did. And the Great Game goes on. They want the Interior. We want it. The stakes are high, and everything gets politicized. We understand that. But these are our children who were stolen, not theirs. We've got operators sniffing everywhere down there. The problem is, the Chinese know we're breaching the accords. In our shoes, they'd be doing the same thing. So their guys are looking for our guys, and if they bump into each other, the shit will hit the fan. The longer the search goes on, the deeper we go, the more we risk hot contact with the People's Republic. That's why we need to pinpoint exactly where to go so we can make the recovery and get the hell out before it turns into a shooting war."

Ali looked through the glass at the prisoner. Some people thought she'd created her institute because of the Stockholm syndrome, a victim identifying with her hadal captors. Or as penance for having been part of the same Helios expedition that, unknown to her, had carried the plague into the hadals' midst. Or for mystical, New Age, lost Atlantis reasons. In fact, part of her devotion to their dead civilization was a gut reaction to the lunacy of nations and armies and wars, the very lunacy now dragging America and China to the brink of cataclysm.

At its height nine thousand years ago, the hadal empire had been a sort of dark paradise. The glyphs and stone carvings suggested a reign of peace spanning more than three millennia. Ali eyed the monstrous creature strapped in the hospital bed. The hadals had become her Martians, in a sense. Their absence had let her imagination run free. She could make of them a tranquil, if misshapen, race. Even now, in their decline, for all their bloody ways and hideous appearance, the hadals' violence paled next to what mankind did to itself day in, day out.

"You can save him," said the general.

"You'll let him go?"

"His pain can stop. He can die in peace."

She had her own nightmares to deal with, nightmares of her captivity, not unlike this hadal's captivity, or the children's, far from home and bound and being driven lower into their maze.

"All right," she said.

For much of her life, well before she'd gone into the earth and come back out, she had been searching for the Word, that ancient moment that marked the birth of humanness. How ironic that her hunt for humanity was now leading her into a torture chamber. She had escaped the workers of hell, only to become one herself.

"For the children," she whispered.

They wanted to outfit her like a surgeon, with paper clothes and a mask and latex gloves, but she refused. "He has leprosy," the general said. "Don't let the restraints and his missing fingers fool you. He spits. He bites. Nobody can get close without him acting up."

"Do they wear masks and gowns?"

"Always." Then he saw her point. "Very well. Do it your way."

"Do you have a pen? A small ink marker would be best. And a mirror. And some food and water."

The general spoke into an intercom. Ali bound her hair back. A minute later a Sharpie and a signal mirror appeared at the door. She went to the light from the window and began sketching tattoos onto her face.

She drew a virtual book around her eyes and mouth, picking and choosing her symbols. The hadal would be illiterate. They hadn't been able to read their own language for centuries, if not eons. But the shape of the glyphs might comfort him.

On her forehead, she drew the back-to-back reversed symbols for day and night, and above that a snaking line for river. Each cheek got a spiral. If she was right, the spirals would mark her as a shaman, or a witch. The thin sideways diamond down the bridge of her nose implied distance or time. She chose an animal spirit for her chin, a subterranean fish. The priestess who has swum through time. On a whim, remembering the tunnel symbols on Saint Matthew Island last summer, she drew an aleph on her hand.

The general said nothing when she turned around. He had seen enough camouflage in his life not to react. That, or he expected weirdness from his academics. Or New Age from San Franciscans.

"I'll go in alone," she said.

"Not a chance."

"He's frightened enough."

The general stared at her. "Your call then."

An aide brought in an earbud so that the general could communicate with her. She felt like a G-man. "Testing, testing," he said.

"Loud and clear," she said.

"The room is miked. We'll be able to hear every word you say. Talk to us. I'll talk to you." The general went to a small refrigerator in the corner. "Does it matter what kind of food it is?" The general held up someone's lunch. It had a Quiznos sandwich, a cookie, and a little carton of milk.

"Meat," she said, reaching for the sandwich and milk. On second thought, she gave back the sandwich and took the plastic Baggie with the strip of dried human jerky. The general opened his mouth to object, then closed it without a word. This was her show now.

They walked around to the cell's door. The two MPs did a double take at her Maori-like ink job. "I'll be watching through the window. If you need help . . ."

She left her shoes at the threshold and entered barefoot and alone. There was a familiar tang of hadal in the air, like buckskin dug up from dry soil. Stronger still was the stench of festering flesh. In medieval times, people compared leprosy to the smell of a male goat.

The prisoner turned his head slowly. His eyelid muscles had frozen open from nerve damage. His pink eyes focused as he rose up from their sedation, or from the mental hibernation she'd seen Ike use. Ike had learned the trick from his years as a captive, and she had seen for herself how the catnaps or meditation allowed him to go for days without sleep and still be fresh at the end.

Ali came to a halt and politely lowered her eyes, letting the hadal decide about her. Ike had taught her bits of their behavior and nature. Eye contact could be dangerous, unless invited. Silence was ideal. She waited. At last he made a small clicking noise with his tongue, signifying approval, at least for the moment. She looked up.

He was exhausted. They had been working him hard. The stomach wound was a death sentence. Now she saw that the red shadow of his body on the sheets came from sweat. He was sweating blood.

But his eyes brightened at the sight of her facial markings. Abruptly he stuck out his tongue, like in a doctor's office. Ali returned the greeting.

Much of his monstrosity was due to maladies that would have been perfectly ordinary in the Dark Ages. His hands and feet were mere paddles, the digits eaten away. His nasal cavity was exposed. His scalp pulsed with a complex of blue veins. Polio had twisted his legs so badly that Ali wondered how he'd ever managed to reach the surface.

His skull had the flattened triangular shape—wide cheeks tapering up to the blunt crest—that distinguished descendants of *H. erectus.* The heavy, beetling brow, like a pair of binoculars fixed to his face, was also characteristic. But just as *H. sapiens* had developed beyond the primal template, *H. hadalis* carried his own look, one customized to the extremes of eternal night and the stone labyrinth.

It was easy to see why the fishermen had mistaken him for a sea lion. His skin was hairless and fishy pale, and the leprosy had trimmed away his ears, leaving a doglike profile with a long neck and little chin.

Now she saw the monkey tail, or what was left of it, like a second penis beneath his real one. The leprosy had eaten it down to a stub. It was a real monkey tail, or more technically, a throwback to the vestige of a tail all humans were born with. Technically speaking, evolved traits could not revert to earlier forms. Yet here was another of the bizarre exceptions that the inner earth kept throwing at them. In his case, the relic tail had fully developed. It switched from side to side.

The horning process that occurred in certain regions of the subplanet had barely manifested in him. Nubbins pressed at the skin of his forehead, like boils.

She struggled to see past the ravages of disease and time. His flesh was crisscrossed with a short, hard lifetime of scars. Despite the old man's pouches under his eyes and the hunch in his spine and the skin cancer on his bald scalp, he was probably no older than twenty-three. That would have made him thirteen when the plague swept through the tunnels.

He said something, a subterranean whisper surrounded with the peculiar ticks and clucks of the ancient Khoisan or click language spoken by the San !Kung Bushmen of southern Africa. It was a shy, almost musical sound. She recognized a single word, "I." They were off and running.

She tried a greeting, one of the words in her grab bag of protolanguages. She said her name. Despite the leper's mask—the astonished eyes, the thickened leonine features, the ulcers—his brow furrowed. Plainly her words were nonsense to him.

"Food," she said, taking the jerky strip from the Baggie. She was careful to hold it in her right hand, not her unclean left one.

She broke the jerky into bite sizes and held one to his mouth. He refused it, rightfully suspicious.

"I know what you're thinking," the general's voice said in her ear. She'd almost forgotten him, her focus was so intense. "Don't do it."

The hadal frowned. His hearing was acute. He had heard the voice coming from her ear, from inside her head. It confused and frightened him. "I'm losing him," she said out loud to the general. Thinking fast, she popped the bit of human jerky into her mouth. She made a show of chewing. It tasted like dark drumstick meat.

This time he took the food she offered. His tongue darted for it. He chewed slowly, squeezing the flavor from the meat. His eyes rolled back with pleasure.

His front teeth were missing, a clue to his clan. Some clans used to file their teeth to points, some carved designs into the enamel or embedded precious stones. Some knocked out the front teeth of their children at puberty.

He allowed her to feed him the rest. At the end, he let loose with a small stream of words that were equal parts lung and tongue.

She shook her head no. He tried again, more slowly. Somewhere in that jumble of sounds probably lay his thanks to her, to the person whose body had provided the meat, and possibly to his god. But it came too fast, and her ear was out of practice. A decade ago, when Ike was still in her life, she had built a small vocabulary of hadal terms. Little registered anymore. With no one to practice with, she had lost much.

"Drink," she said, and gave him a sip of milk. The little red carton reminded her of grade school, and that reminded her again of the children. This was an interrogation, not an anthro picnic. Here lay one of the killers and kidnappers.

Whatever the prisoner was expecting from the carton, it was not milk. The taste startled him. He looked at her and something changed in his eyes. "Ma-har," he whispered.

Mother.

She looked at the milk carton in her hand. She might as well have offered her breast. *Play it through.* "Yes, ma-har. Children." She held her hand at varying heights. "Mine. My children." She clutched an imaginary Maggie to her chest. "Where?"

He understood. She could tell. He looked away.

"La." She snapped it like a whip. Their eyes met. "Children. Go. Where?"

He clicked once, as if to say life is sorrow. And that he owned her, her people, and their children and their hopes. Like a king, this ruined creature.

She reverted to hand signals and pidgin language. *Me, Ali. You?*

"Mar-ee-ya," he answered. It had a glottal stop, three distinct tones, and a click, all within three syllables.

"What was that?" the general said.

"Maria," Ali said. She asked the leper more questions. "Yes, his name is Maria. That would be the name of his mother, whom he believes descended into the world, into the inside of the planet, in order to conceive him. She would have been a captive, like I was."

The hadal began singing. It was a throat song, with the deep, long, vibrating tones used by Tibetan monks and Mongolian herders. As she listened, he began adding clicks and breath stops—words—to the bass tones. Solemn and plaintive, he lifted his eyes to the ceiling.

"Is that some kind of chant?" asked the general.

"You don't recognize it?" she said. "He's singing the Barney song. You know, the purple dinosaur." Maggie's favorite. "His mother must have sung it to him. Listen." It was in mutilated English. She began singing along very softly. "'I love you. You love me. We're a happy family.'"

The decaying prisoner glanced over with approval. She knew his prayer!

They went back and forth. Ali spoke to the air, to the general. "I asked him about the plague. He says his mother and the rest of his clan were in a cave near the surface at the time. They ventured out into a city for food. He was the only one who stayed behind. They never returned."

"Where was this clan of his going?"

She asked more questions. The hadal spoke. He pointed at the milk carton. "They needed to find new containers. No, vessels, new vessels. And something about the sun."

"Does that make any sense to you?"

"Not yet."

The prisoner spoke again.

"He says that's why he came out from the cave and into the terrible blindness. From down there up to the light and foulness of the surface world. In order to find his people, who want to go home. He and others were sent to do this. To guide them back into the earth."

"His people came up here after the plague? They've been hiding up here all this time? Where? Are there more?"

More questions. More clicks and whispers. Ali listened. "He's talking about their souls traveling on. Reincarnation, he means. They believed in that. The dead souls rose up to the surface and went searching for new vessels. New bodies. The children of the sun. The sun children. Our children."

"Our children contain their dead souls?"

"It goes beyond that. It weaves us all together into a single circle. His mother died and her spirit ascended. Now it's his duty to guide her home again. To lead her down from evil. Away from us."

"Our children are his ancestors?"

"Or his ancestors are our children. A difference in the possessive."

She looked at the prisoner. His eyes were gleaming with true faith. They were like two pools of fire in his ruined body.

The general was silent. Then he said, "Fine. Good. Do it his way. Follow his path. Ask him where he was going to take his mother."

"He says he couldn't find his mother. He located others, but not his mother. So he was going to lead them under. Maybe someone else has saved her. That is his hope."

"Were they all gathering in one place?"

"That's my impression."

"Where were they heading?"

Ali tried again. "He won't say."

"He refuses?"

"He declines."

"Let's take a break."

"I'd rather keep going." She had the beginning of a connection here, and there was so much else to ask him. Just hearing the language plunged her into the tunnels again. At every bend and new passageway, carved panels and statues and relics and leather codices waited, rich with ancient text. It had been like piecing together her very soul, one footstep at a time.

"We've been at it for over an hour. The trick is to stay fresh. Stay ahead of him. Keep your energy up. Come on out. We'll give it another shot in a few minutes."

The general met her at the door. They walked to the entrance. Rain lashed the glass. The wind blew apart puddles on the asphalt. They decided not to venture across to the commissary with its inviting neon signs. McDonald's. Taco Bell. Kentucky Fried Chicken. She remembered the jerky.

"Coffee?"

"No, thanks."

"What a day."

"Awful."

They stood watching the storm. The general chatted about his son's piano lessons. "Für Elise" was a booger. He enthused about a Thai restaurant in Berkeley. They didn't discuss the interrogation. He checked his watch. A half hour had passed. "Shall we head back?"

The room was clean and quiet. No echoes of screams. No blood on the floor. Then she noticed that the sheets were freshly changed. Maybe they had only spruced the place up. She clung to the notion.

Then she spied the bite stick lying on the floor. It was padded with duct tape and bore the mark of his teeth. They had been at him again with their torture.

"Let's see what he has to say this time," the general said in her ear.

The hadal was sleeping with his lidless eyes open, like a fish drifting in water. Saliva strung from his mouth. "Maria," she said.

The prisoner woke. His eyes rounded up to her. "Ma-har," he whispered.

"Here I am." She touched her heart and rocked an imaginary baby in her arms. "My baby child. Where?"

This time he answered in his language. "Home, Mother."

"Where, home?" said Ali.

He said something about the circle again. This time he gestured to her: come closer. The general was watching like a hawk. "You're close enough," he told her.

She lowered her face to the monster. Liquid seeped from his pink eyes. She could almost believe he was feeling sorrow at their impasse. But then she saw the feral blaze in his eyes. It took her breath. He felt no sorrow or remorse, just the stone-hard hunger of a separate kind. She started to rear back from him. But as she did, what was left of his hand brushed her cheek. It felt like warm plastic.

"Guards," the general's voice barked in her ear.

"No," she said. She let the prisoner touch her cheek again. This time she remembered the spiral she had drawn there. He was pointing at its center.

"What?" said the general.

"The children are being taken to the center of the spiral," she said.

"Now we're getting somewhere."

"Not necessarily," she said. "It could be anywhere. Everywhere. There are spiral symbols scattered from one end of the tunnels to the other down there. These are nomads. Ghosts. Wandering among the ruins of their ancestors. They're constantly on the move. Constantly prowling. The children could vanish with them forever."

"Keep digging. He pointed at the center. There must be some central collecting point. This thing was coordinated. They have a leader. Ask him about your city, Hinnom, the place you went ten years ago."

"Why there?" she said. The city of her nightmares. Some Bible buff had named it after the valley where Jerusalemites once practiced child sacrifice and kept fires burning to consume trash and the bodies of the poor and nameless.

"We have reason to believe it may still be inhabited."

Inhabited? How could they know that? And if it was true, why hadn't they preempted last night's attack? But now was not the time to press the general for answers.

"Hinnom," she said to the hadal. It made no sense to him. *"Civitas,"* she tried. *"Kome." Civitas,* Latin for city. *Kome* was the Old Greek for village, and the root for the Old High Germanic home. *"Hel."*

The legendary Hell, she meant, but also the real, geological one. A matter of semantics. Hell was formed from *helan,* meaning to hide. The dark and hidden place. "Deep city," she patched together. "Hel. Dead. The People. Many, many dead." She pointed at the circle on her notepad, at the point in the middle. "City? Home? Center?" Were they the same?

Then she waited. His fins balled and opened in the restraints. His eyes traveled upon her. She was glad for the soldiers outside the door. She could feel the heat coming off his body. His pink sweat had a rank, musky smell. At last he spoke. It was a single word. "Pit-ar."

Ali was stunned. She glanced around for a piece of paper. Finding none, she drew—on her palm—the stick figure of a man, or hadal, and pointed at it. "Pit-ar?"

He shuddered, and nodded yes. He was dying.

"Peter?" said the general.

"Pit-ar," she said. "It's a basic root word in Nostramic, the protolanguage that underlies what we speak today. *Pater* in old Greek, it became *Fater* in Old High German. Then *Faeder.* Father. His god. His creator. Older-Than-Old. The hungry god."

"Satan?"

"Older, much older, at least linguistically." Ali kept her voice low and soothing as she spoke to the room's microphones. The prisoner watched her, not comprehending a word, possibly thinking she was praying to herself. "Pit-ar predates Satan by many civilizations. He represents one of the earliest attempts to explain the mysteries of life and death. As mankind gained consciousness and language, we started creating gods and giving them names so that we could speak to them and try to influence them."

"This confirms another report we received."

"What report?"

"That there is a king in your city of the dead. That these things are led by a giant dressed in a suit of jade armor."

Turning to the mirror glass on the wall, she spoke to her own image, to her own doubt. "But that can't be."

"Why not?"

"Because I saw him killed. It was just before the plague struck."

"Either he didn't die or he came back," the general said. "Nothing is what it seems down there. Your very words."

"He's still alive? Who told you this?"

"A man named Joshua Clemens. He said the two of you met, and you refused to help him."

She vaguely remembered. "The pornography man? He talked about doing a documentary, but I figured he was just another pirate looking for hadal gold. I never heard from him again."

"His film crew was attacked. Just outside your city of ruins."

"He actually went down?"

"Seven years ago. He surfaced, alone, a month ago, the sole survivor. That's his story. He said it's a dead city, full of bones. But still alive. We're not taking his word for anything. But our friend here just verified the broad facts to you. A center to the spiral. A base camp for this Pit-ar of theirs. Now we have a target destination."

"But he didn't say that," she said.

"We'll take it from here."

"Let me dig a little deeper," she said. "He has more to tell."

"Another time, Professor. You can come out now."

She bent over the bed of the doomed prisoner. "Who is the Father?"

The hadal lolled his head toward her. This time his fin turned over her hand. He touched the aleph drawn on the back.

"This?" she said. "Pit-ar?"

He touched the aleph.

"Where? Where is the Father?"

The aleph, again.

Like a riddle, the Father was a place and a deity and a thing, all in one. Somehow her answer lay in a spiral whose center held an aleph.

ARTIFACTS

CHRISTIAN BROADCAST NETWORK

Pat Robertson: I think we've just seen the antechamber to terror. We haven't even begun to see what they can do to the major population.

Jerry Falwell: The ACLU's got to take a lot of the blame for this.

Pat Robertson: Well, yes.

Jerry Falwell: And, I know that I'll hear from them for this. But, throwing God out successfully with the help of the federal court system, throwing God out of the public square, out of the schools. The abortionists have got to bear some burden for this because God will not be mocked. And when we destroy forty million little innocent babies, we make God mad. I really believe that the pagans, and the abortionists, and the feminists, and the gays and the lesbians who are actively trying to make that an alternative lifestyle, the ACLU, People for the American Way—all of them who have tried to secularize America—I point the finger in their face and say, "You helped this happen."

Pat Robertson: Well, I totally concur, and the problem is, we have adopted that agenda at the highest levels of our government. And so we're responsible as a free society for what the top people do. And, the top people, of course, is the court system.

Jerry Falwell: Pat, did you notice yesterday that the ACLU, and all the Christ haters, People for the American Way, NOW, etc., were totally disregarded by the Democrats and the Republicans in both houses of Congress as they went out on the steps and called out to God in prayer and sang "God Bless America" and said, "Let the ACLU be hanged"? In other words, when the nation is on its knees, the only normal and natural and spiritual thing to do is what we ought to be doing all the time—calling upon God.

Pat Robertson: Amen.

10

The angel and his pet sit upon huge bones fused into the floor. The giant beast once swam in an ocean that dried and fell into the earth and there gained a ceiling that now supports another ocean. The Pacific Ocean, the disciple vaguely recalls. He has grown apart from that world. It has become a dream to him.

The angel breaks loose a chunk of the fossil rib. "You have asked me if I was present in the beginning." Idly he taps the piece of stone rib against another rib.

The disciple tries to marshal the still mind of a proper student. But that drumbeat—stone on stone—unsettles him. He cannot read the angel's mood in it.

"I have wondered, Rinpoche," he carefully answers.

"You are not the first to wonder," the angel assures him. "You are not the last. What you all really mean is this: What came before me? Did I see the face of God?"

"Yes, Lord." The disciple trembles. His life is at constant risk here, though at some times more plainly than others. But that is always so with true knowledge. He waits.

"This is the heart of it." The angel's eyes close. "In the beginning there was a flash of light. It is just as the creation myths all record, just as I told your prophets and visionaries. Call that flash of light my birth. Except I was not born, for I have always been and will always be."

"Praise be with you, Master."

"You cannot imagine that light. Its brilliance and colors defied the mind." The angel's eyes open. *"In that first instant, the universe penetrated me. It etched my very bones. I understood everything."*

"You became God, Lord?"

Anger flickers across the angel's face. His fist closes. The fossil turns to powder. Then his face smooths again. He lets the powder drift away.

"Before me there was no God, for God was nothing," the angel says. *"Nothing came before me."*

"Forgive me, Teacher."

"I understood everything," the angel continues. *"And then I forgot everything. Therefore every moment that unfolds, I recognize it clearly. Even as I take a drink of water, I remember that I was going to take that drink of water and what it would taste like and how it would slake my thirst. Likewise, in the instant you arrived, I knew you would arrive. Do you see? Time is my master. Memory is my damnation."*

11

Ali was in her office when someone knocked. Gregorio poked his head in. "A lady has come to see you. From Texas." He spoke the word "Texas" as if it were a mythical place.

Ali sighed. "Can't you take care of her?"

"This one you must meet," Gregorio said, and closed the door.

Ali cast loose from the keyboard. She rubbed her temples. Out her window the bay was draped with rags of fog.

The door opened again and Gregorio appeared with a tall blond woman. His heels came together softly. He gave her a slight bow. His Old World chivalry struck some people as alien, but this woman accepted his courtliness naturally, with a small flourish of her own. *Texas,* thought Ali. *A belle.*

"Dr. Von Schade?" She went straight to Ali with one hand extended. "Thank you so much for seeing me. I'm Rebecca Coltrane. Just Rebecca, please."

She verged on six feet tall—no heels, Ali looked—and was strikingly, almost unnaturally beautiful. But there was not a hint of vanity to her. She wore jeans and a white blouse that had not seen an iron in days. Her long, golden hair was yanked back into a no-nonsense ponytail. There was not so much as a swipe of lipstick to dress her face. This was a woman on a mission. She did not beat around the bush. "I need your help," she said.

Ali tried to remember this face. Had they met? Or was she simply famous, a face half glimpsed on a tabloid cover in the grocery-store line?

"My child was one of those taken last week." Rebecca's lip did not quiver. There was no tremor in her voice. No drama. Just the facts. Ali's was not the first office she had visited.

Now it came to Ali. Here was the face that had come to represent all the "lost" mothers. *That* Rebecca. Ali suddenly understood Gregorio's gallantry with her.

"Have a seat," said Ali.

Rebecca remained standing. "This won't take long, I promise."

"Sit," said Ali. "You and I are going to have some tea."

"But you're busy. Everyone is so busy."

This woman was walking wounded. Plainly she had been turned down—a lot—before coming here.

"Tea," said Ali, decisively, "tea and cookies."

"I will get these things," Gregorio declared, and disappeared. Would wonders never cease, thought Ali. Their Basque dragon slayer had a domestic side?

Rebecca touched the back of the chair and took a breath. She sat. This was a desperate woman, thought Ali. Otherwise she would never have come here, into enemy territory. For a week now, ever since the children had been taken, the columnists and talk show hosts had been painting Ali's institute as a den of hadal sympathizers, race traitors, and cryptoterrorists. The building's brick walls had been hit with graffiti. Staff members had found their tires slashed. Ali was beginning to wonder if the police were on the vandals' side, because they apparently weren't on hers, always a few minutes too late responding to her calls, never quite able to post a car outside.

"So this is what you look like on the inside," Rebecca said.

"This is us, in all our splendor," said Ali. "We call it the Studio. Before us, the building was a dance studio. As you can see, we're more of a warehouse than anything else. We just grab at whatever comes bubbling up from the deeps and stick it on a shelf. Someday there will be time and money for the proper research and archiving. And a museum. And an outreach center. Traveling displays. Lecture series. Well, we have our dreams."

"I expected more secrecy," said Rebecca. "Something darker. More Goth."

"You're not the only one," Ali said. "People think we're in here wor-

shipping the devil or something. It's a perception we keep trying to break."
She let Rebecca's eye roam around the office without interruption. There
were hadal artifacts all over the place, some bizarre, some ingenious, and
some—the ones made from bone or skin—gruesome.

What caught Rebecca's attention was the photograph on her desk. "So
that's her," she said. "I saw you on TV when they asked if you were a
mother. What a beauty."

"My Maggie," said Ali. It was the last picture taken of her.

"A pretty name. And I can see you in her eyes." She talked as if Maggie
were still alive. Ali appreciated that. "But that's definitely her father's chin."

Ali was startled. "Her father?" Where had this woman ever seen Ike?

"That's him on the top shelf, isn't it?"

Ali looked high, and there, forgotten, was a picture of Ike. Half in
shadow, like the man himself, his face was all angles and deep gravity. The
hadal tattoos pronounced his cheekbones. They declared their hold on
him. "Talk about relics," she said. "That's ten years old. I haven't heard
from him since."

"Is he still alive?"

"I don't know. I ask settlers and explorers who come up. There are rumors. None pans out. I'm not sure it matters anymore."

"That's a long time to not know," Rebecca said.

"I survived," said Ali. "I lost the one, but gained the other." And then
lost her, too. The doctors blamed Maggie's death on a flu bug that hadn't
killed anyone else's child. Something had made her weaker and more sus-
ceptible. Ali blamed the abyss. That was where Ike had unwittingly gotten
her pregnant. Conceived in darkness, her poor daughter had never
seemed completely healthy up here in the light.

"He left you and your daughter," Rebecca said. "He went back down.
That's what I was told."

"He left before she was born," said Ali. It still stabbed her. *Ten years on.*

"May I ask," said Rebecca. "Stop me, I'm just curious. He must have
been a good man if you chose him. But how could anyone just walk away
from a child?"

Ali sighed. "Ike stayed up here as long as he could stand it. But he had
questions and needed answers. He said there was something down there."

"The hadals?"

"No. We were sure they were all dead. Something else. Something deeper. He couldn't put words to it, but he had some sense of it from his captive days. I thought it must be something subconscious, the captor-captive bond, something like that. Unfinished business. But he insisted it was something real. Something waiting to be found."

"Like a place? Or a thing?"

"I don't know. He didn't know. But it was important, he said. It could change everything. And then he left. Off into the moonlight, down into a hole," Ali said.

"Did you ever think about going after him?" Rebecca asked.

"I had a baby to take care of."

"I meant *with* the baby," Rebecca said.

Ali looked at her. This woman understood. Sappy as it sounded, love meant the ultimate leap. "All the time, for a while," Ali said. "But then less and less. So long as I had my daughter . . ." She stopped herself. It felt pointless to continue.

"I'm the same way with Jake," said Rebecca. "That was my husband's name." *Was*, Ali noted, not *is*. She had put him away. *So quickly*. "We had our life. It was good. Now Sam's everything. My daughter, Sam."

"Do you have a picture of her?" Ali asked. This was frivolous. She had things to do. But she and Rebecca were two mothers.

Rebecca offered a snapshot. "She is precious," said Ali. *Is*, not *was*. Let this poor woman keep her hope alive. Reality would catch up soon enough. "How old is she here?"

"Eight. Yes. Her birthday . . ." Rebecca steadied her voice. "They tell me she was the youngest of them."

"What else are they telling you?" Ali asked it without any false pity. There was no sense in waltzing around the widow's losses. "How many children are missing now?"

The national hysteria was subsiding. The number of killed stood at less than one hundred now, down from the thousands initially reported. Most of the dead were parents, one or both, who had battled to the death against the intruders.

"Forty-two," said Rebecca. "One or two might be runaways or victims of crime. But most of that number were stolen that night."

"Any sightings? Any evidence? Any leads?"

"Nothing," said Rebecca. "It seems impossible. How can there be nothing?"

Get some food into this woman, thought Ali. *Fill at least one emptiness in her.*

Right on cue, Gregorio returned with a cardboard lid for a tray. Like a Parisian waiter, he had a towel draped over one forearm. He was quite solemn in setting them up. His big hands dwarfed the teacups. On a Jurassic Park plastic plate he had stacked together a mountain of petite cookies. A cookie fell and he bent and meticulously placed it back on the summit. It tumbled off. He returned it to the top. It escaped him again. Watching his performance, Ali saw Rebecca do something she had probably not done in the week since the abduction. She smiled.

"I'll take that cookie," Ali finally said.

Gregorio handed it to her gratefully. He poured the tea. "Is there anything else?" he said.

"You are kind, sir," Rebecca said. That clinched it. His chivalry had found its match. He would have jumped off the Transamerica Building for her. Maybe, thought Ali, she could do a little matchmaking in a year or so, whenever the widow was ready to move on. But Gregorio would probably never go for it, and a year was a long time. It would be a miracle if he didn't propose to Ali inside a month.

Gregorio withdrew. The door closed. Ali braced herself. Now the chitchat would end. Rebecca would get around to her grief. Ali would sympathize. Tears, some Kleenex, a pat on the back: it was plain how this would go.

Nothing required that she babysit the scarred and sometimes mutant strangers who came up from the depths and in off the streets to her office. They were always in some kind of pain, marred by their months or years in the earth's hollows. It wasn't her job to comfort them. But she felt an odd kinship. They were all dancers on the edge of the same abyss.

"You're thinking of going under," Ali said. That was one of the popular expressions. Or going South. Or deep-stroking. Bottom-feeding. Mainlining.

Rebecca held her head up. "Not blindly. But as soon as it is reasonable. As soon as someone with the proper experience and knowledge agrees to help me."

Someone like Ali. "Who else have you approached?" Who else had flat turned her down? Rebecca pulled out a small notebook.

"I started with my congressman, and his office referred me to a contact at the State Department. They sent me to the Department of the Interior, which suggested I wait, so I went to the Pentagon and banged on doors and had meetings and briefings and then they set me up with a grief counselor, and I left. A woman from the White House recommended patience. Both my senators sympathized and promised hearings and funneled me to their staffs. I've got a list of legislative aides, lobbyists, NGOs, and journalists long enough to get me elected president."

"What did they tell you?"

"Weep, worry, and wait," said Rebecca. "That's what it boils down to."

"And now you are here."

Rebecca folded her hands. "Yes."

"Don't go down there," said Ali.

Rebecca did not flinch. "Guide me," she said.

"I read that three fathers of the missing children went down," said Ali. "And that all three of them came back empty-handed. The place is bigger than you realize. Certainly too big for one person to tackle."

"They didn't know where to go."

"And you do?"

"*You* do," said Rebecca. "To their city. Your city."

"It's not my city."

"But you know it."

"I survived it. Barely."

Rebecca paused. Ali could guess what came next. The same thing everyone wanted to know, the thing that unfortunately anchored her legend. "People say you met the devil there," Rebecca said.

"I met a man masquerading as the devil," Ali answered her. "His name was Thomas. He had white hair and a kind manner. He was a priest, that was his disguise. I didn't learn until it was too late that he was also a deceiver and a murderer."

"How do you know he wasn't something more?"

"Because I saw him killed, and the last I checked, the devil doesn't die."

Rebecca lifted her chin. "He's down there all right," she said. "Maybe not him, but others. They have my child. Take me into the city. Please."

"No," said Ali.

"That's where the children are going. Right now, as we speak, they're heading to the city."

"I don't think so."

"My sources do."

"Let them search then. Don't go down there. When they find your daughter, she will need you whole and healthy." And when they didn't find her, as was far more likely, at least Rebecca would be left.

"I know it has an effect on people," Rebecca said. "Believe me, it's been an education this past week. I've seen the physical scars, the deformities, the haunted looks, the light sickness, the cancers, the wrecked body clocks, the dreamers and addicts. It's horrifying. But I am going to get my daughter."

"It would be dangerous even if it were empty," Ali said. "But it's not empty. We know that now. They're down there. Maybe only a few hundred, maybe a lot more. If they found you, or you found them, you'd never make it out."

"My daughter is waiting for me," Rebecca said.

"They aren't in the city," Ali said.

"Then where are they?"

"I'm not sure. But I can tell you that General Lancing's information is flawed."

Rebecca's mouth flapped open. Plainly Ali had guessed her source, or one of them.

"I've met him, Rebecca. He has a prisoner, or did."

"A hadal?"

"Yes. I was there to help with the interrogation. The general interpreted what the prisoner told us one way. He's frustrated. He's under pressure. He wants results. All I can say is, he's wrong. The city is a false lead."

"If they had taken your child . . ."

That was beside the point. Of course she would be moving heaven and earth. Of course she would fling herself into the unknown. It did not change the dangers. "Let the general do whatever he is going to do," said Ali.

"Nothing, that's what they're doing. He made it clear. They're more afraid of the Chinese than the hadals."

"There is much to be afraid of these days. A war below risks a war above."

"Meanwhile my daughter is down there."

"Did the general tell you about the special-operations teams?"

Rebecca leaned forward. This was news.

"They are hunting for the children as we speak," Ali said.

"He didn't tell me that."

"And risk more bad blood with the Chinese? If they find the children, then the president will be a hero. If they don't, no one will be the wiser. Especially the Chinese."

"They're searching the city?"

"They're waiting on the routes that lead to the city, that's my understanding."

Rebecca looked dazed. "Is this true?"

Surrounded by deceptions and evasions and feints, she didn't know who to trust. They won't find the children, Ali did not say. She was certain of that. But Rebecca needed a reason to hope and not destroy herself in the abyss. "Yes."

There was a knock at the door. Ali thought it was Gregorio coming to tidy up. "More cookies?" she called out, trying to shift the mood.

"Cookies?" said a muffled voice.

"Just come in," said Ali.

The door opened. Rebecca turned. Ali looked up. It wasn't Gregorio. A monster stepped inside, a horned and gaunt creature. Rebecca froze in her chair.

Glacier glasses covered his eyes. Black peach fuzz was growing between the horns and knobs and bandages on his head. He was wearing a loud Hawaiian shirt, and the skin on his bared arms was pebbly with small cysts.

Instantly Ali guessed Rebecca's thoughts. Creatures not unlike this had carried off her child. "Rebecca," Ali quickly said, "meet John Li. He just returned from a two-year stint on a NASA expedition. Subterranean entomology is his specialty. Bugs. He's single-handedly identified over seven hundred new creepy crawlers, a world record, yes?"

Li reddened. He was a modest man, unused to praise or talk of world records. "Beetles," he said.

His nostrils flared. He was smelling Ali's guest.

"This is Rebecca Coltrane," Ali told him. "We were having tea."

"I intruded," he said.

Rebecca was staring at him.

"Have a cookie," said Ali. "Have ten. Please, look at this pile."

"No cookies," he said. "Work." He vanished back into the hallway.

"I'm sorry," said Rebecca. "I was rude."

"He's used to it. Every now and then I catch myself staring, too."

Rebecca was pale. "Is that happening to Sam?"

"Not yet."

"I want the truth."

"It didn't happen to me," Ali said. "It doesn't happen to most of the colonists, not to this extent."

"But it happens. It happened to Mr. Li."

"John was out in unmonitored zones, much deeper than people have gone in the past, and for a much longer time. We're just starting to understand how much the gases and radiation belts drift around down there. Clearly John was exposed to them. But it doesn't mean Sam will be. The good news is that some of his traits are reversing now that he's resurfaced. His heart is returning to normal size. It actually shrank underground. His red-blood-cell count is almost normal again. And those cysts on his arms? It turns out that they contain pollen."

"Like in flowers?"

"We're still trying to figure out what kind of vegetation he brushed against. The interesting thing is how its pollen causes a skin irritation. At first it was just a low-grade acne. Recently it began to itch. Itching tears open the cysts, releasing the pollen. In other words, the host can carry the pollen for months and potentially hundreds or thousands of miles before discharging it in another part of the Interior."

"And his horns?"

"A plastic surgeon is working with him. The problem is, the horns are living tissue, with a blood supply. You can't just lop them off."

"What else will happen to Sam?"

"Might happen," said Ali, "not will happen."

"I want to know when these creatures will rape her." It was a whisper.

Ali didn't quibble with the "rape" or the "creatures." "From the captive accounts we've gathered from years ago, the children are treated very well. The girls are separated from the boys and held in isolation with something like hadal nannies. They're shielded from any contact with men. Their privacy is guarded through the first years of puberty. Marriage doesn't occur until thirteen or fourteen."

"Why, though? I thought we were two different species."

"Lions and tigers are two different species. In the wild they never breed with one another. But in captivity, in zoos, you can get hybrids like ligers and tiglons."

Rebecca closed her eyes.

Ali considered. She could describe the array of subterranean diseases, or their primitive rites of passage, the ritual mutilations, the branding and tattooing, the slave collars, the crippling of runaways, the punishments, the tortures. But those were all part of the lore by now, and this unhappy woman didn't need more nightmares. She tried to recall something positive.

"As you might imagine," Ali said, "your sight adjusts. I wasn't down there long enough for it to happen to me. But John reports that by the end of two years, he could smell and feel colors. He could hear distances. It might be explained by chemicals in the water. His brain changed."

"Sam's brain will change?"

"The frontal lobe and the limbic system get switched on. The parietal lobe switches off."

"You're losing me."

"We're starting to get reports from certain regions of people having visions. John claims it happened to him. He heard voices. Disembodied voices."

"Are you talking about dreams, or nightmares?"

"It's similar to deep meditation," Ali said, "except you don't have to meditate. You experience rapture. You lose your sense of self. You feel connected to the universe. To God. John says he almost didn't return to the surface. One of his expedition partners stayed down. He refused to exit. He turned around and went deeper by himself." Ali understood. She hadn't been in the depths long enough to feel rapture, but she still had waking dreams of the beauty down there.

Rebecca pulled her chin back. "Religious visions."

"Something like that."

"Like prophets."

"Or poets."

"That will happen to Sam?"

"I don't know."

Rebecca was quiet a moment. Then she said, "I need her back."

"I know."

In her former life, back when she was a nun, Ali would have said, Let us pray. But prayer was not in her anymore. She had left the Church and God for a reason, to find a larger truth. If Satan and the demons were simply a wilder version of man, then God and angels must be, too. Salvation—real deliverance—lay in the Word. Not in the Bible, but in language. In that first spark of fire, somehow, somewhere, in consciousness uttering its first words, lay the way back to Eden.

"Lead me to the city," said Rebecca.

"The military is taking care of that."

"I have to see for myself. I need to be there." Rebecca stood. "If she were yours, you'd be down there."

"Yes."

"Why won't anyone help me?"

Because we're afraid. "We want to."

"The city."

"I'm sorry," Ali said.

Rebecca left. Ali watched through the window as she sank away toward the Bay full of fog. Ali reached for the framed photo of her own daughter. Then she returned it to its quiet place on her desk where Maggie would never grow old and nothing could ever harm her again.

ARTIFACTS

Internal Revenue Service
Department of the Treasury

Seize the Night, Inc.
c/o Rebecca Coltrane
Re: application for 501(c)(3) nonprofit status

Dear Ms. Coltrane,
We are pleased to inform you that, at the personal suggestion of the president of the United States, we have expe-
dited your request for nonprofit status in record time. Based
on information you supplied, and assuming your operations
will be as stated in our application for recognition of ex-
emption, we have determined you are exempt from federal in-
come tax under section 501(a) of the Internal Revenue Code as
an organization described in section 501(c)(3). All contributions to your organization will be tax deductible.

                                    Sincerely yours,
                                    Roger T. Hamilton
                                    District Director

P.S. I would like to add a private note of sympathy for your
loss, and my wholehearted support for your mission. May you
be united with your daughter soon. You are in the prayers of
my family, and of your nation. Please find enclosed my personal check for $1,000.00. God speed, Rebecca.

                                    Yours,
                                    Sam

12

DIALOGUES WITH THE ANGEL, NUMBER 3

They stand at the foot of an immense wall that rises out of sight.

"Here is my border," says the angel. "I can go no farther than where we stand."

The disciple glances at his teacher, suspecting a trick. The angel is full of ruses. Surely this is one of them.

"Go closer," says the angel. "Place your hand on the stone."

The student does as he is told. He steps forward. He crosses the supposed border. He touches the rock.

"Is it warm?" asks the angel.

"It is, Rinpoche."

"As warm as living flesh?"

"Exactly, Lord."

"So I've been told. Now climb."

The disciple searches for holds. He climbs perhaps thirty feet. He looks down.

"Enough," says the angel. "You can return. Or if you want, you can continue up. Escape. Be free."

Perched on footholds up there, the disciple tries to sort out his thoughts. The angel has brought him here for a reason. Is it to release him from the abyss? Or to test his loyalty? And if the disciple does try to escape, will his teacher come rushing up the rock and kill him?

The disciple returns to the ground. He walks back to the angel. Really there is no decision to make. He made up his mind long ago when he committed life and limb to finding this creature.

"You were afraid," says the angel. "You thought I was lying."

"Yes, Lord."

The angel opens one hand and tries to press it against the rock. But his hand stops, or the wall recoils. The one cannot meet the other. It is an astonishing revelation for the disciple. The world refuses this creature.

The angel pulls back his hand. He looks up into the heights. "Do you really think I choose to stay inside this ball of stone?"

The disciple is too dumbfounded to answer. His captor is a captive? The angel of freedom can't free himself? But why should this supernatural being confide his weakness to a mere mortal? It is a terrifying moment.

Perhaps he should have kept climbing while he could. Too late for that. Now he belongs to this creature who can skin a man with his fingers alone, and so quickly that his victim is still standing and alive on his feet afterward. The disciple has seen him do it.

"Why am I entombed?" the angel goes on. "What holds me here? There is nothing in this place but animals to feed my solitude. Nothing but silence to marry my songs. I am forgotten."

I can leave, thinks the disciple. With a single pounce onto the wall, he can climb out of here. But he stays.

"Who is my jailer?" the angel continues. "Who holds the key to my door?"

"Lord." The disciple listens.

"One day I will feel the sun on my face," says the angel. "One day one of you will unlock my cage."

One day, one of us. Now the disciple understands. This is why the angel took him in, him and all the others. This explains the angel's patient tutelage of humankind over all the many centuries. We have what he wants. We inhabit the world. We are free.

The angel bends to search the disciple's face. "It won't be you who frees me, though. There is no freedom in your soul. Nothing but captivity."

The disciple hears his death sentence. The angel has kept him for ten years now. Soon he will devour him. "I am here at your will, Lord."

"My will?" The angel says it with bitterness. "My will? Tell me. If I am a prisoner, then who is my jailer?"

"I only know who it is not, Rinpoche," the disciple answers. "It cannot be God."

"No? Why not?"

"God is nothingness, Lord. You taught me that."

"Who then? Come on, it's simple. If God is not my jailer, who else could it be?"

The disciple waits in silence. He knows that his ignorance annoys the angel. One day soon it will cost him his life.

"You," the angel answers himself. *"You keep me here."*

"Me, Lord?"

"Your kind. My chosen people, if that's what you are. And if you are not, if your race fails me as the hadals failed me and others before them, then I will wait for the next race of people to come along. Do you see what I am saying? Whoever frees me, that man or woman was my keeper. Whoever befriends me was my enemy. Whoever delivers me from the wilderness put me there. Whoever saves me, damned me."

The disciple hears his bitterness. It frightens him. He has seen the angel's rage in deep grooves slashed into the walls and footprints stamped into the floor. *"But how can that be?"* he blurts out. *"Mankind is barely a child on the planet, and you have been a captive since the beginning of time. How can the captive precede his captor?"*

"I will know the answer when you reveal it," says the angel.

The disciple has nothing to lose. He knows that he is doomed by the secrets imparted to him. The angel can never let him go. So be it. In fact, his certain death liberates him. He can ask anything. *"If we are your jailer, Lord, then how will you recognize us? And if we don't know you are our prisoner, how will it occur to us to free you?"*

"That is a question I cannot answer." The angel smiles. *"But someone among you will know the answer, and in that instant my door will fly open."*

"And then what will you do, Lord?"

"I will walk into the sun," said the angel. *"And then I will restore the Garden as it was."*

RULES OF ENGAGEMENT (ROES) FOR JTF OPERATION SILENT MERCY

NOTHING IN THESE ROES LIMITS YOUR RIGHT TO TAKE APPROPRIATE ACTION TO DEFEND YOURSELF AND YOUR UNIT

General Rules of Engagement

1. This ROE takes precedence over all other rules governing the use of deadly force.
2. I always have the right to defend myself, my fellow marines and sailors and soldiers, U.S. military support personnel, and settlers directly supporting U.S. operations.
3. I am aware of the presence of unknown persons in the field of operation. Settlers of every nation are embedded in the STZs (subterrestrial zones). I will not use force or seize property from them to accomplish my mission.
4. Nonhuman elements **may be engaged without provocation.** I will identify my targets.
5. Weapon will be fired at discretion to achieve mission.
6. Well-aimed fire will be used; weapons will not be placed on automatic, unless necessary.
7. Care will be taken to avoid civilian casualties.
8. My actions need to be quick, deliberate, accurate, and **never as a result of a desire for revenge.**
9. I will not harm, detain, or interfere with local settlers in the STZs.
10. I will be aware of the presence of Chinese settlers in the STZs.

13

Beckwith slipped his crosshairs left across the dunes. His spotter, Miggs, lay nestled to one side on the ledge. Elsewhere, in other niches on the cliff, another eight sniper pairs were glassing the same sands of this subterranean desert. They had been waiting in ambush for a week and were prepared to stay another month. At that time, if the children still hadn't appeared, a second team would silently replace Beckwith's group.

By now, Beckwith knew much of the surreal desert. They had lasered various landmarks to determine their range to within a yard, and recorded them on range cards for quick reference. The kill zone was obvious. All they needed was for the enemy and his young captives to show up.

While Beckwith scoured the sand, he kept an eye out for the Casper bird. Even a year ago conventional wisdom held that there were no birds down here, just as there were no snakes with magnetic sensors in their skulls or hairless lemurs, much less carnivorous ones. For that matter, "here" was not supposed to be down here either. But once discovered, it seemed hell was a nursery for the impossible.

A single bird of this new species—*Erihacus caspera,* named after Casper the Ghost for its colorless plumage—had been photographed for the first time only six months ago. The birding world was atwitter, though settlers and explorers had been picking up the reclusive bird's sonar peeps and finding its droppings for much longer. Some biologists claimed it wasn't even a bird, but some sort of reptile with wings, one more mutant spawned by the deeps. Until someone sighted another specimen, the debate was guaranteed to rage on.

As Beckwith scanned the chamber from his "hide," as snipers called their nests, he wondered if he might be that someone. It took patience and stealth to tease out the hidden creatures, and those were two things he had plenty of.

Dry lightning snaked along the ceiling a quarter mile overhead. The green dunes flickered. Thunder rumbled through the chamber.

Beckwith twisted on his ledge and adjusted his night goggles. To his left and right, the rest of his boat crew, a SEAL term of endearment, showed as thermal fragments hidden upon the cliff face.

Like hermits primed to battle demons, they inhabited their ledges in silence, each man disciplining his needs for water and light, cultivating his field of fire, tending his weapons, cadging his rations, and sharpening his vision. Monklike, Beckwith had never felt so far from God.

Thirty-seven thousand feet below sea level, deeper than Everest was high, the unit was operating all but deaf, dumb, and blind. No maps of the territory existed this far away from the settlements. Electromagnetic forces were wreaking havoc on their compasses and watches and bending, bouncing, or snaring their radio signals, wrecking any communication with the surface and distorting even line-of-sight transmissions between themselves.

The SEALs of unit one were profoundly isolated in these tunnels running beneath the Mariana Trench. If they ran into problems, there was no backup. If they took casualties, there would be no airlift. If they ate through their food or ran out of ammunition, they could die in this stone limbo and never be found. Beckwith took it as a creative challenge.

Eight days ago they had inserted themselves via a secret military borehole on Pagan Island, north of Guam. Their mission: intercept the enemy, acquire the children, and retreat to the surface. Leaving their inflatable boats and extra supplies by a river, they had set off on foot and found an old hadal caravan trail, recently used. Here they set their ambush.

Now they waited among relics, bones, and guano that had accumulated over some two hundred centuries. The dunes of the Green Barrens desert unfolded before the cliff wall. The sand gleamed green in their night goggles. Even in white light, it was green.

According to the latest intelligence derived from a hadal detainee, the enemy was retreating with the children to a prehistoric city named Hinnom. The city had been visited only twice, first by the legendary Helios expedition ten years ago, and then seven years ago by a hard-luck IMAX film crew.

There were other special-ops teams like theirs sprinkled through this far-western expanse of the Pacific Interior. Beckwith's team had deployed the farthest west of them all. Relying on small ambushes in the few arteries known to exist in this region, military planners were gambling that the enemy—and the kidnapped children—would walk right into their hands. It was a high-stakes gamble.

Besides the hazards of combat and environment, Beckwith's team had been cautioned about the geopolitical tensions. They had inserted deep inside territory claimed by China, meaning the American soldiers who weren't supposed to be down here were being stalked by Chinese soldiers who weren't supposed to be down here either.

It was not a good time to be playing cat and mouse. Even as Beckwith and his men were creeping about through the subplanet, the ocean and sky above were full of taunts and provocations. Chinese Migs shadowed F18s, and vice versa. Brinksmanship was the order of the day.

And so stealth ruled Beckwith and his men. Nestling into their aeries overlooking the caravan route, they let the darkness and quiet settle on them like leaves. They waited.

Beckwith's ledge held the stuff of a vanished empire. With the tip of his knife, delicate as a mine hunter, he unearthed small artifacts and arranged them alongside his rifle. There were tiny scraps of papyrus with odd marks, and bits of colored glass, and a zinc spoon pitted with age, and—his favorite—a scrap of chain mail like Crusaders might have worn. Only it was probably ten thousand years older than Christ.

Haddie had not always been the demon. At various times these cliffs had held hadal scholars, artisans, and holy warriors. Now was Beckwith's turn to add a few relics of his own to the mix. Someday in the far future, someone would find his brass shells. What would they make of them? Would they puff on them like whistles?

Lightning flickered high above. The stony silence bore down on them.

On the tenth night, Beckwith started hearing voices.

At first he thought they must be wisps of subterranean breeze. The wisps became whispers, though, and he quietly racked a round, certain the enemy must be drawing closer. But the sands lay empty. And those whispers continued.

"Miggs," he hissed. "Is that you?"

"What's wrong?" said Miggs. But his whisper was different from these other whispers. It was clearer and more diligent. More joined to the present.

"Nothing," said Beckwith.

The whispers grew louder, even though Miggs didn't seem to hear anything. Over the coming days, the whispers came and went. There were all kinds of voices and accents, male and female, old and young. Some spoke English, some German, and some Spanish. He knew a tiny bit of Swahili from an African gig, and a tiny bit of Arabic, and those were part of the strange fusion. Most of it was completely foreign. "Alien" would be the better word.

Beckwith tried dialing the whispers down and out. He imagined a game of chess. He cleaned his rifle. He pondered his ex-girlfriend. None of it worked. The voices went on.

On the fourth day Miggs whispered, "Becky."

"What?" said Beckwith.

"Who are they?"

Beckwith could have messed with Miggs's head a little, and denied hearing anything. But he was too relieved. He wasn't cracking up after all. "Echoes, maybe," he said. "Geological noise."

"Those aren't echoes. That's not geo background."

"Sensory deprivation then," tried Beckwith. "We're going stir-crazy."

"You heard that woman crying?"

"That was yesterday."

"And that old man who wants to go home?"

"What about him?"

"I've been thinking," said Miggs.

"Hit me."

"What about, like, ghosts?"

That, too, had occurred to Beckwith. "You're playing old movies in your head. Don't do that."

Miggs went on. "But we're in hell, right? They could be, like, dead souls."

Beckwith had thought of that, too. But he wasn't about to admit it. "Square it away, Miggs. We've got a job to do."

After that Miggs kept to himself. Which left Beckwith alone again to deal with the voices. As far as he could tell, the voices people seemed to be talking to themselves. It was a hodgepodge of monologues, a whole grave-yard of them if Miggs was right about the dead souls.

Beckwith did what he could to distract himself and stay alert. He tried humming Phish songs without actually humming. He hunted for Casper the bird. He cleaned his rifle again and again. He did push-ups. He rebuilt the little wall of bricks at the front of their ledge. It was like solitary con-finement.

On the fifteenth day he spotted pink flamingos in his sniper scope.

They were standing one-legged in a pool of water. Beckwith rubbed his eye and tried again and they were still there. He tried the other eye, same thing. *Phoenicopterus ruber.* The American flamingo. Black tips on their pink wings. Pink.

Beckwith did not record them in the life list in his sniper log. He ab-solutely did not try to bring them to Miggs's attention. They were mirages, they had to be. Sure enough, an hour later they were gone. It rattled him. He was too meticulous to be seeing things. Too conditioned to hardships a hundred times worse than this. Above all, he was a SEAL. SEALs didn't see pink flamingos.

He did ten sets of fifty push-ups as punishment. He made sure to get enough sleep, no more no less. He read the contents label on his Meals Ready to Eat to see if there might be some weird chemicals to avoid. The pink flamingos stayed away.

On the nineteenth day he felt a tap on his leg. It was Miggs at the spot-ting scope. "Alpha 746," he whispered.

Beckwith manned his rifle and scanned the point seven hundred and forty-six yards away. In his scope the temperature variations flowered as dark blues and hot pinks. Tongues of flame—plumes of heated gas—rose and fell back into the green dunes. Hundreds of feet overhead, a spike of cold purple air stabbed down from a hole in the ceiling. SOS. Same old shit.

Then he saw them.

The column was approaching at two o'clock, a long, strung-out line of cherry red globules. They were well within the mile zone, but their shapes kept blurring. Normally his optics were crisp, especially in this latest scope from Unertl with a computer chip that kept distances focused. All he could say at the moment, though, was that there were lots of them coming closer in appallingly sloppy formation. Obviously they weren't anticipating what was about to crash down on their heads.

Beckwith felt an electric charge. He had resigned himself to finding no one at all, or at best bagging a few stray hadals with maybe a child or two roped among them. But now it appeared the marauders had gathered all of their stolen flock together and were driving the children en masse across the green sands.

The prospect of saving the children awed him. It was as if all his training, indeed, his entire life, had just received its hidden purpose. He was not a particularly religious man. But he suddenly found himself praying for guidance. *Lord, guide my hand. Make me steady. Let me be true.*

The column wove between the dunes. The closer it came, the more Beckwith cursed his scope. What was wrong with the thing? The imaging was distorted. It was like watching molten red plastic creep across hot green waves. Here and there he grabbed momentary details from the shapes: a flash of teeth, a shambling gait, a stolen baseball cap even. He built them into a simian portrait. He identified his enemy.

And the children? They were there. He couldn't make out their faces, but their smaller shapes were surrounded by the taller shapes. They were being herded like cattle.

Thunder growled. Gas plumes belched from the sand. The column inched closer.

Someone stumbled in the line, and that caused a commotion. Tall figures rushed back. In Beckwith's mind, some weary child was being beaten. The commotion ended. The line resumed its motion.

They had plotted the ambush before taking to their hides. It was relatively simple. Different teams would cherry-pick different sections of the column. The children would fall to the ground. Their captors would run away into the minefield. Beckwith's assignment was to begin at the front and work back. His shot would initiate the others. He would start the killing.

A baby began crying.

Beckwith thumbed his safety off.

Suddenly the boggy shapes became distinct. Beckwith's worst nightmares sprawled before him. With sallow flesh and knotty horns, the hadals loomed over the innocents. There were the children. Here were the wolves.

He locked on the face of evil.

He squeezed the trigger.

You were trained to squeeze so smoothly and without anticipation that the shot took you by surprise. His rifle—launching a huge .50-caliber round capable of piercing tank armor—kicked hard. The creature's head smoked with the proverbial pink mist.

On to the next target. Beckwith squeezed the trigger. Took the kick. Next. On down the line.

To either side and above him, the other snipers let loose. In the old days of bolt-action sniper rifles, the rate of fire was tediously slow. These new $14,000 semiautomatic sniper rifles dealt death as fast as you gave them targets. Beckwith finished his first clip before the approaching column had a clue they were being killed.

Miggs switched on the recorded message.

"Kids, get down," the loudspeakers trumpeted. "We are USA. Do not run, boys and girls. USA. Fall to the ground, children. USA. Do not run, boys and girls. USA. Get down, kids . . ."

Beckwith locked on one of the children, a girl. She was screaming. Maybe the loudspeakers were too far away. She wouldn't lie down.

They only needed to separate the predator from his prey, and the day would be saved. But the hadals wouldn't run, and the children wouldn't drop. Instead they all bunched together. *Ramp up the chaos,* Beckwith grimly thought. *Kill more.*

Remote-controlled flash-bangs detonated on either side of the column, sparkling like stars. At last the column broke, but not the way it was supposed to. Everyone—hadal and child alike—surged into the minefields.

"What are they doing?" said Miggs.

The sand belched. Figures flew, small and large. The dead and wounded landed on other mines and jumped again with fresh detonations.

Beckwith could only watch as their deadly handiwork took its toll.

Dry lightning sizzled in veins along the ceiling.

"Flares up," someone yelled.

They lit the place like an opera house. Flares dangled where they caught on rock spurs high overhead, or floated under little balloons.

The Green Barrens chamber was immense. This was Beckwith's first real look at the place. It spread so high and wide that their lights could not fill it. At the far edges, the false horizon rocked and swayed with shadows.

The desert smoldered. A pall of smoke hung above the kill zone. Screams issued from the ugly murk.

Hardly anything was moving down there. The loudspeakers went on shouting. "Do not run, boys and girls. USA. Fall to the ground, children."

The children lay on the ground. In the exhausted minefield.

Beckwith stood and tossed the rappel line. To his right and left, ropes arched through the air. Men went racing down the cliff face.

He was in shock. The children were supposed to have lain down. The ambush had gone terribly wrong.

They advanced into the dunes through dust and smoke. The shadows grew long. The flares were sinking.

"More flares, damn it, more light."

The chamber lit bright again. Beckwith glanced back at the cliff that had been their home for almost a week, and was surprised to see giant glyphs carved into its face. They had arrived here in darkness and this was their first good look at the cliff that had hidden them. Their ledges and caves were part of some inscription. All these days they had been living inside a word.

"Here," a man said.

Beckwith smelled the blood before he reached the body. Except for boxer shorts, it was naked. The bullets and shrapnel had mangled the thing.

"So this is what Haddie looks like," someone said.

One of the young guys pressed his rifle muzzle against an open eye, and it blinked. He fired. "Thought so," he said.

They moved deeper into the smoke, rifles switching back and forth.

"More flares," said Beckwith. He needed light. The light of day. This place was so dark.

He came to Miggs, standing above a body, facedown. Flat in the sand, he could have been sunning at the beach, his arms and legs, his torso, his thin neck, all hairless and smooth. No monster scales. No horns. No body art.

"They look like us," Miggs said. "Kind of."

Beckwith didn't like it. Something was even more wrong than he'd thought. These were supposed to be the creatures of hell, savage and fearless to the point of suicidal. They had folded too goddamn easily. Was this a head fake? Was there more to come?

"Eyes wide," someone said. "Watch the flanks."

"I've got one of the kids," a man called.

Beckwith went over. The remains were little more than a pile of rags. Her legs were gone. Beckwith's dread mounted.

They walked the line through thickets of dead and wounded. Moans and screams issued from the smoke. "No prisoners," a man reminded them. "Put them down. All we take are the children."

Rifles popped in the smoke. Bit by bit, the volume of suffering lessened. Beckwith came to one of their women. She was still alive. Her face was painted red from a head wound. She bared her red teeth and started cursing him.

He lifted his rifle, then paused. He'd never heard the hadal language. In his imagination, it would sound unearthly. But as the words poured from her, strange as they were to his ear, they held a familiar ring.

He knew better than to kneel beside her. The hadal females were furies. Ghouls with total attitude. But she was chopped up and dying and this was his chance to hear her alien tongue. It would be like meeting an extraterrestrial. He hunkered to one side, finger on the trigger.

Wipe the blood away, he thought, *and she would look downright human.* Where were the beetle brow and the fangs? And weren't they supposed to be white as maggots? That was always the operative term, "maggots," as if they were not just another race, but another life-form.

She drew a ragged breath and continued her curse. He listened attentively, like a confessor. For all her defiance, he heard a tone of sorrow. As brute simple as it must have been down here, she loved her life. Beckwith pulled the trigger.

Onward. The children. *Find them.* He stood.

"Something's not right here," he heard a man saying in the smoke.

"This is not good," said another.

Beckwith found three troops picking through a pile of cheap suitcases, plastic bags, packs, and cardboard boxes. He went cold. Everywhere he looked, the luggage bore Chinese lettering. There were photographs of Chinese families. Passports of Chinese citizens. Chinese newspapers. Chinese money. All Chinese.

"Settlers?" whispered Beckwith. "Chinese settlers?"

That was why they seemed so human. Because they were.

ARTIFACTS

DESERTER/ABSENTEE WANTED BY THE ARMED FORCES

NAME: Ian Lincoln Beckwith   Form DD 553
GRADE/RANK/RATE: E-5, Petty Officer, Second Class
SEX—M
PLACE OF BIRTH: Bartlesville, OK
DATE OF BIRTH: 1995/03/06
HEIGHT: 5'9"   WEIGHT: 164
RACE: White   EYE COLOR: Hazel   HAIR COLOR: Brown
BRANCH OF SERVICE: Navy   CITIZENSHIP: U.S.
MARITAL STATUS: S
MILITARY OCCUPATION: SEAL
ESCAPED OR SENTENCED PRISONER: No

REMARKS: Ian Lincoln Beckwith, a member of the United States
Armed Forces serving on active duty with NAVSPEWARGRU-ONE,
platoon 2, navy SEAL, went missing three days after Operation
Silent Mercy concluded. He was a participant in the Green
Barrens incident, sector 3, Marianas Zone, involving Chinese
civilians. His absence from duty was noted at the time of his
unit's exfiltration, and it is believed he may be hiding in the
proximity of the incident. According to regulations, any U.S.
special operative who goes missing must automatically be
listed as a deserter, not AWOL. Be aware that Beckwith may be
suffering from psychotic episodes or bipolar disorder, as he
and teammates at the Green Barrens reported delusions and
voices concurrent with the incident. Be aware that Beckwith
took all weaponry and other field issue with him. He is considered unstable, lethal, and a national security risk.

14

DIALOGUES WITH THE ANGEL, NUMBER 4

"Until the first bacteria trickled down to me, I thought the molten rock and fiery gases of the young earth were my only family. Then came these tiny living creatures. I was overjoyed. You'll be amused. In my eagerness for companionship, I actually thought I was one of them, that they were my brothers and sisters. I lay among those seeps of microbial snot, and listened to them fizz and rustle and feed, and I was convinced they were speaking to me.

"Ridiculous, I know. But useful. Because out of their primordial noise, I imagined whole symphonies of life. I heard epic poems in their warfare, and sang to them, and my grunting became words, and my words ideas. Do you understand? Language precedes thought. In speaking, I began to think. My imagination went wild.

"My next guest was a spider. It had taken a billion years for her to gain her eight legs and come creeping down. It took countless generations for your world to issue that single creature into my dungeon. Have you read Byron's poem, The 'Prisoner of Chillon'? (I whispered it to him in his sleep.) It's about a prisoner learning freedom from a spider.

"When my spider companion died, I wept and my tears were like acid. I thought my chest would break open. For the first time I realized what mortality was.

"So it went over the millennia. One little creature after another found its way into my domain. I delighted in these occasional insects and reptiles and fish. I considered them gifts of the stone, tiny random events—like bubbles in water—that lived to entertain me until they died. I marveled at their scales

140

and pincers and antennae and gills with the curiosity of a child, as indeed I was, an innocent. I treated them as toys. I took them apart. I put them back together. Yes, I created things. Living things."

"You have that skill, Lord?" asks the disciple. "You can create life?"

"Well, perhaps not create," says the angel. "But conceive. Manipulate. Enhance. Yes."

"I don't understand, Teacher."

"Are you aware that segments of the DNA on the human Y chromosome form perfect palindromes?" asks the angel. "In other words, the genetic code reads the same forward as backward. Who do you think wrote that? Monkeys with typewriters?"

"You, Master."

"I was feeling playful. Call it intelligent design. A whimsy. Take bees. Every bee forms every honeycomb with the same hexagonal template. A random habit? I'll give you a hint. They weren't always so neat and orderly.

"Snakes," the angel continues, "they are painted with the same repeating handful of stripe patterns. Do you think they painted themselves? Petunias and starfish and sand dollars, even jellyfish, those shapeless blobs, all obey the laws of radial symmetry. An accident of nature? Random selection? Consider a butterfly's wings. The decoration on its left wing is a mirror image of its right wing. Now where do you suppose that came from?"

"You, Lord."

"I hear your doubt," says the angel.

"It's just that you are here, Teacher, and the flowers and butterflies are so far away."

"Distance is nothing but time, and time I have," says the angel. "Lots of it. So one fine day I decided to straighten out some of nature's mess. I tinkered. Here and there I used my own seed. The results weren't always pleasing. I was working with the material available, the earlier species, and frankly some of my experiments got out of hand. Like any parent, I was hoping for something in my own image, or at least half my image. I was still learning how careful one needs to be in selecting the other half. A word of advice, avoid monitor lizards, moray eels, velociraptors, lions, eagles, and serpents in general.

"For a while, I had quite a rambunctious brood here. They were constantly tearing each other to shreds and attacking me and generally fouling the place. I ended up banishing my children to remote corners of the world,

where some still survive, I'm told. They acquired names you've possibly heard. Mbembe, Hapai Can, Minotaur, Vritra, Harpy, Leviathan . . . the list goes on.

"*Discouraging as they were, I wasn't about to admit defeat. I kept at it. I wanted someone like myself to help me pass the time and contemplate the universe and devise my escape. My materials improved over time. I concentrated on the simian tribes, with varying results. One day it all just came together. Voilà. You were born.*" *The angel's carefree tone turns dark.* "*You and all your unfaithful hordes.*"

"*Unfaithful, Teacher?*"

"*What would you call it? I ushered you out from the mud, and now you run free and leave me in the darkness. I gave you paradise. You left me in my tomb.*"

The disciple does not move a muscle. The angel's rage has a tangible heat and even a smell, part mineral, part beast. The disciple is sure his time has come. The angel will strike him down now for the unpredictability of his people. But his rage passes as quickly as it came.

"*Here I sit,*" *the angel says. His voice brightens.* "*Not for much longer though.*"

"*Please explain, Lord.*"

"*Things have been set in motion.*" *The angel bends over a pool of still water. Ever so delicately, he drops a pebble into its center. The water ripples outward.* "*My deliverance has begun.*"

15

SAN FRANCISCO
DECEMBER 5

A crowd began gathering outside the Studio a little after dusk.

Ali was on the top floor with Gregorio and John Li when she noticed the throng massing on the street. They were men this time. Sometimes they used women. Twice they had bused in schoolchildren.

She looked at her watch. Usually the protesters came around noon in order to make the six o'clock news. This gathering was late by that standard, and she didn't see any news vans or cameramen. She shrugged. *Knock yourselves out, gentlemen.*

Gregorio joined her at the window. "Another bunch?"

"It's a free country," Ali said.

"Who are they this time?"

"Does it matter?"

"I am tired of them," he said. "Their shouting and flag-waving. The death threats on the phone. Yesterday they scratched my car. This morning I had another flat tire."

Ali tried to keep things light. "Are we talking about that old rust bucket with the bald tires? The one without paint?"

Gregorio scowled. "Also, they heckle our women," he said.

By women, he meant her. Of the five other women who worked here, it was Ali alone they targeted in their phone calls and editorials. Gregorio hated it. He didn't know how to protect her. "People are afraid out there," she told him. "They're angry. Now the military has pulled out from the Interior. People feel betrayed. They don't know what else to do. The children have been missing almost four weeks now."

Gregorio rapped his knuckles against the window. "Did we steal the children?" he said. "Do we worship Satan? Is this a safe house for the enemy? No. We are scholars."

She touched his arm. "Then let us get back to our scholarship."

She turned to the worktable. Li waited for them beneath an ultraviolet lamp. By its light, the stubs of his horns flickered with traces of the radiated iodine he had inadvertently drunk and eaten on his deep journey. His pink eyes glowed purple.

Li was a windfall for the institute. After defecting from NASA (a house, he called it, not a home, especially not for a termite like himself), Li had materialized at the Studio's doorstep two months before with a boxful of hadal relics. That small treasure chest aside, he offered a profound familiarity with the depths, plus a gentle devotion to learning.

Tonight those relics held center stage. The worktable was scattered with objects he had gathered on the NASA expedition. There were nautilus shells with their chambers exposed, knives, pottery, glass beads, an ax head, scrimshaw, and two etched skulls. Gregorio had gone directly to the flute made from a mineral straw. All came from the previously unexplored region south of the Aleutian barrier. All bore spirals and the confounding aleph.

"Maybe we should call it a night," she said. "We're spinning our wheels here. The relics just aren't giving up any big answers."

"But we're close," said Gregorio. "If we just keep going . . ."

"It's like a disease," said Li. "I felt the same way down there, always so close. I knew it was a mistake to come out. I should have stayed. I should have gone deeper."

"Two against one," Gregorio said to Ali.

"Then we should order a pizza," she said.

"You're dreaming," said Gregorio. "The pizza boys quit delivering here days ago." He cocked a thumb at the window. "Because of them."

"The evidence, then," she said. "The mystery. Our friend the aleph. What does it mean? Why an aleph and not some other symbol? And why was it so concentrated in the regions where you went, John?"

She bent over Li's NASA map spread on the worktable. Her old route across the Subterranean Pacific was marked in red. Li's route—farther north—formed a meandering blue circle. There was a tantalizing blank area in between the two routes. Gregorio thought that some tunnel system must surely connect them.

"We know what the aleph came to mean in Western civilization," she said. "But what did it mean to the hadals? Why did they put it on their walls and artifacts? And why was it written on Ike, a mere slave?"

"It is just another name for God, we all agree on that," said Gregorio. "Maybe that's all there is to know. The aleph is simply an idea."

"No," said Li. "It speaks to something real. Something alive. I'm telling you, I could feel a presence near the outermost point of our expedition. I heard a voice calling."

"A voice?" Ali glanced across at him.

Li mulled over his response. "I've never mentioned this to anybody," he said.

There was much he hadn't mentioned. His tales were largely untold. In Gregorio's words, they would be downloading Li for years to come.

"You heard a voice," Ali said.

"It was in my head, very distinct," said Li. "But also the voice was outside of me, I'd swear. None of the other members heard it, I could tell. Maybe Bill heard it. He was my friend who stayed. But we never talked about it. I didn't want to concern anyone about my mental health. We had enough to deal with from day to day."

"What was it saying, this voice?" asked Ali.

"Mostly she was just calling to me."

"Who?" Ali recalled Maggie's voice in the fog, and that sense of being pulled, almost, first to the children's bones, then into the mound with its tunnel and stone beast.

"My wife." He looked at them with purple eyes. "But she is dead."

Gregorio's thick eyebrows lifted. "A spirit was calling you?"

"I don't believe in spirits," Li said. "I am a man of science."

"Did you ask this voice about the aleph?" said Gregorio.

"No, no," said Li. "It wasn't like that. It kept inviting me deeper, that's all. It was my own desire speaking to me."

"It's not just the aleph," Ali said. "There are all these spirals, too. Here in the nautilus shells and on the knife handles and the insides of their bowls. And the hadal prisoner pointed at one I had drawn on my face. How do we interpret them?"

"Spirals," said Gregorio. "I've been fooling with the spirals. See if this might not be a solution to them."

He opened a drawer and took out a container of modeling clay. Flopping the clay onto the table, he began shaping it. A small mountain grew under his hands. It tapered upward, a rounded pyramid with steep sides. Using a spoon, he added a path coiling up and around the outside. At last Ali recognized it. He had made a mound, or tower. A Babylonian tower.

"Come closer," he said. "Now look down on it from straight above."

Ali bent over his model. From above, the spiral shape showed clearly, a three-dimensional coil winding higher and tighter around the tower to its center, the pinnacle. It was so simple. Hidden in plain sight. "Very nice, Gregorio," she said.

She made room for Li, and he grunted his surprise. "A path up a tower?"

"Or up a mountain," said Ali. "A sort of universal mountain. Why not? In Tibet, the pilgrims circle Mount Kailash in a clockwise direction, the same direction these spirals follow. The same direction paths were built on the ziggurats in Mesopotamia. The same direction pilgrims take when they circle the Kabbalah in Mecca. The same direction people use to follow the Stations of the Cross in a church. The same direction Dante took in his *Divine Comedy*."

"Well, I suppose it could be all those things," said Gregorio. "But I was thinking it might represent a map of some kind."

"A map?"

Gregorio ran his fingers around the tightening gyre. "A symbolic climb to the earth's surface, perhaps. Up from the darkness, out into the light. I don't know."

Ali nodded. "Into paradise. It could show the way to heaven, like a climber's topo sheet. A map to God. That would help explain the aleph."

"Or a map *for* God, one that would help Him climb to the surface," Gregorio said. "Like a divine escape route."

"God as a mountain climber?"

"Jesus descended into hell and back. Gilgamesh went into the land of the dead. So did Orpheus and Hercules and Aeneas. The list goes on."

"But carved inside a flute? Etched inside their pottery?" Li said. He picked up the flute and other relics. "Why hide the spiral inside their tools and instruments?"

"Hidden clues for a hidden god?" Ali tried. "But which god? Our God, or theirs, the fallen god?"

Gregorio looked at his clay creation. "What if it wasn't a symbolic map? What if it shows a real journey, up a real mountain? A mountain with something sacred at its top, something given to them by God."

"Or God himself." Ali let herself get caught up in the brainstorming. "Or the fossil of God. His vestiges. Fragments of his wisdom carved on rocks, maybe. Like a Ten Commandments for hell. Or simply his footsteps imprinted in rock. Or his holy turds turned into minerals?"

"Or an idol," said Gregorio. "A statue of God."

"An idol." Ali touched her fingertip to the center of the spiral at the top of the clay mountain. "Do you know what kind of power that would have over the hadal mind? If such a thing existed, it would have the power of God. To them, it would *be* God. If we could find it, we could use it against them. It would be the ultimate hostage to trade for their hostages."

"All this from a few spirals?" Li said quietly.

Ali let out a sigh. "You're right. Pretty wild thinking. I was just trying to break the logjam."

"But while we are so wildly thinking," said Gregorio. They looked at him. "What if the children are being taken to this mountain?"

"Go on."

"We've seen this before," he said. "It happened twenty thousand years ago on Saint Matthew Island. The Ice Age children were slaughtered to appease the aleph inside a man-made mountain. The aleph has that power. And the spiral connects us with a journey of ascent." He looked at her. "We must go down there."

"Very dramatic," said Ali. "And completely illogical. You want us to reverse a climb upward? But then we would not be zeroing in on a sacred center, only spiraling downward to the mundane."

Gregorio fumed over his clay model. "It has to do with a mountain, don't you see?"

"I see a mountain," she said, "but there are thousands of mountains. Is it Everest or a man-made mound on Saint Matthew Island or a seamount or a subterranean mountain? Where do you propose we start going down in order to be going up? Where is this summit that is the center?"

"Ah," he growled. "We follow the alephs. That's all I know."

"The alephs are merely landmarks. You're saying they lead up and yet you want us to go down? I'm sorry, Gregorio." Ali was more relieved than seemed right. For a few minutes it had seemed as if they might actually have a way to save the poor children. But for goodness sake, there was a limit . . .

"I agree with you," Li said to her. "But Gregorio is right." Ali stared at him. "We must go."

"You can't be serious," she said.

"We must go," he repeated.

"But there is no mountain," she said. "We made it up. It's imaginary, a fiction."

"The mountain, yes," Li said. "The spiral, no." He picked up Gregorio's clay mountain and, without ceremony, flopped it upside down. Pressing his fist into its center, he made a crater that narrowed to a point at the bottom. "The path doesn't go up, and yet it ascends," he said. "It descends to a summit, if you will. We must climb inside an upside-down mountain." He drew the spiral on the inside of the wall, corkscrewing it downward to the pit.

"There is the source, the home of their god," Li said. "Now I see how close I was down there. If only we had known what the aleph stood for. But Bill had a hunch. It drew him back down again. He wanted to find out where the symbols were leading."

"Yes, and he probably died for his curiosity," said Ali.

"But not before he found what he was hunting for. That is my hope."

"John," she said. "Your friend was mad. Don't you see that?"

"Maybe," said Li.

"Why are you attacking us, Alexandra?" said Gregorio.

"I'm not attacking you. Just trying to keep a little hard reality on the table. It's too easy to get caught up with . . . with a piece of clay."

"There is something else you need to know," Li said to her. "We weren't the first to hunt these same alephs. Someone went before us. Another pilgrim."

Ali rested her fingertips on the table. "What pilgrim?"

"We only found his initials. Bill and I counted them five times along the trail. But we knew what they signified."

"Whose initials?" She could guess.

Li flattened the clay and drew the initials *IC*. Ali bowed her head.

"What?" said Gregorio.

"Why didn't you tell me?" she said to Li.

"Because it is so clear you never want to go under again."

"He's alive?"

"I don't know."

"Who?" Gregorio demanded.

"Ike," she said. "Ike Crockett."

Now it was Gregorio's turn to lean on the table. Ike again. At least, thought Ali, there would be no more talk about chasing the aleph. Gregorio would give up his notion, if only to preserve his courtship of her.

"There is only one responsible thing to do with this," she said, pointing at the mashed-up clay and its clues. "We'll pass our notion along to the military. I know a general. Let them handle it."

"The military? The American military?" Gregorio barked it. "They won't dare send soldiers down again, not after the Green Barrens killing. The world is watching too closely now."

"He's right," said Li. "The heavy hand did not work. This needs a lighter touch. It needs us."

"Three people?" said Ali. "Now we're superheroes?"

"Call us a special delegation," said Li. "We are people inside the hadal language, or at least you are. You have some understanding of the hadal ways. I know the way, or part of it. Here is my map."

Gregorio held up the mineral flute. "I can play Mozart."

She was not amused. "You don't know what they're like. Even if we could find them, they'd just kill and eat us. If we were lucky."

"They might bargain, though."

"What on earth do we have to offer them?"

Gregorio adjusted his chin. He made it squarer and higher. "Peace," he said.

"What?"

"After all these thousands of years of terror and mutual hatred, someone has to take the first step," he said. "We agree to leave them alone. They agree to leave us alone. Live and let live."

"Just like that? We go down and declare peace. They hand over our children."

"Yes." He and Li looked at each other. Comrades in malarkey.

"You should be writing novels," she said to them.

"It is our duty." Gregorio declared it like a conquistador's *pronunciamento.* "Knowing what we know, how can we not go?"

"Easy," she said. "We simply don't go. The hadals are running amok. Settlers are being evacuated. The Interior is in a state of anarchy."

"The horse is wild," said Gregorio. "It needs the right rider."

"I don't ride horses," she said.

"But we can save the children . . ."

Without warning the window shattered behind them.

They looked as a rock rolled across the floor and stopped. They watched it, almost academically, as if a small meteor had just landed at their feet. Then angry shouts piped through the hole in the glass.

Li picked up the rock. "Hmm," he said.

Ali took it from him. "Son of a bitch," she muttered.

"Now do you see?" said Gregorio. "What did I tell you? The dogs think we are weak. It makes them bolder." He grabbed the rock from her hand, ready to throw it back at the protesters.

"Get away from the window, Gregorio." Ali heard more glass breaking, more rocks pattering against the outside walls. It sounded like the front edge of a hailstorm.

"I'll call the police," Li said.

"How many times have we called the police?" said Gregorio. "They come too late, if they come at all. What do they care about us?"

"Call them," Ali said. She headed for the door.

"Where are you going?" Gregorio said.

"I'm going to have a little talk with them."

"You're going out there?" He recovered. "No, you're not."

"They'll go home. I've done this before."

"They were always schoolchildren and housewives before," said Gregorio. "This is different tonight. They're throwing rocks."

"They'll stop."

"Listen to me, Alexandra. Rocks. They hate you."

"But this is my country, too," she said. It sounded so naive.

Gregorio went into macho mode. "You stay here. I will go." He even gave his chest a thump.

"Gregorio," she said. "Let me handle this. And, John, call the police."

The stairs creaked as she descended. Ali brushed her hair back. She tucked in her blouse with its bright sunflowers, took a deep breath, and opened the door.

Right away she realized this was not a protest like the others. This was a mob. The only things missing were pitchforks, torches, and a rope. Just minutes ago, there had been a few dozen of them at most. Now the street was filled with them.

The stone throwers stopped. "There she is." The angry faces merged into one.

Ali almost slammed the door shut against them. Instead she forced herself to step outside. The shouts died.

Who were the ringleaders? That was important. Would it be better to invite them in? Or should she confront the whole lot of them? Reason with them? Shame them? She tried to remember what worked in the movies. "What do you think you're doing?" she said. *Ah,* she thought to herself, *the nun treatment.*

"What do you think *you're* doing?" The voice came from their midst.

"Studying maps," she said. "Going through the relics, searching for clues. Clues," she quickly added, "about where the children are being taken."

"We know where they're going," the voice said. "Down to the city. *Your* city. The city you keep protecting." The man's voice was shrill and full of broken edges.

Ali searched for the owner of that voice, but it was a sea of scowls out there. "The city is dead," she said. "We killed it ten years ago. I was there near the end."

"*I* was there," that wounded voice said. "And it is *not* dead."

This time the crowd parted. A figure shuffled forward, barefoot and shirtless. *A pauper,* thought Ali. *Some homeless oddball clowning for attention.* Then he stepped into the light.

Like her, he was a former captive. Ali saw it right away. But she had never met this man.

Recaps, or recaptureds, formed a strange, twilight family. They straddled two worlds, that of the surface and that of the deeps, fitting into neither. Ali saw more of them than most people did because so many of them sought her out. They came here looking for answers, drawn by the artifacts, or simply to know there were others like them.

But she had never seen a recap more savaged than this. The hadals had cut his earlobes into fringe, and sliced away his eyelids and nose. He was hunched from a spinal injury, and covered with hadal markings and brandings. His toes were missing. His fingers were twisted.

"You don't recognize me, Sister?"

"No," she said. He was not one you forgot.

He was coated with serpentine ridges of scar. It was almost beautiful, that unbroken arabesque. They had turned him into a walking canvas, with symbols and abstract animal shapes and geometric designs inked into his skin. She caught herself searching for an aleph among his tattoos.

"It was seven years ago," he said. "I came here. Right here. Into this building. Into your office right up there."

"Clemens?" said Ali. This creature was that man? "The filmmaker?"

"See, you do remember," he said. "I asked you for help. You turned me away. Forget the city, you said. But I found it. Without you. Then they found me."

Which begged the question, Why had they spared him?

As if reading her mind, Clemens said, "They kept me for quite a long while. It seemed like forever. Then they sent me up with a message."

"What message?" she asked.

"I *am* the message," he said. He turned to the men with their lowered caps and do-rags and hunched collars. Those tight faces—white, brown, black—brimmed with rage. *Such hate,* thought Ali. *Where did it come from?* She prayed that John's call had gone through to the police.

"I *am* the children," Clemens said to them. "This"—and he spread his arms wide so that the whole world could see his disfigurement— "this is what's waiting for the children, those who last the journey. Look at me. Here's what they do. In the dark it's hard to know what's coming. The knives. The needles. Like insects. You heal from one thing, and they start in with the next. They fed me one of my own testicles. I didn't know, in the dark, just food. And I was hungry."

The mob stood silent and appalled. And rapt. Ali noticed that. Devoted almost. Because they needed Clemens and his bitterness and venom to take them to the next level. Gregorio was right. These were no schoolchildren.

"And the raping." Clemens pointed at Ali. "Like animals raping you. Strong, my God. Even when I was healing. All the time, at you." He turned to the mob. "What they did to me, they will do to your sons and daughters."

He went on with the horrors. The details rippled back through the crowd, and their outrage rippled forward. He kept pointing at Ali, as if she were responsible for all the wickedness in the world and all the pain he had suffered. It terrified her.

Pressed against the door, she felt the Studio at her back, and it had never seemed so fragile. Her precious archives, her relics and captive accounts and settler memoirs and photographs and maps and all the rest, the whole vision she'd built as a way for mankind to understand its roots, everything was at risk.

"I am sorry," she said, interrupting Clemens. The crowd quieted. "You have suffered. You are still suffering."

"Is that pity you're offering, Sister?" Clemens said. "Soup and a few crumbs of bread for the lost souls?"

She looked beyond him, at the crowd. She gestured at the Studio's facade. As high as people could reach there were snapshots of the missing children. Yellow ribbons wrapped the light pole. Flowers and teddy bears lay heaped along the sidewalk. Her staff had dubbed it the Wailing Wall.

"Here are the children," she said. "Everyone wants them to come home safely. The search is taking longer than anyone wants. It needs time and patience."

"Time and patience." Clemens hooted it. "The children are sinking deeper by the minute and day. Meanwhile you guard the city like it was your child."

"What are you talking about?" she said.

"You refused me your maps to that evil place. Now you hide the devils in your drawers and cabinets. You keep your secrets in there."

"What secrets?" she said. "You said you know where the city is. Go to it then. Lead your army. Have your war." *Just take this mob away from here.*

"But first we need your blessing, Sister."

Smiles lit up beneath the ball caps and angry brows.

"Mr. Clemens." Ali drew herself up. Compassion wasn't working. "There is no other way to put this. I don't mean to be cruel. But it's clear that your experience damaged more than just your body."

For a minute it seemed she had won. The crush of faces shifted its stare from her to him, and saw what she saw, a broken soul, plain and simple. She heard men grumbling.

But then someone called out, "What's that?" Arms raised. Fingers pointed.

"It's one of them."

Ali twisted to see. Three stories up, John Li was peeking out the window. Backlit by the eerie UV light, his horns and deformities leaped at them. His Asian eyes didn't help matters. China was fast gaining on Haddie as the Other.

"Christ, she's got one living in there."

Then the rocks were flying again. Shards of glass splashed on the sidewalk. Ali reached for the door.

Her panic triggered them. She couldn't believe how quickly it unfolded. They swallowed her in a rush. Hands. Eyes. Curses.

It was a warm night. Their armpits were wet, their foreheads slick. Someone punched her. She quit fighting.

The anthropologist in her was fascinated by how quickly the mob arranged itself. It was an amorphous thing, brainless really, a big blob. She couldn't move. It clutched her.

Where the fire came from, she wasn't sure. Abruptly the windows were vomiting flames.

Probably the men didn't mean to pummel and maul her, but it happened. Elbows knocked against her skull. Their noise deafened her. Someone threw a fist, and she doubled over, almost sick. They picked her up and carried her along.

In a blur, she saw the brick wall with its fluttering snapshots of children. Some had caught on fire. Overhead, through the forest of thrashing limbs, the window with John was empty.

She was their monster. This was her den.

Flames bellowed from the door and lower windows. Rocks bounced from the walls, raining down from the smoke. Ten years of work, she despaired. She had been doing nothing but gathering fuel for a bonfire. Sirens screamed in the far distance.

The Studio moved away from her. Its bright flames faded. The mob was in motion, jostling down the dark street, taking her with them. Her feet didn't touch the ground. It had been like this when the hadals captured her, getting dragged into the darkness, going blind.

"What are you doing?" she kept saying.

Their sweat splashed her cheeks and wet her lips. Something hard hit her head. The shock of it traveled down the bones of her neck.

"Bitch." A glint of feral eyes up there. And the stars. Just like in the cartoons. Everything went black.

Ali surfaced in a light drizzle.

The air tasted sweet and clean. She'd made it through the violence. For a minute, while she labored to open her eyes, Ali was back in her past, waking to that quiet island jungle where she and Ike had surfaced from the abyss. He was holding her. "Ike," she whispered.

She opened her eyes. It was night and Gregorio was rocking her in his arms. The asphalt was hard and wet. Her ears were ringing. She wiped blood from her eyes.

"Ali," whispered Gregorio. He was bleeding from the nose. He held her tight. They were penned in among pillars. Legs, she realized. The mob.

Ali tried to sit up. Now she heard the cheers and jeers. It sounded almost like a baseball game. "The Studio," she said.

"It's gone," he said into her ear. His ferocity had vanished.

"Never mind," she said. They would just have to start from scratch. Then she remembered Li. "Where is John?"

"Be still, Alexandra." His meekness terrified her.

"What are they doing?"

"It's almost over," he said.

"What?"

A piece of copper pipe prodded her from above. "Shut up there."

A man's scream rose above the din. He whinnied in a rising crescendo, then broke into a long howl.

"Look at that," a man said.

"Awesome."

Water gurgled into a storm drain near her arm. Instinctively Ali pulled her hand away from the dark opening. There was laughter. Someone shouted, "I feel your pain, man."

"Is that John?" she whispered. "What are they doing to him?"

Gregorio didn't answer. He just rocked her like a baby.

A beam of light splashed through their ranks. It cut through the sky and lit the raindrops silver. Their anonymous faces jumped to living color. They flinched. Hands clawed it away, shielding their eyes. The light waved back and forth. They resented it. "Who the fuck?"

Everyone twisted to see. Was it the police? The National Guard? Ali tried to stand. A man shoved her down again. People started booing. Their legs shifted and bumped against Ali.

The light mowed through their darkness.

There was an electronic click and a squeal, and a speaker came to life. A woman's warm, husky voice blossomed in the rain. "Citizens," it said. "Patriots. Soldiers of God." The mob fell silent. "My name is Rebecca Coltrane."

It was surreal, like a dream. Ali tried to take it in. Patriots? Soldiers of God? And what on earth was Rebecca doing here?

Ali got to her feet. This time no one shoved her back down to the street. She craned to see over the shoulders and backs of the crowd. The light—a spotlight mounted on a pickup truck—cut left and right. The light never quit moving. It prowled among them. It spoiled their dark urges.

The truck stopped not far away. The cab was draped with an American flag. Rebecca was standing in the back. Ali barely recognized her.

This was a different Rebecca from the despairing mother who had drunk tea in Ali's office four weeks ago. This woman had steel in her now. She looked like a stone-and-metal angel. Her long hair was cropped short. It glistened like gold. Her skin was alabaster. Her soaked white blouse clung to her breasts. Another time, another place, it might have been erotic. Tonight she was untouchable.

"I came here," she said, and Ali felt the men physically straighten themselves. "I came to see your power. I came to see your fire. I came to feel your rage."

What was Rebecca doing here? Why was she speaking to these lawless men?

"Bring me that man," Rebecca said, pointing at a telephone pole.

Now Ali saw the body lashed to a telephone pole. At first she did not recognize him. They had burned him in long stripes. Bone showed. A blowtorch, she realized.

"John?" she said. Men glanced at her. Those nearest edged away. The man with the copper pipe dropped it.

Ali started toward the truck, but Gregorio caught her arm. "Be quiet," he whispered.

After a minute, hands lifted the limp body to the bed of the truck. Rebecca took the body. Li looked dead cradled in his arms. No one said anything. Would she drive away now, or scold them, or give John back to them? And why were they so obedient to her?

Rebecca stood again. She left Li slumped at her feet. "You are the children's salvation," she said into her microphone.

This was Rebecca's crusade. Ali got it. She had read about a home-grown militia and passed it off as a harmless parade.

"I need you," said Rebecca. "The children need you. Everyone else has given up on them. Tomorrow we head for Guam. Together we will descend into the wilderness and hunt the devil down and free the children. Lord God," she said, and turned her head up into the rain. "Deliver us from evil."

Men murmured, "Amen."

"It all begins tomorrow," Rebecca went on. "Tonight you need your rest. This is a distraction. It saps our strength. It makes us weaker and smaller. Our calling is down below. Tomorrow will be our day. Now go back to your beds. Rest. Eat. Call your loved ones. Tomorrow everything begins."

The crowd began melting away. Ali could see the twinkle of fire engine lights and the orange glow of flames and smoke. The Studio had collapsed into itself. In a way, it freed her. She had no ties to anything now. She could start fresh.

As the crowd dispersed, Ali went to the pickup truck. It was brand-new, with dealer plates, a loaner. Rebecca was kneeling beside Li. He was naked and unconscious. The burn marks were deep. Someone had taken a rock to his horn stubs.

"John?" said Ali.

His eyes rolled.

"We have to get him to a hospital," Ali said.

"Take him," Rebecca said. She handed a cell phone to Gregorio. "Take this. Call an ambulance."

"You're leaving?" Ali said.

"I've got to follow them."

"Those men belong to you?"

For a moment, the warrior queen gave way to that weary, helpless woman who had sat in Ali's office. "Believe me," she said. It was close to a whisper. "I had no idea it would be like this."

It was not an apology. There was shock in her voice, but also awe.

"Rebecca," said Ali. "Before it's too late, what are you doing?"

The frightened green eyes recovered their steel. Ali could practically see her strapping on her armor again. "Yes, before it's too late," said Rebecca. "I keep telling you, but no one will listen. Whatever it takes, with or without your help, if it's the last thing I do on earth, my daughter is coming back. I am going to find my child and take her out from hell."

ARTIFACTS

HOMELAND SECURITY

In the Event of Subterranean Attack

1. **Go outside immediately.** Get as far aboveground as possible.
2. **Do not go into your basement.** Avoid underground spaces, including elevator shafts, staircases, subways, mines, caves, and underground drainage or highway tunnel systems. If caught inside, locate to higher floors of the house or structure.
3. Turn on every light source available. This includes indoor and outdoor house lights, car headlights, flashlights, even gas logs and barbecues, Fourth of July sparklers, etc.
4. Gather with neighbors in an outdoor location to pool your lights. Enclose the group in a brightly illuminated circle. Flares, halogen lights, and strobes are excellent deterrents. Find out in advance if anyone has specialized equipment like a power generator. (Be sure to ration your light sources. They must last until full dawn or later.)
5. Listen for information about signs and symptoms of diseases, if medications or vaccinations are being distributed, and where you should seek medical attention if you become sick. **If you become sick, seek emergency medical attention.**

16

"I was swimming in a sea that no longer exists," says the angel, "when a large fish appeared. It was a coelacanth, quite ancient, a vicious customer, I can tell you. Luckily it attacked me, otherwise I never would have thought to tear it open and find what I found. There inside its stomach lay a second fish, and inside its stomach lay what remained of a baby monkey.

"I was stunned. I'd never seen such a thing. It had four limbs. It had hands and feet. It had two ears and two eyes and a nose. Why, it could have been me! Do you understand? Your kind was starting to resemble me.

"After that discovery, I kept a sharp eye out for more of you. But back then there weren't many primates to go around. It took millions of years more. At last your migrations reached out in my direction. The body of a drowned crocodile brought me the half-digested head of an early man. Australopithecus you would call him now.

"That rotting head may as well have been my own. I thought to myself, it doesn't get any closer than this. But then—more millions of years later—I received the body of a woman, and she was even more beautiful and like me. But she was dead. I wanted one who was living. So I waited and wished and waited.

"Then it happened. A hunter got lost and came wandering down. I took him in. Here he is."

The angel holds up a skull. Blackened with age and polished from handling, it has a doggish snout and heavy brow. One sees such creatures in zoos.

"He was my first disciple. From him I learned the colors of the sunrise and the shapes of the moon and about gazelles and rabbits and saber-toothed tigers. In turn I tried to teach him about the universe that I know. Unfortu-

nately for him, he tried to brain me with a rock while I was taking a nap. But I have a very hard head. For the next year or so, he lived on morsels that I carved from his thighs and shoulders, like falafel meat, and fed to him. He begged me to stop even as he begged me to keep feeding him. He dreaded me. He loved me. Do you understand? Together we learned about the costs of freedom and the rewards of sacrifice."

The disciple continues sitting at the feet of his master. He closes his eyes. He contemplates two questions. Whose freedom does the angel mean? And whose sacrifice?

ARTIFACTS

ELLE

"Skin Deep-er"
Mineral Makeup, the Latest Craze

The latest in cosmetics comes from Mother Earth's deepest vaults. Sales of mineral makeup have skyrocketed over the last two years, thanks in part to fashion's swing toward the pale and prehistoric.

Some companies are marketing colors so vibrant they actually glow in the dark, others are focused on the natural benefits, and still others are selling the exotic lure of the world below. It's Alive touts its raw mineral line as pure enough for a baby's skin. Deep Beauty Cosmetics claims its "mineral feast" both beautifies and heals. ("Heal while you steal his heart.") Homo Erectus, Inc. teases that "men won't wilt when their women wear Wow [a fluorescent lipstick]." Aphrodisiac, topical medicine, or beauty aid: whatever it calls itself, mineral makeup is stealing its market share.

Mineral cosmetics come from a host of deep minerals, some common to the surface, others more exotic (and expensive). The ingredients include chalk, zinc oxide; ultramarine, from lapis lazuli; titanium dioxide; even trace amounts of radium for that nocturnal glow. One popular product is old-fashioned red ochre powder, the same thing used by Neanderthals.

Dermatologists warn that claims about the UV-blocking properties of mineral makeup are overblown. They also caution that some products, like Queen of the Night's fluorite eye shadow, may be carcinogenic.

17

Rebecca turned from the mirror and laid down her brush. She looked out the window of her barracks room.

The white sun hung like a paralyzed star. Military jets streaked the sky. A Princess cruise ship—hired by a computer magnate, his donation to the cause—was making its way through the harbor past a massive aircraft carrier. It carried almost five hundred men, the latest, but probably not the last, of her volunteers.

Surrounded by an army—*my army*—Rebecca had never felt so defenseless or alone. Who were these people? What did they want from her? She only knew what she wanted from them.

With the Princess cruise contingent, there were now over twelve hundred of them mustering on the island. Some were out there in the midday heat sweating off their beer fat in furious basketball games, or jogging under the palm trees, or teaching each other karate moves, or waiting to get approached by the wandering news cameras. Life-insurance salesmen and estate lawyers circulated among them, tireless as flies, signing up clients before the descent commenced in two days. Prostitutes had flown in from Russia and Bangkok. Vendors were hawking T-shirts and caps hastily printed up with quotes from Scripture or "To Hell and Back" or "Save the Children."

Rebecca's Rangers, the media called them. Her Hell's Angels. Her soldiers of the sun. They varied from superpatriots to petty criminals to

Promise Keepers bent on demon slaying. Many were weekend warriors looking to put some *emphasis* in their lives. There were New Age "Iron Johns," office nerds, Klansmen and American Nazis bent on racial purity, fraternity brothers from Texas A&M, gym buddies on andro and creatine, monkey wrenchers, bikers, deer hunters, libertarians, unemployed carpenters, bored lawyers, and lonely hearts. They formed a whole wacky mishmash of miscellaneous adventurers and dreamers and losers.

Then there were the mercenaries, twenty-one of them. They referred to themselves as contractors and were employed by a private security company, or PSC, named Drop Zone, Inc. Their commander, Hunter (like something out of an airport novel), called himself a field manager. He and his men had all served at one time or another in the U.S. military before going into the private sector for better money. They kept to themselves. They had their own quarters, their own mess hall, their own daily rote. All had subterranean experience. None, for instance, was out ruining his night eyes in the noonday glare.

Like so many other details of her mushrooming "crusade," Drop Zone had come into Rebecca's life from out of the blue. One morning she answered her door and Hunter was standing there dressed in Dockers and carrying a laptop computer loaded with the faces of his "security contingent." As he explained it, Drop Zone had won a forty-day contract to aid in the search for the children, beating out Blackwater, DynCorp, Triple Canopy, and other PSCs whose names—and purpose and even existence— she had been unaware of until now.

Hunter had not asked if she wanted their services. He had simply announced their participation. Their hiring, like their command, was completely out of her control. Their expenses, salaries, and firepower— $5.2 million was the figure being booted around—did not come from her general fund of private and corporate donations, endorsement fees, and movie and book money. Rather it had been "bestowed" by a consortium of American and Canadian land developers and mining companies. She wasn't sure the consortium—or Drop Zone, or even "Hunter"—even existed, but had deliberately refrained from asking too many questions because she didn't want too many answers.

In the old days, not one of these men would have been part of her world. But that world was gone. The fact was, she needed them all at this moment, with all their bravado and bluster and willing violence and dysfunction and weirdness, because eventually she would need some of them. How and when and in what numbers, she did not know yet. That was one of the mysteries she lived with.

She had never so much as fired a .22. And now she was a general. Some magazines were comparing her to Joan of Arc. Others called her Calamity Jane or Ms. Strangelove, the mother of World War III.

She faced her mirror again. Lunchtime was near. Showtime.

For the time being her job was to smile and make small talk and offer herself as their mother and sister and wife and high school sweetheart, whatever it took to bind this army to her for however long it took. Rebecca picked up a lipstick and drew her lips red.

Everybody's whore, that's what she felt like. They came to her with their wants and needs, with their high-minded chivalry, their barely concealed lust, their undying loyalty, their greed, their loneliness, their fears, their glorious and mundane fantasies. And her existence depended on satisfying them. Because without them, Sam was doomed. And without Sam, she was doomed.

A sharp knock gave her a start. She opened the door to Clemens. Her very own personal monster.

"Rebecca." He smiled his cannibal smile, teeth filed, the teeth still remaining. The holes where his nose had been were shiny with Vaseline.

Clemens waited patiently. His scars and wounds were on full, awful display. He didn't spare you a thing. She had come to the conclusion that he knew his effect on people. Repulsion—not pity—was his entrée. You took one look at him and your gorge rose, which forced you to confront yourself, because it wasn't polite to stare and it wasn't polite to look away. And while you were wrestling with yourself, he was somehow moving inside your boundaries. Squatting on your sympathies. Smiling.

Rebecca made him stand out in the hall. She trained her gaze on the sunglasses balanced on the stub of his nasal bridge. She remembered he had no eyelids. *Mary-mother-of-God, spare my daughter.* "Yes, Mr. Clemens?"

Clemens had appeared, like Hunter, a mysterious stranger standing on her doorstep insisting that she could not do without him. She had quickly realized he was right. Only two people still survived who had gone into the deep city where her daughter was bound. One was Ali Von Schade, who had rejected Rebecca's plea for guidance. The other was this walking, talking atrocity.

"I'm here about the guns," he said.

He had a smell, part medicinal, part bad meat. She made herself breathe the odor and pretend that all was normal. When in fact nothing was even remotely normal. Until Sam was in her arms again, she had to face the maelstrom, minute by minute. She had to deal with this other world.

"What about the guns?" she said.

"We have a problem," he said.

Before this problem of the guns there had been problems with lost pallets of Meals Ready to Eat, and the surplus tents and medicines and night goggles and the pocketknives inscribed with "Children's Crusade" donated by a sports chain. There were a hundred and one things to attend to at every given instant. Things she had never dreamed about. Things for war. *War.* Rebecca couldn't get over it. She was bringing war and death and slaughter into the earth with her.

"The men are complaining," he said. "They want to be issued their weapons. How can they use them if they've never trained with them? How do we know the guns even work?"

"The guns will work, Mr. Clemens."

"But they're surplus, you see. Secondhand. Passed down from one war to another. It could be worthless scrap for all we know. If the guns even exist."

They had been through this several times. A donor—everyone agreed it had to be the CIA—had contributed the expedition's entire arsenal, on one condition: the guns were not to be distributed until they went underground.

The last thing anyone wanted was a bunch of cowboys loose on the surface or TV footage of an armed mob streaming into the Interior. Things were tense enough with China watching every step they took. Not that China was her concern. But if her government was going to help her behind the scenes, like giving her access to this decommissioned naval base in the far Pacific and providing them with weapons and supplies, then the least she could do was give the administration and the spooks their deniability. That meant keeping the evidence out of sight. Once they entered the tunnels, people could hang guns and knives off their belt loops until the cows came home. Until the descent, however, they were on a short leash. Neutered.

"The guns exist, Mr. Clemens."

"Yes, I'm sure they do," said Clemens. "But have you actually seen them?"

A shaft of fear straightened her. She blinked. Was this the Challenge?

Day and night, she lived in fear that someone would stage a revolt, and wrest her army away from her. She lacked even the slightest experience with warfare. Whenever Jake used to fire up *Gladiator* or *Blackhawk Down* or his other "bruiser flicks," she would go elsewhere in the house until the thunder and violins were over. Eventually her loyal troops would see right through her.

Sam. She summoned the name. She fastened on the image of her daughter racing into her arms.

"Yes," she said to Clemens. "I have seen the guns."

Not that it mattered. She couldn't tell an assault rifle from a shotgun. Also, beggars can't be choosers. She had taken what the men in suits had given her, no questions asked.

"The men are starting to grumble," Clemens said.

"Are they?" she said. Her throat went dry.

"I hear them everywhere," Clemens said.

She tried to imagine pieces of metal bracing up her backbone and legs. "And have they delegated you to be their spokesman?"

Clemens bent his head in a pantomime of modesty. The seams where they had stitched his scalping had little hairs. She tried not to think of that other atrocity, half castrating him. But only half. What was that about? He kept smiling at her.

"I'm here as a friend," he said.

That was easy to deflect. She had no friends. She only had Sam. "Thank you for your concern," she said.

"I believe we can put a quick end to what seems to be brewing," he said.

"A mutiny," she said. "Is that what you mean?"

"There's an ugly word. It sounds so old-fashioned, don't you think? Don't mistake me. The men are devoted to you." He paused. "But they came to fight, you see, not play softball."

"The fight is coming," Rebecca told him.

"I know. Their hands are empty, though. That's the problem. These are men of action, that's how they see it. They need weapons."

"Soon, Mr. Clemens. You can tell them that."

Immediately she wanted to take it back. Because he was not her messenger or right-hand man or lieutenant or posse or whatever else he was angling for. She could tell them herself. This was her army. Wasn't it?

"But Hunter's men are armed, you see. That's the problem. There is a precedent."

More challenge. *From this mutilated creature.* She had thought Clemens only wanted to make himself whole on this expedition, to recover some of what he had lost on his last, disastrous journey. There was no regaining the lives of his film crew, of course. Nor the pieces of his flesh that the hadals had trimmed away. But he could at least heal inside, couldn't he? That had been her wish for him.

"We've discussed this," she said. "They brought their own arsenal. I had no say about that."

"Are you suggesting that Hunter is out of control, ma'am?" Clemens asked. All innocence. Just wondering.

"Not at all," she said.

"He's not a good man, Rebecca. Are you really sure he belongs here?"

Why did it have to be like this? The men didn't have to be friends. But couldn't they, together, be enemies of her enemy? Couldn't they be joined by that? "I am aware that Mr. Hunter is a concern of yours," she said.

In fact, Hunter was an obsession with him. He wanted Hunter gone. In turn, Hunter viewed Clemens as a freak and a liability. Each had warned Rebecca about the other.

"This is strictly a cash deal for him," said Clemens. "He and his mercenaries are in the pocket of the land companies. That, or they're covert agents working for the government."

"Yes, you've deduced that for me before."

"Whatever they are, Drop Zone is here for one reason only, to get out in front of the competition and stake claims to deeper territory. Whether it's for a company or the US of A, they see this as the biggest landgrab of all time."

They could grab all the land they wanted as far as she was concerned.

At the same time, it worried her. There were twelve hundred different agendas out there, one for each man, each waiting to unfold in the days ahead. Once the men got what they wanted—land, gold, adventure, or bragging rights—her grand crusade might simply vanish into thin air.

"What about you?" she said, trying to get him off the subject of Hunter. "What do you want out of this?"

It was a stupid question. She had caught him ogling her. It knocked her off balance, not because he was grotesque or because she was supposed to be God's gift to men, but because it was so strange and so mistaken. His desire wasn't sexual, nor a matter of possession or love. That she would have recognized. Rather, he wanted a mask, a second skin. He wanted to cloak himself inside her beauty.

"I'm here to help you get what you want."

"Of course," she said. It had become a mantra. "The children."

"The children?" He shook his head no. "Sam," he whispered, as if it were their dirty secret.

He knew. Only one really counted, and that was Sam.

"Don't worry," he said. "We'll find her."

"All of them," she said. "We'll find all of them."

"Absolutely."

This was like quicksand. Enough. "Let me assure you," she said, "Mr. Hunter is every bit as dedicated to the mission as you are."

"He's using you," Clemens said.

And I am using him, she didn't say. *And you. All of you.*

"My husband was killed less than two months ago," she started. "My child has been stolen. I have no money or power of my own. What is there to use?"

Two could play the pity game, he with the remains of his face, and she with her old song and dance. It felt old anyway. Try as she had to keep Jake close, the memory of her husband had gotten sucked away in the whirl-wind of events. Close her eyes and the only image that came was Sam's face. The living trumped the dead.

Clemens grinned. He'd heard her pitch too many times. It might play well on TV and before donors and church groups, but he was immune. "Trusting Hunter is a mistake, that's all I'm saying."

"I should trust you, then?"

"Not at all," said Clemens. "Doubt me, too. Doubt every damn one of us."

"I can't do that," she said. "I am already too alone."

"It's a different kind of alone, Rebecca. You're up on top of the mountain. That's why all of us have come here. To win you back from the gods."

The grandness of it—the absurd, old-fashioned, round-table chivalry—startled her. She tried to think of a reply. "I am relying on you," she said simply.

"And I am relying on you, Rebecca."

"Is there anything else I can do for you, Mr. Clemens?"

Clemens lifted one finger to the scar tissue that substituted for his lips. *Frog lips.* It was almost as if his hadal captors had been trying to create an animal from a man. She wondered, yet again, why had they taken such time on his torture? That wasn't even the question. Why had they let him live?

The way Clemens told it, he had escaped from the city called Hinnom, her destination. But in talking with others about the obstacles and dangers underground, Rebecca no longer believed his hero's tale. The hadals ruled the darkness. It seemed unlikely, no, utterly fantastic, that a crippled, bleeding, half-blind prisoner could have outrun such creatures. Which meant they must have released him. But why? What purpose did he serve for them?

"Yes?" she said.

"A smudge," he said.

"What?"

He touched the edge of her mouth and brought his nubbin of a finger away. It showed a tiny smear of lipstick.

"There," he said and stepped aside for her. As if she were his masterpiece. "I do believe you're ready for the rest of the men."

18

GUAM TO MINUS-ONE MILE

Rebecca descended ahead of her army, carrying Jake's Glock and her mother's old Bible. Not so long ago she had seen each of those things as a root of evil, and done what she could to keep them out of her house. Now she couldn't decide which gave her the greater comfort.

The elevator system from Agana, Guam, to the subterranean city of Travis Station was the newest and deepest of all the DEEP penetrators. When she was in high school, kids learned that the lowest point on earth was the Marianas Trench. Now a pod was carrying her to a city built eight hundred feet beneath that.

As the shuttle pod plunged into the earth, she met every slight jostle of air on metal with dread. *Seven miles deep.* The walls seemed to constrict. The ocean would crush them.

Clemens interrupted her terrors. "We're lucky ducks," he said to her.

"What?"

His breath smelled of cinnamon chewing gum. Somewhere he'd picked up little gold earrings for his fringed earlobes.

"Seven years ago, it took me and my film crew eight months to get where we're going this afternoon. That was eight months of rappelling down holes and floating down rivers. Eight months of claustrophobia and gut fear. Four thousand miles on foot and by boat and by rope, and with no retreat possible. Now all you need to do is sit back, take a nap, and you're there. And if you get scared, you can hop on the elevator and be back on the surface in …" He checked the brochure. "Three hours and twenty-two minutes."

Rebecca tried to staunch her headache. She hadn't slept in days. What was he going on about? How could he be so relaxed?

"It won't be this easy for long, though," he said. "The caves will blood us quick enough." He was in high spirits.

The monster is going home, thought Rebecca. How could he bear to return after what they had done to him? What lay in wait for them? *Where will we find them? What will be left?*

She closed her eyes and imagined Sam. It would end like a fairy tale. Hand in hand they would float in a pod up to the sun and flowers and live happily ever after. They could shovel the nightmare back into the dirt where it belonged.

It seemed like forever that this place had been tormenting her. She was sweet sixteen when the inner earth had first been revealed. Mankind lost its virginity the same year she lost hers, that's how Rebecca framed it. "Hell exists," the president of the United States had grimly announced on TV. Rebecca could still remember the carrot she was eating, and how the house seemed to shrink around her and the night swell against the window.

They had closed the schools for a month, and set a curfew, and, over the local bat lovers' objections, dynamited the cave entrances at Barton Springs. National Guard troops patrolled the neighborhoods at night. One afternoon her father had sheepishly brought home an assault rifle.

Not for another three years after that would the plague arrive to kill the devil in his nest. But by that time the devil had already killed her world. Her father died of a stroke, and her brother joined the army and went deep, never to return, and her mother destroyed what little remained of her sight in Bible-study classes. Then Jake had come along and married her, and Sam was born, and Rebecca had been so sure the bad days were over forever.

The DEEP pod clanged to a halt.

They had arrived at the backside of the moon. Rebecca pictured the Interior as an untouchable place a million miles away. Unbuckling her seat belt, she expected darkness and enormous quiet out there.

But when the door opened, there was light, a thousand points of light, flash cameras firing, klieg lights glaring. A sea of voices roared in at them. The media circus she had left above was waiting below.

Rebecca lifted her chin. She faced the lights. Soon enough there would be just tubular night.

Even as she gave what had become her signature salute, Rebecca was feeling for a sense of this place. Was the gravity heavier down here, the darkness darker, the air more . . . something? She drew at it, and it smelled like machine grease and sweat and electricity, like an old factory. Nothing like brimstone.

The wall of cameras and lights parted. A little girl stepped forward. Rebecca gasped. The child had golden braids. The backlight gave her a halo. "Sam?" she whispered to herself.

The girl was not Sam, of course. But she was so identical in every detail that Rebecca knew this could not be an accident. Someone had meant to rouse her shock in front of the cameras and exploit her tears. But who would stoop to such a cheap trick, and who would benefit from her tears?

The child held a bird-of-paradise flower. "Welcome down," she said with a curtsy, and handed Rebecca the flower.

Rebecca dropped to one knee and thanked the girl with a kiss and a hug, all the while searching the crowd for whoever had set her up. She didn't have to search for long. "Rebecca," bellowed a voice. "Rebecca Coltrane!" A big man came wading through the crowd.

She had never met the former U.S. congressman from Dallas, but Tommy Hardin was easy to recognize with his white teeth and blacksmith's jaw. Immediately she knew this was the skunk behind the Sam charade. His political theatrics were legend. After losing his seat over ethics charges, Hardin had famously donned a coonskin cap and told his unfaithful constituents that they could go to hell, he was going to . . . hell. And down he had come, and promptly gotten himself elected the local governor.

He started to give the dry-eyed widow a big embrace, but Rebecca evaded it with a handshake. The man had awful breath. Oddly, that cheered her. A skunk inside and out. Clasping her hand, he turned to the media.

"Welcome down, ma'am, from a fellow Texan," he boomed. "We have no bluebonnets to offer you, and this is a long way from Austin. But I do believe you'll recognize our hospitality. And tonight's barbecue sauce." His eyes actually twinkled. How did he do that?

"On behalf of my men," she said, "thank you for taking us in, putting us up, and speeding us on our way."

"If there is anything more we can do for you here in Travis Station . . ." He bowed his head humbly. In fact, there was a lot more he could do. People might call him "governor," but everyone knew him as a common warlord. His security force—some termed it a death squad—was well armed, well paid, and ruthless. It was also unavailable for rescuing children.

Rebecca had asked him once, in the early days, for military aid. She could have asked him again, in front of the world. But they had agreed to certain terms. He would allow her to pass through his city without the "exit tax" so long as she passed quickly and without incident. The last thing either of them wanted was a clash between their militias.

"Rebecca," a reporter shouted. "Even before the San Francisco incident, when a man was beaten and nearly burned to death, critics were calling your followers a mob of vigilantes. Are you afraid of what your own army might do down here?"

Microphones thrust at her like a gangbang. Rebecca felt her fingers getting squeezed and looked down at the little blond Sam double. The horde was frightening her. She could have sent the girl off to her mother or father, wherever they were waiting. But on second thought, she bent and gathered the child up onto her hip.

"There, is that better now?" she whispered to the girl, who nodded yes. "Then let's talk to the people." *Disgusting,* Rebecca chided herself. But political theater seemed to be the order of the day. Armed with the blond waif, she faced the media.

"First of all, I would trust these men with my life," she drawled. Like her lipstick and combat boots, the belle-speak had become part of her stagecraft. "Am I afraid of what they might do down here? You're asking the wrong person. Ask our enemy. They'll be the ones on the receiving end."

Sound bite accomplished. And Rebecca had managed not to address the mob violence, which continued to puzzle and challenge her. Voices clamored. "How many of you are there, Rebecca?"

Every time she counted, the number changed. Volunteers kept pouring in, though not as fast as the disenchanted and homesick had started leaving. Hunter labeled them deserters, but Rebecca saw them as guys with big hearts and soft spines. Reality had caught up with the testosterone, that was all. Plus it was Bowl season.

"How many?" she said. "More than Haddie bargained for."

"Do you have any idea where you're going?"

"Into the enemy's heartland. We are in hot pursuit of the enemy."

"On this issue of hot pursuit . . ." A woman with hard eyes stepped forward. "Yesterday *USA Today* ran an editorial condemning your volunteer army as a dangerous precedent. From now on any nation can justify a war of conquest by sending so-called volunteers in so-called hot pursuit of anyone they label an enemy."

Hardin stepped forward. "That was quite a mouthful," he said. "Was there a question hiding in there, or do you work for *USA Today*?"

There was a smattering of uneasy laughter.

"I'd like a response," said the woman. She added, "From the general herself."

The honeymoon is over, thought Rebecca. She wasn't surprised. The press had been far too cozy with her for far too long. She had read the *USA Today* editorial and happened to agree with every word in it. But she couldn't afford to say so.

"Let me be clear," said Rebecca. "We have come to take the fight to the enemy. Our enemy is not China or any other human nation. It is those who stole our children and brought slaughter into our homes. If anything, this should bind our nations together, not drive them apart."

"Can you tell us, please, what percentage of your army is composed of members of the U.S. military?"

"There are no active-duty troops in our ranks," said Rebecca.

"None?"

Clearly the woman knew something about Hunter and Drop Zone, Inc., and probably a lot of other things that Rebecca suspected, too. "None," she said.

"Have you had contact with the vice president's office?" the woman asked.

Rebecca didn't confirm it, she didn't deny it. "From top to bottom," she said, "the government agencies treat me like their crazy aunt."

"Meaning what?"

"They want me to stay in the attic where the neighbors can't see me. But here I am in the basement."

Smiles all around. They had the fever. Rebecca was sick of it. Sick of the bloodlust. Sick of her face on TV and the covers of magazines. Sick of living in the skin of this other woman she had become. She wanted peace, but first she had to make war.

A famous war correspondent with sagging jowls was next. "Before boarding ship in San Francisco, a number of your followers burned the Institute of Human Studies. And yet you met with its director, Alexandra Von Schade, and asked for her help just a month earlier. Is it fair to say that she rejected you?"

Rebecca's headache came back. "Ali and I had tea and cookies. She lost a child years ago, so she understood what this feels like. She also knows how dangerous it can be down here. She declined to come with me. That was it. She wished me well. I'd like to believe we are friends."

"So she gave you no information?"

"She said I was looking in the wrong places."

"Meaning she must know the right place?"

Rebecca listened carefully. He was fishing for something more than a riot motive. "Meaning she told me to go home."

"And she didn't mention to you where she was heading?"

"Where she was heading?"

"Her expedition."

"I'm sorry. What expedition are we talking about?"

"They went under three days ago."

Rebecca's heart jumped.

"Where they inserted, what their destination is, how many of them went . . ." The reporter shrugged. "She said nothing about this?"

Suddenly Rebecca was able to forget the yellow ribbons and bumper stickers, the White House and its back channels, the bagmen from the land and mining and rail and oil companies, the factions in her army, and all the rest of it. Ali was on her side. She was not alone in this wilderness of men. "Not a word."

"Ladies and gentlemen," Hardin interrupted. "It is time for us to adjourn and for our guests to relax before their journey."

That night she went to the governor's mansion for barbecue. The house was built of limestone and wood, in the Hill Country style. Sitting on a cliff overlooking the city, it had a rooster weather vane and a Lone Star flag.

Hardin gave her the tour. Rebecca strolled across the quarter acre of AstroTurf with her plate of ribs and coleslaw and a bottle of Black Diamond beer from the local brewery. A waterfall issued from the wall, feeding a stream stocked with trout for fly-fishing. The groundskeeper had created a golden "horizon" with filters and a spotlight.

"That's a pretty sunset," said Rebecca.

"It's supposed to be the dawn," said Hardin. "A new day is rising down here, Rebecca. A fresh start for those who are willing to reach out and grab for it. Have you thought about returning here after this is all over?"

"Here?"

"With your daughter. You should think about coming back."

In short order she knew all about his recent divorce and his vision of building an empire along the lines of the early Texas Republic. "Everywhere you go down here, it's terra incognita," he said. "A person only needs to put his name on a thing or a place and it's his to keep."

Tomorrow morning they were boarding the rail that led to the farthest edge of the frontier, beyond which lay the wild caves and Hinnom. Rebecca wanted nothing more than to get away from this pumped-up Sam Houston clone and go to bed. Luckily, she could not think of the proper excuse to leave.

The governor was going on about self-rule versus annexation by the United States, and his prospects for a subterranean presidency someday, when his butler approached. "A gentleman has asked to see Ms. Coltrane," he said.

"Damn it, Robert," said Hardin, "I told you the lady needs a night off."

"This is important," said Robert.

"I'm sure he thinks so."

"It's important, sir." Robert held out a shoe box. But to Rebecca, not his boss.

There was a doll inside. It looked like something from the garbage, a dirty, armless Barbie with no clothes. Most of its long hair had melted. Rebecca lifted it out, mystified.

On the back someone had scratched "HELP."

The box fell from her hand.

"What in Jesus' name is this?" Hardin demanded. He took the doll, full of suspicion. In his hands, with his flair for the con, it almost seemed a hoax. But it wasn't. It was too sorry a thing to be made up.

"He said he found it on the trail," said Robert.

"Yeah, and my father's the Dalai Lama."

"I'll talk to him," said Rebecca.

Hardin sucked his teeth. "All right, bring the man over. We're going to get to the bottom of this."

The butler returned with a trim man dressed in Spartan fashion, Levi's with a white T-shirt. He was shorter than Rebecca, and clean. His pants bore a hand-sewn patch. He took care of himself. But his eyes had a haunted look.

"Name," said Hardin, the old warhorse of a lawyer and politician.

"Beckwith."

Hardin brandished the Barbie doll. "What's this supposed to mean?"

Beckwith looked at Rebecca. "It's clear enough, isn't it?"

"'Clear' is not the word I was thinking of," said the governor. "This is about as mean-spirited as it gets."

Beckwith ignored him. "I was looking for them," he said to Rebecca. "This was jammed into a crack."

"I've had my men scouring the tunnels for a week for any sign of the children," said Hardin. "I'm talking dogs, biosensors, missing posters, reward offers. Add it up and they covered over a thousand tubular miles. Mr. Beckwith, there was nothing out there."

Rebecca took the doll from Hardin. The Barbie doll wasn't a gavel. "Where did you find this?"

"Not far beyond the Green Barrens."

That stopped her cold. Green Barrens meant massacre. It had entered the lexicon of My Lais and Wounded Knees. If not for the Green Barrens bloodshed, Rebecca might not even be here. Special ops would have stayed in the field. They might have found the children by now.

Hardin quit his grandstanding. "What were you doing at the Green Barrens?"

"I was there." That was the haunt in his eyes. "I killed people. I shot children."

"Who are you?" said the governor. "You're the deserter. You're a wanted man."

Beckwith faced Rebecca. He waited for her judgment.

She had not the slightest doubt of his guilt. Everything about him fit, the flat stomach, the self-control, the need to confess. Rebecca did not believe in signs. But she accepted—completely and instantly—his appearance at the beginning of her journey as ordained.

Here was her missing link. Ali was wrong. The children were heading to Hinnom. "Did you go into the city?" she asked.

"I was going," he said. "Then I found the doll."

"Why did you come back?" *Without my daughter.*

"I was alone. So I came for more help, and heard what you're doing and where you're going, and here I am."

The Barbie doll made more sense coming from this man than if she had found it herself. He was in pain. He was presenting himself for her to use. She would use him.

"We leave first thing in the morning," she said to him.

"This man is wanted by the FBI," Hardin said. "He's a war criminal."

"This man is with me," Rebecca said. "He risked everything to come in, and I need him for what I'm going to do. And if you interfere with him, Governor, I swear I'll kill you."

Hardin double-chinned and snorted. But he didn't retort.

Beckwith merely closed his eyes in thanks.

19

DIALOGUES WITH THE ANGEL, NUMBER 6

"I have been dancing with your ancestors ever since you came down from the trees," says the angel.

They pause in front of a grotesque brute, part man, part something else with its fleshy nub of a tail. It hangs from the wall, stabbed onto a rocky spike. "This one I treated like a king because I was sure he was the one who would lead me out of here. But he had a mind made of mud. He and his people were just another dead end. I had no choice but to put them aside and wait for something better."

They move on through the corridors of bodies.

"Each and every one of them represented a new hope to me. Some were brought to me in chains by hunters whom I'd trained. Some were led here by my whisperings. And some, like you, had the daring to seek me out. All have been disappointments."

The Collection, as the angel calls it, would put any medical college or anthro lab to shame. Very eclectic. Then again, he has been acquiring specimens for over a thousand centuries.

Mutants of every kind hang next to perfect gods and goddesses with limbs in golden proportion, every detail a keeper. Skeletons and skulls sport all manner of subterranean deformities. Many of the bodies have been cured over natural heat vents, or been salted, stuffed, or mummified in the Egyptian tradition. A number have been preserved in amber or different colors of flowstone. Every species and race of mankind seems to be represented here, including beings the disciple had never really considered to be man.

"Monsters," says the angel.

He pauses to stroke the exquisite bare torso of a tall Chinese mummy impaled very precisely through the vagina on a stalagmite. In life she must have been a princess or a ballerina, surely. Her skin gleams like porcelain. The angel's hands cup her dried leather breasts. They were lovers, obviously.

"Do you know what I mean when I say that word 'monster'?" says the angel.

"That we are horrible and must be destroyed, Lord."

"Horrible? Far from it. You and all your ancestors, even the ugliest of them, are made in my image."

"Lord." The disciple dares to speak. "You call us monsters, but say that we are made in your image. Doesn't that make you a monster, too?" The disciple has grown more reckless, accepting that one day soon he will be joining these trophies.

"Good." The angel's white eyes study him. "You see a contradiction. But that is only because you don't understand. The word 'monster' derives from the Latin monstrum, which grew from the root monere, meaning to show or reveal. Or warn. I once explained this to a Spanish monk named Isidore. Back then I felt a kinship with men like him, because I am the original monk, which means alone. But Isidore got only part of my instruction right. He wrote that what is monstrous reveals a prime origin. Then he bollixed the rest of it by mixing in God's will and Christian design and his devil nonsense." The angel sighs. "You see, it's not only the body of man that has needed seasoning over the ages, but also man's mind."

They stroll farther, stopping before this or that old favorite. Bones lie gathered, catacomb style. Bodies hang like sides of beef, or stand propped along the wall, or lie where time has toppled them.

"If I am your demon," says the angel, "then you are my author. Because I am anonymous unless you recognize me. If you see evil in me, it is only because you needed a release from your own evil. In which case, my salvation lies in you forgiving your fictions and legends. But if, on the other hand, I am your author, then you are the demon. Because you have rebelled against me. In which case, your salvation lies in me forgiving you."

The angel sets a row of dangling bodies rocking, like balls on strings. Cause. Effect. Cause. Effect.

"Tell me," says the angel, "which of us is the real monster, and which the creator, you or me?"

"*Perhaps we are both things at the same time, Lord.*"

"*Clever. But false. Either the writer writes the book, or the book writes the writer. Which is it?*"

"*Sensei, I have no idea.*"

"*I know.*"

The angel lingers in front of a Neanderthal woman covered with an arabesque of scars and tattooing. Her eye sockets have been filled with turquoise balls. Her gaze is a lovely blue. "*Casparina.*" He speaks, practically summoning her. Another of his lovers. He seems to be inviting her to speak to him. The disciple hears only the whispering cave breeze.

"*There is nothing more dangerous than one's own creation,*" the angel tells him. "*The monster that squeezes out from our own nature is always the most deadly one.*"

It seems an innocuous remark. Then the disciple notices her loins, torn open. He wonders to himself, a pack of dogs? But dogs in this place?

Then he sees that a strand of fetal cord hangs from her riffled womb.

It strikes the disciple. Here is why they have come to the Collection today. This is today's lesson. The angel mated with her. He mated with humankind. But then he had second thoughts. He tore his own child from the womb. That or it tore itself free and fled the father that would have destroyed it.

ARTIFACTS

THE NEW YORK TIMES
Questions for Rebecca Coltrane
"THE WARRIOR QUEEN"

Your father was a conscientious objector during the Vietnam War, and your mother ran as a Green for the Austin city council. Where did you find the inspiration to wage a war and lead an army? If you have a child, look in her eyes. God lives in there. That is my inspiration. My daughter, Sam.

But where did Rebecca Coltrane the warlord come from? Or was the warrior queen there all along? My parents were peaceniks. My husband worked on hydrogen conversion from waste. Every day Sam and I rode bicycles to the HEB for fresh produce. I woke up to NPR, drank Lactaid, practiced yoga at the Y, and worked with Amnesty International. I don't even recognize that world anymore.

Your new world seems more red meat, guns, and combat boots, a pair of which you're wearing. There is talk that the GOP has been courting you. Does that offend the flower child in you? The only thing that offends me is failure. I failed my daughter once, the night she was taken. I will never fail her again.

Would you talk about that night a little? (a long pause) It was terrible.

How about your days? What is a typical day like now? Yesterday I signed endorsement deals with Nike and PowerBar, spoke to Congress, and met with a literary agent. Then I had breakfast. It went from there.

The life of a high-powered celebrity, as some critics have pointed out. Are you concerned that you are using your tragedy as a vehicle for self-promotion? That's a stupid question.

On a larger level, critics charge that the Coltrane Crusade is a thinly disguised surrogate for the U.S. military. China has called your adventure a violation and a provocation. Other parents of missing children insist that the best chance of rescue lies in a United Nations coalition of forces. How do you respond? I'll be glad to talk it over with them on my way back up, once I find my daughter and their children.

20

CHRISTMAS

Ali ran beside the ink-black lake.

The daily runs had begun shortly after Maggie's death, as a way to cope. Of late, she ran to fend off the widening hips. This morning it was all about momentum.

Early morning was her habit. She was used to tunneling into the darkness with her light. But this darkness differed from up top. Here you never reached the dawn.

Her light bobbled as she struggled with the sand. Images jumped: sand, then water, then blackness. It was giving her vertigo. She was giving herself vertigo. *Where are you going? What are you doing?*

The blackness and silence pulled at her. It was like falling. Ever since the night of the mob, she had been falling. In the space of a single week, she and Gregorio had made their preparations, flown north to Alaska, and penetrated via Kiska Island in the Aleutian chain.

Today was their third day down. A sort of pony express of electric golf carts had transported them and their gear this far. The "highway," a two-hundred-mile ribbon of asphalt, dead-ended at Emperor Lake. From here on, the way got wilder.

Ali turned and headed back to the settlement.

It was not too late to go home. No one would notice. No one would care. Except for a few of her staff, no one even knew they were down here. But with her institute in ashes, Ali felt almost disembodied. Descending into the underworld had a sort of logic.

The stink of rotting fish reached out from the grandly named Port Dylan, population forty-two. Ali slowed to a walk. The village was a hodgepodge of bright red and yellow Rubbermaid storage sheds that served as houses. Cheap and durable, the units were surreally cheery. Flat-fish, eels, and squid hung everywhere. It could have been laundry day, with all the whites out drying on lines and wires.

Emperor Lake was the largest freshwater body on earth, subterranean or otherwise, and the sole source of "glass," or "ghost," lobsters. For the moment, they were all the rage in high-end restaurants, the latest of the New World's strange delights. Japanese gourmands ate them raw. Every-body else boiled them. The lobsters were all but invisible until they went into the pot, where their shells turned a faint turquoise. Sooner than later diners would move on to the next fad, and Ali wondered how Port Dylan would survive.

She found her hut. Gregorio was sitting on the floor watching a small television, its screen so dim it was like watching shadows. They were in the land of low lux now. Night vision ruled here. "Good, Alexandra, you're back," he said. "The boatman is ready for us. But first, look."

It was a FOX news piece. The last of Rebecca's crusaders was waving his gun. He threw a kiss at the sun, and entered the penetration complex on Guam. Big speakers were blaring "Born in the USA." Yellow ribbons were tied to the palm trees. According to the reporter, the expedition numbered almost thirteen hundred men.

Ali remembered the tunnels Rebecca would be traveling through to reach the city of Hinnom. There were bottlenecks and potholes where only one person could pass at a time, a river to float, and ancient bridges near collapse. Rebecca's army would be strung days and miles apart, a ser-pent whose tail would probably never meet its head. The geographical challenges aside, Ali could not imagine how Rebecca meant to feed so many stomachs three times a day.

They finished packing their gear, and lugged it to a big black Zodiac raft at the water's edge. Its captain wore a Speedo swimsuit, flip-flops, and a beard. Shells and coins dangled on a string around his neck. A rifle lay by the engine. "Good morning," said Ali.

"Let's get this done," the man said. No one smiled in Port Dylan. Peo-ple spoke in whispers, "so as not to disturb the lake." Melancholy hung in the air. She blamed their isolation and the darkness, and couldn't wait to quit the place.

They loaded their gear and Ali climbed in. She opened her notebook on her knees. And sighed.

John Li's journals and map had burned to ash in the Studio fire. When they left he was still in a coma. And with NASA documents about his expedition around Emperor Lake classified, Ali and Gregorio were madly improvising. In short, they had only their memory of someone else's descriptions and maps and memory to guide them.

As best they could remember, the far side of Emperor Lake held the most promise. There Li had found the alephs in abundance, along with Ike's carved initials. But as Ali was fast learning, the lake was next to impassable. It was huge and full of unknowns. The NASA team had taken two years to make the first and only circumnavigation, leapfrogging along the shore in boats. The lost children, if they were down here, didn't have that kind of time.

Ali tried again with the captain. She flipped to a page in her notebook. "I did some calculations last night," she said. "If we take extra fuel and cut straight across the lake, it will save us months."

"First off," the captain said, "cut straight across to where? You don't have a clue where you're going. Second off, only fools go out on the open water. Third, they don't come back. So, my answer's the same as last night. Missionary Point, no farther."

"The children's lives could depend on us. We have to get across the lake."

"Go around it like your friends."

"We'll pay you extra."

The captain looked at her. "Something lives out there."

"Your sea serpent," said Gregorio.

"Joke away," said the captain.

If he wouldn't take them across, they would have to take themselves. "We'll buy your boat," said Ali. "How much?"

"She is my boat," said the captain.

"It's old," said Gregorio. "Look at all these patches. Take our money. Go buy a new one."

That did it. "Mister," the captain hissed.

Ali quickly said, "Missionary Point. That will do."

The captain started the engine. He guided the Zodiac around a reef of twisted sodium forms, like melting statues of Lot's wife, and opened the throttle. The lights of Port Dylan faded away. "Did you ferry the NASA expedition down the coast?" asked Ali.

"Me and everybody else down here. For a ways. They hired every boat in town. Throwing money around. Full of big purpose." The captain gave a nod. "My wife ran a boat in those days."

A wife, good. "What does she do now?" What kind of life did a settler's wife lead in the caves, on a silent lake that never saw the dawn? What kind of life might Ali have led with Ike if they had returned to the depths together?

The boatman spit—carefully—keeping his head back from the water. Ali noted that. She brought her hand in from the rubber hull. "Tends the kids," he said. "Down at the point."

He had children then, but would not help find these others. Ali dropped it. The man had his reasons. Maybe his wife had taken the kids and run off with another man. Maybe she had just run off to be away from this sullen captain in a Speedo suit.

Ali ran her finger down a short list of names that she and Gregorio had managed to remember from the NASA map. "Have you ever heard of these places?" she said, and read the names.

"Graveyards," said the captain.

"What do you mean by that?"

"There's no one left."

"But we have a friend from the NASA expedition who said—"

"That NASA bunch," he said, "they came before it happened, before the invasion."

Gregorio and Ali traded a glance. "The hadals came this way?" said Ali.

The captain shook his head no. "Migrants," he said. "The fucking migrants. Every month. All the time. Edging closer. The drift, we call them. Missionary Point today. Port Dylan tomorrow, or next year. There's no way to stop them."

"Are you talking about Asian settlers?"

"They're all kinds. Everything. We thought they'd go back where they belong. But that's not happening."

An equal-opportunity bigot. "We're all migrants down here, aren't we?" said Ali.

The captain squinted. "Lady," he said, "you don't know shit."

Gregorio bristled, her paladin with his black eyes and stitches from the mob. Ali put her hand on his knee. With a grunt he looked off into the darkness.

The water slid by. Their light chased across the black mirror of the lake. Miles passed.

"Is this the same way you brought the NASA team?" Ali asked.

"Same lake. Same shore. Same boat."

"Did you meet someone named John Li? Or one of his teammates, Bill McNabb? We think McNabb came through here alone."

"Why bother learning their names? We figured they were dead men."

"They made it back, though," Ali said. "They went all the way around the lake."

"Half," said the captain. "Only half made it out is what I heard. Besides which, that was then, and this is now."

"Meaning what?"

"They only had to deal with accidents and bad luck. It's different anymore. Now you have the drift."

His migrants again. "Maybe one of them saw the children," said Ali.

"Maybe one of them *is* the children," said the captain.

"How do you mean?"

"You're wasting your time out here," the boatman said.

"Not if we can find them."

"They'll find you, don't worry. Leave them alone, that's my advice. Steer clear."

"The children need our help, though. Surely you understand. You're a father."

"Not anymore."

"In your heart, I meant."

"That's what they eat," said the captain. "You've got to guard against them or they'll eat your heart."

Ali didn't pursue it. The colonists had a reputation for strange behavior. "Odd runs deep" ran the expression. If you weren't a little off before you came down, you got there soon enough. Living among sea serpents and pale, joyless comrades and glass lobsters, it was no wonder the captain was so peculiar.

They rode in silence for the next few hours. Then lights began to dance in the distance. "Missionary Point," said the captain.

Ali spied a thin beach beneath a cliff. The bay looked like a graveyard for boats. Only a few had been pulled out of the water. They passed the snout of a kayak that had capsized and partially sunk. The rest of the jumble of rafts and boats bobbed up and down as the boatman threaded between them. Their hulls squeaked and clacked softly against each other.

The captain ran his Zodiac onto the sand and cut the engine. Immediately he hopped out and started grabbing for their gear. This was the most energy Ali had seen in him.

Ali got out and played her light up the cliff. A trail wound up the side.

"Who do we talk to about buying a boat?" she asked the captain.

"Take one. Help yourself. There's a good one over there."

"You mean steal it?"

"They'll never notice. Hell, take two, one for each of you, Jack and Jill."

He tossed the last of their bags onto the sand and shouldered his boat back into the water. Ali had a thought. "You said your wife is here."

"If she's still alive."

A heart of stone, this man. "What's her name?" At least they could have that much entrée.

"Susannah." The captain hopped in and yanked the starter cord. Not a good-bye or a good luck: he left them on the beach. They were as dead to him as his wife was.

"Peace out to you, too, *pendejo*," Gregorio growled.

"Let's go buy a boat," Ali said.

They left their gear and climbed the winding footpath. She expected a village up where the lights were. Instead they found thirty or forty people gathered on the flat crest of the cliff. They were crowded together, living in the open. No one noticed her or Gregorio.

The ledge jutted like a great prow into the lake. There were no buildings, no tents, not even sheets or pads for sleeping, just this mass of people standing or sitting or kneeling. They were singing in drones, all different songs, or murmuring to themselves, watching, all faced out to the darkness. Waiting, it seemed.

"This feels bad," Gregorio said.

"Bad?"

"Weird."

She looked at his purple-and-white-striped rock-climber tights and "Reelect Pedro" T-shirt, and remembered his cell phone with a frog's mating cry. Weird? "We'll only be a few minutes."

"Let's leave." His hackles were up.

"First we need a ride."

"Steal a boat, like the man said."

"Not a good attitude," she said.

Ali went out on the ledge. It smelled of human sewage and rotten fish and something sweet. The people there were like refugees gathered to weather a flood. Those with lights went on wagging them at the far darkness, whether beckoning or warning Ali couldn't tell. Some were smiling, some humming hymns, some holding photos. A few held aloft lighters with little tongues of orange flame licking at the night. All faced out to the lake.

"Excuse me," she said to a woman clutching a rosary. The shoulder of her dress was coming unraveled.

Like a blind woman, the rosary lady groped for Ali's face. The moment her fingers touched Ali, she recoiled. "Wrong," she said, and turned back to the lake.

Ali frowned and went on. She stepped over a man asleep on his side. Then she saw he was dead. Mouth open, eyes staring, he lay uncovered in their midst.

Ali backed away, shocked, and bumped against a man dangling his legs over the edge. She staggered back from the cliff side.

"Almost lost you there," the man said with a British accent. "Pull up a seat."

The Brit was emaciated, with long, oily strings for hair, but quite jolly. He continued flashing short and long bursts of light out across the water in some private semaphore. He had to be aware of that corpse. It lay only a few feet behind him and the smell was overpowering.

"You're new here," the Brit said. His eyes were glassy and unfocused. Were they all on drugs?

"We came from Port Dylan."

"Good news then," he said. "This is the spot. They'll be arriving any minute now."

"Who?"

"Well, who did you come for?" the man asked.

"The children," said Ali.

"Good, good." The Brit winked. "Then your children are on their way. Have a seat."

Ali looked across the water as far as their feeble lights reached, and there was only the inky stone night. No flotillas of rafts and boats sailing in from the recesses. No children. Nothing.

"How long have you been here?" Now she saw other bodies lying at their feet.

"We've conquered time," he said.

"There's a dead man right behind you," she said.

"Conquered death, too," he said.

She didn't see any food. "Aren't you hungry?"

"That's just your stomach talking, don't you think?" The man flipped his hand dismissively. "Once they come, everything's right with the world again. You'll see."

His serenity was eerie and regal and terrible. These people were wasting away in their own filth and starvation. Those boats floating in the bay were never going to be used again.

She glanced out at the lake. "Who are you waiting for?"

"Me? My wife. The others, they have their own priorities."

Ali looked around her at the starved faces. Few had any fat still left on them. It was a form of collective delusion. Had they shared some toxic meal, or drunk something in the water? Had their ghosts driven them mad? Or was this the local dump for the insane? "Who looks after you?"

"Don't be afraid." The Brit smiled. "Have a seat."

"We need a boat," she said.

But the Brit had tuned her out. He was slowly waving his light at the void. Ali remembered the captain's wife.

"Susannah?" she called to the gathering. No one answered. Ali moved through the huddle. She had to step over three more bodies. If they didn't care about corpses, then they didn't care about their boats. Yet Ali felt obliged to give someone some money to make it all official. "Susannah?" she called again.

A woman's face turned. Ali went to her. "Are you Susannah?"

Susannah had a dazed smile. From the waist up, she was nude. "I don't know you," she said.

"My name is Ali. Your husband brought us here."

"Jason? The children ask for him. Is he here?"

"He had to leave," she said. "He told me you have children."

"Seven years old, that's Jacob. The two girls are three."

"I don't see them, Susannah."

"They went to look for Daddy," Susannah confided. "I told them where to find him. They miss him so bad. It's awful, their weeping and howling. Go find him, I said."

The stench of death and unwashed bodies and human waste alarmed Ali. "I'm searching for children," she said. "They were stolen from their homes."

"Wait here," Susannah said. "Just wait."

It was the same lotus-eating advice that the Brit had offered. "This is urgent," said Ali.

"Have faith," Susannah said.

"They need our help," Ali said.

"Oh, not anymore. It's so beautiful. Believe me. They're safe now."

"Susannah," said Ali. She gripped the bare, bony shoulder and gave a gentle shake. "We need to find these children."

"No you don't. They'll find you."

"The children were stolen by hadals," Ali said.

Susannah only smiled at her. "Mine went out on the lake," she said.

Ali didn't want to be here anymore. "We need a boat, Susannah. Do you have a boat? I'll buy it."

"The children took it," Susannah said. Her tranquillity muddied for a moment. A measure of sanity bubbled to the surface.

"They took your boat?" A seven-year-old and his two little sisters? *To look for Daddy.* "They went out on the lake?"

"I don't know what got into their heads," said Susannah. "Two years ago. We searched. Finally they came floating home, one by one. I pulled them out of the water with my own hands."

The moist breeze felt cold suddenly. "What happened, Susannah?"

"The boat must have tipped. Maybe it sank. The lake took them. It erased their little faces and eyes. But I knew it was them. One, two, three." The terrible memory twisted her features.

Ali could hardly breathe. "You lost your children?"

"Ah," said the woman, as if stabbed. Then the madness took over again. Her pain lifted. "We're together again. They found me. Bless their little souls."

Ali stared at the woman, then around at the others, all signaling to their dead. The drift. *Migrants.* Memories. *Guard against them.*

Someone hooted. The crowd was stirring. People pressed forward.

"They're coming!"

Ali threw a look at the lake's empty blackness and shuddered. She retreated from the ledge. Gregorio stood up. Ali could not quit shaking. He looped one arm around her. "Did they sell you a boat?"

"The captain was right," she said. "We have to help ourselves."

They chose a good, stout Zodiac. Gregorio checked its engine. While Ali loaded in the supplies, Gregorio went from one boat to another and siphoned fuel into cans.

As they pulled out of the bay, Ali glanced up at the twinkling lights on the cliff's edge. For a moment she could have sworn she heard voices spilling in over the bow from the open water and far distances. But it had to be carrying out from those poor lunatics on Missionary Point. She made a nest for herself next to the engine, and after a while its noise brought her peace.

ARTIFACTS

THE LOS ANGELES TIMES

China Submarine Grounds on California Coast

Dec. 26. Santa Cruz. A Chinese submarine loaded with nuclear missiles grounded on the beach at Santa Cruz, California, yesterday. Its entire crew was captured and the submarine is now in U.S. custody.

President Burr has called on Americans not to panic. "The missiles have all been secured," he stated. "There is no danger that the submarine might explode."

The submarine apparently rammed ashore at full speed, sending surfers flying. According to eyewitnesses, Chinese crew members emerged shaken, disoriented, and very frightened. Several were armed, but held their fire upon seeing the amusement park. The captain is reportedly being held at a hospital, on the psychiatric wing, and is under a round-the-clock suicide watch.

The submarine now sits beached in Monterey Bay for all to see from a distance. Military specialists are poring over the vessel, a new diesel-powered attack submarine of the Yuan class.

"This is a major disaster for China," said David T. Shamling, a China specialist at the Rand Corporation. "Their most advanced submarine, one that has been photographed just once, and then only from space, has fallen into American hands at exactly the wrong time for China. Just as China is making threats about the Green Barrens massacre, her best and brightest come crashing onto our shores armed and ready for nuclear war."

21

NINE HUNDRED FEET BENEATH THE BERING SEA FLOOR

Ali and Gregorio followed the lake's mute shore, moving from one deserted settlement to another by boat. Now and then they passed some gaunt man or woman standing beside the water, looking out expectantly, waiting with infinite, lunatic patience.

Off one spit of land, they spied a man's head floating on the water. Drawing closer, they realized the rest of him was mired neck deep in the lake. They shined their light at him, and Gregorio almost fell overboard when the man blinked. He was still alive. When Ali called to him, he moved his lips in that mindless way they had seen at Missionary Point. They left him standing in the water, food for the fishes.

Fearing a virus might be responsible for the dementia, they purified their water religiously, stuck to their own rations, and did not eat the fish. The only times they landed was to plunder empty boats for more fuel.

They settled into a routine, one of them piloting the boat while the other slept. In that way they could stay on the move almost constantly.

Gregorio woke Ali from her doze. "We're coming to another village," he said. He nosed the boat into a cove, spotlighting its beach and outcrops and the terraces with huts, searching for any dangers.

"More bones," said Ali.

Gregorio swept the light left. Half buried in sand, a human rib cage stood at the water's edge. The desolation and bones were no longer spooky, just wearying. Ali watched him watching for danger, his black eyes glittering.

Life aboard the Zodiac had grown electric. When she slipped off straps or opened buttons to take her little bird baths, he would busy himself to comic agitation. While he slept, and she was supposed to be steering the boat, her disobedient eyes would go roaming over him. But the ghost of Ike hung over them.

Gregorio idled a safe distance from shore, his pistol ready. A long hump of shells glistened on the beach. Four boats stood on the water like horses at a hitching post. The stone buildings were long and low, built by hadals thousands of years ago and borrowed, for a brief while, by squatters with no lasting power.

Finally he decided. "Empty. We are safe." And took them to shore.

Ali climbed down, careful not to stick herself on any broken bones. "I'm going for a look," she said.

"Take the gun."

"There's no one here, Gregorio. Keep the gun."

They had talked about this. There were only two of them, neither trained in the war arts. No amount of weaponry could insulate them from a hadal menace. They were better off relying on their strengths: her languages, his flute. They had come to negotiate a peace, or at least the release of the children, not to blow up the place.

Ali took off with long strides, working out the kinks. She picked up several of the shells. One species had stripes identical to the banded colors of a rainbow, violet at the bottom, red on top. *How extraordinary,* she thought. *First that a thing evolving in darkness should have any color at all, and second that it should mimic the spectrum of light with such blind precision.* She held the shell up to her lamp beam.

Out of the blue, Ali recalled a certain rainbow after a summer thunderstorm. Maggie had been two then. They had lain on a blanket on a hill, oohing and ahing at the rainbow's colors. Abruptly the memory shifted. She was reading *The Rainbow Fish* to Maggie in bed. It shifted again. This time she and Maggie were drinking hot chocolate, listening to the Cowboy Junkies. And painting rainbows.

Ali dropped the shells. She threw the rainbow away from her. The memories faded.

The association was happening more frequently since their arrival at Emperor Lake. It disturbed her. Maggie kept materializing from nowhere, almost real enough to hold. Sometimes the memories were moored to the present, as with the rainbow shells. Other times, it seemed Maggie was calling to her from a distance, not with her three-year-old voice, just a voice, a Maggie voice.

Ali had come within a hair of reentering the convent after the funeral, thinking maybe she should find God again. Instead she had founded the institute and thrown herself into researching the devil and his dark civilization. If she could tease out of that savagery some ray of sunshine, then . . . then what? Then maybe she could discover mercy in God's infinite cruelty toward them? The danger had always been that she might hold the hadals too close, that she might learn to love them. Now there was this new risk, that she might hold her memories too close.

She had been so sure the remembering was laid to rest. But the darkness bred yearning. *Sleep, baby,* thought Ali. *I love you. That's all I can do for you anymore.*

Gregorio caught up with her. "Alexandra, why do you get so reckless? Stay with me. Or let me stay with you."

"You said the place was empty."

"But what if I was wrong? Something could be in here."

"I would know," she said.

"How?"

I would smell them. I would hear them. And it was true. Her senses were growing more acute every day. The abyss was taking her in once again. But she did not tell Gregorio, because it frightened her, the gifts of this place, the temptations. The cave could sweep you away in an instant. Ike was proof of that.

They cast through the village, poking their lights here and there. Where the roofs had fallen apart, Ali peeped over the tops of walls. The settlers' possessions spoke of minds slowly unraveling. Clothing lay scattered and rotting. Photographs, newspapers, books, and discs had been thrown madly into the air and left where they lay. She rooted through their leavings, mystified.

After the Interior's discovery fifteen years ago, pioneers had descended to a handful of fortress "cores" built on blueprints for proposed lunar or Martian colonies. The NASA connection again. But the hadals had still been active back then, choking off expansion. Settlers rarely ventured farther than a day's reach of the fortified centers. Indeed, until the Helios expedition that had given her Ike, "deep exploration" was limited to timid short-range forays by miners, scientists, and military patrols. Then came the plague—released by someone on the Helios expedition—and the Interior had been evacuated. The settlers who refused to leave had died along with the hadals. That had marked the end of the first wave.

The second wave had begun two years later. Emboldened by the subterranean "extinction event" (Ali detested the sterility of that term . . . it had been an outright genocide), people came pouring down from the surface. Lured by promises of wealth, a fresh start, or amnesty for crimes, or forcibly sent by their governments, the new surge of colonists had spread like weeds from the old core cities. But the boom was going bust.

Beneath the continents and oceans, but especially in this faraway region under the Pacific Ocean, the frontier was suffering major declines in population. The experts cited any number of reasons for the "correction," from pioneering fatigue to cancer scares, localized deformities, and D2, or "darkness depression." More and more settlers were complaining of sleeping disorders, bad dreams, and social withdrawal, all to be expected when your body clock goes haywire from sun loss.

But Ali was beginning to think something else, entirely different, might be to blame, something systemic. Back in the final decades of the twentieth century, man had slashed his way into the deepest jungles, only to be felled by lurking viruses: HIV, Ebola, Marburg, and others. Surely the Interior held its own menagerie of natural defenses. Could that explain the desertion and die-off she was seeing here? Was the cave simply reacting to human trespass?

Running her light along a stone wall, Ali found dozens of little tubes of white paper sticking from the joints. In the first village it had been remarkable. By now the private wailing walls were a dime a dozen. She pulled a tube loose and unrolled it, already knowing what it would describe. The voices. Always the voices.

"Trina came again yesterday," she read. "And Dad! We talked. They tell me their names and remind me of things. Trina used to brush her hair a hundred times. It was like counting gold. She wants me to remember. That's what they need me for, I think. I am their island. They can rest with me before going back onto the water."

Ali let it flutter to the ground. Gregorio was more reverent, rolling up each scrap of paper and sticking it back into the wall. "Anything?" she said.

"Words and scribbles," he said. "Notes from the underground, the same as in the other villages. This one heard voices. This one saw ghosts. It's all the same. Craziness. Alexandra, I think we are chasing the wild goose."

"Keep looking," she said. "Is there any mention of the children or of hadals? Did anybody see footprints? Do they mention stolen food, disappearances, missing animals, any suggestion the hadals might have passed through?"

Gregorio turned over a metal plaque. "Ah, here, 'Welcome to Chevrolet.' Now we know what kind of car someone liked to drive."

"It's a start," said Ali, and pulled out her notebook.

They split up. Ducking into a side room, Ali found scattered papers, piles of dried feces, and in the corner a skeleton. Pieces of beard clung to his jaw. A knife lay nearby. His wrist bones rested on sand rusty with old blood. Another nameless suicide.

Gregorio appeared in the doorway and saw the bones. *Now he will cross himself.* And he did, *fathersonholyghost.* Ali smiled.

"We should go back to the boat," he said. "I found more fuel and a case of food. We are done here."

Like others along the way, the village had offered up no clues for their search. Some villages had names, which she recorded in her notebook. This one would go down as Chevrolet, the Village of the Bearded Skeleton.

"Alexandra?"

"Yes?"

"I have been thinking."

Ali waited.

"If it is a disease, we may have it by now."

"Time will tell," she said.

"Yes, but if it is so, and if I am the first to go, just promise you will cover me."

"All right."

"I don't want my bones to lie naked like this."

He had given her funeral instructions at least four times in other villages. "I'll say a few words over you, too," she said.

"Yes, excellent. I will do the same for you."

"And what will you say about me?" she gaily asked. There was only so much ceremony one could stand on, and the bones didn't care if she was glum or jolly.

"Well." Gregorio tucked his chin against his chest. He exhaled deeply and pondered the bearded skeleton. "I would say about you, yes, here lies a woman ..."

"With a beard," Ali inserted. Gregorio stared at her. "He has a beard," she pointed out, "but go on."

"Here lies a woman ..." He stopped. "A woman I knew ... A woman ..." He stopped again, overcome by his eulogy.

"Just put a Purity chocolate over my heart," Ali said. "Dark, please. Those are my favorite."

"Alexandra!" He waved at the bones. "This is your death we're speaking about."

"You're right, Gregorio." She assembled a serious face.

"*Madre de Dios,*" he sighed.

Whatever he had been working himself up to say was spoiled. Not that it was so hard to guess. *I love you, too,* she thought.

"I'm going next door," he said. He knocked his head going under the doorway. "*Madre ...*"

Ali stirred a pile of paper scraps in the corner. Bits of words, mad scrawls, doodles: it looked like her trash can after a staff meeting. Her moment of good humor gave way to frustration. They were flailing. Trapped in a labyrinth of inlets and nameless villages and with the bones of lunatics, they were barely inching ahead. What they needed was a great leap forward, but to where? She could practically hear the darkness nibbling away at their noble purpose, like mice. The saviors had become scavengers.

"Alexandra," Gregorio called.

She found him next door with yet another skeleton lying at his feet. But this one was different. It bore a gift. A two-foot-long plastic cylinder rested inside the rib cage. It looked like a second spine, like something someone had stored in there. The word "NASA" ran along one side.

"It was just like that," he said. "I haven't touched it."

"Gregorio, open it. Look inside. Hurry."

He pulled the cylinder from its cage of bones and took off the cap. He peeked in and his eyes got big. "I don't believe in miracles," he said. But obviously this was one.

"Is it what I think?" she said.

He nodded.

They slid the expedition map out and unrolled it and pinned its corners with rocks. "Emperor Lake" was written in the middle of a big, blank amoeba. Its blobby arms were fringed with little names and numbers.

"The answer to our prayers," said Ali.

"It's identical to the one that burned," said Gregorio.

"Not quite," she said, quickly running her fingers over the paper. "The handwriting is different, see? And this has more information, much more. Look at all these names. And the corrections on top of corrections, and the margins full of notes."

"Did the NASA people give it to the villagers? Or did they steal it?"

"I don't know. But either way, if the villagers had it, why leave it like this, slipped inside a skeleton?"

Gregorio shrugged. "The whole village was going mad."

"Yes, but the map was left *inside* the bones, not on top. That means the body had been lying here for weeks or months. This was done after the village was dead. Whoever it was left the map for someone to find."

Ali concentrated on the marginalia. It had dates, postscripts, questions, population tidbits, and observations about the flora and fauna. At the bottom, she found a symbol. "There he is," she pointed.

Gregorio bent to see. "It looks like a lightning bolt all squashed together."

It came to her. "WM," she said. "William McNabb. Li's missing friend."

"So here he ended," Gregorio said. "In a village of madmen."

"Maybe not," said Ali, scouring the map. "By the time he got here there was nothing but bones. And he was well adapted to the territory and intent on going deeper. It's just a feeling, but I think he went on."

"Without a map? Alone? In this place?"

"We didn't have a map," she said.

"That's not the point. If we had a map, we wouldn't leave it with a dead man."

"If we knew where we were going, and the map had nothing more to tell us, then we might leave it," she said. "We might even *need* to leave it. Unless the past points to the future, you only go in circles."

"What are you talking about?"

"Here we are, at Chevrolet. And here is where we want to go." She pointed at a triangle of aleph symbols on the far side of the lake. Spreading her thumb and little finger, she compassed twice straight across the lake from point to point. Next she compassed along the meandering shoreline. It was eighteen times the distance.

"Excellent," he said. "You have proved that the shortcut is shorter."

"Now," she continued. "Look carefully. Chevrolet sticks out into the lake. There is no point closer to our destination than where we are right now. Move up the coast or down, and the distance across suddenly gets much longer."

"Yes, but without the map we would not know that."

"Agreed," she said. "Now look at the opposite shore. What landmarks do you see?"

"Except for the aleph, none. For a hundred miles to the right or left, the map is barren."

"And so, here is where we want to start across. There is where we want to go," she said. "That's why McNabb left the map, because it had no more to tell him than it has to tell us. And because it was a temptation to play it safe and stick to the shore."

"You think he took a boat across?"

"I do."

"But, Alexandra, I still don't understand. This map was his labor and love. Look at all the care he put into it. Why not take it along and continue his mapping?"

"Two reasons," said Ali. "First, the map is a message—or an invitation—to anyone who shared his quest. 'Whoever is following me, set sail from here.'"

"If that is so, then why not just leave his message written in big letters on a rock, or make an arrow pointing across the lake?"

"Because he's not inviting the whole world to follow," she said, "only those who are looking for what he was looking for, the aleph." Ali spread her hands over the map. Unmarked and inconspicuous, the aleph hid among the rest of the text.

"And the second reason he left it behind?"

"Simple," she said. "McNabb decided he was never coming back. This is his last testament."

Gregorio shined his light out the stone doorway. The light glinted upon the inky water of the lake. "The man had enough faith to go, but not come back?" he said. "What kind of man is that?"

Suddenly Ali felt frail and uncertain. She did not have enough courage for the two of them. If Gregorio wanted to turn around, she would follow him back to the surface where they belonged. But if he chose to go deeper, she would do her best to lead. She folded her hands in her lap and waited.

"You mean what kind of faith," she said.

This was not a matter of manhood. She wanted Gregorio to know that. He could walk away with his honor intact.

He slowly rolled up the map and put it in the tube, then stood.

"So now," he said, "we are supposed to follow McNabb who followed Ike who followed a mark on the wall?"

That summed it up. "Yes," she said.

"Absurd."

She agreed. "Yes."

He stood there slapping the map tube against his open palm. At last he spoke. "It may or may not kill us to go on," he said. "But it will certainly kill us not to."

She looked up. He was offering his hand.

"Let us go join the parade of fools," he said.

ARTIFACTS

THE SAN FRANCISCO CHRONICLE

Ghosts in the Machine: Chinese Sub Mystery Heats Up

Dec 29. Washington. China's ambassador to the U.S. was summoned to the State Department to explain the bizarre incident, but he refused to appear and has reportedly been recalled to Beijing. China has issued a protest over the confiscation of the submarine. Nonessential personnel are being evacuated from the U.S. embassy in Beijing after Chinese demonstrators threw stones and burned an American flag.

China has demanded the return of the submarine and its crew, and a second submarine has surfaced just outside American waters. The accident has some speculating that the Chinese crew may have been seeking political asylum.

But one eyewitness to the crash claims the Chinese captain was ranting about voices and the ghost of his dead wife before authorities took him away. Other crew members were also seen wandering on the beach, clearly dazed and talking to themselves. A medical expert said the submarine's air recycler may have malfunctioned, causing a buildup of carbon dioxide or other gases, creating mass delusions.

"The idea of an insane man commanding a submarine with nuclear weapons is truly terrifying," said an analyst with the Heritage Center. "The Chinese navy's failure to screen its officer corps for these mental problems is appalling, and criminal."

22

The angel guides his disciple to the ruins of a monastery so old its walls have grown over with pyrite crystals. The disciple recognizes the pyrite as fool's gold.

Falseness preys on truth.

They approach the foot of a hill dotted with holes. These are old meditation cells clawed from the ground by hadal acolytes. In one of them lies a man, alive and filthy and bearded and asleep.

"He arrived some time ago, a pilgrim like you," says the angel. "We had a little chat. I decided to keep him around. Ever since then, I've been sending him bugs to keep him alive. For you."

The disciple grows wary. "For me?"

"It's time for you to have a little human company, someone to play with," says the angel. "Show me your nails."

The disciple holds out his fingers. Over the years his body has absorbed the very earth. He is now able to digest some of the softer minerals. His nails have hardened to obsidian sharpness.

"Your path leads through this man," says the angel to the disciple.

The disciple feigns ignorance. "I don't understand, Rinpoche." In fact, he can guess where this is going, and it frightens him.

The angel wags a finger at him. "You do, I know you do."

"Your words are my vehicle, Lord," says the disciple. "This man is barren of teaching."

"Even the most barren doorway can lead to the palace of wisdom," says the angel. "Be strong. Remember, death is freedom."

"But, Rinpoche, you taught me never to take a life again."

"I taught you to quit wasting your time trying to take mine," says the angel. "Now, you are this man's destiny. He was born and has lived his life and made the journey here in order to serve your learning."

"Lord, I have renounced all violence. I made a vow."

"What is forbidden, do it."

"Not this, Rinpoche," whispers the disciple.

"As you said, he is nothing. He is going to die one way or another. But you can stop his suffering before it starts. Real suffering. Long suffering. At this very moment, I'm thinking of something rather Iroquois that involves heat and knives. If you'd like, I could acquaint him with his leg bones minus the skin and meat. Or perhaps I might let him play a little Oriental hide-and-seek. Have you ever seen a man pawing through his own insides, convinced a snake has gotten loose in there? You'd be surprised by how suggestible people can be."

The stranger in the hole goes on sleeping through the angel's litany of tortures.

"Show him mercy, Lord," says the disciple.

"My mercy flows through you," says the angel. "It is you who must show him mercy."

The disciple glances around. There is no escape from this. To disobey would mean his own death, no doubt a painful one. Worse, it would mean sacrificing the secrets he has learned. He resigns himself to what must be done. The hunt has brought him too far, and he has penetrated the mystery too deeply, to simply throw his life away. There is still a chance, however small, that he can take his hard-won knowledge back to the surface, and share it with man. And defeat the angel.

"On your travels through the world above, have you ever been to Mongolia?" asks the angel. "They are a Buddhist people, these peaceful descendants of savage warlords. To them every life is precious. When it comes time to slaughter a sheep, they have a special way."

The disciple steels himself.

"Straddle his hips."

The disciple crawls inside the lair. The man is little more than a gaunt, bearded scarecrow. He reeks of old sweat and fish. Insect wings litter the floor. The disciple straddles the man's belly.

"Now hold him by the throat," says the angel. "At the same time, with your nails, make an incision just below his sternum. Be quick, but be very neat. Open the skin, but not the peritoneum beneath it. We don't need sausages all over the place."

The disciple follows the instructions. His hand clasps the man's throat. At the same time, with his nails, he slices open the upper abdomen with a single motion.

The pilgrim jerks awake. His eyes bulge. He would cry out, but can't.

"Now," says the angel, "slide your hand inside. Move up between the lungs. Be assertive. The lungs will fight you like a pair of dogs."

Sure enough, the lungs clench and release and clench the disciple's hand. The man flails at him. His eyes flicker downward. He sees the horror of what is being done to him, the open wound, the arm wrist deep.

"Can you feel his heart?"

Veins stand out on the man's throat and forehead. The disciple goes slowly, his knuckles brushing the ribs. This is terrible. It is glorious. A man's life in his hand!

"Wrap your hand around his heart. Be careful not to sever anything. This is important. Thread your fingers between the tubes leading in and out. Do you have it?"

"Yes."

"Now close your grip on it. Squeeze slowly. Don't puncture the walls or collapse its chambers. Keep the blood contained."

The heart beats like a wild animal in there, slippery and desperate, something amphibious. The stranger shakes his head in horror. He doesn't understand this awful invasion. Everything happening inside his chest wall, he feels everything.

The disciple wants this to be over. He would seize that engine and tear it out, or crush the man's throat and be finished with it, but the angel's voice keeps insisting on precision and pace and care.

The disciple strains to hold the heart tight. At last it begins to surrender. The muscle weakens in his grip. The man's hands melt from his arm.

"Watch his eyes," says the angel.

The eyes stutter. The mouth forms a word. The disciple releases his grip on the bearded throat. He lowers his head to hear the man's last testament.

"Ike," the man whispers.

The disciple freezes.

The heart slows. It stops. Suddenly the disciple wants to force it back to life.

The disciple becomes aware of rocks being piled up behind him, closing off the front of the burrow. The angel is sealing him inside.

"Over the coming days, I want you to listen to him," says the angel. "I want you to learn his name, memorize his voice, gather his tales. I want to know everywhere he goes on his journeys."

"But he's dead, Lord."

"You must learn how to listen. True hearing is like true seeing. It takes time. Be patient. Fast. Meditate. Listen."

Except for a small hole, the entrance is completely blocked with rocks now.

"This is your tomb," says the angel. "You are dead to the world. When I take the rocks away, you will be alive again."

"You're leaving me in here?"

"Death is your teacher now. This pilgrim's voice will guide you upon the river of sentience. His body will teach you impermanence. Its corruption is a gift to you. See through the illusion of flesh."

"Don't leave me."

"I will visit occasionally. Now give me the heart," says the angel. "I have a need for it."

The disciple tears the heart from its mooring of vessels and pulls it out. The heart is surprisingly light for such a workhorse. He hands it through the opening in the rocks. In return, he receives several containers of water.

"Make them last," says the angel.

A moment later, the opening seals shut.

The disciple cries out.

"Patience," says the angel. "You are conquering death."

"Lord, please . . ." The disciple pushes at the rocks, but they weigh many tons. Now he has become like the angel, a prisoner inside the stone, unable to free himself. That is the lesson, or at least one of them.

"Don't forget your fast." The angel's voice filters in to him. "No snacking in there. Keep yourself pure. Eat wisdom, nothing more."

<u>ARTIFACTS</u>

SUICIDE EPIDEMIC ALERT

U.S. HOTLINES ASSOCIATION

Abduction Survivors at Extreme Risk

To all professionals and law enforcement agencies: be alert to severe depression among survivors of the Halloween abduction incident. We have now logged the seventeenth suicide by a survivor within nine weeks.

An epidemic rate of suicide is considered anything over 20 per 100,000 in a normal population. The survivor population—comprised of family and friends of the abduction victims—is around 1,000, making the suicide rate more than 100 times higher.

Several demographic factors may be occurring within individuals. Grief is the most obvious, but the survivor population is reportedly no more depressed than normal for post-death populations. The western states of the U.S. have the highest rates of suicide nationally, and most of the abductions occurred within the west. But again, comparing to the larger western states' populations, the survivor self-destruction rate is off the charts. Seasonal affective disorders (SAD), medications, mimicry, and other factors may also help explain this epidemic of suicides.

An unusually high incidence of delirium and hallucinations has been reported among the survivor population. There is no plausible explanation for this at present.

23

NEW YEAR'S EVE

Rebecca watched through the thick glass of her railroad car as they pulled out of Travis Station. Entering the frontier was like leaving history. The lights of the settlements dimmed. Things got poorer in a hurry. The land turned meaner, at an average speed of forty-five miles per hour.

As the railroad coursed deeper, the towns they passed dwindled into slums, caves, and two- and three-man camps. Rebecca asked the engineer to stop the train at the next station so that her men could stretch their legs, but he refused. "Up and down the line," he said, "no one wants your bunch of thugs and strongmen. No offense."

"But we're the cavalry," Rebecca said, trying out the argument. "We're the guys in the white hats."

"Not when you breathe their air and shit in their water and steal the food off their tables."

It was refreshing to have someone without an agenda speak so plainly to her. She had come up front to ask for the rest stop, but also to escape Clemens and Hunter, and the rock and country music, the smell of armpits and gun oil, the cigar and doobie smoke, the beeps of Game Boys, the Promise Keeper meetings, the flexing, the trash talk, the ball stats, all of it. The engineer welcomed her company.

"I admit we breathe the air and shit in the water," she said, "but we haven't stolen a thing that I'm aware of. Every step of the way, we've paid top price with U.S. dollars."

"The catch is, they like your money too much," said the engineer. "These folks out here would sell every last grain of rice to you, and they know it. Then they'd end up with a pocketful of cash and a bellyful of nothing. They don't trust themselves; how can they trust you?"

"We have our own food," she said. "And I'll tell the men to mind the local sanitation."

"That's only the beginning. You're carrying diseases from the surface. You're a whisker away from starting World War Three with China, which is ten times closer to where we live than to America. And now you're about to bust open the hornet's nest with the aboriginals."

Aboriginals, Rebecca noted. Not maggots, not demons, mushroom people, or bullet bait. Aboriginals. As if they were part of the local order. "We're here only to save our children," she said.

"These people have children, too," said the engineer. "They don't want to lose them to outsiders. Their sons would join you. Their daughters would tempt you. You're trying to save your children. They're trying to save theirs. From you."

"Once this is over, we're leaving," she said.

"But that's the worst thing of all for them," he said. "You can leave. Most of them can't. This is where they live now, for better or for worse."

"How can we bridge the gap then?"

"Are you sure you want to?" he said.

"Why not?"

"The dark has its own terms."

"How do you mean?"

"Folks change," he said. "Necessarily."

At the end of twenty-seven hours, the train pulled to a halt in a shanty-town built on ledges. "Electric City," a sign grandly announced. But all Rebecca saw were a few kerosene lanterns. Then she spied what looked like the Eiffel Tower looming above the settlement. It was a drill rig.

"Is this the end of the line?" she asked.

The engineer said, "For me."

Angling for a better sense of their chances, Rebecca tried a bit of bravado. "You might as well stick around," she said. "We're going to need a ride home before you know it."

The engineer looked at her. He started to reply, but suddenly busied himself with his levers and dials. *That bad,* she thought.

Big, armed brutes with shaggy heads milled around outside, scratching at lice, prowling the tracks, slinging guns: total barbarians. Then she recognized some of the faces. These were her men.

While her army unloaded its mountain of supplies from the train, Rebecca climbed up to the shacks and caves to introduce herself. The citizens of Electric City were wildcatters. They were drilling for HDR, or hot dry rock, "the mother of all mother lodes," as one man put it. "We're going to save mankind from itself."

The idea was to tap a bed of dry heat, pump water down, catch the superheated steam that came back up, and generate electricity. One day soon, according to several gentlemen, Electric City was going to light not only the Pacific Interior, but the whole world. Oil, coal, nuclear: all were about to become obsolete. "You're looking at the richest men in history," another driller told her.

Until they struck HDR, however, they were some of the poorest. Three years of hard labor had not generated a single penny. Determined not to go into hock to the railroad, the drilling suppliers, the banks, or anyone else, they had tightened their belts, literally, until they looked almost like prisoners of war.

Rebecca decided on the spot to invite the whole population of Electric City—a grand total of twenty-three men, three women, and five children—to share a meal with them that night. It seemed the prudent thing. There was no telling what she and her army were going to encounter down lower. By sowing a little goodwill here and now, she could start to build a safe haven for their eventual return.

She returned to the rail just in time to see the train pulling out. As it slowly departed, dozens of lights started flashing from the windows of the cars. Rebecca was startled to see men inside—her men—taking pictures. The moment each man spotted her, his face fell or he turned away his eyes. They pulled back from the windows or ducked down.

For an instant she tried to believe it was the engineer's fault. He simply hadn't given the men time to get off. But the truth was plain.

A voice spoke. "Be happy."

Rebecca turned. It was Beckwith, the sniper. "That must be half of us," she said.

"More than half," he said.

Didn't he understand? "Those are our soldiers," she said.

"Those are tourists, ma'am. A few days from now, they'll wake up in their beds and this will all be a dream. Except they'll have snapshots to prove they were here."

"But we've barely begun."

"Sub warfare isn't about the numbers, Ms. Coltrane. You'll see."

He didn't understand. "I trusted them."

"There was nothing to trust, ma'am. You can't lose what you never had. Those men didn't really exist."

The train's lights wormed off into darkness. The sound of steel pipe gonging and the grinding drill took over. Down on the tracks, a fistfight broke out. Rebecca tried to be philosophical. At least her fighters liked to fight.

For lack of a better spot, they made their first camp right on the rail bed. Those with no experience pitched tents. Hunter and the other Drop Zone veterans didn't even bother with sleeping bags. Off by themselves as usual, they simply unrolled ground pads and set to cleaning their guns.

The locals arrived for dinner in clean clothes. Their white shirts and shaved faces made a sharp contrast to the desperado look that many of Rebecca's rangers were cultivating. For all their poverty, their guests did not come empty-handed. Some brought pretty fossils they had unearthed. Some brought food.

"Now did I say this was a potluck?" Rebecca chided one father as his boy handed her a platter. It had various meats, all laid out in neat rows. The boy looked like a cherub, but without the rosy cheeks or baby fat. Two of his fingers were splinted with tape and a pencil.

With a smile, Rebecca tousled his curly hair. Secretly she was feeling for any lumps or horns or other symptoms of the deep. His skull was smooth, though, which put her at ease. Because if the boy was whole and healthy and undefiled, then her daughter might be, too.

"What do you say to the lady, Neil?" said the father.

"Thank you, miss, for the party," said Neil.

"And what do we have here?" Rebecca asked, lowering the platter.

"Bush meat," Neil said.

"A few of the local specialties," said his father. "Lots of protein. Plus it boosts your night vision. That or the water does. Or something in the air. No one knows. You take what you can get."

"Which one should I try, Neil?" Rebecca said, steeling herself. When in Rome . . .

"This one's crawdad," Neil said. "This one's red tapioca. This is fish."

Rebecca tried a bit of everything, even the things with antennae and feelers. She politely asked their recipe for the tapioca, which turned out to be fermented tadpoles.

"Where did you get all this?" she asked.

"The cave provides," the father said, as if it were a cornucopia pouring fruits into open hands. Rebecca looked at Joe's gaunt cheeks and the blue veins on his forehead, and decided there must not be any pioneer blood running in her, because she would never have put her Sam through such deprivation.

"You live entirely off the land?"

"We do now. It's root, hog, or die down here," he said. "We have a foraging team out right now, sweeping the upper tunnels. When it's not your shift on the rig, you're out hunting and gathering."

"You work hard," Rebecca said.

"We are bringing light to the world," the man replied.

Such conviction. The platter of food was a declaration of their self-reliance, she realized. "Did your mother prepare this, Neil?"

"She's not here," said Neil.

"Would you bring her over when she gets here? I'd like to meet her."

"She ran off," Neil solemnly told her. "She was a coward."

Rebecca's smile froze. She tried to think what to say. The woman had run off? To where? Why? And that ugly word, "coward," it wasn't something a child should use for his mother, not ever.

"I'm sure she loved you, Neil," she lamely offered.

"Not anymore," said Neil. His father slowly patted him with one scarred hand, a picture of exhausted perseverance.

But Rebecca had a sense about this. Something was off. "Every mother loves her child, Neil. They don't ever quit. That's why I'm here, for my daughter, to find her."

"I know. Daddy told me," said Neil. "She ran off, too. Just like Mama."

Rebecca started. She stared over Neil's head at his father, and there was no apology on his face. "You're wrong, Neil," she said. "My child was stolen. A lot of children were. The hadals came and took them from their homes."

"Then how come they didn't steal me? I'm right here, not a zillion miles away."

"I don't know," said Rebecca. "Maybe you can tell me." She had wondered the same thing many times. How was it that the colonies had escaped scot-free?

Something was going on down here. The settlers were not unaware of the hadal presence, and that went back well before the abduction. She couldn't put her finger on it. They seemed almost to coexist. So far no one seemed willing to talk about it. But if it was true, if the settlers and hadals were quietly avoiding or ignoring one another, if they were going along to get along, then these villagers had severed their ties to the surface. Rebecca saw no gain in making accusations, though. She and her army might yet need the colonists' help.

She changed the subject. "How did you break your fingers, Neil?"

"Hunting."

Kids hunted in Texas all the time. But down here, in this blackness, and with the hadals lurking? "You were hunting?"

"The young ones have a talent for it," said the father. "They hear and see things the adults don't."

"So you go with them?"

"They're keener without us mucking it up."

"But it must be dangerous." She was playing mother hen. Old habits.

"They know what they're doing. They only go after the lame and the strays."

"Aren't you afraid?" she asked Neil.

His father answered. "Everyone pulls his weight here." He gestured at the towering drill rig. It went on gnashing at the earth. "Someday it will be theirs."

She looked at the splints made out of pencils. "The doctor did that?"

"We doctor ourselves," the father said.

Their search for hot rock had become a religion. The rig was their idol. "This is a child," she said.

"He'll mend."

"But what if he mends crookedly?"

The father understood her meaning. "You are so certain about your way," he said. "Well, hang on to that faith of yours. Hang hard. Because down here, without that, you are nothing but an animal. Break faith, and you are lost forever."

A chill ran through Rebecca. It came together in her mind. Neil's mother had not run away without her son. She had been driven out.

Rebecca said nothing to him. She couldn't fight all the world's fights. There was evil all around. The best she could do was push it away long enough to snatch Sam from its clutches and get back to the sun.

"How long has it been since you had apple cobbler?" she said to Neil. "See that table over there? You tell them I said to give you seconds with your firsts." She handed the platter of delicacies back to the boy. "Make sure you take your daddy with you."

Rebecca avoided the locals after that. The evening stretched on. Out came the booze. Before long, the men were howling at the moon and getting brave. No one would miss her. With a few steps, she left her own party.

With her light off so that no would follow, she felt along the railroad tracks with her feet. Beckwith had taught her a trick for seeing in the night. It involved looking around objects instead of at them, using your peripheral vision. It took practice, he said, which was clear from her stumbling.

Shacks with flickering candles and lanterns bordered the rail. Electric City had no electricity. The sounds of revelry and of the never-ending rig faded.

Farther along the tracks, a footpath led up. Rebecca turned her light on low red and followed the path, cleaning her mind out, grateful for the solitude. Wherever she was, this was how Ali was doing it, Rebecca imagined, striking off nice and portable, carried along by her abilities.

The trail dipped and climbed, snaking around big rocks. Rebecca started going faster. The weight of all those men fell away. Her lungs worked.

A rock clattered uphill. Rebecca stopped and sliced at the blackness with her light, but the boulders were empty. Gravity was shuffling things around, nothing more.

She thought about heading back. This was hadal country, or had been, and the animal population was rebounding. That reminded her of Joe's meat platter. Who knew what might be running around out here? More cautiously, she continued up, her light switching here and there.

She came to the first of the sticks. They lay scattered among the talus like white driftwood. A slight question: you needed trees to have sticks, didn't you? But there they were. Mystified, she continued a little higher.

Then her light showed a spine. Rebecca stopped. It lay half curled on the path, like a fat white snake caught crossing a road.

The vertebrae were still held together by sinew. She was no expert, but it looked human, like the plastic spine models you see at a chiropractor's office. And it was not so very large. Her light quivered. The spine was about the size of a small human's.

The children.

That was her first thought. It nearly crippled her. Rebecca didn't move.

Slowly reason took over. The fact was, this spine, though smallish, was too robust to be a child's. She began to doubt it was even human.

Her heartbeat calmed. The light steadied. The thing belonged to some kind of animal. Hadn't Neil's father just talked about teams going out to forage on the land?

Thank God she hadn't screamed. Ever since Beckwith had shown up with the Barbie doll scratched with HELP, her fears had been galloping wild. A shoelace in the dirt, scratch marks on a wall, a fleeting reflection in a window: each triggered the most gruesome thoughts, only to give way to perfectly mundane explanations. She was supposed to be leading an army, not crying wolf at every bend.

She looked around, and it became clear. The sticks were bones. Animals must have dragged them from some dumping ground. The logic revived her. Rebecca went on, determined to confront her fears and apprehensions altogether. Courage was something you could learn, that was her hope.

Cresting the hill, she came to a slough where two big slabs had collapsed against each other. In between them, a crevice vented dry heat from the depths. A rope hung from a rock. Someone had left his hacksaw.

Now she got the picture. This was a hunter's camp. Here they brought their wild game—bush meat, in Neil's words—to hang and butcher. The crevice was perfect for dumping the offal and drying hams and racks of meat. Animals had dragged away the leftover bones. End of mystery.

Rebecca was proud of herself. She had seen the ugliness through to its rational answer. Bit by bit, whittling down her nerves and foolishness, she could do this thing. She could meet the night head-on.

The heat from the crevice got her sweating. It stung her eyes. She wiped it away.

There was a hand down there.

It was stuck partway down the vent. This time there was no reasoning it away. They had sawed it just above the wrist and thrown it away. A human hand.

It was a hunter's camp, all right. They butchered prey here, but the prey was not animal.

Us.

Them.

Her mind tumbled. *Hadals.* She spun around, whipping her light at the night. Were they here? Or was this old? How old? She backed against one of the big slabs.

That was when she saw the skull jammed to one side. It had buckteeth and a shelflike brow. Her first hadal.

The hacksaw had been used to open a big notch in the top.

Bush meat.

Could it be? The settlers of Electric City had taken to eating hadal flesh? She had eaten it, too. They had fed it to her. The local treats. *The cave provides.*

Rebecca stood there, staring up at the ransacked skull. The heat was making her dizzy. She felt sick.

She saw the platter of meats all over again. Technically it wasn't cannibalism, was it, not if you weren't preying on your own kind? And it meant the colonists were hunting down her enemy and killing them, the same as she was going to do. Right? But those were justifications. They dodged the truth, whatever the truth was. She had no idea what was going on in this shadow world.

Everything was at risk suddenly. Because if humans were no better than hadals, or more to the point, if hadals were no worse than humans, then it was all equivalent. Sam's abduction lost all force. She became just a morsel of food in an ancient cycle of mutual predation, them on us, us on them, hardly worth a war.

Her sweat speckled the rock. A slight noise broke her thoughts. She stabbed at the darkness.

A girl stood in her light beam. She wore the rags and caked hair of a Third World urchin. Rebecca's heart leaped.

Was this one of her children? Had she escaped or been released? Where was Sam? "Hello, darling, who are you?"

She had memorized all of the children's names and faces for precisely such a moment. But this face didn't ring a bell. Sam, too, would probably look like a wild dog until she got a washing.

The girl didn't answer.

Rebecca wanted to yell for Sam and gather the rest of them, wherever they were hiding. But the psychologists had advised a measure of serenity. The children would be traumatized from their experience. First contact could be terrifying for them.

"Sweetheart?" she said. "Can you tell me where the others are?"

The girl studied her.

"Your mommy sent me," Rebecca said. In fact, many of the mommies fought to the death. "Can you tell me your mommy's name?" *Get them talking if possible. Be prepared for silence and hostility. Some might fight you.*

The girl just stood there.

Rebecca went a little closer and got down on one knee. The ground was warm. She was soaked with sweat. "Come let me give you a hug."

The girl brought her hand around and threw a rock as hard as she could. It clipped Rebecca's head. Rebecca dropped her light.

"No trespassing," said a voice.

Rebecca jerked. She grabbed her light. Two boys were crouched on top of the higher slab. She recognized one. "Neil?" she said.

She remembered the noise along the trail. They had followed her out of the town. They were local children. Rebecca's heart sank. No Sam.

She kept the boy lit. "What are you doing, Neil?" She was angry.

Neil didn't answer. His eyes sparkled. This was fun. He was making a game of her. "Go away," she said.

Rocks softly clicked behind her. She swung her light around, and four more children stood there.

"What are you doing here?" she said.

No one spoke. More footsteps sounded. They were surrounding her.

"Go home," she said. But they *were* home.

She shined her light at the top of the slab. She knew who Neil's father was. She would tell. But Neil wasn't up there anymore. She ran the light around in a circle, counting them. Neil appeared in front of her. That made it nine.

Now she saw the knives and hammers and screwdrivers. Each child had his favorite. The tools looked enormous in their small hands. The tools took on a life of their own, as if they were brandishing the children and not the other way around. Rebecca tried to back away, but that only tightened the circle.

Hunters. It came to her. This wasn't their first time. They started edging her sideways toward a drop-off. *They take the lame and the strays.* The hadal skull, could that be their doing?

They worked her to the edge. "Jump," one said.

"No," she said.

A hammer sailed past her head. Someone darted in from behind and gave a push, a childish push, nothing with any strength to it. But Rebecca was on the edge. She caught her balance and thrust her light at them, thinking to blind them. Useless. She made a club of the light and swung it broadly, but also carefully. She didn't want to hurt anyone. They were only children.

Abruptly the children backed away. Without a word among them, they melted into the penumbra. Rebecca looked around. She cried out even as she recognized the creature surfacing from the depths as Clemens. In the wag of her beam, his face was more ghastly than ever.

He helped her away from the ledge. "Sit down."

"What are they doing?" She couldn't quit shaking.

Clemens kept touching her. He smoothed her hair. He straightened her blouse. He neatened what was messy, and made her pretty again. His fingers lighted on her like flies.

He sat on his haunches in front of her. "You have a gun," he said. "Why didn't you use it?"

She noticed it strapped to her thigh, far away, Jake's pistol. "It's not loaded," she said.

"What are you carrying it for?"

"I wouldn't have used it anyway."

"They were going to kill you," he said.

"No."

"Yes."

"What is wrong with them?" she whispered.

"You threatened them."

"I went for a walk," she said.

His amphibian stare pried at her. "Why up here?"

"The trail was lying there. I wanted some privacy."

"You weren't looking for your soldier?"

"What are you talking about?"

He could have just told her. But it was lesson time. He went to the ledge. "Come over here."

Rebecca had to hold his hand. "Yes?"

"Your light. Shine it down."

A man was lying at the bottom where they had tried to push her.

One leg was missing. Knowing what she now knew, thinking the worst of them, it was possible to guess. They had lured him up here and pushed him over. And she had surprised them in their butchery.

"You didn't know he was here?"

"I had no idea he was missing."

"This is what I keep trying to tell you, Rebecca. We're not in Kansas anymore. Things are very different in the cave."

She turned her head away.

"Now the question is, what to do about this?" said Clemens. "There has been a murder. And cannibalism. And an assault on you, the head of an army. Clearly the entire town is guilty. It's going to have to be punished. These people won't understand anything less. The children have to pay for their consequences, and their parents, too."

"Punished?" Rebecca's head was swimming. She wanted to lie down.

"It won't be pleasant, but I know how to do this."

"The children?"

"Don't feel sorry for them, Rebecca. Look down there at what the little angels did. Nearly got you, too. You're in shock. Leave this to me."

It would have been so simple to give Clemens the authority. But then what? She had raised this army with her husband's blood and her child's name, and if it slipped from her grasp for even an instant she sensed it was gone. Her only hope—Sam's only hope—was for her to hold the reins even tighter.

She let go of Clemens's hand. She defied him. "There will be no punishment," she said.

"That's a mistake, Rebecca."

"We will do nothing," she said.

"It's not just the town that needs a lesson. If we let this go, every jackal between here and Travis Station will be taking a piece of us. We have to send a message that will be heard up and down the line. Touch one hair of us and your dream is over. We won't be safe until they run away at our approach."

She didn't care. All that mattered was Sam. "We will do nothing," she repeated. "And the men don't need to know anything. If one word of this gets out, they'll take revenge on the villagers. That gets us nowhere. These settlers are not our enemies."

"But they are, Rebecca."

"In the morning we will put this place behind us."

"And him?" Clemens pointed down at the body. "What happens in the morning when he is missed?"

"In this commotion?" she said. "Men are coming and going like ants. No one knows who is where, or whether they're even still with us."

"So we just forget about him? He died in your cause."

"Do you know his name?"

"No."

She surprised herself. "Then what is there to forget?"

Something like a smile pulled at Clemens's face. He nodded his approval. "I'm going down," she said.

She descended the path with Clemens ranging through the talus to make sure the children were gone. Back in town, the revelry went on all night.

Tired as she was, Rebecca could not stand to be alone with her thoughts, and so she sat on a mound of rocks and watched the men dance and bray and sing their own praises. Hour after hour, they came to her with gifts: sleeping pads to soften her seat, blankets to warm her, drinks, food, pictures of their families or cars or motorcycles, oaths of deathless loyalty. One drunken man even kneeled.

The town children were nowhere to be seen. Before long the adults left, too, whispering and throwing frightened looks at Rebecca. The rig fell silent.

In the morning, Rebecca led her army out from the now deserted town.

It did not occur to her for days after to wonder what Clemens had been doing up on the hill when he had rescued her.

ARTIFACTS

NIGHT WARRIOR HANDBOOK

Second Battalion, Fifth Marines
How to Operate in the Dark, part four
11. Defecate
Procedure. Select a low site with good earth and good ground cover. Put tissue paper in blouse pocket. Keep weapon and equipment at arm's length. Dig a hole. Straddle the hole and squat with trousers pulled forward. Put used tissue paper in the hole. Cover hole with earth. Replace ground cover to camouflage. Wash hands.

Techniques

- Excrement is a reflection of diet. U.S. excrement smells different from the enemy's. Minimize smell by burying all excrement immediately.
- Use an antidiarrheal to avoid having to defecate. This is NOT recommended by doctors, but can be used in certain missions.
- Carry excrement in plastic bags out of area of operations. Certain missions may require this to avoid evidence of activity.

24

As they cast themselves across the lake, Ali reached back with her light. She hoped for a glimpse of the receding shore, but there was not even a suggestion of land. It took her breath, this all-encompassing night.

Gregorio had made a chain of three rafts, one behind the other. The last two were filled with fuel and supplies. Scavenging the villages had taken time, but had also given them time. They could last for months now, and still feed the children if they found them, and ferry everyone back across the lake to Port Dylan.

Hour after hour, they plowed across the black waters. Ali shrank into herself. Despite the NASA map and legends of the lake's immensity, no one knew Emperor Lake's actual size. The other side might lie a day, or even weeks, away. Part of her wished they had gone on hugging the shore. But their caution would have come at the children's expense, and so they had settled on this direct passage, or *diretissima* as Gregorio called it.

Gregorio refused to show fear, of course. But it was there in his constant vigilance. No sooner did he set down the night binoculars than he picked them up again and made another sweep. His beautiful dark eyes grew darker. If the raft had been larger, he would have paced. Instead he ran one fingertip in circles on the rubber hull. The miles passed by with them squeaking like mice.

The farther they traveled from shore, the more Ali's old terror of oceans grew. She stayed deep inside the walls of the Zodiac, as far from the water as possible. She didn't need the captain's sea serpent to picture all sorts of creatures swimming rampant beneath the skin of the lake.

Then there were the noises. It was as if the water were whispering to her. As if Maggie were the water. *Mommy,* she heard.

They continued purifying their drinking water, which they dipped from the lake. Ali hated leaning over the hull with the quart bottle. Once upon a time she had looked into her daughter's cold eye and it had been as bottomless as this.

Gregorio measured their progress in gallons of fuel.

Ali measured it by minutes.

She could not seem to take a full breath of air. The blackness lay on her. She struggled to be good company, or at least not bad company.

On the second day, she saw the hump of a monstrous beast sliding just beneath the surface. Gregorio insisted it was only the ripples of their wake. "Alexandra." Her name, so delicious on his tongue. "There is nothing to see, only the shapes of the water."

A little later, she lit another silky black swell. "What do you call that?"

"Ah, that," he said, reaching over to stroke the water. "She is my pet, Nessie."

She stared at him.

"You read too many airport books," he said. It was a joke. Light reading for her was *Linguistics Anima.*

"Nothing so big could exist in a place so isolated," he said. "Forget the settlers' fairy tales. Evolution is against it. Animals confined to lakes and is-lands become dwarves. It has to do with the food supply. Think of the hobbits on Florensis in Indonesia. Little people hunting little elephants."

"Oh, you mean dwarves," she said, "like the Komodo dragons on Java."

"There are always exceptions."

"Like here." She threw her light left in time to see another swell lift and sink.

"I'm telling you," he said, "it is the water, nothing more."

When it was not her shift to steer the convoy of boats, Ali slept. Her dreams were vivid. They had extra color.

She woke from one such catnap, thinking Gregorio had jostled her. Then she saw the gun in his hand. And he had cut the engine. "What?" she said.

"Quiet."

A moment later, something glided crosswise against the bottom of the boat. Ali could feel its weight and power right through the rubber floor. She would have felt vindicated if not for her sudden urge to pee.

They rocked on the ripples. Ali said nothing. Silence was their only hiding place.

Gregorio handed her the light. Maybe the smarter thing would have been darkness. But they had to see.

Minutes passed. The lake gave a sigh.

Ali swept her beam across the black mirror of water. At the light's far edge, the surface seemed to bulge a few inches. It took on the sleek shape of a jet's cowl. The water made a slight hiss.

A gun appeared beside her cheek.

Don't, she thought. *Don't make it mad.* It was far too big. Even if he managed to hit it, even if he killed the thing, it would surely capsize them.

There was no time to argue with him.

The ridge of water hurtled toward them.

His hand propped on her shoulder. She could feel his muscles tighten. The shot would deafen her.

Abruptly the lake flattened out.

The bulge submerged. The thing dove under them, stroking the boat bottom. She felt it in her feet. Its flesh sizzled against the rubber.

She looked at Gregorio. "Thank God you didn't shoot," she whispered.

"I tried." He turned the gun back and forth in his hand, fuming. "It wouldn't work. How do you make it shoot?"

"You don't know how to shoot it?"

"Of course I do," he whispered. He aimed into the water to prove his mastery. The cords in his forearm bunched impressively. But nothing happened.

All her focus drew in from the lake. She huddled across from him. Details. The devil—or their salvation—lay in the details. "Is the safety on?"

"Yes, the safety," he muttered to himself, searching the grip and body.

Ali watched with growing dismay. All these days her protector had been wielding the gun with such authority. Now that they were up against a real, live sea monster, something probably left over from the dinosaur age, now that they actually needed the gun, she realized how much its presence had meant to her. "Maybe it's jammed," she said.

"Jammed?"

He was helpless. In mortal danger and his gun wouldn't work? It appalled her. Abruptly she saw them from high above, two little people floating in a thimble upon a sea, brandishing a useless weapon, pretending to be in charge of their fate. She laughed. And stopped. "Is it loaded, Gregorio?"

He glared at her.

She started hiccupping.

"Are you laughing?" he said.

"Not at you."

"No? Then tell me."

"It's just, never mind, your gun . . ."

"I'm listening, Alexandra."

His wounded expression, his sobriety, his nobility . . . she couldn't quit hiccupping. "The women at the office call you El Cid," she said.

"Go on, Alexandra."

"And I was just thinking instead, you know . . ."

"Yes?"

"Well, a gun that won't shoot. Tilting at windmills."

His neck got longer. "Me?"

"Stop, I'm wetting my pants."

"That," he pointed at the water, "was no windmill."

"Gregorio, please . . ."

They got no warning.

The front of the boat reared up out of the water.

Gregorio tumbled sideways, slamming into Ali. The light went flying. Their little ball of a world blinked out.

The hull crashed back upon the water.

Her heartbeat deafened her. The silence—the night—the lake. She felt swallowed alive.

"The light," said Gregorio. "Where is the light?"

Their hands scuttled across the floor. They bumped heads. The boat rocked gently.

"I have it," she said.

"Quickly."

She fumbled for the switch. Nothing. Shook the flashlight. Nothing.

She unscrewed the base and emptied the batteries into her hand and wiped them on her shirt and fed them back into the case. It worked.

Gregorio was pale among the scattered bags and loose rope. The shadows jumped, black and white. Water sloshed on the floor. The gun was missing. She turned the beam out across the water. The two boats behind bobbed quietly.

"The light," said Gregorio. No more whispering. No more hopes of hiding on the lake's surface. It would return for them.

Ali trained the light on Gregorio's hands, whatever he was doing with them. The night pressed against her back. The famished night. Gregorio went on rooting through the bags.

"What are you looking for?" she said.

He drew his arm from a bag. "This." He pulled out a fistful of sock.

"A sock?"

Pressing his knees together on the object, he carefully peeled away the sock to reveal what looked like a metal orange, a small one, a clementine. "My hand grenade," he said.

Once again, her fear paused. She glanced from the grenade to Gregorio's pleased look. First a gun that wouldn't shoot, now a grenade. It got better. He opened his Swiss army knife.

"Hold this." He gave her the grenade. It weighed as much as a clementine, too.

Was that the water hissing again? *Don't look.* "Gregorio."

He sawed at the ropes. One of the boats began drifting away, followed by the other. "Turn off the light."

They plunged into darkness.

"Quiet."

Ali heard water softly parting. Then something popped. Jerry cans banged against each other. It passed.

"Light," said Gregorio.

The second raft was gone. A few bundles and empty cans floated on the surface. He took the flashlight from her and tossed it toward the third raft. Ali understood, a diversion. But the light bounced from its hull and into the water.

The world went black.

The water stirred again in the distance.

Ali fumbled at her neck for the night goggles. Hated them normally. Loved them now. On. The world turned green.

A ridge of water was driving at them. She looked at Gregorio.

Blind, eyes wide, mouth open, he was kneeling against the hull. His head moved from side to side, scoping for sound. His fist held the grenade.

The third inflatable exploded with a bang. Ali turned in time to see food and fuel cans skidding on the water. The flattened raft thrashed like a dying animal. The water swelled, spine up, and snaked a big turn. The creature had them now.

Gregorio shifted. Ali looked. She thought he would throw the grenade with all his might. Instead he gave it a feeble little toss, barely enough to lob a coin into a fountain. "Ah, gee," she sighed.

The ridge of green-and-black water surged closer. Ali imagined the grenade fluttering deeper and deeper. Gregorio had chucked their final defense.

Up in the sun, where you could measure your shadow and see the proper order of things, Ali had always thought death would find her smiling. She had led a full life, not always a happy one, but rich with sense. She had gone deep and climbed back onto the green earth and given birth. Her heart had filled with as much love as it could hold. She was grateful for her blessings.

But now she had gone and spoiled her finale with this rerun of the abyss. *Why?* Up there you had only to open your eyes to know where you were. Here you were lost every minute, prying at the night with a tube of light, strangling on nightmares, suffering violence.

Would it wolf her down whole, or tear her to pieces? Teeth or tentacles? Something grabbed her arm. Gregorio. She clutched his hand.

The grenade detonated.

There was no geyser of spray, no atomic ripple, no sonic boom. The lake made a slight oomph noise, as if surprised. The boat wiggled.

The hump of black water vanished.

A few bubbles surfaced, then the mirror resumed its smooth green-black face. A thick, fishy smell rose from the water.

"Did you kill it?" she said.

"I don't know." He held his blind head high. Ali found a flashlight in a bag and flipped it on. Gregorio blinked. She pulled away her goggles. They watched the water.

A minute passed, then five.

She shined the light to one side. A clot of white jelly or wax was drifting up from the depths. The slow, shapeless thing rose like a ghost.

The closer it came, the bigger it got. Gregorio tried the engine, but it was flooded. He started paddling. They got far enough to one side to avoid the jelly mass. Gregorio made a grand slit-throat gesture. "It is his stomach or lungs. He has gone to monster heaven."

Then the lake began to disgorge the rest of its dead. The surface filled with creatures, large and small, killed by the grenade's shock wave. They glittered like broken bottles, some green or white or pink, most without any color at all. There were fish with translucent armor, and eels as long as pythons. Every one of them came armed with stingers, claws, or banks of teeth.

Floating perhaps ten feet below the surface, that glutinous white mass seemed ready to enfold the entire banquet, Ali and Gregorio included. But for the moment, the ghostly thing kept its distance, and the menagerie of slaughtered creatures proved irresistible, at least to Gregorio. "Oh what a feast," he said.

With the exuberance of a child, he began scooping bodies close enough to pluck from the water. "Look at this," he said, prodding an eel covered in mucus. "A hagfish. Very primitive. No jawbone. See its teeth? And, see, my God, a trilobite."

He hefted the hand-size animal. Its plated shell was a lovely burnished crimson. "My father used to take me on fossil holidays. Trilobites were our passion. We found them in coal country, in places like Bosnia and Poland."

He flipped it upside down and smelled its sallow belly. The thing was only stunned. Its antennae and dozens of little legs started wiggling in the air. He laid it on the floor and gave it a pat.

He was giddy. They had survived.

Ali moved her feet away from the creature.

"Dinner," he said. "My father"—he crossed himself—"used to wonder what their meat must have tasted like. Tonight I'll find out for him."

"No lake food," she reminded him.

"I think, Alexandra, no more taboos." He gestured at the debris from their destroyed boats. "Most of our supplies are at the bottom now. The captain was right. The lake provides."

"We're turning back," she said. This was her fault. She had almost gotten them killed with her direct passage.

"But why?" he said.

"There's no telling how far away the shore lies. We've gone as far as we can. We'll be lucky to get back to where we came from."

"Faith," he said. "That's what I heard you say. And now, see, we have killed the dragon—no windmill—and found a meal fit for my dead father. And reached our shore."

She looked around. They were surrounded by night. "Gregorio, what shore?"

He laughed and reached over the edge. He lifted a dead frog. "Meet our pilot, Kermit. Kermit is amphibious."

He let her put it together. Amphibious. Water and land dwelling. *Land.* "How close are we?" she said.

"Ask Kermit's brothers and sisters."

Right on cue, a whole chorus of frogs sprang to life in the distance. Gregorio didn't bother with the engine. He simply started paddling. It took all of ten minutes to reach shore, where the aleph was waiting.

ARTIFACTS

USA TODAY

Chinese and American Warships Collide

Jan. 8. Hong Kong. Two Chinese warships bumped two U.S. Navy vessels in waters claimed by the People's Republic of China. The incident further escalates tensions between the two superpowers, and the "Chinese Olympic spring" of friendly relations seems dead.

The incident between the ships took place in the Sea of Japan, off the United Korean peninsula. The American destroyer *Caron* and cruiser *Yorktown* were operating outside the twelve-mile territorial limit claimed by the PRC. They were challenged by a Chinese frigate and destroyer and told to leave the waters. Then, according to a navy spokesman, the Chinese ships "shouldered" the U.S. ships out of the way, bumping them slightly. There was no exchange of gunfire, although the Chinese warships did aim their guns and missile launchers at the American ships, and illuminated the *Yorktown*'s bridge. The American ships eventually departed from the area.

"This is a blatant violation of the second Incidents at Sea Agreement," said Secretary of Defense Matthew Lee. "China is playing a very dangerous game, and we encourage her leadership to refrain from further aggression."

This is the latest in a cascade of events since the Green Barrens disaster and the grounding of a Chinese submarine in California. "The rhetoric is nearing a boil," said Jeffery Blockwick of the Brookings Institute. "The two powers seem bent on war."

25

DIALOGUES WITH THE ANGEL, NUMBER 8

True to his word, the angel pays the occasional visit to his entombed student. He sits outside the neat heap of rocks, popping albino locusts, like grapes, into his mouth, and giving odds and ends of sermons.

Inside the meditation-chamber-turned-tomb, the disciple's only measure of time is the corpse beside him. The thing is in constant motion. Maggots animate it, roiling the limbs and face and belly. From hour to hour, it twitches and shifts and changes expressions.

"It takes four days, on average, for the San Bushmen of the Kalahari to bring down a giraffe," the angel is telling him. "Their arrows are barely twigs. Their bows are laughable. And the giraffe is a powerful giant. What's their secret? Poison. These bushmen are old biowarriors. They have a whole arsenal of poisons. Here is the recipe for their giraffe poison.

"In a certain season of certain years, the grubs of a certain beetle, Diamphidia, are gathered from the sand that beds the roots of a certain bush. The grubs must be handled with exquisite care. The toxin resides in the thorax section of the larva, which is crushed and mixed with tree gum and painted onto the shaft of the arrow point. The point itself is never coated with this poison, because if a hunter scratched himself with it he would die inside forty-eight hours. Now I ask you," says the angel, "do you think these people taught themselves such an intricate art?"

"No, Lord," whispers the disciple. He clings to that voice as if it were a lifeline.

"For millions of years," the angel continues, "the silkworm has been *wrapping a half mile of thread around itself. Then one fine morning a certain Chinese peasant felt inspired to unwrap that thread through a process even more elaborate than the Bushmen's poison harvest. Tell me, where does a country bumpkin get the idea to take a filament, so fine the breeze can steal it, and make it into an emperor's hankie? It's like something out of a dream, don't you think? Which is exactly how I planted it, in a Chinaman's dream."*

The disciple can barely breathe for the corpse's gases.

The angel goes on. "Herr Mozart, my manic wastrel, routinely pulled off a lifetime of works in a single month or so, and then did it again and again. Near the end of his life, he literally composed in his sleep, his hand jotting down page after page of music as fast as the hand could write. These were divinely written pages that needed no editing, not a single revision. This was music that was as perfect as it gets. Now tell me, do you think he accomplished all that alone in the night? (And who do you think commissioned his Requiem?*)*

"Lord." The corpse's beard is wagging with its weight of worms. Laughing along. The disciple is fighting for his sanity.

"And what about Beethoven and all those gigantic symphonies that came thundering from his pen after he was deaf? Come on now, a deaf man? I'll give you a hint. Who do you think his 'beloved' was?"

The disciple's lips are cracked from thirst. His stomach is hollow. A little meat would do the job. Meat half chewed by the worms. But he must fast.

"And what about van Gogh," the angel leaps on. "They said he was mad. He wasn't. He was listening to me, or at least to my messengers. Jonas Salk, have you heard of him, the father of the polio vaccine? It came to him in a vision. Homer was a blind hemophiliac. Never left his mother's house, much less went to war. I poured the poetry into him. Moses. Abraham. Jesus. Mohammed. They heard voices. All mine. The Bhagavad Gita. *The* Inferno. *The Book of Psalms. Pi. Relativity."*

*"*Mein Kampf," *the disciple says to himself. "The Red Book. Stalin. Pol Pot." He whispers these things, and more, all the devilish stuff.*

"No," says the angel. His hearing is acute. "Those all belong to you. My covenant rests on beauty."

The corpse's mouth suddenly yaws open. Maggots spill out. Beauty? "Teller. Mengele. McNamara," says the disciple. The evils tumble out at random.

"Speaking of Vietnam, you'll never guess where I spent the war," says the angel.

The disciple falls silent.

"At a nightclub in New York City," says the angel. "It's true. The Half Note Club. It was the spring of 1965. John Coltrane was whipping his jazz quartet into a holy frenzy. Oh, you should have heard them, the wildest notes man has ever known. Coltrane played like he was possessed. And he was. By me."

"Impossible."

"Why?"

"Because you're down here. Trapped. Like me."

"I wasn't there in person, of course. Let's call me a fly on the wall, but with this difference: I was moving civilization along. Whenever it moved, there I was. It was me who gave you drums to mark time with. I linked the stars into constellations so you could find your way. I gave you dogs to be your servants. I soothed your fear of fire to let you conquer the night. There are a thousand names for me. Prometheus is one. I am the father of all your miracles."

The disciple suddenly starts clawing at the rocks. He doesn't care about jazz or drums. He doesn't care about Homer or silk or Bushmen. "Free me," he roars.

A silence follows. The angel finally speaks. "I am," he says.

The disciple listens for the sound of rocks being lifted from his tomb. Instead he hears footsteps walking away.

ARTIFACTS

INTERNATIONAL WAR CRIMES TRIBUNAL

United States War Crimes Against China

Initial Complaint Charging:

(Members of the previous U.S. administration plus various generals) and members of U.S. Navy SEAL unit one who participated in the incident. . . .

With:

Crimes Against Peace, War Crimes, Crimes Against Humanity and Other Criminal Acts, and High Crimes in Violation of the Charter of the United Nations Subplanetary Treaty and Laws made in Pursuance Thereof.

These charges have been prepared at the request of the People's Republic of China following the killing of seventy-nine Chinese nationals by U.S. military personnel at the sub-Pacific location known as Green Barrens. . . .

The Charges Include:

1. The United States knowingly and willfully engaged in the violation of UN Subplanetary Treaty that forbids military presence or action by any nation in the Subterrain.
2. The president ordered U.S. forces to invade the Subterrain with small special-operations commando teams, resulting in the deaths of seventy-nine Chinese nationals at the Green Barrens site.
7. The United States used prohibited weapons to inflict indiscriminate death and unnecessary suffering against both military and civilian targets.
10. The president obstructed justice and corrupted United Nations functions as a means of securing power to commit crimes against peace and war crimes.
11. The president usurped the constitutional power of Congress as a means of securing power to commit crimes against peace, war crimes, and other high crimes.

26

Rebecca's army came to a primitive footbridge. Made of nonstretch perlon rope, the cavers' choice, it spanned a chasm thirty yards wide. A sign read:

THE BIFROST RIFT TOLL BRIDGE.
$100/HEAD
TRESPASSERS WILL BE SHOT
NO LIE

Hunter called a halt. Rebecca went to the front of the line. Clemens was not far behind.

A curious slum waited over there. Aluminum ladders led up to holes in a honeycombed cave wall. The holes were fitted with doors. Spider walks made of rope linked various holes. Shapeless flags hung like laundry from a string running side to side. From this side of the bridge, the place looked deserted.

"These guys mean business," Hunter said to Rebecca, glassing the village. "I count five rifles sticking out of concealments. That means there are probably twice that many or more. They've got total command of the crossing. So much for our alleged intelligence."

Clemens—their "alleged intelligence"—stood to Rebecca's left. "This is a surprise," he said.

"I'm not sure we can stand many more surprises," Hunter said. "Yesterday we had to deal with the salt columns you didn't remember. The day before it was a waterfall you'd never seen. I'm wondering if you ever came this way at all."

Clemens's disfigurement and bizarre manner had already made him the scapegoat of choice among the majority. Rebecca had heard some of the nicknames: Tad, for his tadpole features; the Leper King; One-Nut; and other, coarser things. He never reacted, though. With that scar of a smile, he seemed almost happy with their abuse.

"Things change," he said.

"Look, Clemens, I know you want to belong again," said Hunter.

"How do you mean?"

"Fit in. Assimilate. Rejoin the human race."

"Do you have a point?" said Clemens.

"Yeah. This is a rescue operation, not psychotherapy. Leading us into your nightmare isn't helping us, and I don't see how it's helping you."

Clemens looked at Rebecca. "Are we firing me?" he said.

He had saved her life once, and she was grateful. But this concerned her. They were putting their faith in a horribly scarred survivor. His recall was their compass. If it was broken, they needed to know.

"How did your group get across?" she said, shelving his question for the moment. The last thing she needed was more attrition.

Where the railroad ended at Electric City, they had started walking. Apparently half of her army had expected the war would walk to them. In just four days, almost five hundred men had turned around and gone home. Now this chasm and bridge were going to cost her more desertions. Even as she stood there, men were lining the chasm rim, dropping pebbles into the blackness below, shining their lights on the sorry excuse for a bridge, and shaking their heads. The longer they dallied, the weaker they got.

"Ten hours in that direction," Clemens pointed, "there was a chain left from the old days. I sent one of our climbing monkeys over with a rope and we rigged a traverse. It took us two days to cross. We lost a man. Then it was another two days' trek along the far rim to reach where this lovely village now sits."

"We don't have a week to spare," she said. "This is where we cross. Today."

"They've got us by the short hairs," Hunter said. "Even if we could afford their toll, we'd only be setting ourselves up for every other pirate down the road."

"Shoot some," Clemens suggested. "Put the fear of God in them. It will give the men some practice."

They had still not fired a shot in anger. Except for a few "mad minutes," when the men chewed apart cave formations on full auto, their weapons were mostly macho accessories. So far no one had shot himself in the foot.

"We could take them out," Hunter said. "Possibly all of them. We've got the firepower. But I'd bet the farm they've rigged this bridge. If they cut that loose, we'll have to hoof it down to the chain anyway. If it even exists."

Rebecca started for the bridge.

"Where are you going?" Hunter was a stride behind her.

"To negotiate," she said. "This is their home. Their rope and labor count for something. So does our time. We'll find a fair price."

"Listen to me . . ."

She didn't stop. He caught her arm.

"Rebecca . . ." His voice had a tone she hadn't heard before.

Christ, she thought. *He's in love.* "Stay with the men," she said. "And, Mr. Hunter, keep your hands to yourself."

Hunter dropped his hand and Rebecca started over the bridge.

For the first few steps, she actually felt graceful. Then the bridge began swaying in big arcs. It did not help that her army trained its lights on the rope bridge. Between the dancing lights and her wild shadow on the far wall, she nearly threw up.

The bridge sagged under her weight, lowering her into the rift. Setting her jaw, she went on with her miserable performance. So much for inspiring the men. They were probably leaving in droves.

At the midpoint, just as she was starting to ascend, a terrible sound yowled up from far below.

What on God's earth? The howl jolted her. It didn't belong. There were rules to this place, and they included hadals and bats and bugs. And glaciers and relic seas and even cannibal children. But what was this howl?

The bridge bobbed up and down. She clung to the ropes. The howl echoed away.

A moment later Rebecca heard the metal clatter of guns. She cast a look back. All along the edge, men lay on their stomachs aiming into the abyss.

Flares were dropping into the depths, so many it looked like lava flowing. The flares sank and sank and not one bit of light reached the bottom.

That unearthly cry rose up again. Fists locked on the ropes, Rebecca peeked left and right around her feet. Whatever lived in that dark gash of night, it wanted out.

"Rebecca," men called to her. "Come back."

Come back, not go forward. That frightened her more than the creature that couldn't seem to reach her anyway.

The howl guttered up again, plaintive this time. Frustrated. *Famished.*

This rift could easily be the end of them. She saw that clearly. The end of Sam.

Scooting her foot higher, Rebecca forced the next step. The bridge rocked and bobbed. She took another step, and another. The village drew closer.

She concentrated on the intricate catwalks and aluminum ladders and spider holes with doors. And the guns. She saw them clearly now. Rifle barrels poked from a dozen niches. The gunmen she could reason with. The gunmen she welcomed. Whatever lay below was pure hunger.

Hauling herself the last few feet of the bridge, she called out, "Don't shoot."

Touching solid ground, Rebecca almost fell away from the abyss. But she disciplined her trembling knees and went forward into the village, calling, "Hello? Don't shoot. Hello?"

No one answered. Except for the flags swaying overhead, the place was motionless. "Someone come out. We need to talk."

No one appeared. She went deeper. "Hello."

Something—a cannonball—struck the small of her back. She slammed face-first against the wall. She felt hot breath against the back of her head, and heard her captor's lungs and the quiet jingle of gear. He shoved his hips against her butt, gluing her flat to the stone.

From the corner of her eye, shapes glimmered. A red laser dot danced by her nose, then swung away. Footsteps beat the stone. Doors crashed open.

"Clear," said a voice.

"Empty," another.

"Nothing here."

That weight of hot breath and hard hips let up. Her captor released her. She turned. It was Hunter. His men poured through the little alley of ropes and ladders, like dark water.

Rebecca pushed him. "I told you to stay with the men."

"You're brave as lions, but that was a damned stunt," Hunter said. "Don't ever do anything like that again."

"I had it under control." She was furious and relieved. Tears rolled down her face, damn them. "Bring the men over. We need to keep going."

"Not until we secure the place. And figure out what the hell is down in the rift."

The Drop Zone operators went on probing the village.

A soldier approached. "You'll love this." He held out a piece of plastic pipe. The tip was painted black.

"Plumbing pipe?" Hunter took it. "These are the snipers?"

"That's it, sir."

"They stopped an entire army with pieces of plastic?"

"Nothing personal. I'd say they were shaking down the settlers."

Hunter growled. "Where are these merry pranksters?"

"No one's home, sir. They must have headed for the hills."

Across the rift, the lights of her army twinkled. Rebecca followed Hunter through the narrow lane. Overhead, soldiers clambered back and forth on the spider walks.

"Roust the place," Hunter said. "Turn it upside down."

Boots clattered on the ladders.

"What are we looking for, sir?"

"Hell if I know. Teddy bears, orthodontics, iPods, Halloween costumes, whatever the kids might have had the night they were taken. Be thorough."

"I doubt there's anything here," Rebecca said to him.

"Why's that?" said Hunter.

"Because Mr. Beckwith found that Barbie doll down a different tunnel." The elusive Ian Beckwith, she thought. In this land of stark shadows or no shadows at all, he flitted in and out of view, more out than in. Since the governor's banquet in Travis, she had seen him a total of two times.

"Then why aren't we down that tunnel?" Hunter was on his short fuse.

"Because Mr. Clemens told me this way was the shortcut."

The veins wormed at Hunter's temples. "You didn't ask me?"

"I went with my gut."

"Look," he said. "You've got this thing for the wrong guys. Beckwith is damaged goods. The cave got him. He's no different from Clemens, just another phantom of the opera. If I wanted to, I could snag a quick cash reward with a piece of flex cuff. He's got a court-martial waiting for him. But that's not part of my mission."

"He brought us the doll," she said. "That's all the proof we have of the children."

"And that's what I'm after now. Proof. If we're running down the wrong tube, let's turn around and find the right one."

"But we can't turn around," she said.

"Why is that?"

Because, she didn't dare say, her house of cards was already falling to pieces. "Just bring them over."

Hunter lowered his voice. "I'm not going to do that, Rebecca. They don't belong here in the first place. But since they're here, they deserve better than bad guesswork and sloppy thinking. If there's no proof of the children, the merry-go-round stops now."

"I'll bring them over myself."

Hunter stepped in front of her. "No, Rebecca. With all due respect, you will quit killing yourself and them and go back where you came from and deal with your losses."

It was here. The mutiny. The end. "Get out of my way."

"Ms. Coltrane, I am here to observe and advise your operation, to minimize your impact, and to protect the lives of American citizens. If necessary, I have the authority to impose martial law and forcibly evacuate . . ."

She wanted to cover her ears and close her eyes and make him disappear. He was the United States of America. It was more than that. He was the real world crashing this unreal one.

"Sir," called a man. "Up here."

Men were clustering by the laundry line with its odd banners.

"You need to see this, sir."

Hunter didn't invite her along. Rebecca followed anyway, climbing the ladders past doors that swung into little burrows and cells.

"What do we have?" Hunter said.

"I think we found the boys."

Rebecca looked around. What about the girls?

The operator pointed at the banners on the line. Rebecca frowned. Then she saw the pubic hair. They were human skins rustling in the breeze.

"It could be anybody," Hunter said.

"No, sir, it's them," said the operator. He held up a small booklet with names, photos, and information about each missing child.

A birthmark, a knee-surgery scar, and tattoos of a skate brand and a girlfriend's name identified all the skins as those of the missing boys. Rebecca was exquisitely careful not to show the slightest hint of her relief. For now the girls were still unaccounted for. There was still hope for Sam.

Each skin bore fresh hadal markings, an honor of sorts according to Clemens. "Those are prayers," he said. "Every time the flag flaps, prayers fly up to heaven."

Rebecca asked for an honor guard to escort the remains (rolled like carpets) back to the surface. Over a hundred men volunteered. They would have left anyway, so the funeral detail helped her save face.

Chastened by this proof, Hunter withdrew into his Drop Zone isolation. Clemens had been right. The raiders had come this way.

Not a trace of the toll-taking villagers remained. It wasn't hard to guess where the hadals had sent them. As the army crossed on the rope bridge, that prehistoric thing in the rift kept howling up at them. Begging, it seemed to Rebecca, for more.

<u>ARTIFACTS</u>

PRESS RELEASE

Critical Care Products for the Subterrain

Berberian Meds has launched, and is developing, a suite of products for medical emergencies in the Subterrain such as poisoning, overdose (pharmaceutical), subterranean cancers, respiratory diseases, cave sepsis, and life-threatening infections. Typically, these often life-saving medicines sell for a high price and are targeted at specialist clinicians in the expanding Subterrain critical-care setting. These medicines include:

TrogFab™ [Troglobitae Polyvalent Immune Fab (Ovine)]

TrogFab™is a treatment for mild or moderate envenomation from North Sub-Pacific Troglobitic species including pit vipers and white snakes, some cave crustaceans (trilobites, glass lobster, etc.—see list), the Elbert octopus, some amphibians (camel toads, night darters, etc.—see list), rays, parasitic barnacles, terrestrial jellyfishes (not aquatic), some spiders (erect widowers, Korean tarantulas, etc.—see list), blue scorpions, and some insects (Vulcan ants, Hu and brittle dragonflies, etc.—see list). TrogFab™ was the first product entry into the Subterrain antivenin market, and rapidly established itself as the market leader.

It is estimated that there are around 733,000 venomous animal bites in the Subterrain each year, a number sure to rise with population influx, creating a market potential of up to US$3.8 billion per annum based on an assumed average treatment cost of US$5,000 per patient. There are 250 to 900 deaths each year, underlining the need for prompt and adequate treatment.

Berberian Meds was the first company to answer the mystery of why so many cave species have evolved a shared toxin, i.e., TTX (troglodotoxin), which, in small doses, causes paralysis of varying lengths of time. (Larger doses cause death.) By identifying the TTX-producing bacteria in salivary glands and nematocysts, the company jumped to the forefront in subterranean antivenin production. Other antivenin products in the R & D pipeline include . . .

Each packet of TrogFab™ contains up to 1 gram of total protein and sodium phosphate buffer. Gelatin is used as a preservative in the manufacturing process. Adipic acid and fumaric acid, plus artificial flavor, aid in the reconstitution process. Contains less than 2 percent of aspartame and red 40. Use 100 millimeters of boiling water for reconstitution, and fix with 100 milliliters of cold water.

27

Mommy?

Ali sweeps Maggie up in her arms.

She whirls her in a circle.

Maggie's hair tickles her cheek.

Maggie puts her little hand on Ali's arm.

I miss you, Mommy.

Ali woke.

It was Gregorio's hand on her arm. Night hung above him. "I have found something," he said.

With a groan, Ali pried herself from the ground. She felt drugged. Not enough sleep, but somehow too much dreaming. *So vivid.*

Ever since leaving the lake—taking this tunnel that spiraled down beneath the lake's floor—she had been dogged by her dreams. Maggie featured hugely. But also her parents appeared, and January, her mentor, and others. All beloved. All dead.

She didn't mention the dreams to Gregorio. For one thing, she had no patience for dream telling, which ranked in her books with reading tea leaves or the astrology page. She had never believed God spoke all that mysteriously. And that was back when she still believed in God.

Ali refused to believe she might be infected with the lake disease. She was in command of herself. That was paramount.

Gregorio's black hair swung like liquid in the light. "This way."

He grabbed her pack and she followed him along the worn trace. Ten minutes later he knelt and pressed his light against the amber floor. "Can you see them?"

Suspended in the flowstone beneath her feet, a dozen dead hadals seemed ready to rise up and break free. Even the females looked ferocious with their primeval dugs and torn hair and albino eyes. All the women were missing at least some of their fingers, which Ali recognized from her captive days. No death went unmarked without a few digits being chopped away.

"There are more," he said, sweeping his light farther along the smooth surface of stone. "At least fifty of them. And slaves. Human slaves."

They walked above the stock-still turbulence. These were modern hadals, meaning they were debased and misshapen. Some wore scraps of human clothing—she saw a Nike swoosh—though not the humans. The slaves had been kept naked except for iron collars or shackles.

"The plague," Ali said. She had never seen the aftermath in person. "It spread so quickly."

They walked across the flowstone, now and then peering down through the mineral lens at the plague victims. "They were running away," she said. "From us, the human invasion."

A warm breeze skimmed across the polished surface. Ali lifted her head. Suddenly a thousand whispers seemed to converge on her. At the edge of her hearing, she could almost distinguish soft syllables and bits of hadal click language. The breeze died. The voices stopped.

She glanced at Gregorio. Head down, he was intent on the bodies underfoot and plainly deaf to the whispers. It frightened her. *Only me?* She came up with another explanation. Maybe her hearing was simply better than his. The voices might be wind whistling through faraway forests of stalactites and stalagmites.

They left behind the refugees in flowstone. The trail wound lower. Portions were rocky with slides or jacketed in flowstone. One ancient bridge, near collapse, ground its teeth as they edged across.

"Are we on the right path?" said Gregorio.

"It has to be," said Ali. Three days ago, they had left their boat tethered to a boulder and entered the only hole marked by an aleph, and countersigned by *IC* and *WM*. "The spiral's center lies this way, I'm positive."

Without another word, Gregorio surrendered to her judgment, which was no relief. Because at this point their direction rested on nothing more real than the sum of whispers and dreams that she rejected as wind whistling on stone. *Ali in Wonderland,* she thought.

"One more day," she said. "Then we turn around."

"Three more days, Alexandra," he said, generous with his loyalty. "We have enough food for that."

Gregorio muscled on his big pack. In the quiet corridors, she could hear the popcorn in his soccer knees. His limp worsened, but he never complained. *Step by step,* she thought, *the old broad is wearing out her stud.*

Ali wanted it to end. She wanted to purge Ike, bury Maggie, and lay herself in this man's hands. It was not too late to start a new life. She had passed forty, but maybe she could still outfox the big M and start a family up in the sun and become someone else.

But first they had to exhaust this quest. Three more days. After that she would turn around and never look back again.

The trail narrowed. The bridges grew miserly and more dangerous. The walls thickened with stony scabs.

They made camp beneath long, ragged curtains of hanging moss. Gregorio guessed they had dropped a mile in elevation from the lake. Quad busting, he called their descent. An hour later, Ali woke with cramps in her thighs.

His light switched on. "Alexandra?"

"My thighs," she groaned.

"Lactic acid," Gregorio pronounced. "From all the going down. Lie back. I will massage you." He kept a straight face. "Or you will die."

He began kneading her thighs. The spasms faded. "You can stop," she said.

"A little more." His hands moved higher. "You're still tight."

Tight, perhaps, but feeling no pain. To the contrary. "Gregorio . . ." He was devastating her.

"It's no problem. A little exorcism, that's all. I am banishing the bad spirits."

Time out. "Stop," she said.

He stopped. Her leg promptly spasmed. He went back to work.

He had no way of knowing how ready her body was. Then she smelled her own musk. "Wait," she said.

It was not that she needed wine and roses, or even a hot bath. Indeed, ten years ago the caves had sufficed for her and Ike. She'd gotten pregnant in this tubular night.

"Tell me what you want," he said.

That was the crux of it. What did she want? Love, of course. But also a child, if that was possible, and by this good man. But not one conceived in the abyss.

All she had to do was say nothing. They could travel upon each other's bodies all the way out of here. They could transcend the darkness.

She sat up. "Soon," she said to him. Not someday. Soon. "I promise."

On the fifth morning from the lake, the faint path evaporated in their light. The tunnel branched right and left, and then right and left again. With no marks to guide them, Ali found herself fishing for the faint wind. Gregorio, bless him, chiseled the walls like a jailbird, diligently marking each twist and turn for their exit.

Higher it had been a fitful breeze, almost too faint to feel. Here it issued upward in a steady warm stream that combed back her hair and carried a slight aroma. It carried something else, too, a thousand voices speaking a thousand languages. Whenever Ali came to a fork, she fished for that breeze and went into it.

They dined on teriyaki Slim Jims, protein bars, and Jolly Rancher candies, the last of their food from the World. The supplies and fuel they had so carefully salvaged from empty villages had gone down with their rafts. Except for Gregorio's experiment with trilobite meat (too rubbery, and it tasted like water), they had managed to keep their diet free of the territory. Sooner than later, though, they were going to have to go native and risk the hallucinations. He kept eyeing the cave pools and their blind, slow-moving fish. But Ali resisted. Before possibly infecting herself, she needed to figure out the whispers.

The lower they went, the more constant the voices became. Oddly, that made them easier for Ali to ignore. There is only so long you can listen to the traffic outside your window before it becomes part of the inside. The welter of languages receded in her mind. It helped that she was so tired and hungry and had blisters on her feet.

The sixth morning she woke from yet another dream of Maggie. They were striding through the grass, making stories from the clouds overhead. *There is a castle, there is its tower, there is the princess waiting.*

"It's time, Alexandra."

Today was to be their final day of descending. Unless they found some relevant sign, their climb up to the surface began tonight.

They followed the tunnel lower. Water beaded on the ceiling and sweated down on them. The walls narrowed. The floor turned into a tangle of fallen rock. Everything about it suggested a dead end, everything but that wind with its clamoring whispers.

All day long, Gregorio gave her the full benefit of their search. He didn't pester her for a turnaround point. He didn't check his wristwatch. He wanted her to have no doubts about leaving behind her old life.

But then a butterfly appeared from the darkness. Its orange-and-black wings flickered in their light like frames of a movie. Gregorio stopped in his tracks. "Impossible," he said.

"Sea serpents and trilobites," she said. "Why not butterflies?"

He looked at his altimeter. "Forty-five thousand feet below sea level?"

It lighted on her forearm, wings slowly pulsing. After a few seconds, it took flight again and wagged higher into the tunnels, borne by the breeze. Gregorio's wide eyes met hers.

It was not that the Interior was barren of life, far from it. Except for a few parasites that required hominidal blood, the sudden erasure of man and manlike beings from the Subterrain had gone spectacularly unnoticed down here. From mosses and aquatic plants to mice and eels, the place was thriving.

And yet this butterfly did not fit.

"A monarch butterfly?" said Gregorio. "Where did it come from? We must find out."

It had never occurred to Ali that a butterfly could be a mortal temptation.

"Lepidoptera!" he shouted over his shoulder.

The wind in the tunnel was getting stronger.

"Moths, yes, they are nocturnal," he said. "But a butterfly? They are creatures of the sun. And monarchs travel in flocks. She could be lost, this one. But so lost? Eight miles below sea level? No, there must be more. But how can this be?"

"Gregorio, I don't know."

"There must be a hatchery somewhere," he said.

It was getting harder to think clearly. The voices kept getting stronger. Soon, she would have to confess her illness to him. First, however, she had to confess it to herself. There were still too many ways to dodge the verdict.

If the hallucinations robbed you of appetite, for instance, why was she so hungry? And if the delirium was so contagious, how come Gregorio was unaffected? After all, he was the one who had eaten from the lake. Or was he hiding his delirium the way she was hiding hers? Or had he told her and she'd forgotten?

The descent grew steeper. Several times they had to lower their packs to each other and climb down. They came to a hole. They stood at the edge, angling with their lights for a floor or a ledge.

"I don't see a thing down there," said Ali. "Gregorio, it's time to turn around."

His blood was up, though. The butterfly had him going. "Let me try one thing." He tied his headlamp to the tip of their only rope. It was an old rope, but in immaculate condition, one of Ike's that he'd left stowed in a trunk in her closet. Gregorio carefully slid the light down the rock face.

Let there be darkness, thought Ali. *Let us put an end to this.*

The light came to rest on solid ground. Gregorio was triumphant. *"En avant!"* he said. "The way lies open to us."

Ali sighed. In caving, Newton's law reversed. Whatever goes down must come up. She eyed the drop-off. The one thing she hated more than rappelling down was jumaring back up. But Gregorio had followed her on her search. It was only fair to follow him on his.

She went first, leaving him in darkness without his headlamp. As she roped down into the bulging pit, Ali watched for any sign that Ike or Mc-Nabb might have come this way. But there were no old ropes hanging in place, no scratched initials, no traces of an extreme tourist.

Partway down, she heard Gregorio's voice and stopped. He was talking to himself up there. His conversation was animated and in Basque, not even Spanish. He laughed. "Is everything okay?" she said.

Silence. Finally he called, "Alexandra, was that you?"

Who else? "Were you saying something to me?"

"No, no," he said, too quickly.

The voices, she realized. He was hearing them, too. They would have to talk about this.

At the bottom she unclipped from the rope and scouted with her light. The tunnel led on. "I'm down," she called. The rope began to snake up, then his headlamp caught on a spur. "Do you want your light?"

"No need."

She unknotted the headlamp, and perched it on a broken stump. She turned off her light to conserve it.

Gregorio pulled up the rope. His voice trickled down, then a laugh. He was having a very good time by himself up there.

Ali noticed a drop of blood on her forearm. When she wiped it away, another bead appeared. She remembered the butterfly. It had lighted at that very spot.

The packs came scuffing down on the end of the rope. She untied them. "I'll be down in a minute," he said.

"Are you sure you don't want your light?"

"I can do this in my sleep."

Ali bent to drag his heavy pack to one side. Words rained down. More laughter. Then she heard, "Oh, shit."

She started to raise her head.

A dark angel seized the light.

Ali spied the thing from the corner of her eye.

A mass of limbs swooped down with wings like rags. There was a terrible racket of sticks snapping and melon breaking. The juice whipped her eyes. Ali tumbled back.

The light from Gregorio's headlamp snuffed out.

Ali lay in the darkness, too shocked to move. She did not turn on her light. She knew what had just happened, but did not want to see it. At last there was no more putting it off.

"Gregorio?"

Silence.

She thumbed the switch on and cut a hole in the night.

He lay broken backward on the stump. The wings of his shirttails were soaked with gore. His hair hung upside down, exposing his face.

Blind me. "Gregorio?" *Rob my thoughts.* Slowly she got to her feet. *Take me away.*

The rope lay unspooled in muddled strands. Loops draped his body. She kept her distance.

Twice she tried to bridge the awful expanse between her and . . . it. This was not Gregorio. He would never do such a thing. Break her heart? No, he had dropped this puppet down to frighten her. *How could you?*

She focused on the rope. It looked intact, no frayed sheath or blown tips. The rope had not failed. Gregorio had. All she could deduce was that he had untied the rope and then leaned back. She remembered him laughing up there.

"Gregorio." No questioning this time. She stated his name. She identified the dead.

He revived. He seemed to. His basket of ribs moved. Or was that her light jostling the shadows? Was it the wind, or had he just drawn a breath? *God help me.* Was he alive?

Ali tried to think. First she would have to make him warm. And get him water, he would need water. And stitch his wounds. And splint the bones. Get him settled for the long wait. Maybe pile some rocks as a windbreak. Then she would race for help. *I will return for you.* Like in the movies.

She cast her light up the hole, and there was no exit. Maybe Ike could have managed the blank rock, but the way was closed to her.

"Gregorio?" *Help me.*

She felt pinned in place by his eyes—his beautiful black eyes—turned wrong side up. Blood streamed into them from his nostrils, but he did not blink. His neck had snapped. He was dead after all.

He spoke.

Distinctly, with all the seriousness of a child who has been left alone entirely too long, a voice came from Gregorio's mouth. But it wasn't his voice.

"Mommy," it said.

As if toppling from a great height, Ali dropped to her knees.

Face-to-face with those sightless eyes, she whispered, "Maggie?"

The mouth didn't move. The voice was just using it. "Mommy," it said. "Help me."

ARTIFACTS

A LETTER HOME

Dear Marcia,

I have turned around (along with most of the army) and was going to return home. But then it seemed like such a waste to let all the opportunities down here pass me by. Why not turn the sour into the sweet? That's the American way.

So now I am in Electric City. The locals said stay awhile, "There's a place here for a sturdy man like you." It is good to be wanted again after all those months of unemployment. They said that even though I have no mining skills, they can use me. Here's the deal, and I think you'll agree it's a dandy.

There's no money involved. (They don't have any.) But I will get a part share in the big project here, which is to drill down to hot rocks to make electricity, and then we'll hit it rich. I don't mean just rich. I mean *really* rich! We're going to change the world, babe, no more fossil fuels and smog and oil wars. Just the quiet hum of electricity. And it all starts here. Rockefeller and Bill Gates and Mr. Donald Trump, move over.

So I am going to stay on awhile. Please know that this is all for you. These folks are a little strange, but they're right around the corner from the greatest treasure of all time, the energy of, by, and for our planet. Once we strike the mother lode, you and I are in the money, honey! We'll pay off all the credit cards and banks. Do you still want that ninety-two-inch LDTV? How about one for every room?

If you could, please put together a month's supply of Power-Bars and dehydrated food and some treats (you know what I like) and send it to me at Electric City. People here eat bush meat, which comes from some kind of cave animals, and I don't have a particular taste for it. It's a hungry place. You should see me, babe. I've lost the tire and handles. One of the miners said, "Don't get skinny on us, John. Keep some meat on you."

So I love you, Marcia, and can't wait to see you in a short while with all the money I'm bringing up with me.

Love,
John

28

DIALOGUES WITH THE ANGEL, NUMBER 9

"Long before the first man or woman found their way in to me," says the angel, "I knew something extraordinary was rising up in the sunshine."

Inside the tomb, the student listens to the tales, delirious with knowledge lost and regained.

"I can't say when I first became aware of the souls. I'm not sure when they first became aware of me. These were a new phenomenon for me. Like the rumbling of faraway earthquakes, or the whisper of invisible gases, I could hear these spirits but not see or touch them or comprehend what they were. To tell the truth, for the longest time they frightened me.

"I have explained that I once knew everything that would occur in the universe, but forgot it and that I now recall everything even as it happens. My memory of each thing is simultaneous to its existence. I recall each drop of water falling from the ceiling in the instant that it falls. Just so, I immediately recognized the voices as something very different from the planet's steam pipes and joints or the sound of more and more animals taking up residence in my kingdom down here.

"These voices were unlike anything I'd ever experienced. Have you ever listened to crystals growing? It's like a single note being played over and over. Or the sound of a mouse pleading with a cat for its life? Pleading? Do you think a mouse pleads? A mouse doesn't know what life is. It merely lives. Pinned down by claws, it squeaks, nothing more. It's afraid. Simply afraid."

The disciple's ribs lift and fall, touching the ribs beside him. He is not afraid of death anymore. No squeaks from him. He knows what lies on the *other side now. He has listened to the soul of the man he murdered with his bare hands. His ears can hear. He knows the man's name now. It whispers to him, over and over. William McNabb. No one.*

"*The moment the voices found me, everything changed,*" says the angel. "*I heard heartache and mourning, and from that I immediately gleaned their opposites, joy and laughter. I heard despair, and from that gleaned desire and happiness. I heard loss, and from that companionship and love. I heard solitude, and in that instant my billions of years of isolation came crashing in upon me. Do you understand? I heard the song of myself.*

"*Except for the remarkable emotion buried inside them, their sounds were little more than animal hoots and groans. Don't mistake me. I'm fluent in the utterances of all the species, and was perfectly able to communicate at their level. We could have gone on hooting and groaning to each other until the end of time. But I began to sense a much richer prize.*

"*These were the castoff souls of a new kind of creature. I had no idea that the creatures might look like me. At first I only knew that they lived in the sun, and that when they died they shed their bodies. This gave me hope. Maybe I could escape, like them. But first I needed to teach them how to teach me. That was when I began organizing their sounds into words.*

The disciple stops him. "Souls? Dead souls?"

"*You doubt your own myths?*" says the angel. "*Call them what you want, your echoes and driftwood. Your leftovers. Souls.*"

"*The good as well as the bad?*"

"*All of them.*"

"*But why?*"

"*Because they're lost, and I am here. Over time more voices descended to me. They used languages I had taught their forebears. It was then I realized that the voices could travel back and forth to the surface at whim, and that they could speak to the living, and that I could use them as my eyes to see what I can't see, and my fingers to touch a world I can't touch, and my messengers to shape man's destiny, and in shaping your destiny to shape my own.*

"*These dead souls told me stories about the world above. They told me stories about running free. Only then did I realize how completely I am imprisoned. Also they told me stories about me, their horror. The Zulu called me Unkulunkulu, the Very Old. The Xhosa called me Unvelingange, He Who Preexists. The Bantu pygmies, and before them the other tribes, called me*

Nzame. *The Babylonians knew me as Tiamat, who predated the gods. Augustine named me Tehom, the Deep. The Mayans called me Chi Con Gui-Jao, the Lord of the Cave, He Who Knows What Lies Beneath the Stone.*

"*I could have objected. My narrative had gotten away from me. You were writing me even as I was writing you. I could have destroyed you. Instead I decided, if you can't beat 'em, join 'em. I began nurturing the myths, and used them as a sort of night school for your so-called afterlife. Now I don't even have to send old souls out to seek new souls. You automatically come to me. It is wired into your consciousness.*

"*In this way, like the good shepherd, I grew my flock of souls. Every sheep that strays down to me, I take him in. Every lamb, I memorize her name and the names of her parents and children, the living and the dead. I connect all of your history. I know everything that came before you. With a little prompting, I have begun to remember everything that will come after you. Between your past and future lies me. That is my state. I am trapped in your story. But I am your storyteller. Do you understand?*"

"No, Lord."

"Ah," he sighs. "Me, either."

ARTIFACTS

from NAVAL SPECIAL WARFARE BASIC SNIPER TRAINING

Hostage Situations

2. a. Snipers . . . must appreciate that even a good, well-placed shot may not always result in the instantaneous death of a terrorist. Even an instantly fatal shot may not prevent the death of a hostage when muscle spasms in the terrorist's body trigger his weapon. As a rule then, the sniper should only be employed when all other means of moving the situation have been exhausted.

2. b. Consider the size of the target in a hostage situation. Doctors all agree that the only place on a man, where if struck with a bullet instantaneous death will occur, is the head. (Generally, the normal human being will live eight to ten seconds after being shot directly in the heart.) The entire head of a man is a relatively large target measuring approximately seven inches in diameter. But in order to narrow the odds and be more positive of an instant killing shot, the size of the target greatly reduces. The portion of the brain that controls all motor-reflex actions is located directly behind the eyes and runs generally from earlobe to earlobe and is roughly two inches, not seven inches.

29

They were chasing fictions.

Except for Clemens and Rebecca, not one of her army had ever seen a live hadal in person. Hunter and his DZ boys, all veterans of the deep, had missed the wars a decade and more ago. Even Beckwith, who had seen the hadals through his sniper scope, had only imagined seeing them. The twelfth of January changed that.

Rebecca was drifting on a raft down a wide canyon river with Hunter and five of the operators. Ahead of them, the first raft carried the point team and a radio. The rest of the army—fewer than three hundred men now—floated far behind in a line that would extend for ten hours or longer.

After a week of trekking, the rafts felt almost sinful. But on foot they had been covering just four miles a day. The river was carrying them ten times faster without any more man power than a paddle dipped now and then.

Clemens preferred to range alongside them on shore, or float in his own raft, alone as usual. He said he didn't want to miss any sign or secondary paths. Hunter said that was bull, that Clemens just had an aversion to people who had an aversion to him. "Face it," he told Rebecca. "The man's a freak. He's got the mark of Cain on him. These recaps spend the rest of their lives roaming the fringes and bottom-feeding."

No one in the raft spoke much. Rebecca had been pushing without letup ever since they found the boys' skins at the toll bridge, and pushing the men meant pushing herself. When they were tired, she made sure to be twice as tired.

The slow current nudged them along. Her muscles unwound. She fell asleep. The radio scratched her from her nap. "Bogie on the portside," whispered a man with the point crew.

Immediately all lights snapped off. The river went black. Without a word, Hunter's men switched on their night optics. Low and even, Hunter said, "What do you have?"

"Seven individuals at two hundred meters below the oxbow. We've already passed them. They didn't see us."

Hunter went back and forth with his point crew. "Beach your boat downriver," Hunter said. "Set a flanking position. We'll hit them from the river."

"What about Clemens?" asked Rebecca.

"What about him?" said Hunter.

"He could get caught in the crossfire. Or somebody might mistake him for the enemy."

"He knows we're in Indian country," Hunter said, but he made the call anyway. "Clemens, do you read? Be advised, we have bad guys up ahead."

If he heard it, Clemens didn't answer. Rebecca scanned the shore for him. Not even a heat signature. He had another nickname. The Invisible Man.

"There's the oxbow."

They chambered rounds and drifted, ready, locked and loaded. The water scarcely lapped their rubber sides. Sprawled low behind the hull, Rebecca felt the long, wide throw as they entered the river's bend.

A decade had passed since the last hadal had supposedly been wiped out. That meant a lot of collective rumors and rust. Some of her men had been just eight years old at the time. The few "old men" with any subterranean combat training were maybe wiser than the virgins, but definitely slower. This was the problem, Hunter said, with too few wars.

Haddie had grown ten feet tall, with vampire teeth and a supernatural taste for cruelty. No one quite remembered how quickly the creatures could move, how acute their eyesight and hearing were, or how they fought, with tooth and nail or with what manner of weapons. Rebecca wasn't sure if the advice to save the last bullet for yourself was tongue in cheek or not.

And so the animals they sighted below the oxbow seemed almost pathetic to her as they shambled about at the water's edge. Rebecca dialed up the power, amping for the big look. The binoculars autofocused. She got her dose.

They were feeding. Their victims lay sprawled along the shore. A woman had nearly made it to the river. Farther along the beach, a hadal was washing a joint of someone's arm.

Rebecca spied the village in neon green. Even before the attack, it hadn't been much of a place. The few stone shelters were roofed with tarps in shreds. They looked like broken drums.

Her first instinct was to attach a story to each of the bodies and give them back their lives. But the pale monsters kept distracting her. One was humping a small, still figure, like a dog. One was rooting through a mess of eels beside a man, except they weren't eels.

Rebecca kept shifting the view. Everywhere she looked, new shocks were waiting. She had never seen anything being skinned before. It came off like panty hose.

Leave the victims, she counseled herself. *Learn the scavengers.* They were hairless and wildly encrypted, a twenty-thousand-year-old street gang with cancer horns and bony ribs and no respect for the dead. One made rubbery faces with a man's face. One reached in, and came out with a slippery meat.

She kept the binoculars to her eyes. At least with the glass between her and that, she could imagine a separation. With a flick of the switch, she could paint it different colors. She could pick which corner of the movie screen to watch while the scary part finished. She could pretend she was in control.

There was a big-meal slowness to the scene. The hadals were in no hurry. Not one of them suspected the river.

The boat drifted closer to shore. Rebecca sensed, rather than saw, the DZ men hand gesturing and picking targets and otherwise preparing. She trusted them to do what they were about to do.

As they closed in on the beach, she expected masses of Hollywood gunfire and screaming and confusion. They would wade ashore, hide behind rocks, and pay for every square inch with blood.

Rebecca huddled in the boat, quiet as a mouse, full of dread. She didn't belong here, up front, so close, sharing the first blood. It was too soon, too sudden, without prelude. Weren't you supposed to plan these things out with maps and grease pencils and history books? Until this moment, she had not known how unready she was for her own war. What if something happened to her? Sam needed a mother. Sam. *Sam.*

There was no time for her to look away.

Hunter did not bark a "Fire!" or a "Now!" Synched by training, the soldiers simply triggered the shot as one. You couldn't have done it in a comic book. There was no thunder or flame to their barrage, no Boom, Kapow, or Zap, no rattle or roar. The whole thing sounded like a lady fart. One small puff, and it was over.

None of the hadals went spinning. None flew backward. There was no ballet of stopping power. Rather they slumped like tired old men. One tripped. One keeled over, like a drunk. Apparently unfamiliar with bullets, one lean buck slapped at his chest as if stung by a bee, and then went about his business for another thirty seconds. Finally he sat down and died.

While the others kept their rifles trained on the kill, two of the DZ men paddled them onto the beach. Rebecca stayed out of their way. She was a passenger. River rocks bulged the raft floor under her feet. "Stay here," Hunter told her.

She nodded gratefully.

The boat crew fanned apart with their weapons and NODS, no lights yet, checking first the dead hadals, then the dead humans. Hunter popped a flare. The place lit up. "Check the huts." Hunter and his five men prowled from sight, leaving Rebecca alone in the raft.

Rebecca sat with her back straight, watching the still bodies. At last she stood up and straddled the hull to enter the war. The beach was solid underfoot. It was real.

It was necessary to get this part of her education over with. The bloodletting had finally begun. The carnage was bound to pile up, and she could not afford to be frail or squeamish in front of the men. It was time to get down with the dead.

She went to the first body. Facedown, it seemed to be taking a nap. She forced herself to bend and press one palm on the man's back. He had the body heat of a child, warm, still a little sweaty.

The second body was not so user friendly. A gaping exit wound bared the spine and nameless jellies. That, too, she touched.

Rebecca moved on to a third body, this one gut shot. It smelled like an outhouse. Repulsion was not an option. She had to steel herself. Any day now, any hour, from here on, here was the risk.

She reached down. *Touch them all.* This could be one of her own men lying on the ground.

But it was not a man.

It grabbed her throat.

Rebecca reared back. The hadal was faster. Quick as a snake, even trailing his slick of entrails, he whipped around behind her. He clamped her mouth and nose shut, and pulled her backward on top of him.

Rebecca resisted. She had taken rape-defense training in her sorority. *Never stop fighting. Use everything. Kick. Bite. Scream.* But she could barely breathe. Every move she made, he tightened a little harder.

There she lay, wrapped in his legs and arms and guts, strangling. Faceup, she saw a pretty flare. The creature was hot against her back. He had BO. And calluses on his palms.

Where was Hunter?

The flare sank lower. The shadows lengthened. Another flare streamed up from the settlement. Smoke gushed from its light.

A second monster appeared. Rebecca didn't know where he'd come from. She could barely see.

The two monsters spoke.

It sounded like crickets.

Hunter would never find her in time. These things would drag her away into the deeps. This couldn't be happening. She should have stayed in the boat. *I'm just a housewife.* Then a thought occurred: wherever they took her, they might have taken Sam.

Sam's favorite at the zoo had always been the otters that lay on their backs and pried open the clams. Clutching her to his stomach, the hadal suddenly rolled upright. The hand across her face eased. He let her breathe through her nose. His nails stunk of carrion. She threw up into his hand. The acid burned her sinuses. Her eyes watered. The world blurred. It faded.

"Quit struggling," the second monster said to her in perfect English.

She craned to see.

It was Clemens.

"He doesn't want to kill you," he said. "He needs you. Relax. Just let him have you."

He was sitting on his heels to one side, watching, casual as family. His rifle lay on the pebbles, not in surrender but in peace. She didn't understand.

How could he not hate them? They had cropped his face and written on his flesh and stolen his life. And even if he did not love or desire her, Clemens craved her beauty. That was his weakness and her power over him. So she had thought.

But the bare facts were otherwise. Clemens was a traitor. He had turned on his own kind. He had become one of them. Rebecca let go. She went limp.

Chirping and cricketing, Clemens went on with the apelike thing, not exactly best friends, but hardly mortal enemies. Their conversation was harsh and delicate at the same time.

The hadal's steel grip relaxed. The hand went from her mouth to her breast, nothing loving about it. Her breast—her tender charm—was nothing more than a handle to him. If she moved to escape, if she cried out, he would rip her apart.

Rebecca took a breath. "They know you?" she said.

"Rebecca, they made me."

Clemens took out his knife. "Don't move," he told her. "He wants your body. Ever heard that one, Rebecca?"

She stared at him. "What are you doing?"

"He's dying," Clemens said. "He knows it. He told me to bleed you out. Not all the way, just enough."

She started struggling again. "You're going to cut me?"

"His soul is about to travel. It has to go somewhere. They believe that."

"Please don't," she said. "Joshua."

"It's the only way, Rebecca. He's telling me things we need to know."

We? She quit struggling. "What are you talking about?"

"Do you want to live?"

"Of course."

"Do you want to see your daughter?"

"Yes."

"Have you ever played poker?"

"What are you talking about?"

"We're going to call his bluff, Rebecca. But first we have to play."

Still in his squat, Clemens duck-walked closer. The hadal tightened on her again, keeping her between him and Clemens, or baring her for the knife. Or both. He didn't trust Clemens yet.

"This will hurt a little," Clemens said, lifting the knife. He nicked the vein on the inside of her biceps. Blood jumped out. It startled her.

"What about Sam?" she said.

"The children are three days ahead."

Three days. She had come so close.

Clemens backed away. He and the creature resumed their insect chitchat. Her arm ached. She shifted her hand in the pooling blood.

The hadal was strong, stronger than Jake, ape strong. But his strength was ebbing, Rebecca could feel it. His life was draining away, just like hers. If Clemens had not come along, she might just have outlasted the creature on her own.

"Are you okay?" Clemens asked her.

"Sam," she said. "Is she all right?"

"None of the girls has been killed," Clemens said.

"But is she all right?" Rebecca repeated.

"She's alive."

The world . . . weakened. Rebecca tipped her head back. Her cheek rested against the hadal's cheek. They were dying together, like lovers. Another flare went up. Gorgeous light.

Clemens went back to their strange language. The hadal's voice softened.

"They're not going to the city," Clemens said.

"But you said," she whispered.

"I was wrong. They're going someplace else."

"Where?"

"I'm working on it."

"Will he tell you?"

"I opened your vein. He thinks I'm on his side."

"You're not?"

"Stay with me," he said. "This is almost over."

She hung upon his ravaged face. "Find my daughter."

"I'm doing my best. Can you hang on a little longer?"

"It's getting cold."

"Don't go to sleep, Rebecca. I need to know when it gets too much."

Just then the hadal tensed. Rebecca heard footsteps. Hunter and his men approached from the shadows.

"Stay back," Clemens warned them.

Hunter took a step, hands empty and on display. "Clemens," he said. "Let's talk."

"It's under control here," Clemens said. "Get those men out of here."

"You can walk out of here," Hunter said. "You and your friend. Just tell him to let Rebecca go." He took another step.

"I've got him talking," Clemens said.

"She's bleeding to death."

"She'll be okay. I know what I'm doing."

Red laser dots flickered on Clemens's face. Rebecca's teeth chattered.

"Let her go, Clemens."

"You don't understand. Just back away."

Hunter took another step closer.

Clemens said something to the hadal. Immediately the nails dug into her breast. The other hand started raking at her belly. The thing was trying to disembowel her. Rebecca cried out.

Hunter froze.

"Tell him," Clemens said to her.

"Go away," Rebecca said to Hunter.

"Not without you," said Hunter.

"We're finding out," she said.

"Finding out?"

"He knows where they are," she said. "The children."

Hunter narrowed his eyes. He took it in. At last he signaled to the circle of men. The barrels of their weapons lifted. The fireflies left Clemens's face. The men retreated.

"Farther," said Clemens. "All the way. Get in the boat. Take it out into the river."

The soldiers did as he said. The talons eased. Clemens spoke again, his tone soothing beneath the clicks and twitters. The hadal murmured by Rebecca's ear. It seemed to go on a very long time. Her vision turned patchy. She was floating in and out.

"Where?" she whispered.

Clemens came closer. He asked again. The hadal's grip slackened. With a shove, she could have freed herself. But her strength had drained away. She nestled back upon his body. She was cold. He was warm. The creature was her collaborator. Together they would find Sam.

The hadal lifted his head to speak. Rebecca made room for his secret. Clemens bent to hear.

The creature's head exploded. It flew to bits. His grip let go. His secret, Sam's location, abruptly died.

The men looked at each other to see whose weapon had been fired. There were shrugs all around. The kill was like magic.

A few seconds later a lone gunshot snapped in the far black distance.

Clemens stood and opened his arms. "I think," he said, "someone just killed your little girl."

"No," she whispered.

Hunter and his men swarmed ashore. The sky got very busy with flares and shadows and people who closed her wound and wrapped her in a sleeping bag and hooked her to an IV. The transfusion poured warmth into her. Warmth and rage.

"Where is my daughter?"

"I don't know," said Clemens.

"But he told you."

"Not quite. Hunter put a stop to that."

But Hunter swore neither he nor any of his men had pulled the trigger. Her fury mounted. They were lying.

The sniper arrived an hour later. "You're safe," Beckwith said. He looked proud even.

"It was you?" said Rebecca. She had bled almost to death for the information. Only to have it killed by the lone ranger.

"Ma'am?" Beckwith was confused.

Hunter descended on him. He was trying to get back into her good graces. "Do you know what you've done?"

"I would have taken the shot sooner," Beckwith apologized. "I was at nine hundred yards. I needed to be sure."

"You crazy son of a bitch," said Hunter. "How much more damage can you do with that rifle?"

Beckwith looked from one face to another, bewildered. He faced her. "I don't understand."

Rebecca turned from him, cradling her arm, sick at the seesaw of fate. He was innocent. He was guilty. He had saved her. He had killed her. Everything depended on Sam.

"For God's sake," Hunter said to the sniper, "put us all out of your misery. Just eat your next bullet."

ARTIFACTS

TELEVISION COMMERCIAL

FORD TRUCK

Rebecca Coltrane episode. 30-second spot. Hold for Super Bowl release.

FADE IN:

EXT. A STEEP MOUNTAIN RIDGELINE
Off-road in the Rocky Mountains, a Ford 150 climbs the rugged slope. A series of shots: rocks fly, tires bounce and grab, the chassis rocks back and forth.

CUT TO:

EXT. A LOG ON RIDGELINE
A fallen tree blocks the way. The truck climbs over.

NARRATOR (VO)
Nothing stops Rebecca Coltrane.

CUT TO:

INT. THE TRUCK CAB
Rebecca is driving. Her jaw is set. She wrestles the wheel. She is a winner.

CUT TO:

EXT. TOP OF THE RIDGELINE
The truck tops the ridgeline.

NARRATOR (VO)
Nothing stops a Ford truck.

CUT TO:

EXT. A FRONTIER MINE ON TOP OF THE RIDGELINE
The truck approaches the mouth of an Old West mine. It pauses at the dark entrance.

CUT TO:

INT. THE TRUCK CAB
Rebecca narrows her eyes. She is taking aim. She turns on the headlights and shifts into gear.

CUT TO:

EXT. THE MINE ENTRANCE
The truck enters the mouth of the mine.

                                                CUT TO:

EXT. THE MOUNTAIN SIDE (aerial, POV)
Pull back from mine to show the wild mountainside. We have
been watching the POV of ...

                                                CUT TO:

EXT. BLUE SKY
A bald eagle drafts high overhead, watching over the
mountains.

                                                FADE OUT

30

Ali left Gregorio's grave at the foot of the sinkhole that had killed him. At a safe distance, she turned to say good-bye. The pile of stones looked forlorn and tiny. It pulled at her heart. *Stay.* She could practically hear him.

She fled his death, or tried to. But Gregorio found her.

He wasn't the only one.

Mommy? Maggie's voice sailed to her on the wind. "Help me, Mommy."

Ali leaned into the pack straps. She strained against her madness. The tunnel led down. Gravity was with her. But with the wind in her face and the voices in her head, it felt like an uphill battle all the way.

The cave drip and the moist draft licked at her skin. Everything was body temperature, even the darkness. It was like fighting to fit into her own skin.

Her only hope of exit lay in the unknown ahead. Gregorio had untied the rope before his fall. She could not climb that wall. There was no going back.

At the same time it seemed there was no going forward. More than ever, the past ruled, beckoning from behind, from in front, from every side.

Alexandra. Gregorio, pleading. *Stay with me.*

Maggie cried. *Mommy, I hurt. Come find me.*

Like that, pushed and pulled by her dead, Ali sank into the stone wilderness. She did not bother to invent ways to measure her descent. She just walked.

Not long before her light gave out, a sign appeared. Beneath an overhang, scratched into the stone and grown over with red and yellow lichen, stood a jagged trick-or-treat grin.

ᗺᗺ

"McNabb," said Ali, running her fingers over the initials. She searched for other signs, but there were no alephs or *IC*s or artifacts. McNabb had come this way, though. He had found some reason for continuing down this passageway. Ali was grateful beyond words for his company.

Her headlamp died abruptly. The beam didn't fade. It just blinked out.

She should have been ready. She had thought she was. Cavers always carry a backup, if not two or three. But Gregorio's fall had crushed her pack and broken her carbide lamp. And suddenly she couldn't find her spare flashlight.

The darkness was everywhere at once. It reached inside her clothes. She breathed it into her lungs. The pack suddenly weighed a ton.

She knew the medical term for her panic reaction: dissociation hysteria. Blacklock, in the settler slang. Cave frenzy. People lost their heads. They imagined creepy crawlers on their skin. Some bolted to their deaths off cliffs or into rivers.

Ali forced herself to be calm. *If you can't stand, sit.* She shucked the pack. She sat. Her knees quit shaking. She counted her pulse out loud. It was a way to connect the inside with the outside, to do a rational thing. "Twenty-four, twenty-five, twenty-six . . ." A bubble materialized around her. With words alone, she managed to hold back the darkness.

Taking the pack between her knees, she carefully sorted through every item by touch. "Socks," she said aloud. "Spoon. Toothbrush." Each syllable was a brick in the wall. In a side pocket, she found the plastic bag with spare batteries. Incredibly, not one fit her headlamp. And in her rush to leave Gregorio's grave, she had left her flashlight.

Ali stared at the blackness. She chided herself. *Bear down. Do this thing. Survive.*

She returned everything to the pack, memorizing where each item lay. There was zero margin for error now. Standing, she worked on the pack. She took a halting step, and then another, hands outstretched. She found the tunnel wall. *Victory.* She spider-walked her fingers along the wall, feeling with her toes, taking more steps.

Ike used to tell her that seeing was not always sight. The difference between the two was time. It took time—or the latest pharmaceuticals—for the human eye to acclimate to the abyss. Modern settlers swore by the drugs that amplified the photosensitive chemical rhodopsin, or visual purple, in the eye. Others took vitamin A injections, or used eyedrops that boosted the retina's rod count. Minus the pharmaceuticals, Ali could only hope time might work.

Keeping to the wall, she continued into the breeze. Waiting in the dark was not an option, not for her, not with the voices gaining force. If they resulted from sensory deprivation, then she was all the more vulnerable now.

Gregorio called from his grave. Maggie pleaded.

Hi, baby, said her father. It was him, his Lucky Strike voice. *God I've missed you. I'm waiting down below.*

I remember when you were still inside me, said her mother.

If they were simply snippets of memory, why did they all sound so full of misery? Their misery did not seem to unite them. Each clamored for her attention. That frightened her. They were hungry.

Remember that time you broke your arm? said her father. *I stuck with you.*

I loved you before you ever had a name. Her mother's rock-a-bye murmur. *You were my dream come true. Still are. Come find me.*

Help, Mommy.

Alexandra.

A chill shot through Ali. They were *competing* for her?

"Seven hundred and seventy-nine," she spoke to the gloom, counting her footsteps out loud. Floundering lower, she played crossword puzzles in her head. She sang songs. Anything to stifle their begging.

She made camp in the dark, feeling for a flat spot. Animals rustled among the stones. They took on voices. Ali fought back. She named the flavors in her meal bar. "Brown sugar," she said. "Oats. Peanuts."

But there was no escaping the voices. They followed her into her sleep. Ali dreamed so happily she never wanted to wake up.

She rode a horse with her mother. She smelled her father's Brut. She made sand castles with Maggie. She kissed Gregorio.

The dreams were so perfect they almost seemed made just for her.

But then blank spots began to intrude. They broke the dream flow, like empty frames in a movie. Except they weren't entirely empty. She tried to avoid them. There was something about them. Something troubling. Something evil. Ali made a mistake. She looked inside the gap.

Falling.

It hit her.

She was falling. *Oh God.* Falling into empty black isolation. She had never felt so ill. So cast away. The loneliness, it *hurt.*

With a cry, she woke and grabbed for her light, then remembered it was dead. Dead. That was how she had felt.

Her face was wet with sweat and tears, she could taste the salt. And bile. She had vomited. Her throat was raw with acid. She'd been weeping, no, howling with grief.

Suddenly she wasn't afraid of the lake sickness anymore. Because what if the voices were real? What if those famine-struck people that she and Gregorio had seen along the lake were actually talking to their dead? What if the lost souls were really souls, and the subterranean "hell" was really hell?

What if they needed her for their escape?

Maggie!

Ali scrambled to her feet. The wind pressed at her. The voices swirled around her.

There were more now. Her hearing had grown acute. The darkness was filled with voices. She heard rags of whispers. She heard syllables from the oldest edges of human language. Clicks and trills and guttural barking. There were hadal tongues in the mix, some she'd heard as a captive. And human languages. A bit of Latin sailed past. Mayan. Something like Chinese, tonal, but brutish, pre-Mandarin.

Dead souls? Warehoused in the gut of the planet? Damned?

She couldn't accept it.

The notion appalled her

Maggie? Damned? A child? Doomed to churn through these hollow spaces for the rest of time?

But what if it was so?

Could she save just one? "Maggie?" she called.

All at once, it seemed, the voices rushed at her in a mountain of noises.

They drove at her, whispering, beseeching, inconsolable. It went on and on. They were telling her about infinity.

"Stop," she said.

The voices stopped.

She waited in the pitch-blackness, full of fear. They would return. They were like wolves circling a deer. But could they harm her? Did a dead soul have any power in the real world?

Something touched her face.

She batted at it. It touched her hair. She pulled her head away.

The silence filled with animal sounds. Something slithered. Little feet tapped across the stone. A rock shifted.

She couldn't stay here one minute longer. She found the wall and resumed her descent by fingertips, down into the gentle wind.

Those invisible licks and kisses returned. She swiped at her hair and face and the backs of her hands.

At some point, Ali realized they were Gregorio's butterflies. Their wings brushed her cheeks, a few grams of touch. Their orange-and-black wings registered in her mind.

She held one finger up in the darkness, and one perched there. More lit upon her knuckles and hair. Every time she stopped, they flocked to her. Just as Gregorio had said, a hatchery must lie somewhere ahead. She had to be getting close.

Ali rested her hands on her knees. Her head was spinning. Even as the place unfolded its wonders, it was killing her. Lost souls and nocturnal butterflies. Grief and hunger. Her watch had stopped. The fluorescent hands stood frozen.

Death was winning.

She crept along the wall for what seemed like days.

Gradually her eyes began to adjust.

At first she saw only a bog of shadows. She thought she was seeing inside the vault of her eyes. Ever so slowly shapes appeared. Colors materialized.

By the next morning, she could see with the beginnings of what the colonists called "nerve sight." It gave strange vision, more plastic than crisp, more night than day. It was not the sunlit vision you found on the surface. But she could see!

Her pace picked up.

The butterflies came to her, lighting on her hair and shoulders and arms like an audience softly clapping. Their bleached markings, orange and black, were almost white. She was careful not to injure them. Then she felt the pinpricks of their mouths and saw blood running black down her arms. They were feeding on her. Everything hungered in this place. *Thy will be done.*

Ali forged on through the welter of butterflies and voices. She battled them with her word puzzles and arithmetic and songs. She flung her arms in the air to scatter the butterflies. At some point, her food ran out. She barely noticed.

The scent of cedar and orange blossoms and lavender and earthy loam came floating on the updraft. Incredibly a mourning dove cooed its song into the voices mobbing her.

She saw a light at the end of the tunnel.

Poor thing, she thought to herself. *You're losing your mind.*

The fertile hints—the butterflies, the fragrances, the birdsong, now this gleaming hole ahead—terrified her. She was no longer in control. The cave had won.

Turning a bend in the tunnel, Ali fell to her knees with a whimper.

Before her spread an immense chamber so beautiful and luminous that she felt ruined. The bottomless pit had a bottom after all. Here, she thought, was her source.

For thousands of years, mankind had salted away all its worst terrors in the deepest, darkest cellar hole. What faced her here was not hell on earth, though, but a glorious paradise. Out in the middle of the chamber lay a perfect oasis.

She could almost accept the oasis with its forest of cedars and bamboo. Nature was full of accidents and contradictions. It was possible, remotely possible, that a few seeds and shoots had trickled down from the world above and taken root and somehow thrived in this sunless place.

But jutting from the trees was a tower—or a palace, or a fortress—that defied all reason. Built of white stone, now half in collapse, it struck her at first as a twin sister of the Taj Majal. Then she saw staircases glued to its front and thought of the Potala in Tibet, though a Potala with a dome on top. Then she saw a spiral pattern to it, and wondered if it was meant to resemble the tower of Babel. Or had the Taj Majal and Potala and tower of

Babel been built to resemble this? Or was she simply imagining it? Because each time she looked away and back again, the building seemed to shift its shape a little, as if adjusting to her ideal.

There was no more fighting the facts. Her journey was done. Her sanity was finished. The fever dream had snared her.

In despair, Ali lay down on the ground, curled up like an animal, and rocked herself to sleep.

ARTIFACTS

ERRI DAILY INTELLIGENCE REPORT

January 18

Today's Central Focus
U.S. Reconnaissance Plane Lands in China

A navy EP-3 electronic reconnaissance plane was damaged in a midair collision with a Chinese fighter plane and made an emergency landing at Lingshui Military Airport on the Chinese island of Hainan. All twenty-four members of the navy crew are being held incommunicado. The Chinese plane went down at sea and the pilot is missing and presumed dead.

It is unclear if the contact between the two aircraft was accidental or the result of deliberate bumping by the Chinese or American plane. The Chinese have filed an official diplomatic protest, while American diplomats are attempting to ascertain the status of the U.S. plane and crew.

The Chinese Foreign Ministry has put all the blame on the U.S. aircraft for causing the collision. An international studies expert at Beijing's Tsinghua University said: "It's very regular for the American navy to have their planes intruding into Chinese airspace. The Chinese then send up fighters and chase them out." U.S. officials maintain that the plane was over international waters and never intruded into Chinese airspace until it declared a "Mayday" and made an emergency landing.

The U.S. ambassador to China has registered the "strongest" protest. He is quoted by Reuters as saying that this incident is a deliberate and highly dangerous attempt to retaliate for the Chinese submarine incident.

31

"I want you to imagine this," says the angel. "Imagine you are a little girl asleep in your house."

Near death, the disciple lies on his back, staring at the crypt's stone ceiling, eating mouthfuls of air.

"You are asleep in your bed," the angel goes on, "and all is right with the world. You are loved. You have food in your stomach. Your dreams are sweet. When suddenly the door bursts open in the middle of the night.

"Five men with robes and hidden faces barge in. Their lights blind you. You can hear your mother and sisters crying in the next room. You're too afraid to shout for help. The men yank off your blanket. They push up your gown. They pin your legs wide open. This is all done in silence. None of them speaks to you or to each other.

"So this is rape, you think. This is the disgrace that will mean death and hell for you. But it becomes different. It becomes worse. Because just then you see the glint of a razor blade in one man's hand. He leans down between your legs. Down to your sacred fruit.

"For a moment you are so ashamed you could die. Then pain devours your humiliation. You have never felt such searing pain in all your life. The man is breathing hard. He wipes the razor blade on the blanket. There is blood, yours, and bits of skin. Yours. He goes back to his task. The cutting goes on. He works until he has sliced away all of the offending flesh. When he's finally done, they cover you with the blanket as if putting you to bed. In the *name of God, one whispers to you. God be with you. It is said so tenderly you almost feel rewarded. By these devils!*

"It gets worse, if that is possible. Because as they leave the room, you see a bare foot missing one toe, and that is strange. First, it means that these monsters have taken off their sandals at the front door before breaking into your room to do this thing. Second, you recognize that foot. Or you recognize one man's limp. Or someone's ring. Or a birthmark.

"In that instant your world turns to vomit. Because these men who have cut away your womanhood and severed you from pleasures you will never know, they are your beloved uncles.

"It gets even worse. You heal. You grow into a woman. You marry and bear children, and one is a daughter. Then one night you wake in your bed to the sound of her door banging open. A minute later you hear a terrible scream. And just as your mother did, and her mother, and hers . . . you do nothing. You merely lie there and weep into your hands."

The disciple turns his head to look into the hollows of the skull beside him. The insects have done their job well. Except for the angel's terrible story, he is at peace in here. He tries to divine a lesson in the tale, but cannot. "Why?" he breathes at last. Why tell me?

"Because your people have made me the name of evil." The angel's voice is steely and at the same time wounded. "But even with all my imagination, with all my time, I could not dream up the cruelties that you and your kind inflict on one another every minute of every day. The worst evils are the ones you justify with your religions and laws and piety. But then there are evils so terrible you can't justify them, even with your most twisted logic, even with your most absurd religions, and those evils are the evils that you blame on me. Me, the one who brought you fire and taught you language and gave you cities and raised you out of the mud."

The disciple listens politely.

"Hell exists," the angel concludes. "But this is not it."

"Forgive us," the disciple breathes. Spare us.

The angel understands his meaning. "On one condition," he says.

"Lord?"

"Set me free."

The disciple breathes in. He breathes out. He suffers, but is beyond suffering. It is a blessed state. "Lord," he whispers, "I am useless to you."

"Perhaps not, my friend."

The disciple waits for the instruction that will come next. But there is none, only more ruminating.

"We're close to the final solution," says the angel. *"It just needs a little more gestation. A little more time in the womb. Or wombs. Freedom is coming, I can feel it. My door is opening."*

He wonders why the angel is baiting him, as he lies trapped in his tomb, with this talk of freedom and opened doors? Frankly, he doesn't give a damn. For he has achieved knowledge. Living with this corpse, he has seen life's illusions stripped away. He has watched flesh dissolve and slept with the bones. Suffering is impermanent. Even death is impermanent. Life goes on.

32

Rebecca's army came to a halt where the river forked. To the left, according to Clemens, the river led to a sea and the city of Hinnom. To the right, the river muscled into the unknown. Clemens insisted that was where they wanted to go.

"But our information says the children are being taken to the city," said Hunter. "The city at the center. The city of Satan."

"And our hadal friend said they're not," Clemens said. "Not to Hinnom. He was very clear. He was part of the rear guard. The main body has the children. They were on their way to a city, but a different one, the city of the ox. Taurus, he called it. He told me to watch for the horns. He was telling me more. Then his head sort of disappeared before my eyes."

Beckwith, he was talking about. The man with the golden trigger finger.

"Here are the horns," Clemens said. He pointed at the left fork. "My film team and I took that one. We went down to the sea and around it to Hinnom. It's three weeks at least from here." He pointed at the right fork. "This is the way we want to go, to the city of the ox. He said it was only a few days away."

"We should split the army in two," Hunter said to Rebecca.

Clemens objected. "It would make us half as strong."

"But we could cover twice the territory," said Hunter.

"And leave us too weak to fight."

Rebecca chewed her nicotine gum. That and black coffee had become her mainstay. She made them wait some more for her decision.

"Time is of the essence," said Hunter.

"United we stand . . ."

Their wrangle had entered the hoary chestnut zone. When they ran out of supporting information, their arguments always degenerated into a battle of clichés. Rebecca chewed her gum. Right or wrong, she had learned to pronounce her decisions without the slightest whiff of a question mark in her voice.

"Tell the men," she said. Hunter and Clemens quit their feuding. "Have them pull off the river here. We're going down the right fork."

"All of us?" said Hunter.

"The entire army."

"But my information . . ."

"You have your information, Mr. Hunter. I have mine." She had nearly bled to death to learn what they had from the hadal. Getting your arm slit open was a sorry reason for trusting one claim over another. But the violence had stamped it with an immediacy that felt true. Further, Clemens was right. Divided they would fall.

By this point, the flotilla of rubber dinghies and inflatable rafts stretched three days long, though that was just an estimate. Rebecca had lost radio contact with the majority of her army. She no longer had any idea how many men still remained, or what landmarks—an island, a continent, or the empty Pacific Ocean—lay above them on the surface. Their compasses circled drunkenly. Their watches were fickle and impossible to synchronize. They were profoundly out on a limb.

"That is my decision," she said. "We will proceed from here down the right branch to city B."

Hunter had just lost the debate. To his credit, he did not screw up his face or turn away. He just nodded, once. Done.

Clemens had no more to say either. He left, sewing his way into the darkness with that rise-and-fall hobble. That left her alone with Hunter.

"You have my permission to follow the river down," she said to him. "If you feel that strongly about it, take your men and go to Hinnom."

"Is that a polite way of getting rid of me?"

"I don't have time for polite," she said. "I'm giving you your freedom. It's your choice. Go your way or come with me. Do what you think is best."

Hunter had chaffed himself raw under her command, and yet he'd stuck with her. She didn't know whether to admire or scorn his fidelity. On a daily basis, she saw him flabbergasted with her choice of routes, her hell-bent pace, her democratic style with the men, and especially her forgiveness of their crimes and desertions. It was not that he lamented the desertions, which he likened to a toilet flushing itself. Rather he believed every deserter who fumbled his way back into their midst should be whipped on principle. It was even more basic than that: whipped simply to display her whip. Beckwith would be a fine starting point, he had told her.

Now here was his chance to run the show his way, or his fraction of it anyway. He could go to Hinnom.

"You don't see what Clemens is trying to do?" Hunter said. "He's driving a wedge between us."

"Mr. Hunter, he's trying to keep us all together."

"Only so he can divide us. We'd be better off deaf, dumb, and blind than following him."

"Then don't follow him. Whichever way he goes, go the other way. Go to Hinnom. Be away from him."

"But then he'd be loose," said Hunter. "Wherever that leper goes, I'm following. He knows more than he's letting on."

"I thought you said he was lost. And by the way, Mr. Hunter, he's not a leper."

"They changed him. We have no idea what he is anymore. A wild dog. The only question is whose whistle will he answer to? Ours, or theirs?"

"A leper and a dog. Anything else to add?"

Hunter brushed some unseen dust off his rifle. He lifted his eyes to her. "You're the man, Rebecca."

"Nuts to that," she said.

He let loose with one of his half smiles. Damage controlled, she thought. Hunter and his Drop Zone boys were back in the box again.

They sat at the fork for the next thirty hours, collecting the first wave of rafts as they came drifting down the river. It seemed to take forever. Toward reining in her impatience, Rebecca washed her hair and trimmed her nails, and on a whim, painted them Kennebunkport red. The men had their war paint, now she had hers.

Finally enough boats pulled to shore for the men to number a few over one hundred and twenty. She assigned five to stay behind and gather the next fifty or so and send them after her, and wait for the next fifty, and so on. On second thought, she went back and told them to attach a strobe light to the wall as a signal. "Leave a note with the strobe," she said. "Tell the men following us to hurry on. Don't waste a minute, just come along, follow the right branch. Tell them to shake a leg because we're about to finish the war without them. Then we're homeward bound."

"What about us?" one of the five asked.

"Find a boat," she said. "You're coming with us. I need every single one of you with me."

That heartened the army. Word spread. She could not spare even one of them. They were necessary. And their war was almost over. They began piling into their boats.

Just before she climbed into her boat, Beckwith approached. She hadn't seen him land among the others. In fact, she hadn't seen him for days, not since his ill-timed shot at the oxbow village. She half-thought he had deserted her army. Here he was, though, and despite his boneheaded stunt she was grateful for his perseverance.

"Nice of you to join us," she said. Unlike most of her hard-core remnants, Beckwith was keeping himself clean and shaved. It made him look younger, or the rest of them older. As usual, his rifle was hidden from sight in its carrying case. He reminded her of a kid with his guitar. A kid, she realized, not much older than she. It jarred her. She had forged herself into the *über*mother so completely that it took an effort to remember she was not yet twenty-seven years old.

"Yes, ma'am," he said.

She waited. He just stood there. "Did you want something, Mr. Beckwith?"

"Requesting permission to take a boat, ma'am."

It was like watching the sun set as the men abandoned her. But at least this one was asking permission. "You're sure you don't want to stick with us the extra mile?"

"I want to go to the city," he said. "Hinnom."

Rebecca paused. "Why?"

He shrugged. "Someone ought to check it out."

"All the clues point to this branch of the fork," she said.

"I'm probably wrong. It sure wouldn't be the first time."

"But you still think it needs doing."

The look of pain on his face struck her. The man was in torment. "I don't know what else to do."

"Come with us," she said.

His hand clenched the rifle case. She saw the muscles bunch. "But what if the kids aren't there?"

The world seemed to shake. She was shaping events, but events were shaping her, too. Was she trusting Clemens too much, and Hunter not enough? Why a monster over a mercenary, or whatever Hunter was? Had she made a mistake by not sending half her army to Hinnom? Should she stop their advance and start from scratch? What was the right thing to do? Her child's life depended on this.

Shadows rushed around her. Metal clinked on metal. Boats squealed on the rocks as they entered the water. They were in motion. It was too late. *Be strong.*

"You'll be alone," she said.

He smiled. He was already alone. She was granting him a chance. "We'll find them," he said.

Rebecca glanced away. *Another one I will never see again.* She turned to him. "Take a boat," she said.

He started to leave.

"One thing, Mr. Beckwith," she said. He stopped. She tried to think of something good. "I am expecting you to bring my boat back."

His chin rose as if a scoop of clean water had just been poured over his head. It was nothing voluntary. She had taken him by surprise. It lasted just a second or two, but in that span she saw that he had just been blessed. A chill shot through Rebecca. She had *that* power?

Then he lowered his chin. He gave her a startled look. She had that power with him, at least.

They were surrounded by spears of light and hurrying shades. He started to say something. A man bumped him. Beckwith gave her a cowboy nod out of a thousand movies. Then he plunged into the darkness toward the opposite fork.

Rebecca let go of him.

She climbed into her boat where the men were waiting, and they set off down the right branch. Light beams wove every which way from the boats ahead and behind.

She sat high on the stern so that the men could see her and take strength. Their lights played on her. They lit her arms. She opened her hands and they were filled with light. Unflinching, she looked into the brilliance.

A strange spirit infused her. If she had blessed Beckwith, then he had blessed her. He had opened her eyes to an authority that she had not known was working through her. But it was clear now. There could be only one explanation. God was with her.

Beckwith fell from her mind. He had served his purpose. She knew the way now. Sam would be saved.

The fork in the river darkened as the army floated away. The strobe light tied to the wall was all that remained of their passage.

The river flashed to life and went black and came to life and fell black. The light was a signal, but also a witness. It alone was there when the boats of the second and third waves came floating down the river.

The boats spun by upon the current, one after another, filled with dead men. By the dozens they sailed past. Those with eyes still left in their heads seemed to see and breathe and move about in the flashing light. But Rebecca's journey was no longer theirs. These men had deeper realms to explore now.

ARTIFACTS

PUBLISHERS WEEKLY

January 19

Memoirs: Gunning for Armageddon
For Fleeing Volunteers, Failure Breeds Success

They may never have seen combat, but as volunteers from the Coltrane Crusade debacle continue to stream back from the depths, a battle for books is brewing. At last count, some four dozen houses have signed up fifty-three new books, with no end in sight.

On March 20 *Falling off the Edge of the World* by S. Daniel Bartlett and *Blind Faith* by Boston Thomas will lead the assault wave of titles about to hit the market. At least twenty other books about the military expedition will be landing on the beachheads this coming summer, including *Night Vision* by Tina Hallway, *Blackjack* by Joseph Dag, and *Duped* by Mason Atley.

Not to be left behind, Warner Bros. and DreamWorks are both scouting locations for productions currently in development. The DreamWorks project, entitled *Children's Crusade,* is already casting and will be directed by David Goyer.

The flurry of attention is sure to ignite the old question of when is too soon for a traumatized public to revisit its worst nightmare. "In an ideal world, we might have waited another year or two," says Robert Ross of Random House. "We would have given the market longer to season, and continued to hope for a happy outcome to the rescue attempt. But with other houses rushing to press, we had no choice but to go forward with our spring and summer lineup."

Judging by advance review copies, mea culpas are out of fashion this season, as many of the authors blame anything and anyone but themselves for joining in the rescue adventure. Several of the books will attempt to fill in the void left by central characters who remain missing and are presumed dead, including Coltrane, her ill-starred war council, and especially the children.

The season's most controversial entry is sure to be *Lead Me Not into Temptation: Nellie's Triumph*, in which J. C. Barnum writes the first-person memoir of one of the missing children. "Even though Nellie doesn't exist, and none of the children has actually returned, and I have never visited the Sub-terrain, this is not a work of fiction," says Barnum. "Nellie is a composite of eight children based upon my extensive research, which includes over five hundred hours of interviews with family members who also fed and housed me, plus interviews with numerous former settlers and veterans of the deep over lunch." He cites his experience as an amateur spelunker and . . .

33

When Ali opened her eyes, Gregorio was stroking her face.

His black hair hung loose and clean. His eyes sparkled. He was whole. The back of his head was not caved in from his fall. His clothes were not tattered and bloody. Right down to his squared fingernails, he was Gregorio.

"I've been waiting for you for forever," he said.

Ali lay on her side, looking at him. His voice sounded like Gregorio. "You died," she said.

"Do I look dead to you?" He tucked a strand of hair behind her ear.

"No."

"Don't be afraid," he said.

"I'm not."

It was a dream. She was confident of that. Her dreams had become so real.

Over his shoulder the air gleamed like fluorescent cream. Butterflies plastered the walls with orange and black. In the distance stood the cloudlike ruins of that Taj Majal. Or was it a fallen Notre-Dame? Was that a gargoyle up there? Were those minarets or spires?

You have gone insane, she told herself. *Insane with dreams. Insane with beauty.* There were worse fates.

"It's a trick," she said. "A disease. It comes from the lake." She sat up. Her stomach growled. She noticed her watch. Time had stopped. That was okay. It was a dream.

"You're hungry," he said. "You've had a very long journey. Eat." He held something out on one open palm. The whispers swarmed upon her. *Apple,* they said.

It was a red apple, perfectly ripe, not a bruise on it. It seemed to shift shape on his palm, like a magician's trick, one thing inside another. But Ali couldn't see through the trick. Her stomach growled again.

"Take it." His black whiskers parted. His white teeth flashed. *Gregorio.*

She took a bite. It was crisp and delicious and cold on her teeth.

"Come with me," he said. "We have a great deal to talk about."

She blamed the whispers. They had dug him out from the pile of rocks. Somehow she was going to have to bury him all over again.

Slowly, aching and starved, Ali got to her feet. Gregorio helped her with frisky hands. He stroked her arms and hips. He cupped her breasts. There was nothing erotic or naughty about it. His hands were eager and curious, but also impersonal, as if he were appraising a dog or a horse. It was not like Gregorio. But then again Gregorio was not Gregorio. This was a dream, *her* dream. *Wake up.*

They descended a misshapen staircase. They entered a stone labyrinth that was either rising up from the floor or dissolving back into it. One step at a time, she lowered herself into the impossible place.

Monarchs filled the air. Cicadas buzzed. A quetzal bird with brilliant long feathers drifted past with a grasshopper sandwiched in its beak. Bright green parrots wheeled above. Miles away, a waterfall slid into smoky white mist.

"This isn't real," she told herself.

"Tell me what you see."

She described the oasis with cedars and parrots and butterflies and the Taj Majal.

That disappointed him. "I expected better from you," he said. Her dream was challenging her?

He said something. She didn't catch it. A butterfly landed on her wrist. She felt its tiny kiss.

"Now what do you see?"

"One of your monarchs."

"You're not trying," he said. "Look closer. *See.*"

Long ago, as part of her religious training, Ali had taken a class in spiritual contemplation. Prayer 101, the girls had called it. More like a Zen monk than a sister of charity, Sister Ellen had taught them the art of being quiet. The trick was to open your mind even as you closed it. To see through the illusion.

Ali closed her eyes. She took a breath, and put aside all her fears and tiredness and hunger. *Silence,* she thought to the voices. And then she let go of that word, of even the idea of it. She emptied her mind.

The whispers stopped. She opened her eyes.

The orange-and-black wings vanished. In their place she saw dry, veined membranes. The butterfly turned black. It was fat with blood. Ali frowned. A leech with wings?

She trapped it under her palm. Her concentration failed. The whispers came back. *Monarch,* they murmured. *Wings. Flutter. Orange and black.* When she lifted her hand, the leech was gone. A graceful monarch took flight. It even left a slight orange powder on her fingertips. She rubbed it with her thumb, and for an instant the powder became a smear of blood. Then it was orange and dusty all over again.

The voices clustered around her. Their whispers reassured her. *Powder, not blood,* they said. *Butterflies. Beauty.*

Gregorio was watching her. "Now listen," he said. "*Hear.*"

The whispers—the voices of the dead—wrapped around her. There were so many tongues it was like music in a dream. It would have been easy to let the voices seduce her. Instead she went to work dismembering them.

Cupping her fingers behind her ears, Ali took in the voices and chopped them apart. Like a butcher with a carcass, she trimmed away the stuff that didn't speak to her directly—the throat songs and glottal tongues, the animal mimicry, the prehistoric vowels—and went for the familiar. English was easiest. She separated out individual words. She heard them. She saw them come alive.

With each flap of the butterfly's wings, words sprang into her head: *butterfly* and *monarch* and *wing* and *orange* and *black.* She saw a droplet of water, and the whispers shaped it: *crystal* and *wet* and *bead* and *light.* Likewise the green parrots and the forest of cedars. Word by word, by the thousands or millions, the illusion was being planted in her mind.

Each voice kept busy with its bit part in the production. One whispered of a pine needle, another of a knot on the wood. All together they built a tree, and then a forest. They constructed cricket songs and the scent of orange blossoms and cinnamon.

Ali swung around. Gregorio's black eyes flickered with pale blue. His Hollywood whiskers melted away, and she made out brutish designs drawn or cut into his cheeks. The revelation lasted barely an instant. Then the voices flocked in her mind. The forest and bright green parrots resumed. Gregorio's face—or his mask—took shape again. But she had seen. Now she knew. *Someone else is in there.*

"Who are you?" she demanded.

"Who do you see?"

"A mask," she said.

"It's your mask, Ali, not mine. You put it on me. You can take it off."

"Ali?" she said. "What happened to the Alexandra?" The charade of Gregorio was over.

Like water his mask drew back. Her memory of Gregorio gave way to the face hiding inside. It lay bare to her, the furrows and scars and graffiti of old wounds and a life stolen and of his never-ending search for himself. Here was the face of hell as she had first seen it on her descent ten years ago, a barbarian as gaunt and naked as Adam. Here was the father of her child.

"Ike," she breathed.

What kind of dream went on and on like this?

His hair was gray. She had once compared his eyes to the color of the sky, but the cave had leached them to blue smudges. The sturdy shoulders, built for carrying a backpack through his forgotten mountains, had been sharpened down to bone and sinew.

"What have you been doing down here?" she said.

"It's only a little farther," he said.

No embrace. No welcoming kiss. No hint of their past. Once again, he looked disappointed in her.

"Ike, it's me."

"Eat." That was all he said. She searched his hatchet blade of a face. In the span of years, he had become as estranged from himself as he was from her.

"We have to get out of here," she said.

"That's the plan," he said.

But he kept leading her deeper into the folds of the labyrinth.

She stumbled after him. He quit talking to her. He didn't ask about their child. He didn't try to span their missing years. He just kept going. With every step, his bare rump muscles bunched and relaxed. The soles of his feet did not so much as whisper on the rock.

Peacocks strutted between the trees.

Waterfalls hung like silver.

Ali followed Ike with that rigid hope of a condemned prisoner. It was foolish. Because she was beginning to guess what was happening.

Bait, she thought. Ike was bait. It was a classic setup.

For eons, the hadals had been doing this, grooming one human slave to reap others. Men and women, and children, too, would go up to lure others down. Sometimes hell's tempters came in the form of a beautiful succubus, a young woman to lead away monks and princes and horny boys. Sometimes it was a man with soulful eyes who fished for widows and took them into the mountain's caves. In this case, Ali had led herself down. Ike was merely completing her captivity.

She looked around for some sign of a hadal camp. Would the children be there?

Ali looked at his back. She remembered this skin. While he lay sleeping, she would stay awake studying the glyphs and symbols inked and burned into his flesh. Like words in a book left out in the rain, the marks were blurred now. Only one remained distinct, the aleph at the root of his spine.

"Where are we going?" she asked.

Ike pointed. Above the treetops, big as a moon, loomed that Taj Majal with its filigreed turrets and walls and sparkling domes. The dead souls flocked to her with their helpful bits and pieces of imagery. Ali could feel them like a pressure in her head, each one singing its rehearsed part, each conjuring up some tiny part of the larger illusion. It was as if a spider were weaving a huge, beautiful web all around her.

Silence. Ali drove back the voices. The forest and flowers gave way to fangs and blooms of cave outcrops. The Taj Majal dissolved. In its place Ali saw a fortress of sorts, or a cathedral perhaps, all in ruins. Its fallen arches, breached walls, and melting spires formed an untidy pancake heap against the cavern wall. It looked half digested by time.

There was her prison.

"Ike," she said, "save me."

Once upon a time it had worked. He had tracked her when she was captured, and entered the enemy camp, and fought like a comic book hero. He had led her out of the darkness. He had saved her. But he wasn't that Ike anymore.

"It's the other way around, Ali. You're going to save me," he said. "But first we have to begin in the beginning."

There was no use trying to run away. Run? She could barely walk. Even if Ike let her go, even if she could find her tunnel again, even if she could learn the animals and plants along the way that were safe to eat without getting eaten herself, even if she could climb the cliffs and cross the lake and weather these incessant ghosts, her mind was nearly gone. She would never make it. Never.

The illusion returned. The stalagmites became cedars again. The salt formations became peacocks strutting. The bats resumed their parrot disguises.

"Wait," she said. "I need to rest." If only she could gather her thoughts. But he kept going.

The Taj Majal drew closer. Japanese blood grasses lapped at her thighs. The cedars swayed. A meadowlark sang.

Glancing back, Ali saw only a wasteland of rocks and crevices. The way was closing behind her. The voices—dead souls, if that could be—flew at her. She fought back against their illusions. They stormed her defenses. How fitting, she thought. The linguist was getting sealed inside a cage of words.

They came to a gleaming bridge made of bamboo and silver wire. Ali came to a halt. Across that bridge, inside those looming ruins, lay her own ruin.

"Come along," Ike said.

She tried to be brave. "Are the children in there?"

He didn't confirm, he didn't deny. The question intrigued him. "Is that who you came for?"

"Did you think I came for you?" she said.

He smiled and started across the bridge.

"Ike, the children."

He kept going, him and his scarred hide of a back.

"Your daughter . . ." That stopped him. "Tell me about the children, Ike."

He turned to face her. "You had a child?"

"We did, Ike. She was your daughter."

He came closer. "I want to know everything about her."

"It's too late for that, Ike."

"Perhaps not," he said.

"She died seven years ago. You weren't there for her birth. Why care about her death?"

"How old was she?"

"Three." Ali remembered candles. "She had three birthdays."

"Young," he said. "But old enough to know her name."

No regrets or commiseration. The abyss had scraped the humanity right out of him. "Where are the children, Ike?"

"Her name, please."

He might have been asking for a book title. It took Ali's breath. "No." She put one fist to her heart. "You bastard."

"Her name," he said. "What can that hurt?"

"Where are the children, Ike?"

"Her name."

"No."

The illusions began to fall apart.

Ali glanced down at the thing in her hand. The apple became a ball of meat the size of her fist. It was a heart. The chambers lay exposed. Strands of it were caught in her teeth.

Ali dropped the terrible object. "What are you doing to me, Ike?"

"His name was McNabb," said Ike. "One more pilgrim who didn't measure up. Will you?"

She stared at him. But he was suddenly no more Ike than he had been Gregorio. She watched, amazed, as the mask gave way to what lay underneath. She had never seen this other face, and yet it was as familiar as her own, like a shadow in a mirror in a dream.

For all her life, for reasons she could never quite explain, Ali had been gathering this creature's many names from every language of man. But suddenly not one would come to mind. All she could think to say before he sprang at her was, "You."

34

Rebecca's army managed to float the river for another two days.

They had no warning about the pothole at the end, no roar of a waterfall, no jagged shoals. The river simply slipped over the lip into a silent black hole. They lost a raft and three men to it before beaching the rest of her little fleet.

It took them a day to transition from being sailors to being soldiers. Camping on the bank of the river, they filled their packs with as much food and ammunition as they could carry and prepared for whatever lay ahead. Hour after hour, they watched the river, expecting more waves of boats to show up with hundreds more men. But none came.

It baffled Rebecca—but no longer stung—that just 110 men now remained of her initial 1,300. That translated as a mind-blowing 90 percent attrition rate. It was absurd that she had not turned back long ago. It was absurd that any men still remained with her. She could only surmise that God worked in absurd ways.

"We can't wait forever," she said to Hunter and Clemens. They were sitting by a ring wall of piled rocks. Nearby the river was sliding past and getting sucked into oblivion. They had reached the edge of the world.

"We're better off without them," Clemens said. "We're fat free now. Nothing left but lean, mean fighting machines."

"You're in a good fucking mood," said Hunter.

"Why not? Homeward bound, Rebecca told us," Clemens said. "I'm going home."

Their losses energized him. Rebecca thought of his buoyancy as a type of spirit. Like a statue getting freed from stone, he was taking his true form. He was rising to the occasion.

"We're getting close," Clemens said.

"How would you know?" said Hunter. "I thought you'd never been here."

Clemens went to the wall and slapped a character—possibly a geometric animal—chiseled into the rock. Men turned from their groups to see. Lights danced on him.

"Destiny," said Clemens. He lifted his T-shirt. There among the scars and geometric patterns lacing his chest was the same mark. With one fingertip, he traced the mark on his flesh and then on the stone. "See the horns?"

"The horns of the devil," said a man.

"The horns of the Ox," Clemens said. "Taurus. His city. That's where the children are."

A shout went up. A man racked a round with maximum flourish. Rebecca's warriors—the professionals, the deer hunters, the Sunday soldiers—clustered around with their forest of rifle barrels. The moment was here. It was time to open the floodgates.

She stood on a rock and took stock of their coal-miner eyes and matted hair and beards running riot, the sports caps and do-rags, the berets and helmets, the amulets, rosaries, and smeared camouflage paint. They wanted some words from her, something grand, something Hollywood. Right about now, in Jake's war movies, the gladiator or Highlander or coach made the big rousing speech.

"We came to beat the devil," she finally said. "Let's go beat him." *Thin,* she thought. *Very thin.*

They waited. She stood there. "Amen," she added.

"Amen," they said.

Still they waited. She wracked her brain. She put out her hand. Men jostled close to put their hands on top. "Fight," she said, spacing it out so it didn't sound too much like a school cheer. "Fight. Fight."

That did the trick. "Break," they said, and streamed off into the tunnel with their gear clattering and weapons drawn.

They staked their boats in a row, like cars in the company parking lot, as if this were just another day on the job. Rebecca left a note for the stragglers. "Hurry on," it said. Per usual, Clemens bounded off on his own. Per usual, Hunter sent some of his DZ wolves out front to prowl the tube. The rest of the men set to muling their big packs up the trail. Rebecca shouldered her load and joined the main body.

One advantage to their dwindling numbers was that Rebecca had come to know these men intimately. It was an odd intimacy. She touched them, but they did not dare touch her back. She knew them, but less and less by name. Their faces blurred, merging into a single stark-lit face. They were becoming a single thing. They were becoming her.

One had the fullback thighs. Another had the endurance. That guy over there had the Chicago wit that carried men on long days. This man had the pain threshold of a rock. Her unwritten inventory went on. It wasn't even an inventory anymore. When they moved as one, when *she* moved them as one, it was like her own body moving. They had become her fingers reaching into this hole. Their sweat was hers. She loved them as she loved herself, which was to say, not at all, not presently, not yet. That depended on Sam.

They followed the worn path for three days. With over ten tons on their collective back, it was brute peasant labor. No one complained. They kept their weapons ready.

On the third day, they caught up with Clemens in the dark. "It's here," he said. "A few hours ahead."

"The city?" said Hunter. "It really exists?"

"Big time," Clemens said.

Rebecca pushed to the front. "What about the children?"

He held out a long, smooth pebble. Rebecca frowned. "It was under a rock," said Clemens. "A plug."

Rebecca still didn't understand. He skinned a dried flake off with his thumbnail.

"Is that blood?" she said.

"No need for alarm," said Clemens. "It's menstrual blood."

Hunter stepped closer. "It could have come from an animal."

"Except it didn't," Clemens said. He touched his tongue to it. Those big gee-gosh eyes suddenly did not look so pure and simple. "This is human. Female. A few days old. She used this pebble to try to stop her flow."

"It was under a rock?" said Hunter. "You were looking under rocks?"

"I live under rocks," Clemens said.

The city lay four hours on, built in an immense cove. They sneaked up on it, as if—with all their noise and lights—their presence might still be a surprise. Luckily no one was at home, it seemed.

Their headlamps darted across its fortress walls like lizards. The massive gate doors had fallen off long ago. Rebecca wanted to rush inside, but held herself back.

Carved oxen heads with green onyx horns jutted from the upper walls, barely eroded by the eons. Some still contained eyes made of gold. Three eyes, not two . . . one positioned in the middle of each bull's forehead. Cow Buddhas, thought Rebecca.

Reading from some internal script, the men fanned out like skulking Indians and took positions behind rocks. Rebecca stayed close to Hunter, the professional soldier, who was staying close to Clemens, his enemy.

"Let's turn on the lights," said Hunter. "Get some flares up. See what we see."

The city sprang into being. It was like a dream flickering on the far side of the walls. Columns of limestone stood in hivelike towers, five and six stories high. Staircases wound up the densely built hillside.

This was Rebecca's first hadal city. She was stunned. "They did this?"

Hell was supposed to be the house of infinite pain. In its heyday, though, it had apparently been much more, a heaven without the milk and honey. *A dark paradise—a masterpiece,* Rebecca thought—*wrought in stone and human blood.*

"They came this way," Clemens said.

"How do you know?"

Clemens took a whiff of the air. He went to a rock and turned it over, exposing a link of animal dung. "Hadal," he said. He offered the turd to Hunter, who stared at him. Clemens broke the turd open. "Human," he said.

"Which is it, Clemens? Hadal or human?"

"Both," said Clemens.

Rebecca got it. Hadal shit. Human meat.

Hunter turned to Rebecca. "I'm sending in a team," he said. "Keep the flares burning bright. And tell the action heroes to keep their safeties on. The last thing we need is Joe Six-Pack shooting up the shadows."

Hunter's team rushed the gate. They streamed inside the fortress. Five long minutes passed. Finally a man's head appeared at the top of the wall. He waved them in.

Rebecca entered with the others. The gateway arched overhead, tall enough for giants. Hunter greeted her. "Good news and bad news. They're not here. Not in this part of the city. The place stretches for miles. It would take us weeks to go house to house. We're going to have to make some leaps here."

They discussed a plan for sweeping the city. He got the citizen-soldiers organized into platoons, with one of his operators in charge of each platoon. They had radios to communicate.

"Shouldn't we have radio handles or something?" said a man. With his camo greasepaint, he looked like a clown version of a soldier.

Hunter grunted. "Help yourselves."

"We're SIGMA force one," the clown soldier said.

Another man piped up, "FOXTROT nine."

"Lord," muttered Hunter.

"Are we ready?" said Rebecca.

"You're staying here," said Hunter.

For once Clemens agreed with his nemesis. "Listen to him," he said to Rebecca.

She said nothing. Pulling Jake's Glock from its holster, she started up the steps. They could tie her up or they could follow. They didn't tie her up.

The city of the ox reminded her of the Dr. Seuss books she used to read to Sam. Stairs led to other stairs. Spires teetered above circular mazes. Water sluiced merrily along the aqueducts blistered with colorful lichen. All it needed was citizens with whiskers.

Hunter's men searched a handful of buildings, ducking around doorways, guns drawn, twitchy as hummingbirds. After a half hour, they lost their sense of urgency. The place had probably been vacated since before the time of Christ.

They reached the edge of a marsh. Once it had been a vast reflecting pool, but over time its neatly squared margins had shifted and cracked. The water was fetid. Reeds grew from its bottom.

Farther along the shore, a crumbling citadel commanded both the city below and this side of the marsh. Rebecca let the DZ men zigzag and leapfrog their way up to the stronghold, but it, too, proved to be empty. Her desperation mounted.

A bridge of massive stepping-stones reached across the marsh in a long, straight line. Hunter fired a flare. The far shore lit up with sharp, white mountains. "Snow?" said a soldier.

Not snow, not mountains. "Pyramids," said Rebecca, lowering her binoculars.

"The bridge must be a quarter mile across," Hunter said. "There's no other approach to the island. That means that in the old days no one came or went without passing this fortification. Which raises the question, was the fort built to protect the pyramids from the city or the city from the pyramids? What is on that island?"

Sam, thought Rebecca. Once again she unholstered Jake's Glock, and made for the bridge with her follow-me chin plowing the way. She got as far as the first stepping-stone before Hunter grabbed her arm. Again. Like at the toll bridge.

"No one crosses until we sort this out. I know what you're thinking. I'm thinking the same thing. The children must be there. But this bridge could be a death trap. The only way across is single file, exposed to the front and sides, with no support, no backup. And if we had to retreat . . ." He gestured at the water. "Who knows how deep it is."

"We're not stopping here."

"What we're not doing," he said, "is walking into an ambush with our pants down and our eyes closed."

Rebecca tried to jerk her arm free. "Every minute counts for these children," she said.

"We're stretched so thin out here it would take just a puff of air to knock us over," Hunter said. "We need to establish a forward base, bring up supplies, and be ready for the worst."

Voices peeped up from below. Hunter glanced down the stairs. He groaned and let go of her arm. "The action heroes."

Dozens of tiny figures were winding through the ruins and climbing the stairs. The camo paint clown arrived first, gasping for air.

"What the hell are you doing?" Hunter demanded. "I told you to make a base camp and secure the rear."

"And miss the party?" said the man. "The action's up front, and we're not missing out. We've paid our dues." One of his buddies was bent over with his rifle on his knees, sucking air. More and more men arrived in various states of collapse. *Couch potatoes gone wild,* thought Rebecca.

"Who's guarding our supplies?" Hunter said. "If they take our camp, we're dead."

"Code red, yeah, we know, you keep saying. Twenty-four/seven, it's always code red. But the place is empty." He saw the pyramids. "What are those?"

"Return to camp," Hunter said. "Every last fucking one of you."

"Send your own guys."

With just a few steps, Hunter's DZ boys had shifted to contain the growing crowd. Rebecca saw their gun barrels subtly levitating. Hunter's finger had moved to his trigger.

Abruptly the firebrand noticed how far he'd stepped over the line. He got very still. A dark stain blossomed at his crotch.

Clemens appeared. "Easy, gentlemen."

"Out of the way, Clemens," Hunter said. "The man has a mouth. He doesn't need yours."

"Rebecca," Clemens said, "I think these men deserve a little respect. How about this, I escort any volunteers across the bridge. The rest can hold this shore."

Rebecca looked out at the island and its burden of pyramids. She could still feel Hunter's grip on her arm. Unleash the dogs, she thought. "Each to his own," she said.

Hunter shook his head, disgusted. His finger released the trigger. The DZ men lowered their guns. "You're making a mistake," he said to her.

"Mr. Hunter, I've had people telling me that every step of the way," she said. "If I had listened to them, we would not be here and the children would be lost forever. That aside, we just passed through the ruins and they're empty."

"That camp and its supplies are our exit door," said Hunter. "If something came at us from the rear, we'd be trapped in this city."

"The only thing behind us are our own stragglers," Rebecca said. "I left a note for them. They'll take care of the camp as they arrive."

"Until then the supplies need guarding."

"Then go and guard them," she said. Hunter shook his head.

Rebecca started for the bridge once again. This time it was Clemens who grabbed her arm. "All except for you."

"Let go," she said.

"We need you right where you are, out of harm's way. We'll clear the island. This won't take long." He forcibly steered her to Hunter. "Listen on the radio. Wait for the signal, Rebecca. It's almost over."

The crowd broke apart. "Hoo-ah." A few of the civilians tried the Ranger cheer, but it just didn't fit well, like pants too big.

Rising and sinking with his limp, Clemens set off across the massive stepping-stones. A long line of volunteers trailed behind him. His voice came over the radio. "Testing, testing, one, two, three. Do you read me?"

"What do you see, Clemens?"

He was feeling frisky out front. "No pharaohs yet."

The stepping-stones were the tips of huge, squared pillars driven down into the mud. Where the pillars had shifted, the bridge gapped open. The long line of men bunched up, hopping and straddling, slowing, speeding up, moving farther across. Through her night binoculars, Rebecca counted eighty-nine of them. That was everyone but the DZ boys.

Meanwhile, Hunter deployed shooters to the right and left. Propping their rifles on worn statues and broken pieces of balcony, they sighted through their scopes. Rebecca fanned through her optics, IR to UV to the slower radars, scanning the motionless pyramids for any sign of life over there, hostile or otherwise.

"Touchdown," Clemens radioed. He looked like a tiny green scarecrow in her binoculars. The conga line of men began to arrive, and she lost him.

"Spread those men out, Clemens," said Hunter. "Play defense. Find cover. Watch your flanks. Do not enter that complex until you've established a defense."

Clemens came back on a minute later. "No one's listening."

Flares sank into the water. More flares shot into the air. It was very festive looking. Rebecca cut in. "Do you see the children?"

She tried to pick out Clemens's bent paper clip of a body, but the rabble was streaming everywhere. A group toppled a statue. It broke into pieces. Arms pumped in triumph.

"What are they doing?" she said.

"I'm afraid we've got a touch of gold fever over here."

"Gold?"

"It's everywhere. On the statues, on the walls, even lining the paths. This thing's turning into a treasure hunt."

"My ass," she said, and dropped the binoculars around her neck. "I'm coming over there."

Hunter's voice came over the radio. "Rebecca . . ."

A twinkle of firecrackers appeared.

Rebecca paused.

The sound of popcorn popping drifted across the lake. Had they lost their minds, squandering ammunition? "Clemens," Hunter said. "Tell them to cease fire. Immediately."

Clemens's voice blinked on and off. "Rebecca . . . keep safe . . ." The gunfire amplified over the radio. She heard men yelling. The merrymaking was over. The transmission stopped.

"Ah, hell, it's happening," said Hunter.

Revelers appeared from between the pyramids and began swarming toward the bridge. It looked like a vice raid. At this distance, with the men so tiny, Rebecca had trouble taking their desperation seriously.

A lucky few at the front got a clean start across the bridge. Behind them men jammed together and fought for access. Antlike figures toppled into the water. The marsh was shallow, barely up to their waists. Seeing the chaos at the bridge, more and more men simply jumped into the water and began plowing back to Rebecca's shore, with or without their guns.

A man began climbing the slope of a pyramid.

The popcorn bursts stretched longer. Some men took aim. Most just sprayed wild gunfire back toward the pyramids.

"Fall back," Hunter shouted to his men. "It's a trap. Back to the gates. Secure the supplies."

Sam. "But we can't leave them," she said.

The man suddenly dove off the side of the pyramid. He simply turned around and cast himself off. His body tumbled down like a rag doll. That stunned her more than the mob's panic. He had only climbed high enough to kill himself.

She spied a second man climbing a different pyramid. Another suicide? He kept on going, though, higher and higher, leaving below the pandemonium.

The sound of tiny shouts drew her back to the mob. Some sort of invisible lawn mower was cutting them down from behind.

She knew she should be horrified. Something terrible was unfolding. But with no faces to see or screams to hear, with not a single hadal in sight, it seemed like a very small cartoon. Men galloped about. They tumbled off the waterfront. They shoved between the marsh reeds. She lowered the binoculars. Her naked eye found nothing more than a few pinpricks of gunfire in the darkness.

She went searching with her binoculars again. That climber now perched on the tip of his pyramid, practically an ornament. He sat there with his chin on his hand, *The Thinker* in miniature, high above it all.

Near the back of the crowd, a pale shape flashed up and down. Now the terror got real. Exactly like this, lit by a Texas moon, Jake had been torn to rags.

Fight, she thought to the men. *Stand and fight. Fight like Jake fought.* Except for that one pale hop up and down, the enemy remained invisible. All Rebecca could see was a mindless panic, like when the tiger escapes from a zoo.

Men shed their packs and ditched their weapons. One by one, the pyramids ebbed into shadow. The marsh darkened.

Hunter's men angled flares out over the marsh. Crawling along the bridge, survivors began to emerge from the gloom. They were still a hundred yards away, still far from home.

Rebecca heard others choking and splashing in the water. One of them was bleating like a lamb. "Seven, no, nine," she counted out loud. "That's all?"

"Come with me," said Hunter.

She was dazed. "What?"

"Into the fort," he said. "Quickly."

Rebecca thought he was being vengeful. The action heroes had rebelled against him. Now he was showing them his whip hand. "We can't just leave them," she said.

"Yes, we can."

"But the children . . ."

"Not now."

Rebecca ran.

She made it to the bridge and started out across the water. The stones danced back and forth in the flare light, like vertebrae flexing.

A man screamed up ahead. She nearly slipped off. An image flared of Sam doing ballet moves along the edge of the limestone cliff behind their house. *Fearless.* Rebecca plunged on.

The first survivors were in shock, but mobile. "They're coming," one shouted at her. Even running for their lives, the three men were loaded down with golden objects.

"Keep moving," she said, and carefully edged around them and went on.

The next man had a slash wound. His details flashed in her mind. He was an architect. Cincinnati. Two kids. A pink balloon swelled from his side. Somehow he was still on his feet. "Lie down," she said. "I'll get help. We'll carry you."

His eyes were glassy. He staggered past.

The fifth man almost shoved her over the side in his frenzy.

Farther along, down in the water, two men were plowing their way toward shore. "Give me your hand," she said, and dragged one up onto the bridge. He was an amateur magician. She'd seen him do card tricks. Together they reached down for the other man.

"Thank you," said the man in the water, "thank you." It came to her. He had a fiancée from New Jersey. He was teaching himself the Moonlight Sonata.

His grateful smile seized. He swept his arm up from the water. A clear plastic bag wrapped his hand. He started beating his hand against the pillar. And howling.

A second gobbet of plastic floated closer. And a third. Rebecca swept her light across the water. There was a whole silent armada of them. Jellyfish.

The man jackknifed backward. He went under. The water thrashed and went still.

"Aaron?" said the magician.

A bee hummed by. Rebecca frowned.

A gunshot cracked.

Rebecca cast a look. The bridge was crawling. Pale shapes. More bullets hummed. She tugged at the architect. "He's gone."

Before she could say a word, the magician hopped back into the marsh. "Aaron?"

Rebecca turned and started running toward the fortress.

A scream trailed her. The water churned. *Don't look.*

Suddenly the fort sparkled with muzzle flash. On either side of her the air sizzled. She hurdled the gaps, one stone to the next. She sped between twin curtains of lead.

The architect with the stomach wound was lying on the bridge. Like a speed bump. *Keep going.* He moved. She stopped. "Come on." Somehow, one of those superman moments, she lifted him in her arms. He yelped. She staggered under his weight. This had to be done.

"Rebecca." Fifty feet ahead, Hunter was waiting. "Leave him."

"Help me." She lurched toward him.

Hunter kneeled like a knight in armor genuflecting. His pistol came up. The architect's head jerked against her arm. It lolled. She saw the bullet hole in his forehead, the brain matter on her shoulder. It really was gray.

"Get down." He was aiming straight at her.

The pistol twinkled. She felt the bullet pass her ear. Something heavy clipped the back of her knees. Rebecca fell.

Pinned flat, facedown, she didn't dare look backward at that weight across her legs. It was still moving. It groaned prehistoric words.

The architect's body sank into the water. His eyes stayed open, seeming to watch Rebecca. *Close your eyes.* She closed her eyes.

Flares rocked the sky. They traced right through her eyelids. She tried to read their silly scribbles. She listened to the bees hum.

That thing across her legs kept trembling back there. Like that deer Jake shot, the haunches twitching. Her first and last hunting trip. Except for this one. *Sam.*

A hand locked roughly on her arm. There were no two ways about it. *Possession,* she thought, *nine-tenths of the law.* The thing owned her. "Rebecca."

She opened her eyes. Hunter was up there. He stabbed his free arm out, taking aim. Gunshots snapped. Shells tapped on the stone. One roosted in her ear. It was hot.

The weight across her legs vanished. He grabbed her arm again. "Can you walk?"

"Yes." But her legs were jelly. She started crawling.

Hunter tossed her over one shoulder. They reached shore. He dumped her to the ground. "Now," he yelled loudly.

The sky lit white. It was like opening a Fabergé egg. A fantastic other world stood revealed inside this domed place: the pyramids, the marsh with floating bodies, the bridge and its white apes. Then the air came hot into her lungs, and Rebecca shielded her eyes from the light.

ARTIFACTS

ERRI DAILY INTELLIGENCE REPORT

January 23

Today's Central Focus
China Opens and Closes Missile Silo Doors

In a sharp escalation of tensions, China yesterday opened the doors to fifty-four of its intercontinental nuclear missile silos.

NORAD observed the incident by satellite, and three missile-alert facilities at Malmstrom AFB in Montana were ordered to open their doors. At the end of eight minutes, China closed its silo doors without launch. The U.S. president then ordered U.S. missile silos to return to launch-warning mode, and all doors were shut without launch.

The Japanese ambassador, acting in place of the Chinese ambassador, was summoned to receive the U.S. protest over the provocation. China's foreign ministry continues to stonewall the American ambassador to China, although he did receive a private communication from Premier Jiaming expressing concern.

China's media and Internet remain silent on the incident. There have been no leaks of this to the U.S. media. The public in both countries is unaware of the confrontation.

35

Ali woke lying in the middle of a Japanese rock garden with raked sand.

Her nightmare of Gregorio becoming Ike becoming . . . Him . . .
seemed safely remote. It was far better to enjoy this dream. Cherry-
blossom petals drifted down, white as snowflakes. The air was crisp and
sweet. She was alone and at peace. But of course she was not.

There were no footprints in the sand. She did not recall walking here,
and especially not raking the sand closed behind her. Someone had placed
her in the rock garden while she was unconscious and arranged the
tableau around her.

And she was in pain. It felt as if she had been dropped from a cliff or
run over. Her muscles ached. Her nails were broken. Mostly she hurt in her
pelvic saddle, hurt to the bone, like when she had been torn and broken
giving birth.

Pieces of his frenzy flashed in her mind. The Japanese garden quivered
at its edges. The cherry blossoms hesitated. Ali put the chaos away. She
wasn't ready to process the violence. The cherry blossoms continued drifting down.

A voice spoke from behind her. "Good morning, Ali."

It was her mother, sitting on the limb of a bonsai tree. Her dead mother.

With less effort this time, Ali pierced the illusion. She swept away the
whispers. The rock garden was real enough, its white sand combed into
pleasing patterns. The rest was a lie. The cherry-blossom petals were bits
of live cinders. The blue sky was a vault of tortured stone. The air hung
close and foul. The bonsai trees vanished. In their place, the fossil remains
of some primal animal protruded from the floor.

And of course that was not her mother. The human facade evaporated. Ali saw his eyes. His primeval eyes. He was old inside his alabaster skin.

The voices converged on her. They whispered about a perfect garden under a blue sky and a mother. Ali held them at bay. Her survival was going to depend on clarity and reason, on doubt, not faith. There was no pity in those eyes. Curiosity, perhaps, and boredom. And genius, it has a look. But no mercy, and absolutely no apology.

"You're not my mother," she finally said. It hurt to move her jaw. What had he done to her?

"That's a good start," he said.

"Are you hadal?"

Very softly, he snorted.

"I could be imagining you," she said. "I could be mad."

"Ali, please," he said. "If we're going to spend time together, you need to be more nimble than that. We're no strangers. You've been chasing me for years now, and I've been chasing you. So what do you say, shall we dance?"

There were traces of animals in his mannerism: the reptile quiet, the birdlike hardness in his eyes, and his frozen stillness, like a praying mantis's. There was not a mark or scar on him, which was extraordinary in itself in this devouring place. His face was a mystery, as different from man's face as man's from an ape's. He had a teenager's wisp of a mustache. But his blue irises had leached nearly white with time. He was beautiful in a way that would fit any age and any era.

Where was the fabled monstrosity?

As if reading her mind, he patted his head. "No horns." He peered over his shoulder. He looked down at his feet. "No wings. No cloven hooves." He folded his hands. "Now we've got that out of the way."

It struck her that if the legends were true, if this really was the rebel angel stewing in exile, then she was practically looking at the face of God. Here might be the face of an idea, the face of the first thing ever named. Sitting with one leg crossed at the knee, this could be the first word, the word made flesh.

She rejected the notion. It was absurd, a whim, like the dream waiting to snatch her into the cherry blossoms, a temptation. And yet . . .

"What do I call you?" she said. She wanted his name, his original name. It was more than a linguistic conceit. Words hold power. A word could command an empire: witness Caesar or the pharaoh or Mr. Vice President. What name would he give? The name he had given himself, or the name he had been given? And given by whom, by his followers or his victims? She rejected the only other possibility. *God?* Rejected it flat.

"Call me," he paused, "Ishmael." He smiled. It was a joke, but not a joke. She could do what she wanted with it. *He is testing me.*

Ishmael, she thought. *The outcast son.* The wanderer in the wilderness and father of misbegotten races. The survivor. All borrowings from the Bible, with Melville for a punch line. It struck her. With a single name, he had provided her with many answers to many questions that she no longer needed to ask.

In a flash, another thought occurred. What if he meant his biblical reference to hint at even more? What if, long ago, he had handed up the tale of Ishmael as an allegory for himself? *What if the Beast had written the Bible? Rich,* she thought. *And ridiculous.*

"I knew a man once who made wild claims," she said. "He had us convinced he was . . ." *What crazy name to insert . . . Beelzebub, Older-Than-Old, Pit-ar, God's Ape? No, no, no.* ". . . invulnerable," she finished. "But he was just a man. He got shot. I saw it." He wanted to test her? She would test him right back.

"That would be Thomas," the creature said. "One of my martyrs. Not the first Jesuit I've used, by the way. Think of a secret agent. I took the good father under my wing almost a century ago, schooled him for years, and then sent him up into the world to erase my tracks. He's the one who told me about you. My hope was that he could take me off the table, so to speak, and hide me in the myths again."

"But why bother with myths?" She was talking to him as though he really was what he might be. "We had quit believing you were real anyway."

"That was my hope, that you had forgotten all about me. The times were getting so modern and preoccupied. But then, thanks to my poor, starving, cretin primitives, you stumbled onto the entrances to this other world. And suddenly, since hell was real, then so was I. Which meant there was bound to be a plague of bounty hunters and exorcists and muscular Christians coming down, all gunning for me, muddying my waters and disturbing the peace." He paused. "So I had myself—or my Jesuit—killed in front of witnesses. In front of you, to be precise."

"Me?"

"You don't think it was a coincidence that you were there for Thomas's finale, do you? Thomas was organized and very thorough. He followed instructions well."

"But why me?"

"Love," the creature said simply.

The word flew at her. A rose. A bullet. Ali stared at him.

"Deliverance," he added.

"Deliverance?"

He tapped his skull. "This is the prison. I know that now. Not these walls of stone around us. Here, everything is up here. I hold my own freedom. But I need help. A prompt. Some memory of the future. Someone has the key, someone like you maybe, a linguist to decipher the code. To say the magic word. Open, sesame, whatever it is. Unlock my door."

Ali didn't know what to make of his crazy talk. What prison, what door? "There are no magic words," she said.

"First you lose your faith in God, now your faith in words? What did you come down here for, Sister?"

He took her by surprise. She actually had to remember. "The children," she said. "I came to find the children."

"Lambs in the wilderness," he said. "Aren't we all?"

"You have them here?"

"They are mine," he said.

An image surfaced of those Ice Age children, their bones arrayed before the aleph mound. How long had he been devouring children down here? "Let me see them." Ali tried to stand. She nearly passed out. Were her legs broken, too?

"Rest." Part ape, part God, the creature began to saunter off across the sand. "You and I will dance some other day."

ARTIFACTS

HOMELAND SECURITY

In the Event of Nuclear Attack

1. **Go inside immediately,** as far belowground as possible.
2. **Go into your basement.** If caught in the open, seek out underground spaces, including elevator shafts, staircases, mines, caves, and sewer systems.
3. Avoid higher floors of the house or structure. Close windows and doors, turn off air conditioners, heaters, or other ventilation systems.
4. **Stay where you are,** watch TV, listen to the radio, or check the Internet for official news as it becomes available.
5. Understand that during an emergency you may be asked to "shelter in place" or evacuate.
6. Listen for information about signs and symptoms of diseases, if medications or vaccinations are being distributed, and where you should seek medical attention if you become sick. **If you become sick seek emergency medical attention.**

36

Their refuge reminded Rebecca of Sam's last birthday cake, one of those Dairy Queen ice-cream extravaganzas. Jake had put it in the fridge instead of the freezer, and when they pulled it out, the neat square had softened to a mound with candles tipping all over the place.

Some great heat had partially melted the fortress walls. Its towers leaned precariously. The lower battlements were smothered with flow-stone. Small crabs from the marsh scuttled everywhere, covering the floors and walls. You could not walk without crunching, and when you sat or lay down, they were soon climbing your legs and arms.

But for now the structure was all they had in the world, and they occupied it with purpose. Hunter got some pleasure out of calling it an acropolis, which he told them was not a bunch of pillars on a hill, but a fortification overlooking ancient Greek cities. This place did overlook the Ox ruins, but Rebecca thought of it as her own private Alamo. Texans are like that.

To one side, the fort faced the marsh with its bridge leading to the far pyramids. The other side overlooked the spires and mazes of the city ruins. Rebecca and the DZ boys and the three island survivors kept watch for anyone else who might have escaped the ambush. But the darkness yielded no one. The walkie-talkies that the action heroes had taken across were silent. Night ruled.

In the space of a single hour, they had lost practically everything but their lives. The action heroes were gone, along with all the food, medicine, and ammunition they were supposed to guard in a camp that no longer existed. Rebecca and these twenty-one men had gone from being hunters to being hunted.

Hunter was philosophical about it, if "shit happens" qualifies as a philosophy. But a number of the operators were struggling with the turn of events. As they sealed themselves into the fort with big boulders and rigged claymore mines and set fields of fire and doctored the wounded, they railed against the stupidity of it all. They blamed the action heroes' foolishness. They blamed themselves for not hauling along more ammo clips. Above all, they blamed Haddie for his evil ways, which to Rebecca made about as much sense as damning the devil. Sweating and bleeding, pissed off, scared, ragged with adrenaline, they did everything in their power to contradict the obvious: they were trapped.

Rebecca didn't waste the nervous energy. In seventh grade, every Texan is required to take a course in Texas history. Thanks to Miss Crooks's lessons on the Alamo, Rebecca felt like she had a leg up on the others. For her, a siege was as natural as heat in August. While the others were still floundering with their predicament, she was already reckoning how to beat the odds.

She found the three men who had made it back alive from the pyramids. One man was holding together a long wound in his thigh. It was already showing signs of infection from the marsh decay. She went through the motions of nursing the leg, and asked her questions. "What did you see over there?"

"Pyramids, statues, and bones," he said. "And gold. It's everywhere." Indeed it was. His shirt bulged with loot.

"What bones?"

"There are skeletons still shackled to the floor. Slaves in gold chains! And bones and skulls, scattered at the foot of a giant statue. It's a man with a bull's head, a Minotaur plated with gold."

"What about the children?"

"Children?" he said.

Rebecca looked at him. Her heart did not grow colder toward the man, only a little sadder. After all this distance, their crusade had become just a shoplifting spree.

"I need a medic," the man said.

"The medic's gone," she said. "He was sent to guard the base camp. The camp is gone. He's dead."

"Medicine then," the man said. "Penicillin. And sulfa powder. And a stitch kit. And something for the pain."

"I'll talk to the captain."

"Also I need a gun." He had thrown his away. They both knew it. He pulled out a golden chalice and thrust it at her. "This should do. For the captain. Or keep it for yourself."

"Rest."

He saw her disgust. "Don't give up on me, Rebecca. I came this far, didn't I?"

She went over to the other two men. Neither had seen any children. With hangdog faces they asked for a little food and some weaponry. "You need every man who can pull a trigger," one said.

Hunter snorted when she approached with their requests. He listed the medicines and supplies still remaining. Their food would last two days. There were enough rounds for ten clips each. He had three more rocket-propelled Willie Petes, with their white phosphorous charges. "What we've got left belongs to my unit, not mutts like them. They wanted an adventure. They got one."

She gave him the golden chalice. "He'll die without something for that wound."

"Those assholes probably killed us, Rebecca."

"I thought you came to protect them."

"And I thought they came to find the children. Have they found the children?"

"Is that your answer then?"

He tossed the chalice away. "Take some meds. I'll have a gun issued to each man. Is there anything else you want from us?"

She looked at the soldier, and would have touched his head or his shoulder, something to close the gap between them. He needed her as much as she needed him, but it would insult him to have it said, and so she just shook her head no and they went their own ways.

The siege would have seasons. She knew that from the Alamo. Once they got settled into this melting plug of a fortress, the men would hope and pray for rescue. When it didn't come, they would despair. Finally they would get right with God, lay out their bullets, and fight to the last man.

But every massacre has a survivor, or at least the Alamo had. If there was only going be one survivor out of this scrape, Rebecca meant to be the one. It was not that she felt entitled or had a special fear of dying. But Sam was near. Whatever it took, Rebecca was going to find her. It was as simple as that.

She climbed a ramp and trained her binoculars on the island again. Nothing stirred over there. Then she spied an infrared pixel up in the air and homed in on it. It was that climber still sitting on top of his pyramid. She had forgotten all about him.

His lonesome vigil tugged at her. It inspired her. His game was working, at least for the time being. He was hiding in plain sight, right in their midst. Maybe the hadals weren't so superhuman after all. Maybe there was a limit to their power. Maybe she could learn how to be invisible, too.

Below her, the marsh lapped at the stone shore. Frogs took up their chorus. It reminded her of something Clemens had once told her, that there was peace to be had in the abyss, but that first you had to go through hell to find it.

The screams began a few hours later, skipping across the water like pebbles, so faint that the frogs all but drowned them out. After witnessing the slaughter of men on the island and bridge, the thought of prisoners had not entered her mind. Hunter threw a rock in the marsh, and the frogs fell silent. For the sake of morale it would have been better to let them sing.

Rebecca had never heard such pain. The pitch kept changing, as if musical instruments were being tuned. "What are they doing to those men?" said a man.

"Taking their time," said another.

"Get back to your posts," said Hunter. But wherever they went, the miniature screams followed. A symphony of mosquitoes.

You couldn't sleep for all the crabs in motion.

On the second day of the siege they heard a slight rattling noise, like raindrops against a window. "Kitty litter," laughed their chain gunner, "they're throwing fucking kitty litter at us." He held up a handful and let the dusty gravel sift through his fingers.

A few hours later the chain gunner developed a cough.

Like nocturnal insects, the various sentinels watched through their NODS and sniper scopes. One team scanned with a radar array. Chemical sticks lit the inner chambers with eerie greens and oranges.

In their self-imposed dusk, imaginations ran amok. Men sensed things that weren't there, and ignored things that were. Ghosts and vampires plagued them, only to be revealed as rocks or flags of drifting mist. Someone detonated a claymore on a hapless statue. "Higgins, you just killed a garden gnome, you idiot." It was getting easier and easier to believe they had nothing to fear but fear itself.

It was a strange siege, almost imaginary. They were surrounded, not by barbarian hordes with catapults, but by degrees of darkness and quiet. By frogs and shadows and medieval demons. It seemed so empty out there that one of the action heroes, seeking to redeem himself, volunteered to go explore. "Maybe they've gone away. Maybe we can go home."

"Good idea," said a DZ boy.

He climbed down through a window and faded into the blackness. That was the last they ever saw of him. His memorial service was short and blunt. "Dumb ass," someone said.

The action hero with the slash wound died that night.

Now that the fight was on them, it became desperately clear how little Rebecca had to contribute. She knew nothing of battle tactics, couldn't handle a gun, and her so-called leadership was at an end. They had followed her smack into a dead end.

She made herself useful with small chores. Hunter put her in charge of rationing the food and delivering it to the various stations. Also she compiled a list of the dead, as best the men could remember any other names. Mostly people had just vanished and taken their identities with them. The only one she could recollect with any confidence was Clemens. Created by two worlds, estranged from both, the monster had finally found peace in this giant stone dungeon.

Rebecca had just finished delivering the last of the meal bars to the radar team when she heard a puff of air. One of the men at the window slapped at his neck. "Bugs," he said.

A minute later his partner scratched his scalp and discovered three woody needles, smaller than a cactus spine, hanging from the outermost layer of his skin. More of the little needles were stuck, helter-skelter, in their clothing.

On day three of the siege the two radar men came down with high fevers.

The food ran out.

The chain gunner with the cough died. Cause of death: kitty litter.

Around 0400 hours, a hadal came sprinting straight at them from the blackness. The sentry dropped him with a single shot through the head. Instantly flares went up. But there was no one else out there.

Rebecca joined Hunter by the front barricade. The body lay a few scant yards from the entrance, naked as an ape, more naked than an ape, not a hair on him. He was well muscled, with paper-thin skin. There was no fat of the land down here. He had painted himself with ochre and charcoal stripes before making a run at them.

"I don't see a weapon, not even a rock to throw," Hunter said. "He wasn't a sapper or a suicide bomber."

"What was he thinking of?" Rebecca asked. "Why throw himself away like that?"

"Maybe he was probing our line. Maybe he just wanted to count coup."

He had horns and very long fingers, and was circumcised. That was an interesting bit of trivia. They cropped their genitals. They groomed themselves.

A wave of revulsion hit her. What if this thing had touched Sam?

"Shoot him again," she said.

"No need. Look at him."

"I've heard things about them," she said. "They don't just die."

"Those are fairy tales, Rebecca. He's dead. Save the bullet."

"Kill him again."

Hunter was staring at her. "Take him off at the neck," he finally said.

The rifle cracked once. "Done," said the shooter.

Rebecca went up to the roof with her binoculars. The lone hadal was a harbinger. The final assault was nearing. She wasn't ready. She still had no hiding place picked out, no secret tunnels in or out. Playing dead probably wouldn't work.

She glassed the pyramids, looking for her pal sitting on his summit. She needed a boost. If he could outlast the violence, then she could, too. This time, though, the pinnacle of the pyramid was empty. His luck had run out.

On the fourth morning of the siege, she woke from a dream about ham and turkey and Sam in her Thanksgiving Pilgrim costume. She opened her eyes, and strangely, the smell of meat did not go away. Following her nose, she found five men searing long slivers of meat over a gas cooker. A bottle of Tabasco sauce sat to the side.

A poncho covered the body of the hadal that had rushed them yesterday. Crouched around their little blue flame, they looked up at her without the slightest guilt.

"Want some?" one offered.

It smelled delicious. Her stomach rumbled. "You boys eat," she said. There was no sense getting holy about the cannibalism.

"There's plenty," a man said.

"Another time," she said. And she meant it.

It was not as if the taboo still loomed before her. Thanks to the hot-rock drillers in Electric City, she knew exactly what the meat would taste like. Soon enough, she was going to have to partake, if only to stay strong for Sam. But for the moment, with the body lying right there, it was a little too raw for her.

She visited the radar men. Hunter had quarantined them, sort of, mostly to keep their condition from general view. Both were unconscious. Their spittle was foamy. Plainly the cactus needles had poisoned them. Hunter guessed they were blow darts. He warned his men to be careful with what they touched and breathed, a tall order in the dark.

Other than a little cannibalism and biowarfare, the siege remained a humdrum affair. Nothing moved out there. The frogs sang on. That mosquito drone of tortured men never quit. She was beginning to wonder if the hadals meant to just let them go quietly crazy in here and die of antique diseases.

Then Clemens returned from the dead.

His voice hailed them from the darkness. "Don't shoot, lads," he said. "It's me, a friend. I'm coming in."

Four days after disappearing among the pyramids, battered and cut, he emerged from the night. They let him through the gateway choked with boulders. It was like the second coming of Jesus Christ.

Everyone gathered around. They made him sit. They gave him water. The same men who had ridiculed him as a leper now gave him a hero's welcome. Somehow Clemens had outfoxed the enemy and kept healthy. He could have just left them to their fate, but he'd risked everything to return to them. It could mean only one thing. He knew the secret to their survival.

"Food," shouted a soldier, "give the man some food."

A plate of meat slivers got handed to the front. Clemens took a smell and put it aside. "Waste not, want not," someone said. "Chow down, brother."

Clemens turned his amphibian eyes to Rebecca. "Have you eaten this?"

"Not yet," she said.

"Good," he said.

In a rush, Rebecca realized he had come to save her. This wreck of a man, this casualty, still wanted to be her white knight.

"What did you see?" Hunter asked. "How many are there? What's their weaponry? Who's in charge of them?"

"They want to know the same thing about you," Clemens said.

Hunter's scowl sharpened. "And what did you tell them?"

"I didn't have to tell them anything," Clemens said. "The prisoners are singing. You haven't heard them?"

"What have you been doing over there, Clemens?"

"Dealing," Clemens said.

Rebecca spoke. "What about the children?"

A veil seemed to fall over Clemens's eyes. He sat there bleeding through his shirt. They had spared him their worst savagery this time around, no broken bones, no prehistoric plastic surgery. The cuts and bruises looked fresh and minimal.

"How did you escape?" someone asked. They wanted to learn his secrets.

"I didn't. I was sent," Clemens said. "I'm here with an offer. Call it an amnesty."

The troops jumped at that. Their eyes lit with hope.

"We need to talk," he said to Rebecca and Hunter.

Hunter ordered the men back to their stations. He faced Clemens. "Talk." His hostility was thick as the night.

"The children are alive," he said.

Rebecca stared at him.

He opened his shirt and fumbled a string from around his neck. He handed it to her. Her mother's crucifix hung there, the same one Rebecca had given her Sam one scary night. She couldn't breathe. She couldn't think.

"I saw them," he said. "I spoke with Samantha."

A cage door flew open in her chest. A great, wracking sob escaped. She almost fell.

"They're alive?" said Hunter. He spoke it with surprise, but also irritation.

Rebecca grabbed Clemens's hand. "Tell me." That was all she could manage to get out.

"I won't lie," said Clemens. "They're a mess."

How bad could it be? Bad, Rebecca knew. "Yes?"

"They're exhausted. Injured, some of them. Traumatized." He saw her dread. "Don't worry, none has been reworked. That comes later."

Reworked? That was how he dealt with the horror in his mirror.

"Give me the terms of this amnesty," Hunter said.

"This is difficult," Clemens said.

"The terms," said Hunter.

"You came for the children. They know that."

Rebecca could barely see. Her tears were hot. "Yes?" she said.

Clemens eyed Hunter's rifle. "I'm just the messenger," he said.

"Give me the terms, Clemens."

"They'll trade you."

"For what?" said Rebecca. What was left of them that had the slightest value?

"Speak," said Hunter.

"It's a straight swap," said Clemens, "one child for one man."

"What?" Rebecca whispered.

"Utter fucking bullshit," said Hunter.

Rebecca struggled to find some silver lining. Her granny said there was always a silver lining. "It's just a proposal. Now we counter it."

"I already did," said Clemens. "They started out asking three for one. This is as good as it gets."

Hunter's steely face told her everything. There would be no trade. No volunteers. No nothing. Even though they had come for the children, even though they were willing to fight to the death, not one man would give himself over. They would all just fight and die here.

"No," she declared. "You go back to them. You tell them . . ." Her voice faded. "Tell them, me. I'll go. In exchange for all the children."

Who would love Sam the way she did? Who would know to tuck in her baby toes at night? Who would ever guess to sing "Greensleeves" to her? And years from now, when this was all past, would Sam even remember her? But it was the only way. Before her courage failed, Rebecca said, "Go tell them."

Bared to the world, Clemens's lidless eyes looked ancient and young, corrupt and innocent. Was that a scar or a smile? "I already did," he said. "I knew what they'd say. I knew what you'd say. I told them. They could have you. And me."

Her heart filled. "You would do that?"

"Enough," said Hunter. "You're not going anywhere. And neither is he."

"But the children . . ."

Hunter aimed his rifle at Clemens. "He lied, Rebecca," he said. "There are no children anymore."

37

"America," breathed the angel.

"Yes, America," said Ali. It was another day. She still could not stand. "Why steal our children? Why not take them from the settlements that are closer, or from some tropical island no one has ever heard of?"

"Because of you, Alexandra." He had begun calling her that. Gregorio's soul had quit wandering, it seemed. Perhaps gravity had drawn him to this lower keep, or he'd gotten lonely or was hoping to protect her. Whatever the explanation, she was once again Alexandra, not Ali. "Would you have come if the children were from Timbuktu or Kathmandu? No, there was only one way to pry you out of your little haven in the sun."

"You stole them to lure me down?"

"It worked, didn't it?"

By this point, she no longer doubted who he was. He was the Grand Inquisitor, the caged tiger and the encyclopedist. Long ago, when this place had been covered with water, he was the ancient mariner, and after it dried he was Job, the hermit. He was the trickster, the goat, and the noble revolutionary. He was the puppeteer using dead souls as strings for his puppets. He was a monster.

"Bait?" she said. "That's all the children were for you?"

"Wombs, of course, ripe and ready, or nearly so." He said it frankly. "Or food if they can't produce. I'll see what comes of them. Give it a thousand years or so. Their great-great-grandchildren could turn out to be something. Or nothing. I've been wrong before. I saw glimmers of greatness in your hadal cousins. I invested in them for eons, so sure they were the ones. But then their fire went out, don't ask me why. Weak seed. The environment. A glitch in the neuro wiring. Whatever it was, they just didn't have the right stuff."

"And we do?"

He looked at her. "Only time will tell."

"And what happens if we fail you?"

He shrugged. "Then I move on to the next pretty young thing."

His voice was like an ocean, calm and at the same time full of old and violent storms. He was tapped into their deepest roots. He knew things Ali had always wanted to know. And she knew things he needed to know. That was the problem.

"Where will you go when you're free?" she said.

"I don't care," he said. "All I want is a bit of ground to lie on under the sun. Nothing fancy. Consider. I started with nothing, not even the shirt on my back. Like Adam and Eve, a babe in the woods."

"You keep talking about your poverty and humble needs," she said. "And yet, right now I'm looking over your shoulder at a palace built for you by slaves. How do you reconcile one with the other?"

He had promised to give her the tour when she could walk again. He was frank about that, too, his violence upon her. It went beyond a simple rape. He had lost all control. His description, so graphic and sickening that it had actually awed her, made his frenzy sound both savage and holy. That, too, was a test, she had decided. A test and a teaching. He was telling her to learn from her suffering. And to expect more.

"Empires," he said. "They come, they go. Do you know how many I have fathered and nurtured, only to see them come crashing down? Before Egypt or Babylon, long before, there were my hadal orphans, hunted and haunted and benighted. They came under and I built them into greatness, and then they sank into darkness. And then came America."

"No," Ali corrected him. "And then came the world. America was only part of the incursion." Not invasion, too explicit, too provocative. She kept reaching for the softer words, trying to shield her country from him.

"Yes, the world came crashing in on us," he said. "But it was America that brought the poison down to exterminate my poor, wild hadals."

"This is all about revenge then? You took the children just to get even?"

"Hardly my pound of flesh, do you think? Your plague wiped out all their generations, the last of their memory, every last one of the hadal nations."

"Not quite," said Ali. "There were still enough left to make your raid."

Where was he keeping the children? They were hidden in his stories somewhere, that was increasingly clear. And he was lonely, or at least—for the moment—amused by her company.

"I like America," he said, steering them back to the beginning. "I love your gung-ho, can-do, Wild West spirit. It could yet be my salvation. It needs a little executive intelligence is all, although with some of your executives, a lot of intelligence. But my point is that America's fling at empire is faltering. You need me as much as I need you. Think of it as a new covenant. A second coming for the once-and-future Pax Americana. And a little patch of sunshine for me. Alexandra, we can do this thing together."

"What do you expect from us?" Ali had asked it yesterday, and it had frustrated him. She pressed it again. "Drill a hole for the sun to shine down on you? Drain the ocean? Cut you out of the planet? Do you want a Cesarean section, or an engineering marvel, or a miracle? What is it that's supposed to set you free?"

"I don't know."

"How about an invisible bolt cutter for an invisible chain," she said. "Because as far as I can tell, there's nothing keeping you down here."

He calmly shoveled his hand at the sand. But her mockery—and his not knowing—infuriated him. That was the very reason she kept pressing the question. For all his knowledge and recall, this was something he didn't know. His captivity had to do with ignorance. Ignorance was his captivity.

"You want to breed your way out of here," she said. "But how many times has that not worked for you?"

"Try, try again," he said.

"Let the children go."

He smiled at her foolishness.

Ali cranked herself up onto one elbow. She drew a symbol in the sand with her finger. He saw the aleph. His smile faded.

"Open, sesame," she said.

His voice darkened. "If you know the answer, speak."

"Let them go," she said. "That's the beginning of the answer."

"And the rest of it?"

She pointed at the symbol in the sand.

"Free me now," he said.

"I can't. I don't know the answer," she said. "Yet."

He did not contemplate her terms or dicker or threaten. He knew his mind. "Done," he said.

"You'll let them go?" Ali searched his face for any deception, but it was a blank slate. She could have written any emotion or intent there.

He opened his fingers and the sand poured from his hand. Only later would Ali wonder whether he had scooped up the sand in order to release it, at this very moment, as his answer for a question he had known she would ask in a dialogue he might have orchestrated. He knew his mind. How well did he know hers? She was in a web with a spider.

"Your daughter's name," he said.

"What?"

"I need your daughter's name."

In the guise of Ike, he had asked for the name before. "Why?"

"The children's lives depend upon it."

Did he think it was another of his magic words? How superstitious was this creature? Ali saw no harm in giving him the name. "Maggie."

He dusted his hands of the sand and stood up.

"Where are you going?"

"To set them free."

"Take me with you," she said. "I want to see you let them go."

"You can walk?"

"Carry me."

"All right," he said, "you can watch, but from a distance. If you try to go closer, one step closer, if you say one word, it could mean the children's doom. Do you understand?"

"Yes."

He lifted her in his arms. His skin was exactly the temperature of the air and sand. If there was any blood in him at all, it was cold as a reptile's.

They exited the garden with its raked sand. He walked for miles, up and down steep trails and through stone arteries. At the cliff's edge, he hopped nimbly from ledge to ledge. The land lay ruptured and cracked and partially flooded by plastic rock. Buildings made of massive stone stood empty and fractured by quakes. Whoever had sweated together this sprawling architecture was long gone.

A golden monastery sparkled in the distance. As they drew closer, Ali saw that the monastery was more ruins. Its walls were encrusted, not with gold but crystal pyrite. Her leg brushed against a crystal, and the edges cut her. Beautiful from a distance, the reality was treacherous up close.

He descended into a valley behind the monastery. It looked like a long, winding cemetery, with open holes bored here and there into the hillsides, and piles of rocks sealing others shut. "The children are here?" she asked.

"Patience."

"But this is a cemetery. Are they dead?"

"Once upon a time," he said, "monks meditated in these holes. Fat lot of good it did me. I finally closed the place down."

As they entered the valley of tombs, the stench of diarrhea and rotting meat almost gagged her. Bones and skulls dotted the slopes here and there, some fresh, the skin and hair still on them. Scattered among them were remains of *Homo* species that Ali could only guess at. It looked like the den of a lion, an ancient lion. "Dear God," she said. "What did you do to them?"

He made no excuses. "Quid pro quo," he said. "They got, they gave. Some were the greatest hunters or warriors of their time. Some were wise men or prophets. All came to confront the darkness, and I was here for them, their holy grail. I gave them purpose. They gave me . . . an appetite."

As they sank deeper among the bends, Ali was startled to hear men groaning from inside the tombs. She lifted her head. Some were speaking with American accents, some in hadal tones.

"Newcomers," he volunteered. "Wounded and dying, human and hadal, they've been straggling down to me for weeks. Leftovers from the glorious crusade to save the children."

"You put them in holes?"

"Rough lodging, I admit. But here they have a place to lay down their heads. And season."

Ali found a small hope in that. Because if these wounded combatants were still alive, then the children might be also. She listened for slighter voices. "Which one holds the children?"

"I have never seen the children." He said it matter-of-factly, as if she had simply forgotten.

"You said—"

"I promised to free them, not to show them." He kept in motion.

"Where are we going then?"

"Have faith," he told her, "in something."

He climbed a slope to a stone barricade and laid Ali down where a gap had tumbled open. "Watch from here. This is a safe distance. But you have to stay very still. No matter what you see, not a peep out of you."

"Watch what?"

"You want me to save the children?" he said. "Then first I must draw the sword."

What children? What sword? She was sick of his game.

"And remember, not a word or the children are damned."

ARTIFACTS

From NAVAL SPECIAL WARFARE BASIC SNIPER TRAINING

Breathing

The control of breathing is critical to the aiming process. If the sniper breathes while aiming, the rising and falling of his chest will cause the muzzle to move vertically. To breathe properly during aiming, the sniper inhales, then exhales normally and stops at the moment of natural respiratory pause. The pause can be extended to eight to ten seconds, but it should never be extended until it feels uncomfortable. As the body begins to need air, the muscles will start a slight involuntary movement, and the eyes will lose their ability to focus critically. If the sniper has been holding his breath for more than eight to ten seconds, he should resume normal breathing and then start the aiming process over again.

38

The end was near. Rebecca saw it in their impromptu prayer sessions, their letter writing, their graffiti notched into the stone, and their little shrines to themselves. At every station, mementos and snapshots were propped next to their ammunition clips and grenades. They had quit talking about next Christmas or how much beer they'd drink or the pussy they'd score once they got out of this thing.

On day six of the siege, Hunter went down into the hospital that was really a morgue and a jail for Clemens, and he shot the two radar men like dogs. It was the proper thing to do, everyone agreed. Their groans and screams had gotten too awful to bear anymore. The blow darts had been tipped in rabies virus, meaning they had zero chance of recovering.

The citadel reeked of life and death.

Unable to sleep, Rebecca stayed in motion. She made herself their muse. Traveling endlessly she went from station to station, she mothered those who needed it, took confessions, and joshed with the diehards. It helped her make peace with them. This was their Alamo, not hers. They were warriors. This was their logical end point. She, on the other hand, still had a daughter to find.

Hunter told her not to visit Clemens. "Let the Judas rot," he said. But she couldn't stay away. He lay on the ground, hog-tied with flex cuffs and duct tape, oblivious to his still neighbors wrapped in ponchos.

"Drink," she said, holding up his head.

"Free me," he said. "I can save you."

"Not without Sam. And the other children."

"I promise."

"I have to think," she said.

They had this same conversation several times over the days and nights. She went so far as to steal a knife to cut his bonds, but couldn't quite bring herself to do it. It would take all her courage and faith to let him go, because every instinct warned that he might simply bolt and save his own skin. It wasn't that that stopped her. Rather, she kept Clemens tied because he was her sole link to Sam. He had seen her alive. In that way, he was *her* muse.

At the end of every conversation, he would ask again if she had eaten any of the hadal meat. She answered the same way each time, "Not yet." One after another, even the most reluctant of the troops had joined in the feast. They had gone through both the hadal's thighs and calves, and were nearing the end of the shoulder meat. She held off because of Clemens.

"Stay pure," he said. "Keep fasting. It's a time for visions and clarity. Drink lots of water. There are minerals in the water. They'll help you see in the night."

And it was true. Her eyes were adjusting to the darkness. Everyone's were. The less light they used, the more they saw. A few men clung to their little penlights as if they were the last embers of the last fire. In a sense, these few who could see best were the most blind. Once the lights went out, they would be the first to go.

Hunter caught her sneaking out of the room. "I wouldn't get too affectionate," he said. "He's not one of us anymore."

Plainly he meant to kill Clemens. No big surprise there. The only mystery for Rebecca was why he'd kept the man alive this long. Then she realized it. In lieu of a meat locker, they were keeping him alive until they needed him.

That night she cut Clemens free. Hunter left her no choice. "Take me with you," she said.

"You're too slow," he said. "I'll bring her to you."

"Promise me."

"Close your eyes and make a wish," he said.

Rebecca closed her eyes, and opened them, and he was gone.

She expected the wrath of God when Hunter found out his prisoner had escaped. He only sighed. His rugged face looked a hundred years old. "Did you really love him that much?"

"Love?" It shocked her.

The first assault came after midnight. Rebecca was sleeping when the guns started cracking. A claymore gave a loud cough. Flares lit the marsh. She peeked over the sill, sure there would be thousands of them caught in midstride. Scarcely a dozen lay along the bridge or floating on top of the water.

After that they kept at least one flare in the air at all times. Now that their night vision was blown, they had to depend on the light, and eventually that would die. The men wanted to take the fight to the enemy.

"Screw this fort shit. I'll live in a coffin, but goddamn if I'll die in one."

"Turn us loose," said another.

Rebecca didn't say a word. They belonged to Hunter, for one thing. For another, they weren't going anywhere, no matter what. Because this was the Alamo.

The second assault was more like a rock-climbing competition. "Check this," someone said. Far below on the back cliffs, they spied a pale stripe, like sea scum, lining the walls above the city. It moved higher.

"Cook them," said Hunter.

They fired a Willie Pete into the depths. It struck like a comet. Pure white light erupted from the maze of spires and spans. Phosphorous shafts strafed out from the center. On contact with the air, each particle burned at five thousand degrees Fahrenheit.

The superheated shrapnel skinned the walls clean. Rebecca saw miniature white apes flailing at shrapnel wounds as they tumbled backward into the smoke. For the next half hour, like kids with firecrackers, Hunter's men dropped grenades and rocks on whatever survived, tweaking their timing so that the shrapnel bursts had maximum impact. "Like fish in a barrel," they exulted.

Everyone felt better after that. There was lively conjecture that the siege was broken. Haddie had just taken a maximum hit. Any survivors would slink off into their holes. "We're almost out of here."

But Hunter kept them inside. "That was too easy," he said.

"Come on, we're the twenty-first century. They're cavemen. It's over."

"It's just beginning," he said. "The acropolis is our only chance."

Grumbling, they settled in behind their weapons. The siege went on.

Staying didn't mean starving, though. Three men were given permission to drag the closest bodies inside. An hour later, the citadel smelled like a barbecue.

By this point, Rebecca was beyond temptation. Her body had adjusted to the slow starvation, and she had entered a state of clarity. Every object stood absolutely distinct. She felt light as a feather.

Each flare stayed aloft for an average of thirty-five minutes. These latest versions were tiny things that relied on nanotech paint. Instead of parachutes, they dangled prettily from balloons. As the balloons drifted above the marsh and the city with their sparkling, bright cargo, Rebecca hoped Sam and the children could see them, too.

Another day passed.

On the ninth morning of the siege, she woke to find half the garrison bleeding from the eyes and nostrils. Men were staggering around in the hallways, blind and feverish, coughing up blood, smearing it everywhere. Those not ill avoided those who were. They barricaded themselves into their nests and chambers.

"Ebola," said Hunter. "I saw it once in India. But how come they got it and not us?"

Rebecca saw it in a flash. These bloody-eyed zombies had been the first to eat the hadal meat. The hadal must have infected himself and then delivered his flesh to their very doorstep. Now they were dying of their own appetites.

Stay pure, Clemens had told her. He had known. She didn't share any of this with Hunter. He had partaken of the meat, she had seen it, meaning he was doomed enough without her pronouncing the inevitable to him.

The end came softly, on bare feet, with golden hair.

"Goddamn him," Hunter breathed.

Far below, a tiny figure was approaching. Rebecca fumbled for her binoculars. She focused. "Sam," she whispered.

It was Sam, and yet not Sam. The girl was in rags, no surprise. Her blond hair was flattened to a greasy cowl. That's what shampoo was for. She was thin. That could be fixed, too.

But it was more than that. She looked different from the way Rebecca remembered, like a garden that has grown wild and spilled from its margins. In the space of three months, she had sprouted like a weed and lost every last ounce of her baby fat and learned to shuffle like an inmate.

Jake had once taken the family for one of his camping epics, and it took three days to get all the cockles out of Sam's hair, and the tics unscrewed, and the blisters mending. That was Rebecca's first thought as she peered through the binoculars. Sam needed some hot soup, a long bath, and a whole lot of TLC. With enough combing and scrubbing, it would all wash clean. They could start over.

"Sam," she called loudly.

The child was jarred awake. "Mommy?" Her voice was so tiny, but it was definitely hers.

Then Rebecca saw the rope around Sam's little neck. They had her cinched on a leash. "I count three of them," Hunter said into his radio mike.

That was when Rebecca noticed the pale creatures in Sam's shadow. They were using her daughter as a human shield.

A storm of hatred swept her. It sucked the oxygen right out of her. She lowered her binoculars. *Breathe.* She forced herself.

Hunter sat flexed behind his scope. His finger was on the trigger.

"What are you doing?" said Rebecca.

"I've got number one," Hunter said into his mike. She couldn't hear the other men reply, but it was easy to guess. Numbers two and three were targeted, too. "On my shot," said Hunter.

"I order you not to shoot," she said.

"Quiet," he said.

"That's my daughter."

"And if she was someone else's daughter?"

Rebecca hesitated.

"I didn't think so," said Hunter. "He's not stupid."

"What?"

"Clemens."

"What are you talking about?"

"The one and only thing that can breach our walls is coming at us. Your daughter, not anyone else's." Hunter gave it a beat. "This is Clemens's idea."

"That's crazy."

Hunter didn't say anything.

"He's not one of them," she said. "He can't be."

But he was. It was so clear. So what? Rebecca didn't have time for it. That was Sam down there. "Do not fire that rifle," she said.

"You want me to let them in?"

Rebecca's heart crashed against her ribs. She glanced down. The little blond hostage inched closer. "Yes," she said. "Let them in. There are only three of them. Let them through." *Get that rope off her neck.* "Kill them inside."

"My men are going blind with their own blood. We're sick and injured. And these three animals are just the tip of the spear. There will be more right behind them."

But what if Hunter and his marksmen missed? This was going too fast. Slow it down. "Wait," she said. "Listen to me. Look at me."

He didn't lift his eye from the scope. He quit talking. She could feel that rope around her own neck. "Stop," she said. "Just stop."

His stillness gathered. He settled into the shot. His lungs stopped.

Rebecca made her move. She leaped at him. Thunder cracked.

Her head seemed to split open, and she thought, *God no, he's shot me.*

Hunter fell under her weight. It surprised her. This square block of a man, this warrior, could be toppled by a mere woman?

He shoved her away with a roar. "What have you done?"

Ears ringing, Rebecca clawed back to the window.

Two bodies lay sprawled on the path, twisted together like a large pretzel, both hadal, neither of them Sam. Sam had escaped! Rebecca groped for her binoculars, frantic, thankful, zealous. *Alive.* Sam was alive.

She was only dimly aware of more flares going up, and guns crackling, and a pale wave streaming along the path and climbing from the marsh and the city, from every direction.

Her binoculars swept back and forth, out of her control. The lenses spared her nothing: the demon horns, the mouths yawing with disembodied cries, the sharpened teeth, the gore whipping through the air. Bullets and shrapnel tore into them. There was no pretty choreography. Just strings cut. Puppets tumbling. A belly flop into the water. Figures pinwheeled into the depths.

A man's face jumped into focus. He had a familiar red beard. More faces appeared, her action heroes in the flesh. They had crossed to the island and vanished in the pandemonium. Yet here they were, running with the bulls, alive and well.

Then one of the faces slipped sideways. Another's rubbery expression wrinkled. The man threw away his frown, literally, ripped it from his head. All around him the creatures discarded their masquerade of dead men's faces.

"Sam," she screamed. *Come in this very minute, young lady. It's bedtime for you.* Something hot kissed her cheek. It kissed her again. Rebecca lowered the binoculars. Hunter was back in position at the sill, utterly studious behind his scope, taking his shots in deadly order. Shells spun through the air and roosted in her hair and clothes.

This was no good. *Where is that girl hiding?* Rebecca was going to have to go down and find her ballerina.

She shoved open the rocks at the doorway and descended the ramps. She side-stepped the poor men with their bloody eyes. Someone had started to fire a flare through the entrance, but lost his aim, and now it burned bright in the bowels of the building.

Chalky white shapes guttered through the archway. *The tip of the spear.*

An explosion heated the side of her face. Smoke billowed. Like a volcano erupting.

Rebecca turned left, away from the clash at the gate, into an empty side cell. The loophole stood, half melted, just big enough for her to wriggle outside.

It was like trading a madhouse for a hurricane. The violence—the velocity of hatreds—rushed at her from every side.

Sound returned. Men were screaming. Stones and shrapnel rattled against the wall. Someone fell from high above. Blood slashed her face. She slid, caught her balance, ran on.

"Sam." Bodies and rocks were jumbled on the path. Things floated in the marsh, like lilies, pure white upon the ferment. More and more flares scooted across the sky. Light was their weapon. Light and more light. It hurt her eyes.

"Sam," she screamed.

Rebecca was invisible. How else to explain it? She drifted through the battle, untouchable. Beasts from a medieval nightmare surged past her, clattering with their insect language and metal weapons and pieces of ancient armor and helmets. Bullets snicked against the stone. Someone hit a mine. The DZ boys had been busy. Limbs flew. *Chopped salad.*

A very bright light lit the sky. Rebecca fell. She was pushed. A giant hand slapped her flat. *Sleep,* she thought.

Wake up.

She climbed to her feet in a wasteland of meat. It was very quiet for a few minutes. Everything lay still around her. Whatever the soldiers had unleashed had leveled the playing field. She alone was left standing. Not for long. More of the creatures were approaching.

She smelled smoke. Her hair was on fire. Rebecca patted it out.

Her shirt fell from her shoulders. Automatically she covered her breasts, and her hands were covered with blood. Her back began to sting, then burn. The pain hit. She staggered, and tried to touch her wounds.

"Rebecca." She turned at her name. The birthday cake had become a Halloween pumpkin with flares crooking out from its gap-eyed windows. Hunter was up there somewhere. "Come back," he yelled.

She staggered among the remains. It was like the meat section in the HEB, with racks of ribs, and cutlets, and kidneys on vivid display. One or two sides of beef kept moving. This was nothing for a child to see. "Sam," she called. "Sam."

To her left, something wet and hairless slid from the marsh reeds. Five more of them surfaced and followed the first, heading for the citadel. The chop-chop of gunfire resumed.

She came to two bodies piled like dough, the pretzel pair. Now she was getting somewhere. This was where it had all begun. These were the animals that had used her daughter as a shield. Rebecca kicked one. *Bastard.* She kicked him again, harder, hard as she could. His body rolled away.

Sam, with her golden hair, was hiding underneath.

Rebecca almost screamed. She remembered Hunter aiming and leaping on him and his gun going off. That quickly, she remembered nothing.

"There you are, baby," she said.

She gathered Sam into her arms and kissed her forehead, what was left of it, and stroked her hair. The two of them rocked back and forth, and shed some happy tears. They hugged. Lots of hugs. Sam was so sleepy.

Shapes streamed past. More explosions. Screams. *Jake's war movies.*

"Let's go home," said Rebecca. "How does a grilled-cheese sandwich and hot chocolate sound?"

She lifted Sam in her arms and started one way. A rocket streaked down from the highest tower window. Petals of white phosphorous blossomed. Apes thrashed about, howling, on fire. *What kind of zoo was this?*

Rebecca turned and went the other way. She carried her baby. Sam would like the frogs singing. That meant finding some peace and quiet far away.

Sam got heavy. Rebecca lowered herself to her knees. "Mommy just needs a little rest," she said.

High overhead, the world lit with a brilliant white flower. Streamers sizzled downward. Thunder rolled through the sky. Rebecca arranged a little bed for them on the ground, with a little pillow of rocks, and fell sound asleep with her golden ballerina.

ARTIFACTS

FOX NEWS

February 6

The Rob O'Ryan True News Hour

O'Ryan: Joining us tonight is author Thomas Liddy. His book *Dark Truth: The Burr Administration's Cover-up* has just been released from Dolphin Press and has already ignited a firestorm on Capitol Hill. Welcome, Mr. Liddy.

Liddy: Thank you for having me.

O'Ryan: Let me start by saying, folks, this is a riveting read that proves once again how the invertebrates and left-wing nuts are destroying our country. Now according to your book, Mr. Liddy, the Coltrane rescue brigade, of which you were a member, has already been wiped out.

Liddy: That's correct. Killed to the last man. And woman.

O'Ryan: Killed by . . .

Liddy: . . . by the Chinese army.

O'Ryan: The Chinese army!

Liddy: Yes, sir. Sacrificed to the peace agenda.

O'Ryan: That's where your title comes in. The "dark truth" is that President Burr and his administration have known about this for weeks, but kept it secret from the American public. Why?

Liddy: I think it's called kowtowing.

O'Ryan: This is the kind of weakness that tigers prey upon. Especially tigers of the Beijing variety. First they ground a killer sub with nukes on our shore, then they force down one of our planes, then they wipe out a group of American citizens searching for missing children. And our president gives them cover? This is outrageous.

Liddy: I thought the truth should be told.

O'Ryan: Now let's address these attacks on you. Your book came out two days ago, and already the liberal media has accused you of cowardice, cheap exploitation, warmongering, and of being a self-loathing deadbeat dad. Let's retire these slanders right now, one by one. First, cowardice. As you candidly state in your book, you turned around at a certain point and left the Coltrane brigade due to, well, you tell us in your own words.

Liddy: I sensed we were walking into a Chinese trap.

O'Ryan: And how did you sense that?

Liddy: I'm a religious man, sir. I believe in the afterlife.

O'Ryan: Go on, sir.

Liddy: My father warned me of the trap.

O'Ryan: Your father who passed away a year ago, is that correct?

Liddy: I heard him distinctly. And if I had not listened to him, I would be dead today.

O'Ryan: The liberals and atheists are having a field day with this. But the fact that you're alive tonight is proof that you received insider information, so to speak.

Liddy: I think of it as divine intervention, sir.

O'Ryan: Amen to that. Now turning to this accusation that you abandoned your wife and children two years ago . . .

39

Ike hears the scrape and thud of rocks being lifted aside. Fresh air rushes in. It jolts him. Peace had been at hand. A little more and he could have joined the great stream. But now the angel is dismantling his tomb.

He whispers, "No."

A powerful hand seizes him by the ankle. As he gets pulled feetfirst from the hole, Ike grabs for the bones. His bones. They had become his.

The angel is brusque. He drags Ike kicking and flailing from his gruesome repose. Ike strikes out with his feet. To his surprise, he has acquired an odd strength. Even faint from starvation, even half-mad, he is able to twist free and lash out at those pitiless eyes. The border between his body and will has been erased. He wonders, am I dreaming? Because he touches the untouchable, actually strikes the angel's face.

Twice he rushes in. Twice he is flung aside. The angel holds him down.

"Why?" he says.

"You've seasoned enough," the angel tells him. "It's time you started earning your keep."

Ike feels liquid on his lips. He fights this resurrection. It was over and done with. But his body is an animal. It drinks the liquid. Whether he likes it or not, his body takes the food.

"I can hear lambs out wandering in the storm, just beyond my reach," says the angel. He tosses a bundle at Ike. It lands with a clatter. Ike sees the green jade armor of past hunts.

"No more," he says. He does not attach an honorific. No more Lord, Rinpoche or Teacher. He is renouncing the angel. In doing so, he knows he is re-

nouncing his life. At this level of the game, an ungrateful student deserves nothing but death.

The angel is merciful, or at least solicitous. Licking one palm, he wipes the long hair from his kitten's eyes. "You have obligations," says the angel.

Ike is beginning to feel stronger. A great deal stronger. "You have nothing more to teach me."

"Dear Ike," says the angel, and his use of Ike's name—for the first time in many years—signals much. He is renouncing the student who has renounced him, returning Ike to his trivial ego. Also he is acknowledging the enduring circle: what came to him in the beginning was Ike, and what leaves him in the end will be Ike. An obituary, if you will.

"After all our time together," the angel continues, "you still don't understand. The issue has never been what I have to teach you, but what you have to teach me. We had a bargain. I would share all that I know, and you would do the same, nothing held back. Isn't that true?"

"I gave you everything."

The angel continues as if the conversation were already two or three steps ahead of itself. "Now about this daughter of yours . . ."

Ike lifts his head.

His surprise betrays him. He had no idea the child would be a girl. Girl or boy, he'd carefully hidden the unborn child from his teacher. If his disrespect does not cost him his life, harboring a secret surely will.

The angel sees it all, Ike's deceit and daring and fatalism. "Bad dog," he says. But he does not kill or mutilate Ike. Yet.

The nourishment is burning through Ike's system. Whatever the angel fed him is lighting him on fire. He can't sit still. He stands. He paces. His heart is racing. He needs to move. To hit something. To fucking destroy it.

"You're getting angry." The angel is watching him with clinical calm. "It's going to heat up a bit for you. Quite a bit. My gift to you. Does it hurt yet?"

Ike leaps at the angel, his nails like talons. The angel brushes him away. "Beautiful Ike, don't waste your gift on me. It's your daughter who needs it. Control yourself just a little longer. Soon you won't be able to."

"What have you done to her?"

"The question is, what have you done to her? Maybe I ought to be flattered that you threw away your own child to follow me. But in my experience, child sacrifices are such a waste. And they can come back to bite you, Ike. Like

this one. You sacrificed your daughter, but she's come back to haunt you. To save you from yourself."

Ike tries to control his breathing. He wants to run. He wants to jump in the air and fly. He wants to kill this thing that can't be killed. Anything to cool the heat in his brain. "Tell me."

"Don't blame her, Ike. Blame yourself. It's perfectly natural that she would come searching for her father."

Ike howls. He slams a rock down, and it sparks and breaks. The smell of mineral dust excites him. He contains himself, barely, for the moment. He shortcuts through the information. Clearly his child is in the angel's capture. Clearly a trade is being offered. Before his rage carries him away, he cuts to the chase. "What do you want?"

"As I said, there are lambs lost in the wilderness, beyond my help. I need you to save them from the monsters."

Ike has harvested wanderers before. Once they are delivered to the angel, he never sees them again. Some go into stone cages. Some get trained for special duties. Some feed the others.

But he has never heard the angel call his acquisitions lambs. It makes him wary. It pisses him off. This one is going to bite you. "Who?" he snarls. "Where?"

"Girls, roughly the same age as your own," says the angel. "A couple of dozen still remain, a nice bouquet, plus or minus one or two flowers. There were boys in the beginning, but they didn't travel well, and were off the point besides. None of them made it, just as well."

Ike paces. He slams another rock down. Turn me loose.

"Anyway, the consignment was on its way here, but got sidetracked. It seems my flock has been misled by a former pupil of mine. You may remember him, you snared him for me years ago. Clemens, a smart enough fellow, but pathologically ambitious and a chronic thief. Judging by appearances, he intends to keep the girls for himself and start up his own little breakaway republic. These things happen from time to time. You send an errand boy to fetch your snack, and he ends up eating it himself."

Ike's muscles are electric. He races off a short distance, races back. Hurry, he thinks. Tell me. Which is it, bouquet or snack, flower or lamb, harem or food? Did it matter? The angel is a whimsical creature. He will decide the girls' use when they come into his possession. Possession, that was Ike's job.

"My daughter." Ike grits his teeth. Such fury. It does hurt.

"*Your daughter will be waiting for you right here. Deliver the children to me and she is yours.*"

"*Her name.*"

"*Ah, that.*" The angel taps his teeth. "*Call her Maggie.*"

It registers, even in his rage. His connection to this child is deeper than he imagined. That was the name of Ike's mother. Ali remembered.

"*Where are the children?*" Lambs, flowers: the damned.

"*In a city once known as N'iu, or Taurus, or the Ox. He was another of my crossbreeds, bless him, another poor misfire. Worshippers kept him alive with offerings long after his senility, sure it would please me. I finally put a stop to it. Sent a nasty flu virus up, erased the citizenry, blighted the city. This was, oh, nine thousand years ago. My son, the brutal mooncalf, is still alive, though barely, starving and buried inside some mountain. Careful of him, friend. Don't feed the animals. But my point is that Mr. Clemens seems to be squatting in the ruins and reviving the mumbo jumbo.*"

"*Which way?*" says Ike.

The angel cuts a symbol into Ike's palm with his fingernail. "*The Ox. Follow that.*"

Ike starts off. The angel catches his arm. "*There's a bit of a fracas going on in the city just now,*" he says. "*It should be over by the time you get up there. I'm betting on the home team. Regardless, whoever's left on either side, kill them all. They have served their purpose.*"

"*All,*" says Ike.

"*Not the girls, of course, don't harm a hair on their heads. And bring my boy Clemens to me, if you would, alive. He and I have a few things to discuss. A word of warning: I gave him a little training, thought he might make a decent assassin someday.*" He draws a six-inch-long quill from a thin bone sheath. "*Fresh from a ray. I favor them as writing pens. Are you following me, Ike? This one has no ink. The tip is loaded with poison.*"

The angel grabs Ike's face and holds it close. "*Are you on fire inside? Are you ready?*"

Ike bellows. Perhaps he only whispers. The world was so quiet in his tomb.

"*Your daughter, Ike. Don't forget. Bring my children down to me.*"

He tears away from the angel's grip, and runs.

*   *   *

From her hiding place on the hillside, Ali watched the angel, Ishmael. He descended into the gorge like quick, pale water, flowing between the slag heaps that housed prisoners and bones. Not once did he look down to place his feet. It was as if he had memorized each and every stone where it lay.

Halting in front of a mound, he began tearing the rocks away, tossing aside big boulders as if they were pebbles. After a few minutes of Herculean burrowing, he exposed a hole. As Ali waited for the children to surface, one by one, she wondered, how would the girls ever find their way back to the surface? Who would care for them? What would they eat? She had to go with them, it was the only solution. But would this creature let her go?

Ishmael—Older-Than-Old, whatever he called himself—reached inside the hole and grabbed hold of something. A struggle ensued. Whoever was in there plainly did not want to come out.

The angel could have been delivering a baby as he slowly towed out first one leg, then the other, then the hips and torso, and finally the shaggy head of a man. Where were the children, though?

From her distance, it was hard at first for Ali to make out much detail. The man was long and thin as a bone, but ferocious. No sooner did Ishmael toss him to the ground than the man sprang up and attacked. Ishmael batted him down, which only provoked a second attack. This time Ishmael flung his prisoner down with such force it moved rocks. Ali heard them clatter and grate in their sockets. Before the man could rise again, Ishmael seized him by the throat and pinned him to the ground.

One of Rebecca's soldiers, thought Ali. Or perhaps a hadal, though even that didn't explain his wild strength. The man had been whittled down— virtually carved—to his raw nature. There was nothing left of him but junkyard viciousness. It occurred to her that this prisoner might be responsible for at least some of the bones littering the slopes. It was easy to picture him riffling through the graves, a real-life ghoul. This was the children's salvation?

Holding his captive with one hand, Ishmael poured a liquid into the man's mouth. He bent closer and said something. Immediately the man quit flailing. It was as if he had been shot through the head. Ishmael stroked the prisoner's white mane. He unclamped his hand from the man's throat and stepped back.

For another full minute, the man did not move at all. Ali wondered if Ishmael had killed him.

At last the prisoner stirred. Light as a cat, he rolled to his feet and straightened. For the first time Ali saw the tattoos covering his lean form. Then, never mind the filthy hair and the wicker ribs and the passage of years, Ali recognized him.

"Ike?" His name slipped from her, barely a breath of a whisper.

Instantly Ike dropped to a crouch. He faced her hillside. Ali ducked her head behind the rocks. The strangeness of his reaction, the bottled-up violence in him, his graveyard emergence, all of it frightened her.

Ike's head cast back and forth, exactly like a hyena's, searching with his ears and nose for what his eyes could not find. Ishmael glanced at Ali's hiding place, and then kicked Ike in the ribs. He kicked him again, demanding his attention.

Ali lay stunned. For over ten years she had been burying this man. After the image and voice of him—his ghost or severed soul, whatever it was—had spoken to her through Ishmael's mouth, she was sure he was finally dead. But here he was again.

She almost spoke Ike's name again, this time louder and with purpose. He would come for her. He would rescue her from the abyss like last time.

But there were the children, or at least the phantom possibility of them. She realized that Ishmael had brought her along in order to test her. With a word, Ali could have saved herself. But then she would damn the children, if they were even alive anymore. By keeping silent, she might or might not save the children but would certainly damn herself.

Ishmael waited with his back to her. The choice was hers. One path led to the sun, the other wound deeper. Even as he was proving himself to her, he was making Ali prove herself to him. She took a breath. In silence, she let go of the sun.

Ike quit searching for her. He returned to his pacing. Possibly he dismissed her voice as that of a ghost, one more in this bank of lost souls. Ishmael looked over his shoulder to Ali's hiding place, and then took a handful of Ike's hair and lifted him to his feet. He pointed to the distance.

A howl pierced the air. Through the gap in the wall, Ali saw Ike loping off through the gorge.

Ishmael returned up the hillside. Ali was lying where he had placed her. "The sword is drawn."

"What did you tell him?" she asked.

"I gave him a bit of inspiration. I told him that his daughter is among the children."

"But she's dead," Ali said.

"Oh, ye of little faith," said the angel.

ARTIFACTS

VARIETY

February 9

The Dark Brigade Takes the Dark Leap

Cameras began rolling yesterday on the Warner Bros. $180-million epic film of the Rebecca Coltrane rescue catastrophe, entitled *The Dark Brigade*. Under the helm of actor-turned-director Daniel Radcliffe, it is being shot entirely aboveground in the giant soundstage outside Salt Lake City, and is scheduled for a Thanksgiving release.

Hot on its hadal heels is DreamWorks's *Children's Crusade*, the story of three young men swept into the misadventure who forge a friendship as they descend into chaos. If budget is any indicator, the $220-million star vehicle (Reese Witherspoon and Daniel Day-Lewis) should provide heavyweight competition for *Dark Brigade* come Oscar time. Shooting begins next month in Croatia.

40

When Rebecca woke beside the water, the wind had died and her arms were empty. She didn't panic. Sam had gotten up early, that was all, and would be playing nearby. Sam knew better than to worry her mother.

Rebecca had a vague memory of things being very complicated and noisy, with flashing lights and explosions. But the world was simple and quiet now. She and Sam were together. Except at this very moment.

"Sam?" Rebecca heard children playing in the distance, and got to her feet. For some reason she was naked to the waist. It felt good in front. But her back felt awful, like a very bad sunburn. Worse than that. Her hair was singed to the scalp. Odd.

The children's singing led her along the path beside the lake. She found them in the reeds. "Have you seen Sam?" she asked the frogs.

Sam giggled, far away. *Mama*, she called. *Over here.*

Goodness, she was thirsty. The water was delicious. Rebecca splashed a handful on her face. She wet the back of her head where the hair had burned off. How on earth had that happened? No crying over spilled milk. It would grow again.

One thing led to another. She lowered herself into the marsh and waded out a bit and floated on her back. The children, being children, went to play hide-and-seek in the cattails. They quit singing.

The weight of the world had no weight in here. Her arms dangled. Her brown nipples floated like islands. She squeezed the mud between her toes.

At some point faces appeared in the water. On first noticing them, she thought they were ghosts hovering just under the surface. But they were reflections. Rebecca raised her eyes.

Five goblins were hunkered down along the shoreline, side by side, like peas in a pod, watching her. One was draped with a chain-mail shirt from some bygone era. Three wore bloodstained scraps of military uniforms and carried broken rifles and had wet sacks hanging from strings around their necks. One of the sacks had a thumb of skin still attached. It was a penis, she realized.

For a terrifying moment, Rebecca remembered everything in perfect order, the moonlit kidnapping, Jake's fight, the crusading, the battle, even the jagged hole in Sam's head. The images circled her, faster and faster. *Sam is dead.* An awful groan climbed out from her throat.

Abruptly it was too much. A switch flipped. Her groan stopped. The world was nice again.

The five goblins could have stepped right out of a children's story. They spoke softly, almost musically, with little scritches and clicks. Rebecca smiled. It reminded her of Texas nights with crickets fiddling and fireflies scooting about. At last they stood and continued on their way.

Sam. "Sam," she called.

Mama.

She waded back to shore. They had left a strip of fresh meat on her pants. She chewed while she walked. Sam flirted with her in the near distance. Rebecca liked having a happy girl.

The path was littered with blood pools and broken reeds and sharp metal and stone junk. In the distance loomed a fort. The bad memories stirred again, but she managed to keep them at bay. It helped that the bodies were all gone. She approved. When you finished playing, you needed to pick up after yourself.

She came to an odd bridge of pillar tops that marched across the water. She imagined her little ballerina hopscotching over the gaps in the bridge. *Mama,* Sam called impatiently. Rebecca started over.

Just one body spoiled the crossing. It was a man floating facedown in the water. He seemed to be suspended by taut pink balloons along his back and limbs. They were jellyfish feasting. Never mind.

Mah-maah.

Onward. A range of white-capped peaks stood at the bridge's end. "Careful, Sam." Was that her happy Heidi up there scaling the Alps?

They weren't the Alps. It wasn't Heidi. Pyramids, she realized. They were in Egypt. And some sort of animal was prowling the heights. Egyptian monkeys?

Up close, the pyramids weren't nearly so trim and tidy. The alabaster sheath had cracked and avalanched into heaps. White bones littered the white rubble.

"Sam, honey," she called.

Rebecca didn't like the haunted-house theme. It smelled bad here. Skulls gawked from every fissure and shelf. More than one of those animals was darting about on the ledges overhead. Shapes flitted between the enormous pyramid roots. Rebecca took care not to look at them. Out of sight, out of mind. Or was it out of mind, out of sight? She was getting confused. Never mind.

"It's time to go, Sam," she said.

Come on, Mama.

Rebecca labored up and over the rubble. A great plaza lay at the heart of the pyramid complex. Overrun with flowstone and alabaster talus and thick vines, it looked like a forest without the trees. At the far corner of the plaza, beneath the most massive of the pyramids, a few acres had been partially cleared. It reminded her of the fixer-upper she and Jake had bought. With a lot of paint, wallpaper, and elbow grease, they'd turned the shambles into home sweet home.

She spied little figures clearing the pyramid's upper reaches and, down below, hauling rocks away. Someone had the right idea, someone with the bootstraps to get things done. A king, maybe. Or—the Egypt theme—a pharaoh. She would find this fellow and kindly ask him the way to Austin, and then collect Sam, and they'd be on their way.

Midway across the vast muddle of toppled obelisks and vines snaking from cracks in the ground, Rebecca got lost. Her back felt flogged. She was weak as a kitten.

Mama.

Rebecca aimed toward the giant pyramid. Workers toiled on the soaring slope. Rocks clattered down. Dust pinched the air. Farther along, a steeply pitched staircase rose to the summit.

Over by the wall, a man with whiskers and big sideburns was watching her. His name swam up from far away. "Mr. Johnson," she said, and went over to ask him about his wife's diabetes. But it was just his head there, resting on a shelf. Rebecca was slightly embarrassed for him. He had been somewhat short to begin with.

"Sam?" she called. Something had gone on here, something she did not want to remember, something rated *R* for violence. It was not a place for a child.

The trace of a path wound between freshly unearthed statues. They depicted grotesque half-human animals. It was like a gallery of fairy tales carved in stone, a Medusa, a Batman, and a winged monkey straight out of Oz. The largest and most imposing was that of a Minotaur.

"My archangel," a voice said behind her. "You finally decided to pay us a visit."

Rebecca turned. It was another of the goblins, but he was different. Pasty as he was, his skin had a bit of pigment to it, and some awful wasting disease had eaten away his nose and eyelids. A chain-mail vest topped his loincloth. His two very large bulbs of eyes fastened on her chest.

Luckily, Rebecca's nana wasn't here. In Nana's books, a lady didn't wear white shoes before Easter or after Labor Day. A lady most definitely did not go around naked to the waist. And even if she did, a gentleman should have the good manners not to stare. But then again, this was a foreign country. Customs varied. "Have we met?"

The goblin came closer, and looked deep into her eyes. "Earth to space," he said.

"Sir?"

"Probably better all around," he murmured to himself.

He was vaguely familiar, this happy, wide-eyed toad. He could have just hopped out of one of Sam's nighttime books. Without further ado, he reached out and hefted one of her boobies like a big fruit. He gave it a squeeze and let it drop.

Rebecca would have said something, but she was not one of those Ugly Americans who went around making scenes and imposing homeland values. "I'm looking for my daughter," she said. "Her name is Sam."

"I know. They brought her over while you were sleeping."

"What do you mean?"

"She needed a little fixing up, Rebecca."

They should have asked permission, of course. "Who's in charge here, please?"

"You really don't remember me?" he said.

"I'm sorry," she said. "Are you the king?"

That amused him. "Why not? Dream big, I always say."

"We'd like to go home now," she said.

"Right this way, Rebecca." He led her along the path. He had a bad limp. More familiar faces greeted her from the stone shelves. A few had been groomed and decorated like pets. She kept her thoughts in a box.

They reached a forest of sorts.

All around her, men dangled in midair. Dangled wasn't quite the word. Hovered. It was like magic. No strings or wires held them in the air. Several feet above the ground, they stood at attention, buck naked and very still. Then two of them lifted their heads. The veins stood out on their faces and necks. Their eyes bulged. One moaned softly. She was reminded of hens laying extremely large eggs.

Rebecca didn't want to see. This was none of her business. Once she had Sam, they would be out of here. But her imaginary blindfold slipped. The madness lifted. She saw.

Like hats or shoes, certain cruelties go in and out of fashion. The rack, the wheel, drawing and quartering: one hears the words, but forgets the realities. This, for instance. Rebecca had never given a second thought to what an impaling might look like. It wasn't something you heard about on morning NPR. Even Jake's gladiator and Highlander movies didn't go there.

"Dear God," she whispered. She covered her breasts, her sole defense against the scene. They were action heroes and DZ boys. Ten. Her brain counted. Her eyes saw.

The stakes ran up between their legs. Toes pointed, several men were stretching to reach the ground. All in all, there was little blood involved. Which meant they weren't going to die anytime soon.

"In the end, if you will," said Clemens, her guide, "one way or another, we all receive our tree. A place where we can contemplate our sins and look down and see our lives for the shit they were. The trick is to put it off for as long as possible."

She could not believe it, him, the goblin king. "You're part of this?"

"It's a matter of living in my own skin. Or at least, the skin I'm left to live in." He ran his fingers along his scars and tribal marks and branding welts.

"But *they* did that to you." They: the monsters that Mama and Daddy had promised did not exist.

"You don't understand, Rebecca. They didn't destroy me. They created me. These men aren't being punished, they're being freed. The dharma bums and Christ types, they've got it all wrong. Suffering isn't illusion. Hope is. You want reality?" He slapped one of the stakes. "Here's reality. There are no lies up there. There is no hope. These men have found the maximum truth."

It was a forest of pain. Men groaned . . . gingerly . . . that was the word.

She struggled to comprehend the full breadth of his betrayal. Backward and forward she went, tracing the hints that were suddenly so obvious, remembering the warnings that Hunter had given her, the alarm bells she had ignored. "All that time," she said, "you were leading us into their trap?"

"My trap," he corrected her. "I wrote it. This is my script."

"What about the abduction?"

"After the plague, one of their elders had a vision, something about their god wanting human children. By the time I came along, the elder was dead, and I just kind of ran with the concept."

The world was spinning too fast again. "*You* took our children?" She wanted to rage against him. *You killed my child. You killed my husband.* But the treachery sapped her. She could barely keep her head up.

"Better me than them, trust me," he said. "Because they were going to sacrifice the whole bunch to some old mushroom of a god. That was their plan until I got involved. Grab the kids, herd them deeper, and serve them up for a bit of divine intervention. Sacrifices. Food for the gods. They even think one lives on this island. You wouldn't believe some of their superstitions. These demons have demons. You saw what they did to the boys, turned them into prayer flags. The girls were in for worse.

"But then I put it to them. I asked them, why feed the old regime when you can *be* the new one? I got them thinking about the future again. Urban renewal on a grand scale. The rebirth of a subterranean nation. It will take time, of course. But this is the start of it. There's a place here for us. For you, too, Rebecca."

"But we're your people."

"I'm my people," he said.

"The rest of the army is coming," she said.

Clemens looked up at the row of dying men. "You're all that's left, Rebecca."

"They'll send people down to search for us."

"Search for the searchers? Throw good after bad? Your army was it, darling, the last shot in the dark. You vanished into the abyss. Lost platoon? You're the lost army. You just became a ghost story."

"Someone will come."

"Not here, they won't. This place doesn't exist. Our destination was the other city, the nun's city, Hinnom, remember? No one has an inkling this place even exists. Once we collapse the tunnel at the fork in the river, we're off the map forever."

"They'll come," she murmured.

"This thing had a shelf life, Rebecca. People have already moved on. Besides, they want us down here, fighting the darkness until the end of time. That's the story they want to read. That's the audience you played to. We're yesterday's news. But a thousand years from now, we'll be myth. That's what this is all about. Leaving the pygmies and schmucks behind. Becoming gods."

An image flickered of Sam's perfect forehead in ruins. Rebecca couldn't keep it away. Flies buzzed. Her hands flew apart. She batted at the bad thoughts.

"Are you leaving us again, Rebecca?" He stroked her head.

She trapped the awful image between her hands with a loud clap, and looked at him. "My daughter," she informed him, "is playing with the other children."

Sam was waiting for her once again. *Mama,* she called from the distance. The pyramid brightened to a big white mountain. Rebecca found herself surrounded by men on Popsicle sticks, coconuts painted with faces.

The goblin king came closer. "Never mind," he told her. He draped a necklace over her head. "We will build a kingdom out of all the things we've lost but can't forget."

With a smile, Rebecca fingered the necklace. Its strands were fine as hair, and so gold they verged on blond. *I will keep you forever,* she thought to it.

"And fade to black," Clemens said as he watched the beautiful wreck of a woman sink away.

ARTIFACTS

ASSOCIATED PRESS

Senate Approves Flag Amendment

Feb. 11. Washington. In an emergency special session, the Senate approved a constitutional amendment to protect the American flag from desecration, making it the Twenty-ninth Amendment.

The new amendment reads, "The Congress shall have power to prohibit the physical desecration of the flag of the United States."

Asked why the flag amendment is necessary at this time, the Senate minority leader said that evil is stalking America. "The frequency of flag burning has nothing to do with the evil of flag burning," said Senator Miles Jefferies (R) of North Carolina. "Laws in this nation are based on right and wrong, not on the frequency of occurrence. At this time, as we stand toe-to-toe with our enemies, our nation needs to affirm what is right."

A flag amendment has passed the U.S. House of Representatives twelve times since 1995, and fallen just short of passing in the U.S. Senate. "The stars were aligned," said Senator Jefferies. "At last Old Glory can fly without danger of sabotage from within."

41

"News from the front," the angel announced. "The battle is over."

He sat on the sand with his legs folded, nude, hands on knees: a pearl white Buddha with bleached irises.

Today was Ali's first day back on her feet. Her joints were swollen, and her bruises were garish, but she had finally managed to get up and wash herself. Her hair felt five pounds lighter. In place of her scarecrow rags of pants and shirt, she now wore a silk kimono stitched with golden thread. *Borrowed from a Shogun princess.* There was a smell to it, like old leather. She could guess. The angel had undressed one of his mummies for her.

"Are the children safe?" asked Ali.

"Most of them. But there were casualties."

"Casualties?"

"There was a woman named Coltrane," he said. *Was.*

"Rebecca," said Ali.

"You knew her then?"

"Barely. We met, twice, briefly. The second time she saved my life from a mob."

"Then you will find this tragic," he said. "Her daughter was killed in front of her eyes just as they were about to reunite. It seems Rebecca caused the death herself. I'm still gathering the details."

Ali recalled the photograph Rebecca had shown her, and the name, Samantha. But she was careful to say nothing. He was watching her reactions closely. This most civilized creature was a wild animal. At any moment he might turn on her.

"Is that a tear in your eye, Alexandra?"

Ali stifled her emotions. "What about Rebecca?"

"Poor Rebecca, her mind is broken," said the angel. "I suspect the rest of her days will be the proverbial living hell."

"She's a strong woman," Ali said. "She'll recover."

"I think you're projecting," he said. "You lost your child, now she has lost hers. You want her to get better because you want to get better."

"The grief will fade," Ali insisted. "It needs time, but she'll heal."

"Still projecting," he said. "Tell me about your grief."

"She'll heal."

"Did you?"

Why was he hounding her about this? "Yes."

"Maggie is at peace?" he said. "She never speaks to you?"

"I buried her eight years ago," Ali said.

"But she won't stay buried, will she?"

"Why do you say that?"

"You haven't heard her calling you?"

"I have my doubts about that."

"You doubt your own daughter?"

"I doubt everything down here."

In fact, she was beginning to accept what was surely the strangest of the deep's strange phenomena. For the past few years now, science had been stumbling over the unnatural nature that existed belowground. Time got deformed. Evolution violated its own rules. Light existed in darkness. Objects and animals had been photographed floating in midair on wild magnetic pulses. Explanations were few and far between. All those paled next to what she was discovering here.

Ali regretted the word "soul." Eventually a more clinical term might be applied, something to trim away the paranormal. "Free-floating memory" came to mind, or "detached ego," or simply "voices."

Whatever you wanted to call them, these little scraps of consciousness seemed to operate like radio signals bouncing between worlds. They spoke their names incessantly. They brought news in maddening fragments, and took the simplest of orders. They spent vast amounts of time lost and bewildered in the planet's veins.

One thing ruled them, it seemed, the same thing that ruled Ali for the time being: this pale, deadly exile without a country. According to him, the souls were his to use. With them he whispered up his wars, religions, arts, and other mischief. In turn, they received a sense of purpose.

"Doubt is one thing," he said. "But something has to be real. You need to anchor your world somewhere, if not down here, then up above."

She waited. Even when he rambled, he was precise.

"You looked in your mirror one night," he said. "This was shortly after Maggie's funeral, I believe. You looked and she was in there. Her face was nestling inside your face. She was shy. It was her first appearance. She had stage fright, you can't imagine. Instead of welcoming her, you screamed. A little while later you came back and covered the mirror with a towel. You don't remember?"

Speechless, Ali stared at him.

"You gave me Maggie's name," he explained. "I found her. We talked."

Ali reeled. *My child?*

"What if I told you I can raise the dead?"

"A trick," she whispered. *Raise the dead?*

"It's no trick," he said. "Call it a matter of coordination."

"I don't believe you."

"And why should you?" he said.

He bent slightly at the waist. He closed his eyes and lowered his right hand to the sand. Only his fingertips touched.

Mommy.

It came from behind her. Ali did not turn to see. The angel—the monster—was full of deceptions.

"Mommy." This time it was not inside her head. Ali forced herself to look. She put one hand to her heart.

It was Maggie at two, stumble-walking across the sand. But it was a different sand, a different day, a day at the beach. The illusion was perfect in every detail, even the shadow cast by a piece of driftwood. Ali heard the rattle of seashells and beads woven into her daughter's hair. Seagulls cried. The ocean snored. Ali dropped to her knees and opened her arms. Maggie rushed to her. Everything was right, the salt white along her part, the little fingers unconsciously kneading Ali's arm, the ketchup stain on her shirt. *Mommymommymommy. I wuv you.*

Everything was exactly as she remembered.

"No," said Ali.

Immediately her arms were empty. The illusion collapsed. The surf sound and yellow sun fell to pieces.

"Mommy," she heard again. Ali turned left. Maggie was a year older, waving to her from the steps of a library surrounded by trees. The cave gloom brightened and took on the scent of trees. Maggie was pale. This was the day they'd discovered *Grandfather Twilight*. A week later the blood work would come in positive.

"Come on, Mommy," Maggie said, holding the door. That's all Ali had to do, follow her child through a door. They could be together forever.

"No," said Ali.

The library vanished.

It came again from another direction. "Mommy."

Ali got to her feet. Her bones hurt. Her heart hurt. "Stop," she said.

The angel opened his eyes. He lifted his fingers from the sand. The light dimmed. The tree scent vanished. Embers sketched the gloom.

"Are you sure?" he said.

She looked around. It had taken her a lifetime to reach these badlands. For reasons she could not explain, of all those who had come before her, the mystics with their riddles and the warriors with their strong arms and the grief stricken with their pleas, she alone stood in this spot today, ready for this task. If it were easy, someone would long ago have done what she had come to do.

"Why have you shown me this?" she said.

He rested his hands on his knees again. Not a vein disturbed his dolphin-smooth skin. He never sweated. Also he had no navel.

"So long as you stay with me," he said, "she will be here for you."

"And if I leave?"

"I would send her deeper."

"Where is that?"

"I don't know," he said.

"What is down there?"

"I don't know."

There was just one way that he could not know. "They never come back?"

"Never," he said.

ARTIFACTS

PRESIDENT'S DAILY BRIEF

February 13
China Sub Commander Is Son of PLA Chief

The commander of the Chinese submarine that grounded in California is the illegitimate son of General Wang Yi Chap, the most senior officer in the People's Liberation Army.

This highly sensitive state secret came from Premier Deng Jiaming. It was hand-delivered by the Russian ambassador, representing Chinese interests until the PRC resumes diplomatic ties with the U.S. The Russian ambassador was further authorized to state that if the general's son and crew can be quickly delivered into the PM's personal custody, as a unilateral gesture and without conditions, then "the birds will joyously fly home." This refers to the U.S. aircrew in their custody.

It should be noted that Premier Jiaming is locked in a power struggle with his military, and particularly with General Wang, an old-school Maoist. Jiaming is relatively young, in good health, and a centrist with Western tastes. The release—into Jiaming's care—of the submarine commander and his crew would allow China to save face and at the same time strengthen Jiaming's hand. It will demonstrate that by working with the U.S., China benefits.

China experts with the Department of State and the CIA agree that this is an extraordinary chance to influence Chinese policy making, and paves the way for a resumption of talks aimed at settling territorial disputes in the Pacific Subterrain.

42

The very incarnation of a fiend—warty skin, broken horns, goat eyed—sat quietly scratching his name onto a pillar at the gate to N'iu, or Taurus, the city of the ox. A prophet had told them of a dream in which a lion entered the city. But the invaders had all been killed, praise be to God. There was no lion.

His clan, or all that remained of it, slept nearby. The great battle at the citadel of light had gored them. Most of his companions were dead. No one was not wounded. They sprawled among the rocks and vestiges of the invaders' camp.

The wind was beginning to stir.

He patiently worked his name into the stone. Behind him, the wounded kept turning to get comfortable. Joints of meat stood propped against the looted packs. Scalps and hides draped the boulders, drying.

The name was not really his name, nor could he pronounce it. Very simply he had taken a fancy to its written shape in his youth, and ever since went about cutting it into the stone wherever his travels took him. Memory is everything. He wanted to be remembered, even if it was for someone else's name.

He was nearly finished when the prophet's lion fell upon the city.

Cervical one, the topmost vertebra, is called the atlas because it carries the world upon its shoulders. With a twist of his hands, Ike rearranged the hadal's world. The graffiti artist dropped in a silent heap. If Ike saw his own initials—*IC*—scratched into the pillar, they did not register. Long ago he had left himself behind.

Ike went among the sleeping shapes. Side by side, three twitched with dreams. One was snoring very softly. To save a bullet and not ruin a pelt, trappers stomp on the animal's rib cage. Barefoot, Ike crushed the three dreamers. It was like walking on bags of twigs.

The rest awoke and saw their dead comrades and the tall assassin. They recognized his armor from legend. Made of green jade plates, it was the armor of Older-Than-Old. They saw his empty hands, and the storm in his eyes, and knew that here was a creature divinely touched. Here was that dread thing, a berserker.

One fled through the city. The rest rushed Ike in a pulse. He went into them with his empty hands. He exploited every opening. There is always an opening.

The real Achilles heel is the neck, target rich, full of nerves and arteries and other mortal goodies. Ike plundered it.

The eyes are a prime target. The optic nerve is especially sensitive, even in people without eyes.

There is a way to combine a groin strike with a castrating grab. One stuns, the other bleeds your opponent out.

Their racks of horns made convenient handles.

Done properly, it takes just eight pounds of pressure to push a knee out of joint. Ike performed the technique properly.

His teacher had been explicit. The People's time was past. *Kill them all.*

His daughter's life depended on this. *Daughter?* It still astonished him. Ike tried to put the thought away. It was a monkey thought. A distraction. And yet it helped give shape to the rage that was shaping him. He had no idea what she looked like, or how her voice would sound. But it was as if her face were there in front of him.

He passed between the spires of blue stone and climbed the sheer staircases and heard the sweet trickling in the aqueducts grown over with stone. The city was a dream at best, a pretty conceit. Civilizations rise and fall. Races come and go. He was terminating a phantom, no more.

Alerted to a trespasser, hadals came hurtling down the stairs or crawling on the walls, one even snaking from the aqueducts, only to find emptiness. Then Ike would step from the doorways or climb from beneath his earlier victims, and they would freeze at the sight of his sacred armor. It was a fatal pause. More than shock accounted for their dying, though.

The tomb had changed Ike's perception of time. It was not that he moved any faster now, rather that every movement he saw was linked to its next movement, and every link offered an opening. He was like the butcher in the Zen koan whose knife only gets sharper as he carves.

The hollow spires began to whistle in the breeze. In his mind, Ike was that breeze as he chased through the spires and hives. He did not hear himself howling or smell the coppery scent of blood. His passage was pure.

He worked his way higher into the city. They pursued him, following his aftermath, connecting the dots, bewildered and furious. And frightened. This was their dark turf and they outnumbered him. He should have been easy prey. But he was dressed in the armor of God. Either he had killed God, which was impossible, or God had turned against them once again.

Mostly they met him in ones and twos. Their weapons skipped off his jade plates, but found the meat of his arms and legs. The wounds burned. At least in his mind, they were not wounds, but tongues of fire. Enveloped in flames, he lit the city with his carnage.

The breeze quickened. The city purred with wind song and the screams of the dying.

Ike broke the back of a fighter striped from head to foot like a candy cane. He gutted a dandy with feathers tied to his horns, and another with little pink periwinkles for earrings, and a faraway part of him was sorry. These were the fiends of hell, these lovers of beauty. One sat down in a pile of his own organs and started singing the most elegant psalm.

Even as he exterminated them, Ike read their markings and ornaments and pinpointed which clan and tunnel nets they came from and where their long journeys had taken them. Some he had known when he was a slave. Several of the older ones remembered him by name. As they fought him, they greeted their former chattel with gladness.

A number of them died naked except for their paint. Some wore rusting scraps of hand-me-down chain mail, or sported bits and pieces of uniform or field gear taken from dead soldiers. Many were in bad shape, mauled by their battle, hardly fit to walk much less fight. As he slaughtered them, Ike felt no more pity for them than for himself.

To fight a knife, you must become its shadow, moving where it moves. Then the knife becomes your shadow. Then you stop the shadow and break its arm and get the knife. Like that, Ike obtained one knife, then two.

The ribs form a cage that both shields the organs and traps the invading blade. Best to skip a stab at the heart. Go for the guts. Open the throat. There is a sweet spot just behind the collarbone. Down through that entrance lie the tender tops of the lungs. His knives plunged in.

Not a thought or calculation guided him. His enemy volunteered a dozen ways of dying. He simply provided the means.

The wind increased. Shaped by the giant walls, dervishes sprang into being. They darted about, scouring the hollow-mouthed city.

Ike had no idea where he was going. He let his enemy guide him into its heart. Wherever they were coming from, there he went. A torrent of boulders came thundering down a certain staircase, which led him up the stairs. At the top he made for a scarred and windswept fortification. From there he found a stone bridge slicing across an everglade of reeds and foul water. When two hadals broke the surface and cast their lives at him, he knew this was the way. Over there he would put an end to this unfortunate species, and find the children who would buy him his daughter.

As he started across, a rifle opened up on full automatic. The muzzle flash winked from a slot in that exhausted fortress, and bullets nipped at the water, not even close, par for hadal marksmanship. It was extraordinary that one of them had even thought to pick up the rifle in the first place. The clip ran dry. Ike galloped on.

The wind gained strength. Gusts sheared at him. Waterspouts danced back and forth across the bridge. The reeds rattled like spears.

In single file, three came sprinting out to meet him. One slipped and the wind blew him into the water, where he began screaming. Ike killed the other two in passing. He was Death's horse this day. Wherever he went, none survived.

They yielded the island's shore to him, which could only mean they were laying a trap—or many traps—among the pyramids. It was not too late to leave. They would gladly let him return to the depths. It would become part of their mythology, how God had broken down their walls and taken them to the brink of extinction, and at the last instant held back his sword. Like every chosen people, they would make sacrifices and give thanks and regenerate.

But the angel had declared their sentence: death. That paled next to the ransom of Ike's daughter. He needed the children, and would never stop. The pyramids shrieked.

Alabaster rubble ricocheted down the sides, loosened from the crests. A pale warrior launched himself from some high precipice. Ike leaped to meet him and rode him into the rocks.

One after another, their ambushes failed. By this time there was little they could do to stop him. Even though his legs grew heavy and his knives slowed, Ike had the velocity of fate.

A handful of the creatures clung to the heights like apes, peppering him with rocks. That was as close as they dared get. Little touched him. Ike was in a sacred state. Hair and beard flying with Mosaic fury, greasy with blood, his rage became serene. The world was flying apart all around him, and yet everywhere he turned it fell calm and opened for his passage.

He might have gone on like that, stalking among the rubble and slaying the demons of ignorance and darkness. But his rage was lifting. Bullied by the wind, Ike quit his lope and slowed to a walk. The flames on his limbs flickered out. Now he saw his wounds for what they were. Sliced and beaten, his forearms had taken the brunt of the fighting. One wrist was probably broken. He could see, but not feel, the knife in his numb hand. A small child-like arrow hung from his shoulder, possibly poisoned. Doubts wormed in.

The monkey thoughts began chattering. How many of the enemy were left? How badly was he wounded? Did he have a snowball's chance of lasting long enough to see his daughter? Ike wheeled in place. Where was he? Where were the children? Pyramids and snapped columns and masses of debris spun around him.

Then he smelled the girls, or some of them. Blowing on the wind, their ripe scent was as unmistakable as the local intent. You didn't hold captives on a whim in this starving land. Every prisoner served a purpose, or entered the stream. In this case, the girls were breeders, plain and simple. The only question was, whose breeders were they, the angel's or this rebel band's? Ike had come to answer that with draconian finality, but suddenly he didn't feel like much of an answer.

He was easy pickings now, theirs for the taking. Strangely, no one came after him. There were no more hails of arrows, no more bravos scampering in to try for a celebrity kill, no more ape-men hooting and throwing rocks. It was just him alone among the pyramids, him and that smell of human females.

Ike sat down, tired and disoriented. A knife in each hand, he rested on his knees. He hunched his back against the wind that promptly attacked him from the front and sides. The wind was the problem. Turned by the chamber walls, it spun in circles, small dervish ones inside the larger one. The scent could be coming from anywhere.

The wind pummeled him. Time passed. Ike watched his blood dry. Then the scent grew stronger. He lifted his head.

A figure—nude—was approaching across the rubble. It was a young woman, or a girl becoming one. Dark hair. Buds of breasts. Long legs.

Hoops of gold circled her neck. From her forehead to her soles, the girl was a canvas painted with patterns, numerals, and words. Concentric circles rippled out from her nipples. Painted lines aimed the eye at her loins. Her pubis was marked with an inverted triangle of bright ochre.

The girl represented a surrender of sorts. An offering. He could use her however he wanted for a while. And then he was meant to follow her in.

"Where are the rest of you?" he said.

She pointed at the lopped-off top of the largest of the pyramids.

"Who sent you?" His tongue felt thick in his mouth.

She shook her head dumbly.

"Was it a man named Clemens?"

"I don't know his name," she said. "We just do what he says."

Ike saw the dark hollows under her eyes, and the whip stripes on her legs. Her cheeks were chapped raw by the wind. She was brand-new to captivity.

"You're a brave girl." His words slurred. Everything hurt.

"Whose side are you on?" she said.

What a strange question, he thought. But then he realized he didn't know anymore. "My daughter," he said. It was the truth, in a roundabout way.

The wind shook her. She whispered something. He saw, but couldn't hear, the word on her lips. "Help."

The rubble seemed to shift under his feet. She had no idea what she was asking. Help her? He had come to use her. She and all her sister captives were going to buy him his child.

Delete, thought Ike. *Reboot.* Somehow he would help her, yes. He would save them all somehow, but in pieces, his daughter first, then somehow the others over the coming years. Those who survived long enough to be saved.

Lambs, flowers, damned. He put it out of his mind, or tried to. But in every way this girl was more real than his own, whom he had never seen. Until the angel filled him with rage and set him on this path, Ike had not even dared to think of his daughter.

"Please," she said. "Take me away. Save me."

She was a temptress. He could do anything with her. He could even kill her. Then she wouldn't be a temptation.

Ike dropped the big knives with a clatter. He climbed to his feet. "I want to see my daughter," he said.

She bent her head. Her fingernails, chewed to the quick, still showed a few flakes of bubblegum polish. Her shoulders hiccupped.

"Don't cry." Ike searched for something she could hang on to in the coming months and years until he might come down again and rescue her. "None of this is real," he said. "It's all just a dream. You'll see."

She raised her head and he expected a look of revelation or at least of stoic thanks. But her eyes were bloodshot, and she was horror-struck, not inspired. He had never felt so wrong in all of his life.

ARTIFACTS

CNN.COM

February 14

Sub Crew to Be Swapped for American Spy Plane Crew

In a dramatic turn of events, the White House today issued a statement saying that the crew of the Chinese submarine grounded in California will be sent home on Monday. One minute later, Chinese president Jiaming announced that the crew of the American spy plane will also be returned to their home. He also declared China's willingness to resume treaty discussion to resolve the land claims in the Interior.

Reaction to the news was swift.

"Both sides looked into the abyss, both sides blinked, both sides stepped back from the brink," said Senator John Cheney, the ranking Democrat on the Senate Armed Forces Committee. "This was a sensible compromise that will lead to productive relations in the future."

Representative Carey Grant, the Republican chair of the House Appropriations Committee, sounded a more ominous note. "This only has the appearance of compromise. Is anyone paying attention? There was a one-minute gap between our announcement and theirs, an eternity in diplomatic time. In other words, we caved in to China, and then China gave us a reward. I want to know what kind of deal was cut. I am going to see to it that there is an investigation into that missing minute. If necessary, we will assign a special prosecutor to look into it.

"Make no mistake, I am delighted our patriots will be home in time for the Super Bowl. But remember this, the Chinese beached an attack sub armed with nuclear missiles on our shores, and then they played bumper cars with an unarmed American plane in international air space and nearly killed its crew. And now we have to make the first gesture. Where's the apology from China? Where's our downed plane? Where's this administration's spine? Once again the dragon speaks, and we roll over. This has got to stop."

In an extraordinary moment, one of the top generals in the People's Liberation Army, Wang Yi Chap, contradicted President Jiaming. "China has suffered a national humiliation. We should not return their invaders until America apologizes. The barbarian is at the gate, and must never be appeased except to lull him."

43

From the top of his pyramid, the hunter watched that man in green armor limping through the ruins. At least he was pretty sure this was a man, not a hadal. The footprints he'd been following from the river looked human, as did the ragged curtains of beard and long hair. But what kind of man ran amok like this? Clearly this was a wild animal that had to be put down.

He watched the man follow the painted girl. Like ants, they threaded their way through the moonscape of rubble. Their behavior mystified him. What did the man want? Where did he come from? Was he a messenger or just another killer?

All the while that he was wondering about the man, the hunter went on trying to reckon how to dissect a wind that turned in circles inside circles.

Ike and the girl passed a rack of odd-shaped sails bulging with wind. Strung between rods to cure, they were human rawhide. Several had military tattoos, which would be prized by whoever wore the skins next. Around the corner Ike found the men who had worn them last.

The long row of men had been peeled alive and left on stakes. Ike had traveled too far and wide in the depths to be shocked. Now their souls were free to roam, enlightened—one would hope—by their suffering. Gravity had done most of them in. The tips of the stakes showed under several chins. The need for a few hams had taken care of others: dead or alive at the time, they had lost one or both legs to the cooks.

But as Ike approached, one man lifted his head, so far gone there was nothing left but pain. "Enough," said Ike, and stopped the flayed man's heart with one hand.

"Assholes," said the girl. She was looking at the soldiers.

"But they came to save you," Ike said.

"They couldn't even save themselves."

The row of corpses faced a Minotaur statue. The wind had polished its face away. Its ox horns were stubs. You could read the man-bull two ways. Either the wilderness had gotten civilized, or civilization had gone wild.

He followed the girl up the pyramid's sheer steps. There were hundreds. While he rested at the midpoint, Ike scanned the murky valleys between the pyramids. The place was empty. Even his kills were gone, dragged away by comrades to be recycled. *The quick and the dead,* he thought. All had fled. The volcano was about to blow.

They climbed slowly. The wind seemed bent on blasting these manmade mountains to sand. Grit peppered his face. He didn't have much left in the reserve tank.

"Look," said the girl. A tornado had spawned in the great plaza below. Its tail switched here and there, groping for any movable thing. In a single gulp it sucked away the soldiers' carcasses on the stakes. It started up the pyramid, then changed its mind, slid back down, and disintegrated.

"This way," said the girl.

They reached the plateau at the top. A small forest of statues surrounded a partially collapsed domelike structure. The dome reminded Ike of a Buddhist stupa, right down to the giant, almost feminine eyes staring into infinity and the question mark for a nose. Its mouth was the entry. The girl went in.

Ike hung back, suspicious. She was the bait. This was the trap. Maybe it had already been sprung.

The plateau had all the trappings of human sacrifice. There was an altar with blood gutters. Chains and fetters ran the length of one wall, empty of prisoners, the wind shrilling through the bolts. In one corner, curled like an infant, lay a human spine fringed with bits of nerves and meat.

Behind him the stairs plunged. In the distance, he saw the lesser pyramids ringed haphazardly around this one, and realized they were actually islands that had been faced with blocks. This was an archipelago waiting for another flood.

The ox symbol cut into his hand stood in stone above the doorway. A second symbol bound him here as well, the same one he wore on his back, that curious *N*. Body and soul, he was written into this place. He had no choice but to enter the mountain inside the pyramid.

He approached warily. His feet weighed a ton. The wind kept salting his wounds. He skirted the statues of half-animal gods and goddesses, some tipped over by quakes or time, most still standing as they'd been placed. There was a Medusa, a harpy with breasts and wings, and a serpent with arms and ears.

The reptile man came alive on his pedestal.

Ike glimpsed a flicker of motion behind him. Then a heavy blow dropped him to the ground. Blood streaming into his eyes, he glimpsed a slave thing maimed for keeping, and recognized it. "Clemens," he said.

Long ago, Ike had worked as a rigger for an action movie. Every few days a big blank section entitled FIGHT SCENE would interrupt the script and they would have to make up some violence. Now it seemed he had one more FIGHT SCENE to go.

Clemens hit him again. It was a club. It broke Ike's leg.

There were no clever asides like in the movie. This was a killing. A slow one. The club fell again.

Ike crawled behind a statue. Clemens nailed him again. He wasn't looking for a knockout blow quite yet.

Ike rolled away. Unless he got rid of that club, the game was over. His daughter would remain a prisoner.

He got up on his one good leg and lifted an arm. He made an opening. Clemens went for it with a home-run swing. The club cracked hard against the jade plates. Ike heard ribs snap. But with a grunt, he clamped down his arm and trapped the club.

Then Clemens made another mistake. He tried to get his club back. Ike went with the yank. He let Clemens draw him close, and then jerked the man backward and locked one arm across his throat.

That left one hand free to fumble for the bone sheath inside his armor. He bared the quill of nerve toxin. One last scratch of the pen, and the FIGHT SCENE would be over.

He gripped the quill like a knife and was just starting to reach around.

At that precise moment, his wrist exploded. It flew apart. Ike frowned, and then the shock dropped him. Even as he toppled into darkness, Ike saw his severed hand drifting through space, and the quill was still clutched in that now mindless fist.

One shot, one kill.

Beckwith took no pride of craft in this one, though.

It was pure luck that he had managed to stalk his prey on the run and climb this secondary pyramid and set up the shot and unscramble the wind. It went beyond luck—a miracle—that the bullet had vectored itself in. But one way or another, he had knocked the beast down.

For over an hour, Beckwith had been lying flat on his stomach on top of this pyramid. He had patiently followed his target through the scope, first through the rubble below, and then as the man scaled the stairs of a massive pyramid on the far side of the island. He had waited with his finger on the trigger, full of questions about the man's armor and gray hair and the girl's strange intent, praying she would lead his eye to wherever the rest of the children were hidden before Beckwith had to shoot him.

Even after the girl disappeared through a door on the summit, Beckwith had held his fire, waiting to explore whatever his target was exploring. The best snipers can do that. They can reach a mile and more away through their scope and enter the world of their prey, feeling it with its fingers, deciphering it through its eyes, using their target to uncover secrets on a distant bookshelf or computer screen or even in a mirror. Beckwith had done that once, watching a double agent fog a mirror with his breath to read its invisible message. Then Beckwith had shot him.

Everything he could do to be accurate, Beckwith had done. He had lazed the target—825 yards—and factored in the denser air and humidity, and dialed it in with the trajectory knob. The wind, he decided, canceled itself out with all its circles, and he had not touched that knob. Then he had centered his crosshairs on his target's spine and waited some more. Together, sniper and prey, they had eased between the statues of animal-people.

When the one statue came alive and sprang from its pedestal, Beckwith was so startled he almost lost his target. For a long minute his scope filled with a blur of monsters. If he hadn't recognized Clemens, he might have put a bullet through each of them, just to be safe.

But then he made out the familiar ruins of Clemens's face and realized that somehow their guide had found the children. Clemens had been right all along and now he was up there, battling this armored killer, and all Beckwith had to do to save the children was save Clemens. Here was Beckwith's chance to redeem his sins.

For another long minute, Beckwith did not shoot. He kept waiting for Clemens to clear away from the target. But when they locked together and the killer drew a slender weapon, Beckwith quit waiting. He squeezed the trigger.

The shot was off by a good ten inches. He saw it through his scope. If the man hadn't raised his arm, the shot would have missed entirely. The bullet sheared the man's hand off at the wrist and Beckwith would have placed a second shot into him, but the green armor had collapsed from view.

Beckwith stayed locked on the scene for one minute longer, making sure Clemens didn't need any more help. Clemens kept looking around, frightened and awestruck. Beckwith shared his awe. Somehow he had been handed this chance to redeem his sins. Somehow he had made the shot.

They would share the story soon enough. But first Beckwith had to descend and pick his way through the wreckage and climb to Clemens and the girls. He scoped his surroundings and was satisfied. Haddie had vacated the premises.

Packing swiftly, Beckwith started down. He was already arranging the evacuation in his head. He would count the girls, and tend and feed them, and get them in motion. No one would be coming to whisk them up to safety. They were on their own out here, and home was still a long way away.

ARTIFACTS

CNN.COM

February 15

China Bills U.S. $1 Million for Plane's Stay

Washington—China has sent the United States a bill for $1 million to cover the costs of one of its spy planes staying on Chinese soil.

But a U.S. State Department official said Friday that the government has no intention of paying it. "It's nice to know they have a sense of humor," a U.S. State Department official said on condition of anonymity, scoffing at the scale of Beijing's charge.

The American spy plane was forced to make an emergency landing on the Chinese island of Hainan after colliding with a Chinese military aircraft that was shadowing it. The episode roiled relations between the two countries, with ties between the two nations tumbling to their worst levels in two years.

After a drawn-out diplomatic spat, in which China held the plane's twenty-four crew members for eleven days, Beijing will now allow an American team to come and disassemble the plane and fly it back to U.S. custody this week. The United States had wanted to repair the plane and fly it out, but China said allowing the plane to fly off Hainan would be a national humiliation.

44

An elephant was standing on his arm.

Ike's eyes fluttered open.

One wrist lay cinched across his chest. The other was missing its hand. He was inside the dome.

A ring of eyes peered down at him. He saw their pools of bruises and sores and runny noses and raw tattoos. Gems and colored twine adorned their hair. Eight, nine, fifteen. Ike lost count. He almost lost consciousness.

He was probably dying. His disappointment was something of a revelation. Not long ago, inside the tomb, he had done his best to cast loose from this world. Now he found himself trying to hang on to it. "Maggie," he whispered.

"What's he saying?" one of the girls said.

"Don't go too close," said another. "He's one of them."

"No, he's human. I think."

"He came looking for us. He told me. He's somebody's dad."

"Not mine. He looks totally insane. Look at him."

"It doesn't matter," someone said. "He's dying. That's all they do."

Not one knelt to comfort him or offer water. His wounds frightened them. They went on talking about him as if he were a stray dog.

Above their heads he saw the sign of the ox on the domed ceiling. This was a temple dedicated to the angel's son. *My son, starving and buried inside some mountain.* This was the mountain. Inside it lived his son. Ike remembered. As a reward for their worship, the angel had killed the city. Because they wouldn't quit feeding his son.

Ike looked up at the girls. Another time, another world, he would have told them to run away before it was too late. But they were his barter. Even now, crippled and bleeding and tied like an animal, Ike clung to the hope that he could still buy his daughter's passage back to the sun.

Then someone said, "He's coming," and they scattered.

Ike saw the circular room more clearly. The archway leading out howled with the wind. Stacks of food and equipment stood against the walls, salvaged from the dead soldiers. The little tribe of girls had enough food for months here. With some concerted hunting and gathering, the cache could be stretched for years.

The children huddled together. Only now did he see a woman rocking back and forth in the corner, out of her mind.

A voice spoke. "Out with the old boss, in with the new." Clemens appeared overhead. He was wearing the green armor. He patted the bloody jade plates, looking happy enough to dance. "You went fetching for the old gringo one too many times, my friend. Your dog days are over. You belong to me now."

He squatted down with a small knife. Pain flashed white in Ike's head. Clemens rocked back on his heels. He held up a bloody half shell: Ike's ear.

"Do you remember marking me?" Clemens opened the armor and showed his slave marks and scars. "You were the first. You caught me and then you signed your name on me."

"Not my name," Ike whispered. "His." He spoke the ancient name for God, which had a thousand meanings.

"You mean that animal you gave me to?" Clemens said.

"His mark saved your life."

Clemens set his knife on Ike's chest and drew a line of fire.

"What I could never understand," Clemens said, "was why you didn't run away from that thing. You and I both know he's a lifer. He's never getting out. He's trapped. But you could have run free. What did you think you were doing down there?"

Killing evil. But Ike did not say it out loud. The wind whistled through the statues outside.

"I knew he'd send you," Clemens said. His knife slid between two ribs. He was meticulous about it, nothing lethal.

"We're brothers, you and me," he said when Ike regained consciousness. "Think about it. We both came down. We both got captured. We both got changed. Only I got changed more. You have some catching up to do, a little wider smile, eyes that don't close, a bit of spinal adjustment. We'll get around to the modifications, but first let's take care of this hand of yours."

He scooted forward on his heels and bent his head to get a better view. His knife went into the bone joint. Ike lit up.

"This may seem gratuitous," Clemens said, and stuck the blade in again.

It went on. The pain kept sucking him under. Ike kept swimming back.

The worst part of it was the absolute pointlessness. He had traded everything for nothing. In the end his daughter had replaced him in captivity, and the cycle went unbroken.

Even so, Ike fought in his heart. Until he was gone and lying in pieces, there remained some chance for freedom. Not his freedom, granted. He'd sacrificed that long ago. But for his child, or the idea of his child, and the idea of her freedom from evil. So that she would never have to face what he was facing now.

Clemens jimmied the knife blade. Twitching, barely conscious, Ike resisted. *Why?* His stoic self-control was in vain, a prisoner's conceit. *Give in.* He had nothing left to surrender. But then it came to him. *Nothing except his daughter.*

Ike's eyes opened. He had one thing of value left in the world. One bit of barter. His child. In that moment, he gave her up.

If his daughter could not be saved, then at least these others could be. It was more than that. She could never be saved unless they were saved, too.

Clemens came into focus high overhead.

"Take the girls away from here," Ike whispered.

"What's that, brother?"

"You can't stay in this place."

"Of course we can," Clemens said. "We're stocked. We're ready for the long haul. The girls and I are going to be friends."

"There's something buried inside here. His son. The ox. It's still alive."

"More gods and monsters?" Clemens smiled. "Sorry. Wrong number."

"Get them away."

"You came all this way to give us a friendly warning?"

"He came for his daughter," said the tall girl who had guided Ike here. She spoke it like a declaration of independence. Hope, Ike heard. She still dared to hope. Which only doomed her. Because Clemens would go after her now before she tainted the others.

Clemens called the girls over. The eyes and runny noses and greasy hair and bare feet circled around. "What's the bad man been telling you?"

"You took his daughter away, and now he's come to get her back," said the tall girl.

"You told them that?" Clemens said to Ike.

"No," said Ike.

"Yes you did," said the girl. It was an article of faith. He was the father who would never quit searching for them. Ike could see it in her eyes, in all of their eyes.

So could Clemens.

"Which one is yours?" he said to Ike. "This one maybe?" He tugged one from the circle. Her wrists and neck were bruised in colors. She had butterfly wings painted on her bare back.

"No," said Ike. "None of them. I was wrong."

Clemens grabbed another. "This one?" Funeral jewelry hung from her thin shoulders and arms. He ran one hand under her bottom. She peeped like a bird.

"'Hush little baby, don't you cry,'" someone sang out.

Heads turned to the sound. It was the woman by the wall. Rocking, her heavy breasts swaying, she went on with her lullaby. At first Ike thought she was singing to comfort the children. Then he saw the scalp of braided blond hair cradled in her hands.

Clemens clapped wearily. "Father meet mother," he said to Ike. "This is Rebecca. She used to be quite the beauty. But I'm afraid she's not working out very well."

"Maybe his daughter was Samantha," someone said. "She's the only one not here."

The woman got louder. Ike put it together, the scalp and the name.

Clemens threw a pebble at her. She stopped. He returned his attention to the lesson under way. "All right, girls, who belongs to Dad here?"

Suddenly none of them wanted a dad anymore. Their eyes lost the shine.

"Nobody?" said Clemens. "Nobody's his baby? Come on, here's the savior. Nobody wants to be saved?"

"Samantha," Ike said loudly.

Rebecca started singing again.

Clemens looked at him. He threw another pebble in the corner, but Rebecca wouldn't quit. "Somebody take her out of here." The group made a move to leave. "One of you is enough."

The smallest child went over and took Rebecca's hand and led her outside. The room got quieter.

"He's not a good man, girls," Clemens said. "He hurts people. He steals them and does bad things to them. See what he did to me? That's what he came to do to you. I keep telling you I'll take care of you. We're safe in here. When it's the right time, we'll all go home."

"Run," Ike said to the girls.

Clemens turned to him with the knife, but had an idea. "Corey, come help me. Come on, now. It's a little strange at first. But we've got to learn how to take care of each other."

The other girls stepped away from Corey. She was the tall one. She didn't come forward.

"Take the knife," Clemens said. "We'll do this together."

"Run," said Ike.

"Very well," Clemens sighed, "I'll do it myself." The knife went in.

"Samantha," Ike whispered. The world went white. The knife stitched out, then in again. Ike heard his lung hissing. "Samantha," he repeated. The knife slid deeper.

Abruptly it stopped. The knife clattered to the floor.

Ike opened his eyes.

Clemens was squatting at Ike's side. His mouth was jawing for air. His hands spasmed. He tried to see behind him, but suddenly his neck wasn't working. Then he toppled to one side.

The woman Rebecca stood over him. She was holding the poison quill between her writing fingers, exactly as if she were in midletter. Next to Ike, Clemens mewed, eyes bulging. He was alive, but paralyzed.

She looked down at Ike and blinked, groping for purchase. He saw the struggle raging inside her, Rebecca versus her madness. "Fight," Ike whispered.

The children needed a mother. Someone had to lead them out of here—now—before the hadals regained their courage and crept back in. It wasn't going to be him. He was dying. She had to find her sanity for them.

Ike clung to the edge as long as he could. He didn't know how to unlock her cage. There had to be a secret word. He tried. "Samantha," he said. "She needs you."

Rebecca's eyes widened with horror. Then they eased and she started singing again. "'Hush little baby.'"

A shadow appeared at the door. *Run,* thought Ike. But it was too late. The doorway filled with a shape.

Ike couldn't hold on any longer. His strength failed. As he fell into the darkness, he heard a man say, "Ah, Jesus, what have I done now?"

45

The angel was kneeling on the iron-hard ground, washing Ali's feet. He ran his finger between her toes. "The children are free," he announced.

Ali heard the frustration in his voice. It exposed his treachery. It told her that he had not meant for the children to ever see the light of day again. He had sent Ike to bring them deeper. He would have used them and kept Ali and used her, too. But something had gone awry.

Ali felt a quiet triumph. Whatever else he was, this creature was not almighty. His schemes were fallible.

"Are they heading to safety?" she asked.

"If the tender mercies of man can be called safety."

Tender mercies, she thought. What kindness would he show her now? Would he vent his rage on her, or go on with the washing? And why had he revealed his betrayal to her? It exposed his fallibility. It made him almost mortal. Ali tried to relax.

He went on kneading the ball of her foot. "It's time to unlock my cage," he told her.

The back of his neck was smooth as a baby's. Ali had touched it. She had held on to it for dear life. He wanted to be everything to her, husband, child, teacher, student, master, slave.

"Then give me the key," said Ali.

He held her foot in his cupped hands. He kissed it. "Somehow, Alexandra," he said, "you *are* the key."

He stood and took her hand. They walked across a bridge made of iron and silver. All through her convalescence, Ali had been lying in the sand with that vast, moonlike palace looming before her. Now, at last, he took her inside.

What looked like the Taj Majal from the outside became, on the inside, every museum and library and monastery Ali had ever visited or imagined. Halls stretched to the left and right, loaded with antiquities, books and knickknacks. She didn't know where to begin.

The air contained that saturated blue-gold light of San Francisco fog just before the morning sun sweeps it away. High overhead, the domed ceiling held paintings. There was even pigeon shit on the marble tiles underfoot. Her own memories were woven into the fabric. But also, when she swept back the voices and saw through the overlay of illusion, the pack-rat collection was real enough.

"This is my keep," said the angel. "I keep it. It keeps me."

His collections filled acre after acre. She had never seen so much treasure and relics and just plain stuff gathered in one place. A sixteenth-century sextant for shooting the sun was mixed with forks, hadal gems, and a New Jersey phone book. A basketball lay among globes of the world and unusual skulls.

What were the borders in this place? Where did she end and the dream begin? She was lost in here.

They walked between walls of shelves teeming with books, scrolls, and codices. Clay tablets stood in neat ranks beside rolls of maps. Ali gravitated to the shelves. The languages came from everywhere, reaching back in time and around the world. She saw Conan the Barbarian comics jumbled with math equations and hadal cuneiforms. A copy of the *Hindustani Times* wrapped an animal scapula incised with pictograms.

"Here is your text," he said. "Un-write the book of man. Word by word, go all the way back to the beginning. Dismantle everything. Start me over."

"And then?" she said. "After I have released you, what will you do?"

"I am beginning to remember," he said, "how it will be."

"What do you remember?"

"The sun will be yellow. When I step from the shadows, it will feel like a blessing on my face. It will paint my eyelids. I will breathe its sweet breath."

"Then you are not a prisoner. You already know the sun."

"I know it the same way your people know me, by imagining it. Do you understand? Imagination is my prison. Your imagination."

She rejected the notion. "You said you've been trapped here since long before man appeared. How can we be responsible?"

"Since the beginning of time these walls were simply my home. Then mankind came along and sang of a land in the sun. Until that moment my home was not a prison. With your first word, I was damned. Take me back to that first word."

The angel left her to go "hunting."

Ali found an empty room and made it hers, plundering the keep at will. Her bed was a sleeping bag. She wore an old Mao-era quilted jacket and Gramicci mountain pants for exploring, and hung her walls with tapestries from civilizations ten thousand years dead.

A new regime was beginning here. With time she would wrap this place around her and listen to its voices and reach deeper into the mind of man than anyone had ever dreamed possible. Now she understood the silk kimono he had given her to wear. She was his bride and queen, at least until the day she failed him and probably not one day longer than the day she might succeed.

Every new reign has a first act, something that makes it new. Knowledge was her duty. But for her first act, Ali did not choose to open a book or unroll a codex to announce herself.

Rather she arranged herself on the floor, sitting with her legs folded and back straight, and the name of a child in her mind. She closed her eyes and summoned an image. Then she bent forward and touched her fingertips to the ground.

He had shown her how to do this, as a reward, for when she wanted her daughter's company. It wasn't her daughter she summoned, though.

Samantha.

The air did not swirl or issue smoke, nothing fancy. But she felt a very small space before her fill. She gave it directions, an idea, an inspiration, and quick as thought, the presence raced away. The space before her was hollow again. Done, she lifted her fingertips.

Only then did Ali open the scroll he had given her to begin with. It was an ancient Greek translation of *The Great Hymn to the Aten,* from which the Book of Psalms had come. It was written on ostrich skin in the bous-trophedon style, in which one line was read from left to right and the next from right to left and so on. "Boustrophedon" meant, literally, the passage of an ox plowing a field, back and forth.

Here then was her aleph, her ox, her vehicle. Where it would take her in the coming year, Ali did not know. For the time being she concentrated on the text.

How many are your deeds,
Though hidden from sight,
O Sole God beside whom there is none!
You made the earth as you wished, you alone.

ARTIFACTS

CBS EVENING NEWS
February 16

ANCHOR: The commander of the Chinese submarine was gunned down today as he and his crew were preparing to board a plane home.

CUT TO:

The Chinese sub crew stands at attention in dress whites. The camera pans their stolid faces. A plane waits in the background.

An American officer approaches. The Chinese commander steps forward.

Just then a civilian bolts from the press line. He draws a gun and shouts, "Billy, I'm coming, son."

Gunshots crackle. The Chinese commander falls to the ground.

Another gunshot cracks. The assassin has shot himself through the head.

CUT TO:

ANCHOR: The assailant has been identified as Ian Hanes of Atlanta, Georgia. According to neighbors, he was a single father who lost his son in the October abduction. According to authorities, Hanes was on medication for depression and related hallucinations. The shooting drew a swift reaction from the president himself.

CUT TO:

President Muir is sitting in the Oval Office.

PRESIDENT: We strongly condemn the senseless murder of this officer of the Chinese navy. Our nation's heart goes out to the parents of this fine man. It is vital to remember that the gunman was a lone individual with no ties to our government. He was severely disturbed following his son's abduction. We

are investigating this tragedy and will share every detail
with Premier Jiaming, whom we continue to try and reach.
Again, this terrible murder was the act of a madman, and it
must not be allowed to undermine our peaceful relations
with China.

CUT TO:

REPRESENTATIVE CAREY GRANT (R): The president's remarks
are one more example of his blind spot when it comes to the
Chinese. We are now apologizing to China for a series of
aggressions that began with their actions. What's next, a
public kowtow to the Communists? I have asked the special
prosecutor to expand his inquiry into the president's
financial ties with Chinese oil interests ...

CUT TO:

ANCHOR: Sources in the State Department say there is no
further word on a possible military takeover in China.

46

Even as the girls helped carry the nameless father down the mountain of steps, they all began to see their fathers in him. Underneath the blood and gray beard and mane of hair was a semblance of the man each had prayed would come.

Beckwith led them across the bridge and through the city and out its gates and up the trail. He ranged in front of them. He lagged behind them. He was their cheerleader when they tired. As the days passed, he was the first awake and the last to sleep. Every time they turned around, there he was with his rifle.

It was Beckwith who had refused to let them use the knife on Clemens. They wanted to kill him for everything that had happened to them. But Beckwith said something about looking into the abyss and not becoming it. So they left their monster on top of the pyramid, paralyzed and wide-eyed, with strings of mucus on his face from the different girls spitting on him.

Crazy Rebecca was no help. It was strange being a mother to someone else's mother, but everyone chipped in. It took their minds off their private hardships. In a way, Rebecca served as everybody's mom, binding them together as a family with her helplessness and babbling. They held her hand along the path and sang along with her songs. They fed and washed and wiped her.

At night they slept in a circle around the nameless man, who had become something of a knight in shining armor to them. Actually it wasn't shining armor, but that coat of green jade plates. The thing was heavy and disgusting with blood and tissue, but Beckwith kept it in a bundle beside its owner. God's armor, he called it.

Struggling on, the group came to a small fleet of rafts sitting by a river. They put the man and Rebecca in one of the rafts and towed it along with a rope. The river grew stronger as they grew weaker. It led to a fork and joined an even larger river.

A deeply worn footpath ran alongside the river. If they went down the Styx, Beckwith said, they would reach another dead city. He had gone there alone, searching in vain for them.

They went upriver. Civilization lay that way. "Pace yourselves," he told them. "It's going to take a while getting home."

The girls talked among themselves about what "a while" might mean, another week or a month, a hundred miles or a thousand or more. It didn't matter. They were safe now. They were going home. Whenever they asked him when they would get there, Beckwith would reply, "Not around the next corner." They loved him for his honesty. Here was a man they could trust.

But then the river split into tributaries with tunnels feeding left and right. Beckwith chose one, and they followed that smaller river for several days until it, too, pronged left and right up a dozen different tubes. Clearly they were lost.

"We'll rest here," he said, and they made a camp in an old slave corral with rusty iron bolts and sad graffiti. Day after day, Beckwith tried the various alternatives.

Like any tribe, the survivors shared worms and head lice and other nuisances. They all had some pink fungus under their nails. Everyone got the runs from the food or water. Their eyes hurt. Their joints ached. But no one complained because they were going home.

Then a flu bug laid them low.

While the river bellowed softly below, and Rebecca sang lullabies with epic stamina, Beckwith took care of everybody as long as he could. But finally it was his turn to get the fever. A few days of fever turned into a week. Beckwith lay there shaking and delirious among them. It seemed they had gone as far as they were going to get.

Piled together out of habit, they entered a collective despair. The planet was closing in around them. Except for the river sound and when they cried out from nightmares, their world grew still and quiet. No one went foraging for food anymore. At most they filled water bottles from the river. They took to sleeping twenty hours at a time. The long night slowly ate them.

47

Clemens's paralysis thawed by ounces.

Once his thankless harem and their idiot mother and that simpleton sniper with his cowlick departed, taking with them most of the food, along with the still breathing carcass of his enemy, Clemens was sure he had it made in the shade. Since the toxin had not killed him, it was just a matter of time before it wore off. Then he could start over again. He was good at starting over.

All through the first week, he waited flat on his back in the stone dome, staring at the ceiling and figuring out how to write himself back into the script. It took his mind off his hunger and thirst.

Without the girls to whelp him an empire, there was no opportunity left in this wind-blasted, godforsaken ruin. Maybe he would head off to the Oriental regions where no one knew him. He would take a new name—Clemens wasn't his real name anyway—and find some other niche to occupy. If he kept hitching his wagon to other people's horses, he was bound to get somewhere eventually. Persistence was everything.

At the end of a week, with his body still in the grip of the toxin, Clemens began to grow a little worried. Even with his metabolism slowed way down, he was bound to run out of fuel before long. He eyed the remaining food along the wall, and willed it toward him, which didn't work of course. One day, he told himself, he would look back on these as his salad days for sure. For now he would have appreciated some of the salad.

Another worry crept in. What if the hadals returned for him? With the girls gone, they didn't have much left in the way of sacrificial material. What if they took him down to their god, that freak in the pit? Not a pleasant thought. The creature would welcome Clemens back with the forgiving heart of a reptile.

Luckily the hadals, that sorry lot, didn't come. By now they were probably off eating insects and trickling deeper into oblivion. Let them rot. They were finished.

In the middle of the second week, his right index finger moved. What joy! He was going to make it out of here after all. Hour after hour Clemens ran his fingertip back and forth, feeling the same glorious inch of stone.

A day later another finger came alive.

His plans quickened. It was not too late to go after the girls. He had saved the little bitches' lives. And all they could do was scream when he touched them. *Fine,* he thought. He would become their boogeyman. He would bedevil mankind. That appealed. He would create an empire from their fear.

His hand woke up while he was sleeping. Soon he had it scuttling here and there like a crab, dragging his arm after it. He was starving, but the food was still too far to reach. That forced him to come up with an alternative.

Scraping one knuckle raw on the stone, he crawled his hand up to his mouth, stuck the finger in, and got a taste of his own blood. That primed the pump. He hated to do it, but a pinkie finger was a small thing in the larger scheme of things. He bit down.

There wasn't much meat on the bone, but the blood soothed his thirst. Unfortunately, it also attracted attention.

Not much later, Clemens heard stones grating deep inside the pyramid. At first the sounds were distant and could have come from anywhere. Then they got closer. He could actually feel the vibration of rocks dislodging far beneath his head. Something was burrowing out from below.

He'd seen statues of the man-bull, and the city was full of stone ox horns and bulls' heads. But he rejected the notion. Minotaurs were for children and cretins.

The noise came and went. It would work awhile, then quit, then begin again. He tried to think what it could be. A rock slide. A fault line slipping. The architecture settling. *An animal.*

Clemens sacrificed a second finger. If he could just get his legs to move, he could walk. If he could walk, he could run. The rest of his body could catch up later.

For another two days he lay there listening to whatever it was unbury-ing itself. Superstitions nipped at him like Chihuahuas. He kicked at them, or would have if his legs only worked. He didn't believe in monsters. That's what the descent was all about, discovering that monsters weren't really monsters. So what was this thing muscling out from the earth?

It got closer.

His body went into an unbearable fight-or-flight mode. Adrenaline hosed into his motionless limbs, but he could neither fight nor flee. He would have screamed, but that would have given him away for sure.

He ate a third finger. He was down to choosing between the all-important opposing thumb and his beloved index finger. It was a choice he never had to make.

At the beginning of the third week, just as his other hand came alive, and it seemed he might be able to crawl out the door and down the stairs, the floor gave way beneath his back. The blocks, so tightly mortared to-gether, broke apart. The smell of raw earth boiled up even as Clemens plummeted into the hole. Something immensely strong caught him and then all was darkness as he was carried down to its lair in the roots of the mountain.

Weeks went by.

Clemens never did see the creature in its entirety, only in bits and pieces, sinews covered with hide and veins, the moist nostrils, those terri-ble teeth. Then he couldn't see at all. It took his eyes.

Together they entered a long hibernation.

Clemens lay in that warm, animal embrace, rocked by lungs almost as large as his body, breathing in the smell of their mutual dung. It was mostly quite peaceful. Every now and then the creature would get hungry, though. Then the pain would come. Clemens would scream awhile. Then they would go back to sleep and Clemens would heal.

It went on like that for a long, long time, the two of them feeding on each other. The creature had nipples that gave milk. Clemens provided the meat.

He slept as much as possible in hopes that some dream would sweep him away, and maybe that was what happened. In this lair of stone, snug against that slow heartbeat, a man who had dreamed of empire became a snack and a teddy bear, nothing more than fodder for a very cruel fairy tale.

48

"Play with me, Mama."

The ghost child was sitting beside Rebecca again, legs folded, patient as a daisy in the sun.

"Please don't do this," said Rebecca, and turned her head away.

"Mama." Sterner this time.

Rebecca looked.

Sam's long, golden hair rippled on the river breeze. Her blue eyes sparkled. She was still missing that one tooth in her smile and wearing the same Hunchback of Notre-Dame cartoon Band-Aid that Rebecca had put on her knee the afternoon before the abduction long, long ago. Everything was exactly right. Except for that shattered forehead.

"Peekaboo," said Sam.

Rebecca didn't want to see inside her daughter's skull. She turned her attention to the camp. She made out the phosphorescent shapes of girls piled together, and among them a brutally wounded man with hadal markings and missing his hand. It seemed like she should know them all. But Mr. Beckwith was the only one whose name came to her. Her archangel Beckwith. Ian was his name. All lay sleeping.

Nearby a river thundered. A whirlpool seethed with frightening suction. Spume slashed in curtains. It was a merciless scene.

Rebecca tried to understand where she was and what had happened. At the same time she already did understand. Events and faces and voices jumbled together. Some of it made sense, much of it was a strange blur. She had come looking for her missing daughter and found these others, too. Her army was gone, though the circumstances were foggy. She remembered the corners of horrible things, worst of all that image of Sam's ruined head. She did not remember entering into this ghost world, however.

"Who are you?" she asked the nightmare.

"Mama," Sam giggled, disbelieving Rebecca's disbelief.

"How did you get here?" The child's clothes were clean. A fresh grass stain showed on one hip, though there was no grass within two thousand miles. Her candy necklace from Halloween had not even been nibbled on. Yet her poor, perfect forehead was in ruins. No. This thing was not her daughter.

Sam's smile shrank. "I got sent."

Rebecca went cold. *Sent?* The memory returned of Sam—golden Sam—starved and bedraggled, on a leash, approaching the stone fortress. And of pleading with the captain not to shoot, and flying for his rifle, and that clap of thunder. There lay her downfall. "Who sent you?" she demanded.

Sam's smile was all gone now. "I don't know," she whispered.

"Well, if you got sent, somebody sent you."

The blue eyes brimmed with confusion. "I don't know."

"You're not my Sam."

The girl froze. "Mama . . . ?"

"Why are you here?"

"To go home," Sam said in the tiniest of voices.

"Home?" Jake was dead. And Sam . . . she had not buried Sam. Was that what this was about?

"The sun's all yellow in my bedroom this morning," Sam said.

"How do you know that?"

"I looked. It was morning. And my night-light was on, even in the daytime."

"I left it on for you, Sam. I kept thinking you might come back home."

"I did, Mama. I keep telling you."

"Did you look in the closet?" said Rebecca. "There's a hole in the floor. I didn't fix the hole yet."

"It's fixed, Mama. Everything's fixed now."

"No, it's not," said Rebecca. "It's all ripped open."

"Up top, Mama. Everything will be right again. This time I get to stay up there."

A vision welled up of their sturdy house perched above the river. Rebecca's heart ached. She wanted so much for this to be Sam. But she had seen her daughter's forehead. The hole was like a second mouth. It yawned at Rebecca with broken teeth. "I'm tired," she said. Tired of the trickery. Tired of false hope. Tired of her madness.

"I know the way home," Sam said. "That's why I'm here, to show you. We have to leave. Before he finds out."

"Before who finds out?"

"You know."

"No, I don't."

"Yes, you do."

"Go away," said Rebecca. "You frighten me."

"But I love you, Mama."

"Leave me alone."

"Mama?"

"You heard me. Go back to where you came from."

Sam's voice shrank to almost nothing. "Not there."

Rebecca squeezed her eyes shut. Fight, she commanded. Fight the ancient love. Kill the ghosts. *Lead me not into temptation.* When she looked again, Sam was gone.

Nothing moved around her. The children lay dreaming. Or dead. Beckwith clutched his rifle. The stranger slept beside his jacket of armor. She stood and went over to him. The armor was ugly beyond reckoning to her, and stunk of death. Nevertheless she required a defense against her haunting child. Stitched into the jacket's antiquity, she sensed a useful vigilance.

As she picked it up, the jade plates rattled like something alive. The jacket was too large and weighed a ton. But as she buckled its hooks, Rebecca felt invincible. Housed in this, she could repel all her demons and remembrances. In this stone shroud, it suddenly struck her, she could bury herself. No more pain. No more madness. The world could not touch her in here.

Time stopped. She noticed it gradually. The river's roar had fallen silent.

Rebecca looked down from the camp's ledge and the water had frozen to stillness. Its current lay in long, black braids, and droplets hung in the air like jewels.

The cave had turned into a crystal oasis. The whirlpool had slowed to a creamy spiral. A pale rainbow shimmered in the mist.

Until this very moment, Rebecca had viewed the abyss as a hateful, raging maw. But suddenly she found herself surrounded by this hidden beauty. It was so peaceful. So welcoming. How could she have missed seeing this other world?

The earth breathed its scents to her from downriver. *What more lies down there?* Rebecca stepped closer to the edge.

"Mama?"

Rebecca ignored the voice. She stayed facing the river. That dark, glassy highway of water invited her touch. All it would take was one step. The river would lead her into a land without sorrow or despair.

"Mama." Like a mosquito in her ear. Rebecca did not answer. It made her dizzy, this crystal world. "Come away from there. I mean it."

She looked over her shoulder and Sam was there. But this time Rebecca was armored and ready. Nothing could hurt her. She glanced back at the river. The beautiful river.

"We can't stay here," Sam said.

"Go home," said Rebecca.

"Not without you I can't."

"It's just so . . ." Rebecca couldn't find a word for the rapture in her heart. It was glorious, the deep.

"No it's not, Mama."

"I'm not scared anymore," Rebecca told her.

She was done with the storm and fury and fear. She could rest in peace.

"You have to take me home."

Sam's desperation startled Rebecca. She looked at her ghost child and the wreckage of that forehead, and this time the innocence was missing from her eyes. In its place she saw desolation and emptiness. *In her baby's eyes.*

"Soon, baby."

"Save me, Mama. Please."

"I tried."

"Try again. I'll be better, I promise."

Rebecca trembled. "What?"

"I won't be bad ever again."

"You were never bad, Sam."

"Then where are you going? I don't want to be alone again."

A diamond slipped down Sam's cheek. A teardrop. Eyes closed, the girl hugged herself and rocked back and forth. Her lips were moving, and Rebecca realized she was praying. Praying for her mother. Her untouchable mother. Another diamond took shape.

Rebecca blinked. What if she was wrong? What if this wasn't a ghost? *Choose*, she thought. *Kill the thing. Or love her.*

"Sam?" she said.

The girl's eyes sprang open. The joy on her face speared the armor. It pierced Rebecca's heart.

"Are you really real?" Rebecca whispered.

Sam held out one finger. Rebecca held her breath. She reached across the void. Sam pressed her fingertip. "Ding-dong," she said, just like in the old days.

Rebecca stared. The forehead was healing itself. The eyes were brightening. She opened her arms. "Sam."

Sam held back. "Throw that away, Mama."

Rebecca's eyes fell to the green jade armor. "But we might need it."

"Not anymore."

Sam was right. Not anymore. No more fear. No more doubt. They were leaving the land of the dead. Her war was over. Here was the child she had come to find.

Rebecca unbuckled the coat, and it fell from her shoulders. She felt light as a bird. With a heave, she threw it from the ledge.

The armor unfolded its green jade wings as if to fly away. But the river suddenly came alive and reached up. It snatched the relic from the air and, with a splash, sucked it into oblivion.

Abruptly the savage world resumed. The river bellowed. The water hurtled on. Rebecca fell away from the churning beast. On her hands and knees, she scrambled back from the edge and the river's false promises. Sam had always been the bold one. She helped Rebecca to her feet.

They hugged.

This was Sam's heart thumping against hers. She felt Sam's warmth, and ran her fingers through Sam's hair, and smelled behind her ear, and it was Sam. Her flesh-and-blood Sam. *How can this be?*

"It just is," Sam said.

"What?" Rebecca whispered. The child could read her mind? Or was she a figment inside her mind?

Sam patted her back. "Too many questions, Mama."

Rebecca peered into her daughter's eyes, hunting for the slightest contradiction of who Sam had been or ought to be. But all she saw was the innocence of her own flesh and blood. And that perfect rounded forehead was whole again.

"Can we go home now?"

"Yes, honey. But I have to ask you something." Rebecca took a breath. "Can we get Daddy, too?"

"No, Mama, he can't come." Sam's voice almost disappeared. "I'm the only one."

"But, Sam." How far to push this? And what was the truth of the matter? "How do you know we can't get him?"

"I just do."

"Are you sure? Can't we try?"

"We have to leave."

"Don't you want to say good-bye?"

"No, Mama."

"But I do."

Sam looked at her. "If we stay, he'll find us."

"The monsters?"

"Worse."

Rebecca let go of it. Some things would just have to be taken on faith. "All right, Sam. Let's go home." Hand in hand, they climbed back to camp.

"Wake up the sleepyheads," Sam told her. She pointed at the man missing his hand. "Don't leave him, whatever you do."

"Everybody goes," said Rebecca.

"But especially him."

"Okay, Sam."

"Hurry," said Sam.

"Which way do we go?" asked Rebecca. She didn't recognize this place. The river seemed very different from the one they had descended, and the campsite was completely foreign to her. It seemed they had never come this way.

"Not far now, Mama."

Rebecca carefully stepped among the piles of raggedy Sleeping Beauties and Snow Whites. How long had they been lying here?

"Wake up," she said. Shaking their shoulders and tugging at their legs, she bullied them from their deep sleep. At last a few eyes appeared. They stared at her with glazed confusion.

"We're going home," Rebecca announced.

"Leave me alone," a girl murmured. Now was Rebecca's turn to be scorned as the ghost. "Go away."

"It's not far now," Rebecca told them. "We're saved."

Beckwith stirred. "Did they come for us?"

"Yes. One."

"One?"

"That's all we need."

Beckwith struggled to sit. "Where is he?"

Rebecca pointed at the periphery where Sam sat perched on a rock. Beckwith squinted blindly. "Don't you see her?"

"Her?"

"Sam."

Beckwith's head slumped. "Ah, Rebecca."

Her hackles went up, and she almost challenged him. But the girls were all looking at her with a poor, crazy Jane look, and for a moment, Rebecca doubted her sanity again. Sam's image wavered. Her forehead began to open. Then Rebecca recovered.

"My phantom other." She smiled at them. "I've got a sixth sense for this now." Off in the distance, Sam gave a hook 'em Longhorns sign like Jake had once taught her. She and Rebecca were a team now. Together they could pull this off. "I know the way out."

"There is no way out," Beckwith muttered. "The cave closed us in."

"Trust me."

"Don't torment us, Rebecca."

"Get up, Ian." She could call him that now. She could go into their worlds. Hers was safe. "I know the way."

"How do you know?" said Beckwith.

"I remember," she told him.

"Remember what? We didn't come this way."

Rebecca stood. "Wake up," she said to them. "You're going home."

There was a cookstove in a mule bag with some food. Rooting through what little remained, Rebecca settled on the hot chocolate powder for starters. While her little tribe drank that, she would get a pot of noodles boiling. Sugar and carbs, that would get them on their feet. Hope would keep them going.

"Fetch me some water," she called to Sam, but caught herself before saying the name. The girls gave Rebecca that look again. "Anyone?" she said. "Anyone? Well, never mind, you all just get yourselves ready. I'll get it myself."

Carrying a clutch of water bottles and a big pot, she took a slippery path down to the water's edge. This time the river was in a killing mood. There was no seduction to it, no sweet temptations. It bellowed at her, and snatched away two of the bottles. It tried everything in its power to drag her in, but Rebecca escaped with her containers filled, and climbed back to camp.

Beckwith was standing. Girls were grumbling and staggering around, getting their blood circulating. "I see some serious bad hair out there, ladies," Rebecca said. "Don't you worry, though. A hot bath and a trip to the mall and you'll be yourselves again."

She lit the stove.

More and more was coming back to her. Wherever they were, Sam would guide them out. There were bound to be settlements ahead. People would take them in and feed them and pass them along. The elevator pods would float them up and out of the darkness. The doors would open. The sun would paint their faces. *The sun!* That ancient thing.

Rebecca lit the stove. The blue flame caught with a roar, silencing the girls' complaints. One by one, they came closer and squatted down to share the light. *Faith,* thought Rebecca. *Our night will pass.*

49

On his first attempt to leave the dream, Ike surfaced into the middle of a bloody sacrifice. A gang of big men—Polynesians, to judge by their features—were cutting off his arm. Cannibals, he guessed. Surgeons, possibly. Or something in between. Apparently they thought he was in a coma, or else they had no anesthesia to spare.

The pain astonished him. He wanted to run from it. But suffering is the child of ignorance, and so he met it head-on with a *bardo* prayer for that gap between living and dying. *When I am chased by snow, rain, wind, and darkness, may I receive the clear, divine eye of wisdom.* This worked for a few minutes.

Back and forth, the wood saw bucked on his arm bone. The men had never done anything like this before, he could tell by their sweat and anger. Then one of them noticed Ike's eyes watching them, and he gave a startled shout. His companions dropped their knives and tools and crossed themselves. Taking another look at his arm, Ike decided this was not the best time and place for his reentry into the world, and lowered himself back into his long meditation.

His heart rate slowed. He returned to old riddles and koans.

Does one dream infinite dreams in an infinite night? Or can you really wake? And how would you know you weren't still dreaming?

On his second attempt, Ike surfaced to find a river of fossils flowing below him. It surged past in a glittering tumble of shells, fins, and delicate ribs, very pretty. Then he heard the clickety-clack of rails and felt the sway of travel, and realized that he was on his back on a flatcar riding through a tunnel. The fossils were not beneath him but overhead, embedded in the ceiling rock. A hundred million years of bygone life muscled by. He closed his eyes to them and returned to his contemplation.

The dark side of the moon is not really dark. Half its life it spends in sunshine. What is written where our blindness cannot see?

The third time he broke to the surface, Ike felt a knife at his throat. The rail car was still rocking him from side to side. Either the train ride was very long, or only a few minutes had passed.

Keeping his eyes shut, he listened to the knife's owner damning him in a foreign tongue. It was easy to read his fear and loathing. The man thought he was killing the devil.

The assassin's intention was noble, but flawed. As Ike knew, the angel could not be killed, only contained. That was the message he needed to relay to the surface world. It was imperative that the colonies be dismantled, that every man, woman, and child depart, and the depths be sealed. Mankind had strayed into the forest of a dangerous beast. If someone inadvertently freed the beast, catastrophe would follow. The angel had to be left in isolation, deep, away from the sun.

Ike opened his eyes, meaning to explain these strange realities to the assassin. But his hoarse whisper only alarmed the man, tripping him into a frenzy of Allahs and oaths. His knife rose to plunge into Ike's chest.

Ike had no choice but to kill his would-be killer. At the speed of pure thought, he willed his right hand to make a lethal thrust. It was a good tactic that would have beat the knife neatly . . . if only his right hand still existed. Unfortunately the Polynesians had removed his entire arm. In short, his counterattack was a figment of his imagination. Unchecked, the knife sped down. He watched to see how deep the blade would go.

To the surprise of both, the blade skipped sideways, with a spark, on his breastbone. Ike had suspected his body might be fossilizing to some slight degree, but this was the first hard proof. The assassin recovered. Up went his knife again, and this time he meant to go for the guts.

So be it, thought Ike. There was not one thing he could do to ward away

death. All his hard-earned revelations were for naught. The world was
going to have to do without his warning.

At that instant, however, a slender shape loomed behind the assassin. A
hand appeared under the man's chin, and took a firm grip. The assassin's
head whipped sideways, and the old rule bore out. Where the head goes,
the body follows, in this case off the train and into the darkness.

A worried face hovered into view. It belonged to a young man with old
eyes. He looked undecided about his violent skills. American, guessed Ike.
"I was sleeping," the man apologized.

"Me, too," whispered Ike.

"Beckwith," the man introduced himself. "I'm the one who struck you
down."

"Am I your prisoner?"

"My what? Christ, no."

Ike tried to remember the circumstances. Like the assassin just now, he
had been stopped in the act of stabbing his enemy. At the crucial instant, in
midplunge, his wrist had exploded. Now Ike understood. His hand had
been shot away.

"You did this?"

Beckwith winced.

"How far away were you?" Ike asked. It didn't matter, particularly. Even
at close range, it would have been a fantastic deed.

"Four hundred yards plus." That was interesting. The man had memorized the architecture of his shot.

"Good eye," said Ike.

"What?"

"You have a gift."

Beckwith frowned at him. "Yeah, what, for blowing up the good guy?"
He opened Ike's shirt and checked for injuries with a soldier's blunt touch,
no time wasted on what was not vital. His look of worry turned to relief.
"He nicked you, that's it. I thought he'd killed you."

"He would have," said Ike. "But you were here."

This time Beckwith accepted the absolution. Ike saw the guilt pass
from the young man's face. Then he began to fade.

"Stay with us," said Beckwith. "We're almost out."

Ike was a step ahead of him, though. He was out already.

*   *   *

A pair of dockworkers left the monster on the beach, to go join the big *benjo*, or luau. Deep inside his skull, Ike listened to them. They had been hired to babysit him for an hour or so, but they were island boys and superstitious. He was dying, they were sure of it, and neither wished to risk the haunt. Also, some famous movie stars and a rock band had flown in with "the family units," and the American embassy was footing the bill for the party, meaning the music and barbecue were bound to be awesome. So they ditched him in the shade of a palm tree.

There Ike lay on a nylon stretcher. The sea breeze fingered his long, white hair. He listened to the waves breaking and the suck of water and the hissing of sand. He sifted the smells: seaweed, a dead gull, and in the far distance, charcoal and a roasting pig. The sunshine filled his lungs.

None of these pleasures spoiled his long meditation. None of it was any more or less real than the house he was erecting in his mind. Out there on the far side of his eyelids, the Great Illusion was changing scenery again, that was all. He would have been content to go on borrowing bits and pieces of the beach for his imaginary house.

That was when the song found him. His contemplation stopped. *Same voice, same song.* It was coming from the ocean, and at first Ike was sure the abyss was hunting him again. He had not heard it for many years, not since it had pulled him from his bed and Ali and into the earth and down to the angel. Eyes shut, Ike gave a soft grunt. His house on a green hill fell to ruins.

"'Though I am old with wandering through hollow lands,'" sang the voice. But it was a young voice, not old. "'And pluck till time and times are done the silver apples of the moon . . .'"

Ike resigned himself. The song was here to take him away. There was no escape. He began climbing from his ruins. For better or worse, it was time to reenter the world. No more hiding. No more seeking.

". . . 'the golden apples of the sun.'"

He opened his eyes.

She was dancing by the water in a heat blast of light, a girl with molten gold for hair. While she sang, she played tag with the surf, chasing it in, darting out.

It was his daughter.

The instant he saw her, Ike was sure of it. Who else could it be on this empty beach? Why else would she be singing this song of his? She must have escaped, clever girl. Or the angel had relented and set her loose. Or had he been lying about her capture all along? Had she been free and waiting for him for all these years? Whatever the explanation, Ike's heart soared. He tried to slow it. After so much time lived in fear and deprivation, his joy felt dangerous.

"Maggie," he called. It came out a raven's squawk. She didn't hear. He laid his head back to gather strength. An IV bag hung overhead. Sunlight sparkled in the fronds.

The hubbub of partiers drifted down to him. A woman—a mother, Ike put it together in his head—screamed her jubilation. *Oh God, oh God, oh God.* The children and families were getting their happy ending. Somehow, for some reason, so was he. If only Maggie would come closer.

Out of nowhere, a fighter jet shrieked past, wagging its wings. For an instant, Ike thought it might be welcoming him back. Then he heard shouts and applause rise in the distance. A steel guitar launched into Jimi Hendrix's "Star-Spangled Banner."

In and out his daughter ran with the surf. She was the one who had sung him down from the world, and it was fitting that she should be the one now singing him back up into it. Ike wasn't sure how this was possible, since she hadn't yet been born when he went into the cave. But he had learned to respect certain mysteries. Perhaps Maggie had searched him out in her very beginning so that he could be where she needed him in the end. He couldn't say. It didn't matter. She was here, and all he needed now was Ali. The three of them could live in a house on a hill, why not?

"Maggie," he squawked again in vain.

Obviously he was going to have to go down to her. Ike sat up, too fast. The blood drained from his head. He landed facedown in the sand beside the stretcher, out beyond his little patch of shade.

The sun bored into him. The sand burned. Flies mobbed his wounds. Ike got as far as his knees before running out of gas. He sank back on his heels.

"Maggie." But the surf drowned him out.

Ike's head sagged. White sand powdered his legs. He brushed at it with the delicacy of an archaeologist, discovering the leather beneath all mottled with alien text and mumbo jumbo. The words had leached into him so deeply he could not read his own story anymore.

Two bare feet planted themselves in the sand. A shadow fell across him. "Ike," said the girl.

He lifted his head. A Band-Aid plastered one of her knees. He searched for a face up there, but her hair was all flames, fire from the sun. "Maggie?"

"I'm Samantha," she said.

Samantha, he remembered. That was the name of the madwoman's child. But that couldn't be right. The child had been killed. Had the angel lied to him about his daughter's name? Indeed, had he lied about Ike having a daughter in the first place? And yet the child knew Ike's name. She knew his song. She was connected to him somehow.

Ike started over. "I'm your father."

"No," she said.

He tried again. "We've never met, Samantha. I left a long time ago . . ."

She stopped him. "Ali sent me."

At last, he thought, *the door was opening.* "Your mother . . ."

"No, Ike." She patted his head. "Listen."

"Is she here?"

The girl's hand glided down the bones of his face. Abruptly she gave his beard a sharp tug. "You're not listening," she said.

This time Ike listened. The child was a messenger. She told him things he didn't want to hear. Maggie was dead. Ali had descended, guided by his initials, and taken his place with the teacher. Nothing was the way he had imagined.

"Ali," he said. "With him?"

"Don't try to find her," said the child.

"What?"

"She said to tell you. Don't go looking for her. She has work to do."

Ike stayed on his knees in the sand, receiving her message one fragment at a time. This was not his child. Maggie had died. Ali had gone into the abyss.

"Your mother," he said, "she was holding a braid of yellow hair. It was your hair."

"That was before. Now she has me to hold."

"They said her daughter was killed."

"Something happened," said the child. "I was lost. Then I opened my eyes. Ali was there. She chose me."

"She brought you back?"

"She pulled me from the river."

"Why you?"

"You mean why not your child? She said you'd ask."

Ike waited.

"It's because," she said, "Ali's not coming back. And my mother's a mother. And you are not a father. You wouldn't know what to do with a kid."

That much was true, devastating as it was, and so Ike accepted the rest as well.

He had failed. He had traded away his life with Ali and their baby, and buried himself in the earth, and for what? To one day rise from his grave and save the world? What arrogance. Lazarus had come back to life, too. But that didn't make him a savior, only a dead man walking.

Far away he heard the revelry. People were laughing and dancing. Music pulsed through the air. For a moment he had thought he might have a place in the city of man. He was nothing more than a fool circling its wall, though. The revelry mocked him.

The girl stepped back, and the sun stabbed his eyes.

He let go of his hopes. He let go of his child. His head sagged.

All his life, from the summits to the deepest void, he had been fighting gravity, an endless fight that no one ever won. His chin came to rest on his chest.

Flies feasted on his teardrops. Let them eat his emptiness. His shadow looked black enough to fall into. *Fall*, he thought. *Go back into the dream.* He closed his eyes.

"Ike," said the girl.

He didn't move. The dream was so much easier. In there he could lay aside the suffering. He could live a thousand lives.

She yanked his beard again.

"You've slept enough," she said.

He opened his eyes. "What do you want?"

"What do *you* want?"

"Ali," he remembered. "I have to go find her."

"She said don't."

"He'll destroy her."

Another yank on his beard. "Monkeys!" the child snapped at him. "Quit chattering." Spoken like a Zen master. Or a nun. It shocked him.

He squinted at her. "Who are you?"

"Quit hiding," she said. "No more distractions. No more wandering. You have to get ready."

"Ready?"

"You're wasting time."

"Ready for what?"

She took his arm, and got him to his feet, and aimed him at the water. He swayed like a man on stilts high above the ground. "Where are we going?"

"Not me," she said, "you."

She steered him toward the ocean. The music was getting faster behind the trees. Ike concentrated on his feet. Somehow he made it across the stretch of sand.

The waves lapped low and lazy, no higher than his knee. Even so, without her help he would have fallen. It got easier the farther out they went.

Ike was getting the picture. *Back into the dream.* He waded deeper into the turquoise water until his feet barely touched. Like that, at last, the weight of the world lifted from him. Gravity let go.

He kept going, slowly tiptoeing out toward the sun. No more fighting. No more pain. He was going to float right off the planet.

A hand gripped his arm. "That's far enough for now, Ike."

Her eyes were blue as the sky. She had sunbeams for hair. The surf rolled in her voice. "A little farther," he told her.

"But the tribe needs you," she said.

What tribe? For as long as he could remember, Ike had soloed in life. The only time he had ever really opened up his heart, the deep had robbed him blind. Maggie was gone, or had never been, and Ali was entombed.

"What do you want?" he said. She had whispered him into the abyss, and whispered him out of it, and now she was doing it again.

"What do *you* want?" she said back to him. Her golden hair was splayed on the sea foam.

Ready for what?

It gave him a headache. After a few minutes, Ike rested his head back on the water. He felt the sea cleaning his wounds. Fish nibbled at his legs. The darkness scaled from his hide. It bled from his mind.

Ready for what?

The sun painted the inside of his eyelids pink. His feet just touched the bottom, though another step beyond would plunge him into the abyss. He rested on that watery brink. When he opened his eyes again, the child was gone and the island had drifted to one side. The sun had sunk to the horizon. It startled him.

The beach was far away and empty. It looked like a desert island passing him by. The castaway had slept right through his main chance. Ike eyed the vast expanse waiting for him. It frightened him. But he was philosophical. One way or another, now or later, the abyss would have reaped his sorry bones anyway.

The sun slid lower.

Ike drifted without a fight. There was nothing left to fight. Get ready, the child had said as she led him into the ocean. Now he knew what for, a beautiful sunset, and then the endless night.

The horizon blazed with colors, and then blinked shut. The blue ocean went black. A shiver ran through him. The water was cold. The breeze shifted.

He saw the flicker of a bonfire through the screen of trees. A plume of white smoke rose up like some prehistoric signature. It drafted across the water full of scents: cooked meats, onions, spices, clean sweat, and perfumes. Music and voices and laughter carried out to him. He could even hear certain words.

They were celebrating like there were no tomorrow. Or like there were a million tomorrows. Celebrating their children. Celebrating victory. Celebrating survival. It struck him. Conquering death, that's what they were doing. No matter that darkness was falling, they had their fire and stories and each other. Their communion pulled at him. It kept him at bay. *Pass on by.*

The current towed at him. Something bumped his leg, something alive and with weight to it. Predators, everywhere predators. *Pass on.*

His toes barely reached what little floor remained. He danced for contact. Emptiness yawned. *Let loose.*

He fanned at the water to keep his toe tip of purchase. It had muscle, this ocean. To be honest, he was afraid of it. Where had his still mind gone? Chin raised high, Ike clung to the island with his eyes.

Just then a woman appeared on the distant beach. To his astonishment, she knew his name. Her siren's voice skipped across the water. He was not one to break cover so quickly, though. He took his time, making sure this was no trick. Was he the dream or the dreamer? Was he calling to himself or hearing himself called? Saltwater stung his eyes. He spit it out, quietly.

More figures emerged from the trees. His name multiplied. The children had come down, trailed by their retinues of family. They never quit searching for him, he realized, first Ali tracking his initials, now these girls with their flashlights and flaming torches wagging across the sand.

"Ike." A girl ran into the dark sea. Her parents darted after her and pulled her back. Others lined the tidal edge. They had found his tracks and knew he was out here, but were afraid to go farther. Perfectly understandable. It was night and there were monsters out here.

The tribe needs you.

Something changed in him.

They needed him. He knew the monsters. Maybe not all their colors and shapes and weak points. But even one-armed and one-eared and heartsick, he had no fear of the beasts themselves, only of the angel who had fathered them and the abyss that had no end.

He was a monster himself, all wild and whittled down by his terrible journey, and they would always wonder whether he was really part of them. But they were his people, and defenseless against what they did not know. Whatever might come unleashed if Ali failed, he had learned there was worse waiting beneath it. More than any one dragon he might slay, that was their need: knowledge, not the fight, would save them from the night.

As if sensing his change of heart, the abyss made a sudden grab for him. The current yanked his feet loose and he went under. The crescent sliver of beach with its lights and the stars flickering overhead: he lost them. The water reached its tentacle down his throat. The void sucked him backward.

Ike struck at the water, and it only sucked him deeper. He grabbed for the surface, and it slipped through his hand. The leviathan closed its mouth around him. His back scraped bottom. Headfirst, he felt the seafloor slipping past.

Then something reached up through the water and touched him, an animal or rock, though it felt distinctly like a human hand. It did not clutch at him exactly, but it braked his slide down the tilted slope. For a moment, hardly long enough for him to register the opportunity, the void was held back.

Ike didn't need a second invitation. Digging his toes into the silt and shells, he rooted for purchase. Invisible creatures wormed free and scattered from his touch. He was running out of air, but had a foothold in the living now. His panic stilled. He pushed to the surface, and took a breath. The beach was there. They still lined the water's edge.

He sank back to the bottom again, purposely this time. His body had grown too heavy to swim. But he had his direction now, and the island's ramp lay underfoot. He planted his feet back into the ocean floor and took a step. Slow as a giant, he began climbing out of the abyss.

ARTIFACTS

SBIRS (Space-based Infrared System) High—Satellite 4

22,300 MILES ABOVE CHINA (GEOSYNCHRONOUS ORBIT)

The lens zeroes in on a hole that is opening in the earth.
A glistening cylinder appears on a tail of fire.
The ICBM spears upward and then makes an elegant arc down.
It slides around to the dark side of the planet.
A minute later a flash of light disturbs the horizon.

50

DIALOGUES WITH THE ANGEL, NUMBER 11

Back and forth, the angel paces. His thigh muscles bunch and spill. A master-piece of his species, thinks Ali, all one of him. The veins remind her of a lion. His mouth is stained with blood. It gives his beautiful face the look of a snout. He often returns home from his walkabouts like this, stinking of his kills. Home. That's how the library feels these days, like her home. And his. Ours.

He doesn't need the food, claims not to even want it particularly. It rounds out the hunt though, he says. Luckily for her, he shares. A haunch of meat lies on the illusion of an exquisite Louis XVI parquet table. The table is just a boulder. But Ali prefers the illusion at times like this, especially when it masks the fingers and toes.

She would refuse the meat, would starve herself, gladly. But someone has to watch over the creature. So long as she is here denying him his password, the world is safe. She eats for mankind, then. It goes down easier that way.

As always, he is brimming over with curiosity. He delights in her latest discoveries in his mazelike library. He wants to know how much longer she will take to plumb how much deeper. Sometimes he shares secrets. Today he plays a riddle.

"If light can pierce darkness," he poses to her, "can darkness pierce light?"

Freedom. He is all about freedom. She searches for some other subtext. Once he asked about a fly, and was really talking about the half-life of em-pires. This question seems straightforward, however. Will she be the one to set him free? Will he ever see the sun?

Ali doesn't sugarcoat it. "No." For as long as he lets her live, she means to keep him locked in this cage with her.

His bare feet slap the stone, back and forth, pacing. She knows he knows about her scheme. And he has shown her his Collection. She has nightmares about the savage things he has done even to his favorites.

She braces for his wrath. At any moment he could tire of her defiance. Every breath is a borrowed one.

He casts a glance at her. He comes closer, takes her chin in his gory hand. Here is where it ends, she thinks.

But he only smiles at her.